Accidents Happen

In 1962 music teacher Frano Selak from Croatia was a passenger aboard a train that derailed and crashed into a river.

In 1963 he was blown out of the door of the first plane he'd ever flown on, and landed on a haystack.

In 1966 a bus he was travelling on crashed into a river.

In 1970 Frano Selak's car caught fire as he was driving on a motorway. He escaped just before it exploded.

In 1973 his car caught fire again in a freak accident, burning away most of his hair.

In 1995 Frano Selak was hit by a bus.

In 1996 he met a truck head-on on a mountain road, and his car crashed down a 300-foot precipice.

Frano Selak survived it all.

Then won the lottery.

When the child woke that Sunday morning, the thing was simply there, beside the window, as if it had always been. It had arrived during the night without sound, without fanfare. It had crept quietly between the rocking horse with its red saddle that Granddad had carved from hickory, and yesterday's clothes, discarded in a pile, the wet clay from the wooded hills outside the house now caked hard along the seams.

It slithered, jagged and full of threat, past the small shelf unit with the rows of books and the snowdome of a mountain, past the cuckoo clock Aunt Nelly brought back from Austria.

The child blinked hard.

Perhaps it was just a shadow, thrown by the flat morning light seeping under the drawn bedroom curtains?

A piece of jumper or a trouser leg, twisted freakishly?

Two blinks, three blinks – and open . . .

No. It was real. Bigger than last time. Angrier, even, with a gaping mouth. A slice of light across the eiderdown from a gap in the curtains pointed straight at it like a dagger. The air in the bedroom felt chill.

Gripping the eiderdown, the child looked around. The clock said 6.34 a.m. Nobody would be up yet. There was time, at least, to think.

The child emerged slowly from the warm sheets, slipped onto the ground and stayed low, as if the thing were about to attack.

3

It seemed to grow as the child edged nearer. Until it was right there, face to face, spitting out its cool poison.

The child inhaled heavily. It was so much bigger than last time. It jaws gaped, revealing a tiny white spot within its depths. Where the poison came from.

That was new. The tiny white spot.

Without planning to, the child simply didn't exhale again. It seemed to help for a moment, to hold the breath inside, as if controlling time. If there was no breath, no seconds counted away, time would stop, wouldn't it?

Nothing would happen.

Mother would not see it.

The clock ticked into the silence of the room. Out here on the hill, a mile from the nearest road, there was nothing else to hear.

Ten, eleven, twelve, thirt—

It was no use. The child's lungs protested.

Releasing the breath in a panic, the child ran to the half-open bedroom door and peeked one eye around the door frame.

The hall was still. The light along it receded until the kitchen door at the far end was just a blurred shadow. Three doors down, Mother's door was firmly shut. A gentle snoring from the small room next door to it confirmed Father was not in there with her.

The child desperately looked ahead out of the feature window that ran the breadth of the long, one-storey chalet. Father had said the window was there because people thought the view of the peaks beyond was pretty. That people would envy their family this incredible position.

They didn't have to live here.

The urge to run out of the front door to hide in the woods was tempered only by the fear of the woods themselves. The dark hollows and weaves of branches that liked to suck you in and spin you around until you didn't know where you were any more.

Moving back into the bedroom, the child shut the door gently.

4

There had to be something. Anything.

On the floor lay yesterday's dressing gown.

On an impulse, the child bent down and flung it, as if it were burning hot, over the rocking horse. By tweaking the corners, you could cover most of it. You could trap its chilly poison behind a curtain of flannel.

What choice was there?

Otherwise, today would be like yesterday, but much worse.

CHAPTER ONE

It was one of those days when you didn't know what was going on. Just that something unexpected had happened. You could tell by the maverick puff of dark grey smoke that hung above the M40 motorway, the kaleidoscope jam of cars glinting under an otherwise blue sky, by the way that the adults craned their necks out of windows to see what was up ahead.

Jack kicked his football boots together in the back seat, feeling carsick.

'Where are we?'

'Nearly there. Oh, will you get out of the bloody way! What is wrong with these . . .?'

He glanced up to see his mother glaring in the rear-view mirror. Behind them in the slow lane, a lorry jutted up the back of their car, its engine growling.

'Him?'

Kate shook her head crossly. 'He's right up my back,' she spat, clicking on her indicator and looking for an empty space in the adjacent lane.

Jack rubbed his face, which was still rubbery and red from running around the football field. The warm May afternoon air that blew in through the window was mucky with exhaust fumes as three thick rows of traffic tried in vain to force their way slowly towards Oxford.

'I can't even see his lights now . . .'

A spasm gripped Jack's stomach. It made the nausea worse. He turned his eyes back to his computer game. 'Mum, chill out. They probably have sensors or something to tell them when they're going to hit something.'

'Do they?' She waved to a tiny hatchback in the middle lane that was flashing her to move in. 'What, even the older ones?'

'Hmm?' he replied, pressing a button.

'Jack? Even old lorries, like that?'

He shrugged. 'I don't know. I mean, they don't *want* to hit you, Mum. They don't *want* to go to jail.'

Without looking up, he knew she was shaking her head again.

'Yeah, well, it's the one who's *not* thinking that you've got to worry about, Jack. Last year, a British couple got killed by a French lorry doing the same thing – he was texting someone in a traffic jam and ran right over them. He didn't even know he'd done it, they were so squashed.'

'You told me,' Jack muttered. He flicked the little man back and forwards, trying to get to the next level, trying to take his mind off his stomach.

'Oh God – I'm going to be late,' his mother said, looking at the car clock.

'What for?'

She hesitated. 'Just this thing at six.'

'What, the doctor's?'

'No. A work thing.'

He glanced at her in the mirror. Her voice did that thing again, like when she told him the reason she went to London last week on the train. It went flat and calm, as if she were forcing it to stay

8

still. There were no ups and downs in it. And her eyes slid a tiny bit off to the side, as if she were looking at him but not.

A flicker of white caught Jack's attention in the side mirror. The offending lorry was indicating to move in behind their car again.

He watched his mother, waiting for her to see it. His stomach cramped even worse.

Perhaps it was the cramp that pushed the words out of his mouth.

'Mum . . .'

'What?'

He saw her note the lorry's flashing indicator in the mirror, and her mouth dropped open angrily.

'Oh Jesus – not again . . . What the . . .?'

Jack banged his football boots together again. Dried mud sprinkled onto the newspaper she'd put down in the back.

'Mum?'

'WHAT?'

When his voice came out it was so quiet, he could barely hear it himself over all the straining car engines.

'I could have come back in the minibus. You could have picked me up at school like everyone else.'

He saw her shoulders jar.

'It's fine. I wanted to see you play; it's the tournament final!' she said, the shrillness entering her voice again. 'What, am I an embarrassing mum?'

'I didn't say that,' he said into his computer game.

'Maybe next time I'll come wearing my pants on my head.'

She made a silly face at him in the mirror. He smiled, even though he knew that the silly face wasn't hers. It was stolen property. He'd seen her studying Gabe's mum when she did it. Gabe's mum did it a lot, and it made them laugh. When Jack's mum did it, it was as if the corners of her lips were pulled up by clothes pegs. Then, two minutes later, they'd slip out of the clothes pegs, back to their normal position, where half of her bottom lip was permanently tucked under the top one, kept firmly in place by her teeth; her face set in a grimace that suggested she was concentrating hard on something private.

'It was nice to see Gabe today,' she said. 'Why don't you ask him round soon?'

Jack kept his eyes on his game. After what she'd done to their house this week, he'd never be able to ask anyone around again.

'Maybe.'

'Oh . . . there it is . . . Can you see?'

He leaned over and looked out of the passenger side of the car. There was a flashing blue light around the bend to the left.

'Police,' he said, straining forward. 'And . . . a fire engine.'

'Really?'

Her voice sounded like splintering glass. He sighed quietly and put down his game.

'Oh, Mum . . . I've got something really good to tell you.'

'Uhuh?'

'Next term, Mr Dixon wants me to play reserve for this junior team he runs after school.'

'Does he?' She glanced at him. 'That's brilliant, Jack . . .'

'But I'll have to train on Wednesdays after school, as well, so perhaps I can go to . . .'

In the mirror, he saw her eyes dart wildly back and forward between the blue light and the lorry now crossing lanes to sit behind them again.

His stomach was starting to feel as if it were strung tightly across the middle, like when he tuned the electric guitar Aunt Sass had bought him for Christmas too high to see what would happen.

'MUM?'

Her eyes darted to him, bewildered.

'WHAT?'

'Why don't you move into the fast lane? Lorries aren't allowed in there.'

And she'd be further away from the burned-out car that was currently coming into view around the bend on the hard shoulder.

His mother stared at him for a second. Finally, she focused back. Then the clothes-peg smile returned.

'Good idea, Captain,' she said brightly. 'But we're fine here. Don't worry about it, Jack.'

He saw her force her eyes to crinkle at the sides, just like Gabe's mum's did. Except Gabe's mum's eyes were warm and blue, set in furrows of laughter lines and friendly freckles. Jack's mum's eyes were still, like amber-coloured glass; they sat in skin as white and smooth as Nana's china, smudged underneath by dark shadows.

He knew his mum's extra-crinkly smile was supposed to re-assure him that there was nothing to worry about. He was only ten and three-quarter years old, it said. She was the grown-up. She was in charge, and everything was fine.

Jack rubbed his stomach, and watched the lorry in the side mirror.

Oh God. She was so late. She couldn't miss this appointment. The motorway traffic had concertinaed onto the A40 and now into the city and jammed that up too.

Kate turned off the packed main road and sped through the back streets of east Oxford, taking routes the tourists wouldn't know. Bouncing over speed bumps, she dodged around shoals of cyclists and badly parked rental vans evacuating ramshackle

11

student houses for the summer. Where there was only room for one vehicle down streets so narrow that cars had parked on the pavement, she forced her way through, waving with a smile at on-coming queues of drivers, ignoring their mouthed insults.

'They're here!' Jack shouted, as she made the last turn into the welcoming width of Hubert Street.

Damn. He was right.

Richard's black 4x4 was parked in its usual gentlemanly way outside her house, leaving the gravelled driveway free for her. A box of pink tissues on the dashboard announced Helen's presence. Of course they were here. They would have been here on the dot of five. Desperate to get their hands on him.

'So they are,' she said, turning into the drive and braking abruptly in front of the side gate. She pulled on the handbrake harder than she meant to. 'Right – run. I'm late.'

They spilled out of the car, hands full of plastic bags of Jack's school clothes, the empty wrappers of post-football snacks and his homework folder for the weekend.

'Hi!' Jack called out, waving. Helen was mouthing 'Hello' from between Kate's sitting room curtains, her indented two front teeth giving her a strangely girlish smile for a woman in her sixties.

Kate growled inwardly. Why hadn't they waited in their car? That house key was for when they were looking after Jack. Not for letting themselves in when she was late. Mentally, she tried to visualize what the house had looked like when she left this morning. What state was the bathroom in? Had she tidied away her bras off the radiators?

Then she remembered what was upstairs.

Oh no.

She slammed the car door and locked it. She was supposed to tell them, before they saw it. Explain.

Keeping her head down, Kate marched after Jack to the front porch.

'Hello! Have you grown again, young man?' Helen called, flinging open the door.

'Not since last week, I don't think, Helen,' Kate said. Why did she do that? They all knew he was small. Pretending he wasn't, was not doing Jack any favours.

'Gosh, you're going to be tall like your dad.' Helen laughed, ignoring her. She placed her arm round Jack, and led him along the hall to the kitchen.

'Everything OK, Kate?' she called back. 'Traffic?'

'Yup. Sorry.'

Kate couldn't help it. She gritted her teeth, as she turned to close the door behind her.

'Let me take those.'

Rapidly, she ungritted them, and turned to see Richard striding towards her, his hands outstretched, without any apparent awkwardness at having let himself into his daughter-in-law's house. His imposing frame filled the hallway. 'How did you get on? Traffic?'

'Hmm, sorry,' she said, giving him Jack's homework. Richard's usual fragrance of pipe smoke and TCP drifted over to her.

They stood for a second, fumbling their fingers between the plastic bag handover. Kate looked up at Richard's brown eyes, waiting for them to check that Jack was out of earshot, then glance up to the upstairs landing above them, then firmly fix back down on her face, serious and questioning. But they didn't. Instead, he turned on his heels and bounced after Helen and Jack to the kitchen at the back of the house, grinning through his grey-flecked beard at the sight of his grandson.

'So did you beat their socks off, sir?' he boomed at Jack, who was stuffing a muffin in his mouth.

Kate glanced upstairs.

It was still there.

Richard just hadn't seen it. This was interesting.

She checked her watch. Five-twenty. The woman wanted to see her at six sharp in north Oxford. The traffic was so bad she was going to have to cycle. Concentrating, Kate worked out a few figures. Thirty-four . . . Eighty-one – or was it eighty-two? Damn it, she needed that new laptop. It was high, anyway.

She shook her head. It would have to be OK.

She followed Richard through to the kitchen, opened a cupboard and bent down to find her helmet.

'Helen, do you mind if I rush off?'

'Of course not, dear,' Helen replied, filling up a jug at the sink. 'Something interesting?'

'Um . . . just a woman who might have some renovation work,' Kate said, avoiding Helen's eyes.

'Where?'

'In Summertown.'

'Oh well, good luck, dear.'

'Thanks.'

Kate turned to see Jack, his mouth still too full of muffin to answer his grandfather's question about the match score in this afternoon's tournament final. He was grinning and sticking up two fingers like Winston Churchill.

'Peace, man?' roared Richard. 'It's the 1960s, is it? No! Two all, then? No? What? A bunny rabbit jumped on to the pitch?' Richard chortled, his arms wrapped round his rugby player's chest, as his grandson shook his head at his jokes. 'What? Two–nil, then?'

Jack nodded, laughing, dropping crumbs out of his mouth.

'Aw – well done!' Helen clapped, cheeks as pink as fairycakes.

'Good lad!' Richard exclaimed. 'Was he good, Mum?'

Kate grabbed her helmet from the back of the cupboard and went to stand up. 'He was. He made a good save, didn't you?'

As she turned round, the sight of Helen and Jack together took her by surprise.

A pit of disappointment opened up in her stomach.

Jack was a clone of her. You couldn't deny it.

Kate buckled up her helmet, watching them. It simply wasn't happening. However desperately she willed her son's hair to darken and coarsen like Hugo's, or his green eyes to turn brown, it was Helen and Saskia whom Jack took after. As he sat, arms touching with his grandmother, the similarities were painfully obvious. The same pale hair that was slightly too fine for the long skater-boy cut he desperately wanted; delicate features that would remain immune to the nasal bumps and widening jaws that would wipe out his friends' childhood beauty; the flawless skin that tanned so easily and would remain unmarked by Kate's dark moles or Richard and Hugo's unruly eyebrows.

No, he was nearly eleven. Nothing was going to change now. Jack would be a physically uncomplicated adult, like his grand-mother and aunt, with none of the familiar landmarks of his father.

Kate stood up straight and tried to think about something else. She walked to the fridge and opened it.

'Oh, by the way, Helen, I've made this for tonight,' she said, pulling out a casserole dish and lifting the lid. 'It's just vegetables and lentils. And some potatoes . . .'

Kate stopped.

She stared at the dark brown glutinous sludge of the stew. It was an inch or two shallower in the dish than she'd left it this morning.

'Jack, did you eat some of this?' Kate asked, turning around alarmed. He shook his head.

Kate's eyes flew to the kitchen window locks and the back door. All intact. She then spun round to check the window at the side return – and came face to face with Helen, who had come up behind her.

Watching her.

Helen gave Kate a smile and took the casserole gently from her, replacing it in the fridge.

'Now, don't worry about us, Kate. We stopped at Marks on the way over. I got some salmon and new potatoes, and a bit of salad.'

Kate noted the salmon sitting in her fridge on the shelf above the casserole and felt the waves of Helen's firm resolve radiate towards her. 'Oh. But I made it for tonight. Really. There's plenty for the three of you. I'm just confused at how so much of it has disappeared. It's as if . . .'

'Oh, it'll have just sunk down in the dish when it was cooling,' Helen interrupted, shooting a reassuring smile at Jack. 'No, Kate. You keep it for tomorrow.'

Kate peered into the fridge. Was Helen right? She lifted the lid again to check if she could see a faint line of dried casserole that would prove its original height.

There was nothing there.

'Absolutely,' Richard boomed. 'Take the weight off.'

Richard and Helen together. Two against one, as always.

'OK,' she heard herself say lamely. She replaced the lid and shut the fridge. They could eat their bloody salmon. Jack didn't even like it. He only ate it to be polite.

'Now, you're probably starving, darling, aren't you?' Helen said to Jack, taking Kate's apron off a hook and putting it on. There was a fragment of tinned tomato on it left over from making the stew this morning. It was about to press against Helen's white summer cardigan.

Kate went to speak, and then didn't.

'OK, then . . .' She hesitated. 'By the way . . .'

They both glanced up.

Jack looked down at the table.

'I've . . . have you been up . . .?' She pointed at the ceiling.

They shook their heads.

'No, dear,' Helen replied. 'Why?'

Jack kept his eyes on the table, slowly finishing his muffin.

'Well, I haven't got time to explain, but anyway, don't worry about it. It's just . . .'

They waited, expectantly. Jack's jaws stopped moving.

'I needed to do it. And it's done now. So – see you later.'

And with that, she marched out of the door of her house – *her* house – cross that she had to explain at all.

CHAPTER TWO

It was a warm May evening and Oxford was bathed in a pale lemon tint. Kate pushed her bike across Donnington Bridge, then freewheeled down the steep path on the other side to cycle along the river.

It was busy. She set off, cycling around a woman with two big wet dogs, and a student on a bike who had clearly not learned to drive yet and wasn't sticking to the left side. Kate pumped her legs hard, averting her eyes from the water on her right, trying to clear her mind of what she was about to do. She pushed against the resistance of each pedal stroke, changing gear when the journey along the flat path became too easy, until she could hear her own breath whistling gently on the summer breeze.

A swarm settled around her head like tiny flies.

One out of five. About 20 per cent, she thought, trying to ignore it.

She hit a steady pace around Christchurch Meadow. The grand old college looked especially beautiful tonight across the river, its stone facade soft and pretty in the low light. The grass in front of it glowed that rich, saturated Oxford green that suggested high teas and country estates. It was scattered with groups of the cheery, hard-working students who imbued the air in

Oxford with their optimism and best efforts, who sprinkled its streets and parks and alleyways with goodwill, like bubbles of sweetness in a fizzy drink. Who made Oxford feel safe.

No, on nights like these, she hardly missed London at all.

After Folly Bridge Kate cleared the crowds and stepped up her speed again. She sailed past the waterside flats at Botley and the circus-coloured canal boats moored around Osney Lock. Behind Jericho, she ducked under a graffitied bridge and carried on along the canal path till she could cross into north Oxford.

There. She had done it. Dismounting to cross the bridge, she checked her watch. Twenty-five minutes flat. She could still make it for six.

As she set off, pushing her bike along the pavement to Summertown, the enormity of what lay ahead hit her.

She was here finally. She was actually going to do it this time.

Before she could change her mind for the tenth time, Kate made herself walk on, pushing the bike along the pavements of quiet side streets before emerging into the rush-hour traffic of Woodstock Road and Banbury Road, which she crossed to arrive in a leafy Summertown avenue.

Peace descended as she entered the exclusive Oxford enclave. The houses were spectacular. Imposing Victorian detacheds, with grand pianos in grand bay windows and walled gardens. Inspector Morse streets, as Helen would call them. As far from the clattering noise and cheerful chaos of east Oxford as you could be. The kind of leafy avenue Helen and Richard had assumed Kate would buy in when she and Jack moved from London – the first thing she had done to annoy them.

To avoid thinking about her destination, Kate observed each house as she passed, searching for a feature Hugo would appreciate. The houses were Victorian Gothic revival. Not his period, but she bet he would have known the correct name for every architectural detail on their splendid frontages.

Before she knew it, the sign was in front of her. Hemingway Avenue.

Kate stopped. Her cheeks were covered in a gentle sheen of perspiration, her lips still slightly numb from riding fast into the breeze.

Her watch said five to six. She had made it.

She was nearly there.

This was nearly it.

The urge to run overwhelmed her so abruptly, she put a hand out and touched a wall.

She was outside No. 1. If she carried on to No. 15 Hemingway Avenue there would be no going back.

Shutting her eyes, she forced herself to summon the memory of Jack's face in her rear-view mirror an hour ago. His cheeks rigid like a mask, his lips thrust forward as he bit the inside of his mouth.

'You are going to do this,' she whispered, pushing herself off the wall.

And on she went, with smaller and smaller steps.

The house was even more impressive than its neighbours. One gable jutted in front of the other. Ivy grew around medieval-style stone window frames. The glass revealed nothing inside but the red silk fringe of standard lamp, then darkness beyond.

Kate pushed her bike into the driveway and locked it to a railing. She removed her helmet and ran her fingers through her hair. It fell forwards, thick with the Celtic blackness Mum told her she had inherited from an Irish aunt, blocking out the early evening sun for a second. She threw her head back and straightened her hair down to her shoulders, then forced herself up the stone steps to a white, carved portico. The front door was magnificent. Hugo would have loved it. An eight-foot-high Gothic revival arch, wooden, with roughly hewn baronial black metal hinges and a thick knocker.

Kate paused.

She lifted her hand before she could run away – and banged it.

The sound made her jump. It resonated around the front garden, like a shotgun. The huge door swung open to reveal a blonde woman in her sixties. She was as tall as Richard, and broad, with a matronly bosom. Her hair was drawn up into an elaborate bun which looked as if it had first been created in the sixties. The woman wore a green print dress and had a strong piece of turquoise jewellery around her neck.

'Kate?'

Her voice was pleasant and soft, like ripe fruit.

Kate nodded, feeling like a child.

'I'm Sylvia. Come in.'

'Thanks.'

Kate walked into an elegant hall, tiled with gold and blue geometric Victorian tiles. 'Do you want to leave your helmet there?' Sylvia said, pointing to a mahogany table adorned by a giant vase of lilies.

Kate nodded again, praying the plastic buckles wouldn't scratch it.

'I'm so glad you finally managed to come,' Sylvia said.

Kate looked at the floor.

'I know. Sorry. Things just kept coming up.'

'You managed to find someone to look after your son?' Sylvia said, opening a door off the hall, and guiding Kate through. There was a fragrance of roses.

'Yes, I did, thanks. His grandparents. My in-laws.'

The sitting room was even more impressive than the hall, furnished with antique tables, bookshelves and over-stuffed chairs and sofas. It smelled of polish. The wallpaper looked original Victorian, too, or at least one of those expensive reproductions

21

Hugo used to buy through specialists. Sage green with an intricate spray of curling dark stems and ruby-red roses.

Sylvia pointed to an armchair.

'Please, have a seat, Kate.'

But Kate couldn't.

She stood in front of the chair. She was here now. It was time to start.

Looking Sylvia in the eye, she made herself speak the words. Maybe it was the numbness in her lips from cycling, but the voice didn't sound like hers. The words came out half-formed and uncertain, as if she had missed off the hard edges and spoken only the soft bits in the middle.

'I told them I was seeing a woman who wanted to discuss renovating her house.'

Sylvia nodded, as she moved to the sofa.

'I see. Well, that's something we can talk about, Kate.'

CHAPTER THREE

There he was. That weirdo again.

Saskia stood second in line at a cash till in Tesco on Cowley Road, watching the student in front put through two microwave-able beefburgers in buns, three tins of hotdogs and a bumper pack of Curly Wurlys.

Yum, she thought, touching a French-polished fingertip on the chilled glass of the sparkling rosé she had placed on the belt. Some lucky girl was going to be wined and dined tonight.

Cautiously, she lifted her eyes, to check he didn't know she was looking. It was the first time she had seen him up close. It was his height that had originally caught her attention on the pavement a few weeks ago. Not that he was particularly taller than any other tall man she knew. Dad, for instance. His legs just seemed overly long, perhaps due to the shapeless black trousers he wore. His T-shirt was black too, and slightly too short, reveal-ing a white slab of belly each time he moved. Inside Tesco, the student looked even odder. His out-dated spiky, dark blond hair and bad glasses marked him out from the cool indie kids from the poly – or Oxford Brookes University, as it was these days. Not that Hugo had ever let Saskia forget the former identity of her college. Oxford Puniversity, he called it, to wind her up.

Five minutes later she left Tesco with her wine, and found herself behind the student again as they both wound through the back streets of east Oxford. He was doing that strange walk again. Bouncing along on his oddly extended legs, his upper torso bobbing with the motion. It gave him the impression of being both physically awkward and arrogant. His strides were so much longer than Saskia's that by the time she reached the corner of Walter Street he had disappeared from sight.

Saskia stopped at an estate agent's window, perusing her reflection for a second. With the early evening sun behind her head, it appeared as if she was wearing a halo, the white-blonde tips of her hair melding into its rays. She flattened down the front of her pale blue summer dress, wondering if Jonathan was missing her at all.

With a sigh, she checked the property values. Hubert Street was holding its own. That was good. Something, at least, for Jack's sake.

Oh no. Jack.

He would be waiting for her, desperate to know her decision.

On impulse, Saskia dived into the newsagent next door and searched through the boys' magazines to find one she hadn't bought him yet. That would distract him till she decided what to do. Because if she did it, Kate would kill her. If she didn't – well, things were bad enough as it was for her nephew.

At the last minute she grabbed some cough sweets for her presentation at work on Monday morning and headed back outside.

As she set off, popping a cough sweet in her mouth, there was a flash of movement to her right.

Saskia jumped.

What the hell was that?

A large black shape shifted between two cars.

24

Walking fast, she waited until she was at a safe distance before turning round.

A black-clad backside peeked out from between the cars. She recognized the slice of white flabby skin that lay above it.

The weirdo. He was crouched down between two cars, facing a row of houses across the road.

Why was he behaving so furtively?

Saskia surveyed the house opposite. It looked like a normal residential house. No piles of bikes or posters in the window to suggest students. A well-painted red door. Cream curtains half-closed. Faint classical music drifting out of an open sash window.

A figure crossed the window. A woman in her thirties with a brunette bob.

Saskia heard a little click, and then another.

A camera?

Was he watching someone? A woman?

Oh, that was gross.

Then, before she could help herself, Saskia felt a tickle of cold air at the back of her throat behind the sweet – and coughed.

The student moved. A flag of spiky hair began to rise above the car's bonnet.

'No, I'll get some pizza,' she exclaimed, walking off and talking into her hand as if it were a phone, realizing too late that a woman with a buggy was coming straight at her, staring at her curiously.

Saskia dropped her hand and continued quickly towards Hubert Street. She had better tell Kate. Although who knew where that would lead – as if they needed any more problems.

Saskia turned into Hubert Street, trying to shake off the sense of unease at what she'd just witnessed. Kate's semi-detached Edwardian house looked pretty in the evening sunshine, the freshly whitewashed windowsills sparkling, the burnt-orange passionflower that Helen had planted trailing around the front door. Saskia glanced at the house next door, to which Kate's was attached. It looked like the un-identical twin. Whereas Kate's frontage was tidy, her bins behind a wooden fence Richard had erected and stained a pale lilac chosen by Helen, the one next door was undoubtedly a student house. It was worn and tired; its windowsills also painted white, but this time, the paint sloshed cheaply over the joins and onto the windowpanes. Bikes lay in heaps, chained together. A wheelie bin was half open, binbags bursting out, the faint smell of rubbish detectable from here.

That was the best thing about living in a Cotswold village. No students. Not for the first time, Saskia wished Mum and Dad had worked harder to persuade Kate not to rush into buying when she moved from London; that they hadn't been so wary of her bloody moods, that they had made her check who lived next door.

Steeling herself, as she always did on arrival at Hubert Street, Saskia walked up to the door and pressed the bell.

'Hello,' a deep voice said behind her. The 'oh' was pronounced as 'aw', with a long, Scandinavian vowel.

The weirdo was walking in through the gate next door. He regarded her impassively from behind his glasses.

'Hi,' she said, as chilly as she could.

Creep.

He'd probably followed her up the road, taking photos of her backside.

To her relief, Jack flung open the door, grinning.

'Hey, Jackasnory!' she exclaimed in relief, walking inside and shutting the front door behind her. She held her hands slightly forward, in case he wanted to hug. She was never sure these days. Did boys of nearly eleven hug?

Luckily, her nephew was in the mood. He came straight to her,

26

wrapping himself tightly around her waist. She put her arms round him and moved his body gently from left to right. He stayed there happily. Or was it desperately? She wasn't sure any more.

'God, you give the best cuddles. Did you win?'

'Two–nil,' Richard shouted from the sitting room. 'And he's in the reserves for a junior league team next term.'

'Oh, are you now? Smartybum.' Saskia grinned, pushing Jack back to see a beaming, upturned face.

Then the smile disappeared and was replaced with a meaning-ful stare.

'What?'

'Please?' he mouthed, holding his hands in the prayer position.

'Oh.' She glanced through to the kitchen, where Helen was lifting a pot. That was odd. Her mother hadn't looked up and given her one of her cheery hellos.

'No. Not now. Later. You'll get me into trouble, Snores. I'm still thinking about it,' she whispered, pushing him towards the sitting room. 'Take this.' She gave him the magazine. 'Go and keep Granddad company. Stop him annoying me.'

Jack obeyed, as he always did, thrusting out his lip to make her laugh.

Saskia checked her mother again in the kitchen. She was seemingly unaware that Saskia had arrived. What was different about her? Her shoulders? They were rigid. And even from here her face appeared rosier than normal.

Saskia went to hang her bag on the balustrade.

There was a silver flash above her head.

She blinked, as her mind tried to process what she had just seen.

She looked up again.

As she stood staring, her father walked out of the sitting room and placed his hands on her shoulders.

She turned and saw his jovial face as serious as it had ever been.

'*What. The. Hell?*' she mouthed, incredulous, pointing up-stairs.

'Later,' he murmured, nodding towards the sitting room, where Jack was.

Her dad headed off down the hallway, shoulders hunched, towards her mother, who, Saskia realized, had been crying. It was all she could do not to shout, 'Kate?' and run off around Oxford looking for her stupid bloody idiot of a sister-in-law.

CHAPTER FOUR

It was a while until Kate began to talk to Sylvia. They sat in silence, as she knew they might. It was an old-fashioned silence, Kate thought. Inside these thick walls there were none of the normal city sounds. No kids shouting in the street. No sirens. The silence felt thick and upper class and dusty.

She scanned the room. In the centre was an oversized stone fireplace, its heart blackened and empty. A Chinese urn sat on an oak table. This was the type of house a housekeeper used to run, Kate thought. Sylvia still probably had a woman who cleaned every day. She couldn't see elegant Sylvia kneeling down and scrubbing away coal dust.

Sylvia sat opposite her on a sofa. The fabric was strewn with a faint orange-and-green botanical print. Just the right tone of faded, Hugo would have said.

Above the fireplace was an oil painting of a woman in a wine-coloured velvet dress, with Veronica Lake blonde hair, sitting with her hands in her lap, staring out.

'That's amazing,' Kate said, pointing.

Sylvia smiled. 'Thank you.'

Kate shifted in her seat. She crossed her legs, then her arms, then tried to uncross them again. That was amateur stuff. Everyone knew that. The defensive move.

Sylvia kept looking at her. She had a face both long and broad, with generous cheekbones. Her lips were painted a pale red. Kate suspected she was a woman who had grown comfortable in her large frame in later years.

She shifted in her seat, trying to find something to say. 'It reminds me of those horror films when you were a child. Where you move around the room and the eyes in the painting follow you.'

Sylvia nodded.

Kate sighed. This was hopeless.

The ticking of a grandfather clock filled the room like a heavy heartbeat.

Kate looked out the window.

She forced her lips apart. 'It is going to sound silly.'

'Why don't you try?'

Kate placed her elbows on her knees and dropped her face into her hands.

'OK. Well. It appears . . .'

She heard Sylvia breathing steadily.

'. . . that I am cursed.'

The word sang out into the old-fashioned room.

Kate gasped. Sitting up abruptly, she covered her mouth. But she was too late. Laughter burst out. 'Oh God. I'm sorry. That just sounded funny.' She pointed up. 'You know, with the painting, and everything.'

Sylvia smiled.

'Like I'm in a Vincent Price movie, or something . . . You know, "I'm CURSED, I tell you!"' She rolled the syllables like a comedy horror actor, curling her fingers like talons beside her face.

Sylvia held her gaze.

'Sorry. I'm nervous,' Kate said. She stopped fighting her arms and let them wrap around her chest.

Sylvia dropped her head to one side, like a bird.

'Can you tell me what you mean by cursed, Kate?'

How could she explain this? It sounded so crazy. 'OK. Well, I mean, that I'm someone to whom bad things happen.'

She lifted her thumb to her mouth and bit the nail. It tasted gritty and the little biting noises seemed to fill the room.

'What kind of bad things, Kate.'

Out of the blue, a tear pricked at her eye. Damn. Where had that come from? Kate swallowed hard. 'Uh, it happens all the time. For instance, ten days ago I was burgled. They broke into the back of the house when I was out at a work meeting and stole my laptop and my son's Wii.'

Sylvia nodded sympathetically. 'I'm sorry to hear that. But it's not unusual to be burgled, Kate.'

Kate pushed her hands into her knees. 'No, but it's the second time I've been burgled in five months. Every time I come home, I'm terrified I'm going to walk in and find there's been another break-in. Even if there hasn't been, I keep thinking that things have been taken or moved. I can't find things I thought I'd left on a table or on a shelf. I'm sure I've left a cupboard door shut, then I find it open.'

'Burglary can be traumatic.' Sylvia nodded. 'It can leave you feeling very invaded.'

Kate threw her head back, trying not to sound irritated. 'Yes, but it's not just that. It's not just the burglary. You asked for an example. I was just giving you one. No one else in my street has been burgled this year. Out of fifty houses. Just me. Twice.' She frowned as Sylvia's face remained impassive. 'Oh. I don't know how to explain it . . . OK. You know how most people will never be in a train crash, but a tiny number will be in two? Well, I'm always the person who's in two train crashes.'

Sylvia nodded. 'OK. Could you give me another example?'

Kate sighed. This was harder than she'd imagined.

'OK. Well. Five years ago my h—'

She stopped. The tears were welling again. Threatening to betray her. To expose soft wounds beneath toughened bones.

She tried again but the word remained stuck in her mouth. Sylvia waited.

'I find it difficult to say the word.'

'Take your time.'

She swallowed hard and forced the syllables forwards. 'My *hus*-band.' The word came out strangled and sore.

'Your husband?'

Kate stared.

Of course, Sylvia didn't know.

For a second, the word 'husband' sounded real in this woman's mouth. As if it applied to now. As if it were still precious and present. It was such a shock that Kate forgot about fighting the tears. One burst free and ran down her cheek.

'Please.' Sylvia leaned forwards, offering tissues.

'Oh,' Kate groaned involuntarily, taking one. She sniffed and wiped her cheek. 'No. My husband . . . was killed.'

The flash of violence, silver and sharp. She automatically touched her stomach.

'Oh, Kate. How terrible for you. I'm so sorry,' Sylvia said.

Kate held up one hand and took a breath so deep to control herself that she felt her lungs would burst.

'And my parents.'

It was no good. When the breath returned back out of her lips, it had transformed into a sob. It forced its way out of her chest and burst noisily into the room.

She sat back in the chair, horrified.

'Sorry,' she gasped, trying to force it back.

'Kate, it's fine to cry.'

Kate shook her head vigorously. She tried to form the words 'It's not' with her lips, but the motion threatened to allow the tears to escape properly. She shut her eyes and fought hard, focusing on the torrent that she knew was trying to force through the tunnels of her interior, weakening the walls that kept her upright and functioning on the worst days, before knocking them down with an effortless wave, to send her wearily, exhausted, to another lost day under the covers in bed.

No.

Angrily, Kate sniffed even harder.

She *did not cry any more*.

She *would* not.

'One thousand.' She forced herself to count internally. 'Two thousand . . . Three thousand . . . Four . . .'

The heave of her chest settled gradually.

Sylvia clasped her hands in her lap. 'Kate. I can see this is very difficult for you. Would you like to tell me what happened?'

'No,' Kate said, gratefully feeling her composure gradually return. 'It was years ago. Anyway, that's not why I'm here. Not right now.'

She sat up, determined, facing Sylvia. It was time.

'I'm here because I do sums.'

'Sums?'

'Yes. Obsessively. All the time, in my head.'

'Could you tell me what kind of sums?'

Kate shrugged.

'I calculate stuff . . . statistics. Constantly. To stop more bad things happening to us.'

'You and your son?'

'Jack. Yes.'

'Could you give me an example?'

'Well, I could. But before I do, I need to know something.'

'Please.'

Kate sat forwards. 'If I tell you, do you have the power to take away my son?'

Sylvia blinked. Just once. 'Kate, if I feel a child is in immediate danger, I have an obligation to take some action. But the fact that you are here, seeking help in relation to your son, makes me think you are a good mother.'

Kate nodded, surprised. 'I try to be,' she said, fighting back fresh tears.

'Well, why don't we concentrate on you? Can you tell me more about these sums?'

Kate looked out of the window. For a whole minute, she didn't speak.

'OK, there was a lot of traffic tonight so I decided to cycle. But before I cycled, I did a sum. I worked out that because it's May, my chances of having a bike accident are higher because it's summer, and about 80 per cent of accidents take place during daylight hours, but more than half of cycling fatalities happen at road junctions, so if I went off-road I could lower it drastically. So I did. And because I am thirty-five, I have more chance of having an accident than another woman in Oxfordshire in her twenties, but because I was wearing my helmet, I have – according to one American report I read, anyway – about an 85 per cent chance of reducing my risk of head injury. Then, when I was cycling I balanced my chances of having an accident with the fact that by doing half an hour of sustained cardio cycling, I can lower my risk of getting cancer. Of course, that meant I increased my chances of being sexually attacked by being alone on a quiet canal path, but as I have roughly a one in a thousand chance in Oxfordshire, I think it's worth taking.'

She thought she saw Sylvia flinch.

'And then when I was cycling here, I kept doing calculations. When I passed through Osney weir, I didn't think how pretty it was; I looked for the tree I'd cling on to if I accidentally fell in, and planned how I'd swim with the current, not against it, because if you plan your escape you improve your chances of survival. And when I passed the waterside flats at Botley, I didn't think how lovely it must be to live there, I thought about how I'd just read that three thousand properties are at risk of a one-in-a-hundred-year flood in Oxford. Same when I passed the cottages backing on to the river path at Jericho: I thought about how more burglaries take place at the rear of a house, and . . .'

Her breath ran out, as if her lungs had been squeezed like an airbed to be packed away.

'They just come at me like swarms. I can't explain it any other way. They come out of nowhere.'

Sylvia kept her arms and legs uncrossed, pointed resolutely at Kate.

'Where do you get these figures from?'

'I Google them – I get them from insurance websites, newspapers. Every day the newspapers have new figures about how to lower or increase the chances of things happening to you – not that it's always clear, because they contradict each other sometimes, and I get them muddled up, but . . .'

'And you compile them, what, into lists?'

'Yes. But when the laptop got stolen, I lost my list, so I've been trying to remember until the new one is delivered next week. I can remember quite a lot, roughly anyway, and I use my iPhone when I can. And I know it's stupid, but I'm worried that I might be getting some figures completely wrong and changing my chances of things happening. Like today – I picked my son up from football because his PE teacher is in his twenties, which I think – if I remember rightly – makes him more likely to have an accident than I am. But my phone battery needed charging, and the kids were travelling in a minibus, and I didn't know how safe that was, so I picked Jack up anyway, in front of his friends, and he just looked so . . .'

She slumped.

'Oh God. I know what it sounds like.'

'What does it sound like, Kate?'

'Crazy.' She sniffed. 'It sounds crazy.'

'Crazy that you want to protect your son?'

Kate looked up, surprised. She wiped her eyes again. 'Thank you. My in-laws think I'm crazy. They don't understand that's all I'm trying to do. After his dad . . .' Her voice faded away. 'I see their faces when I talk about these things, especially in front of Jack. The thing is, I want him to know. I want him to be careful because I'm so scared of anything happening to him too. It's my responsibility to keep him safe. And yet, at the same time, I know it worries him.' She wiped her nose. The words she'd hidden for so long were coming thick and fast now. 'The thing is, I find it hard to judge any more if I'm being rational or not. Like last week – I spent over a thousand pounds in a private clinic in London having a whole-body scan.'

Sylvia shifted in her seat. 'Oh, I'm sorry, Kate, are you . . .?'

Kate waved her hand. 'No. Not at all. I do one every year to check that I'm not becoming ill. That I don't have even the *start* of a tumour. Because I keep reading that catching tumours early can increase your chances of survival. I have to be there for Jack, now Hugo has gone, you see.' She pushed the wet tissues below her eyes as if physically holding back any more tears. 'I mean, is that normal? I don't know any more.' She placed the tissues on her lap and sniffed. 'When Hugo was here he'd rein me in. When my parents died, and Jack was a baby, I was all over the place, but he never let it get out of hand. He'd let me go into

36

meltdown when I needed to – but then he'd also expect me to be normal sometimes, too. That made me expect it, too.'

Sylvia nodded. 'He gave you perspective.'

'Mmm. I had bad days and good days, then eventually more good days. But now, it's not even about bad days. It's gone so far past that that it's like I'm in free fall. That I'll never get back.'

Kate put her head in her hands, concentrating on the swirl of the rug below. From between her knees, she heard the forbidden words emerge from her mouth.

'I miss Hugo so much.'

Sylvia allowed the words to echo around the room.

Kate touched a hand to her hot cheeks.

They sat together silently for a while.

'I'm sorry,' Kate said finally, sitting back. 'I'm all over the place today.'

Sylvia regarded her warmly. 'First sessions can be very emotional, Kate. You've waited a long time to talk about some very private and distressing feelings.'

Kate nodded. 'Thanks. You must think I'm a complete lunatic.'

Sylvia sat very still, giving nothing away with her body language, Kate noted.

'I certainly don't think you're a lunatic. I think you have been very brave coming here. From the little you've told me, I think you are a young woman who has experienced extreme trauma and has understandably been left with overwhelming feelings of anxiety. But you're here now, and that's the first step.'

Kate licked her dry lips. 'Really?'

Sylvia nodded. 'Absolutely. Now, before we go on, can I fetch you a glass of water?'

Kate nodded gratefully.

Sylvia stood up. She walked out of the sitting room, leaving the door ajar.

Kate sat back into the comfortable chair. She looked round the room again. This wouldn't be a bad place to sit for an hour or two a week. This woman might really help her find her way back to Jack.

As she allowed the silence to calm her, the sound of laughter drifted from a room in the back of the house.

A man laughing. Followed by a murmuring of voices.

Sylvia's voice, and a man's voice. Kate strained her ears to hear what they were saying.

They were talking. Sylvia and a man. He was laughing.

She sat up straight.

A second later, she heard Sylvia's heavy step on the hall tiles. She entered the room with a glass of water and shut the door.

'Sorry about that.'

Kate stared. 'Is there someone else here?'

Sylvia sat down. 'Um, Kate, that's something we should clarify. As you know, I see clients in the evening, but because I work from home, I should explain that there may be people around from time to time. But I can assure you that nobody can hear our discussions. Everything we say in here is confidential.'

Kate paused to choose her words carefully.

'You were laughing.'

Sylvia folded her hands on her lap. 'Oh. Kate. I promise you that I was not laughing. And it was nothing at all to do with you.'

'But who was it?'

'Is that important to you?'

'Yes. It is.'

Sylvia kept her jaw strong. 'It was my husband. He just walked in through the garage door talking to a colleague on his mobile. I'm sorry, I wasn't expecting him home this early. He didn't realize that I had a client.'

My husband.

38

Kate flinched. When this woman said the word 'husband', it didn't stick in her mouth. It didn't hurt. It spoke of a life where husbands came home early, not of a life where they never came home.

Different.

Very different.

Same as everyone else.

Pushing her hands on the firm chair, Kate reluctantly stood up.

Sylvia blinked. 'Kate, we still have forty minutes left.'

Kate fumbled in her pockets. 'You know, when Hugo died, they told me not to start bereavement counselling too early. They said I needed to process things first. And by that point, it hurt so badly, I didn't want to talk about it. I didn't want to cry any more. And I think that maybe that was a mistake now.' She pulled out some money. 'I came here because of the damage that decision has done to my son. And what do you do? I tell you these awful things, that I've told no one in five years, and you go into the kitchen . . .' She gave Sylvia an astonished look. '. . . And you laugh.'

Sylvia stood up. 'Kate. I'm so sorry. Please sit down and we can talk a little more.'

'No,' Kate said, placing the money on the oak table and walking to the door. She waved a hand around the room.

'You know, I imagine some of your clients might feel intimidated by this house. But the irony is that, if I wanted, I could buy it. That's what happens when all the people around you are killed. You'd be amazed at how much money people give you. Like this horrible consolation prize. But, you know what? I'd give it all up to escape from this.' She pointed at her head. 'To feel like I used to, even for one day. To be a normal person again, and a decent mother.'

A lump came into her throat. What had she said to this woman? What had she been thinking even coming here?

'Kate!' Sylvia exclaimed, standing up. 'Please. I'm so sorry if you feel I've let you down. Could we discuss it a little more?'

Kate held up her hand. 'If you tell anyone what I told you, or talk to anyone about my son, I'll deny I was ever here.'

With that, she marched into the hall, picked up her helmet without caring whether it scratched the table or not, swung open the wooden door and slammed it behind her.

Saskia came downstairs, shaking head in disbelief. She walked into the kitchen. Richard was reading a newspaper. Helen stabbed potatoes with a knife.

'Have you talked to Jack about it?' she asked quietly.

Richard carried on reading, raising his eyebrows.

'Dad tried, but he just looked embarrassed, poor pet,' Helen replied. She stuck the knife in again. 'Oh help, I've overdone these. Sorry, you lot.'

The dots on her cheeks were a deep raspberry now, like a Russian doll's. Her pale green eyes were watery.

Saskia rested her hands on her father's chair. 'But it's ridiculous,' she whispered. 'We've got to do something.'

'Now now,' Richard murmured, indicating the sitting room.

'When then? He can't live like this.'

'I said, NOT NOW, darling.'

His eyes darted to the hall. Jack was sticking his head round the door frame, watching. The theme tune from *The Simpsons* blared behind him.

'Five minutes, Snores,' Saskia called cheerily. 'Go and wash your hands.'

He nodded and disappeared upstairs.

'What do you want me to do?' she asked.

'Set the table, will you, darling?' her mother said. 'I'll have to mash these over the heat to dry them out.' As she carried the pot to the sink, Saskia could see she was struggling not to drop it.

Saskia spun round. She was sick of it. Seeing Dad, the powerful businessman who took nonsense from no one, walking around Kate on eggshells. Him and Mum summoning bright smiles and constantly calling her 'dear' and 'darling' in an attempt to diffuse the tense atmosphere their daughter-in-law created. Well, if they weren't going to force Kate to see sense, she would.

Saskia's eyes settled on a closed door next to the sitting room. She checked the clock. Kate would be back after seven.

That would do it. Send a message.

Quietly, Saskia took down a tray from above the fridge and placed glasses, a jug of water and cutlery on it. Then she walked past the kitchen table where her father sat, and carried it to the hallway.

She turned the handle of the closed door. As she expected, it was locked.

'Sass, darling, don't . . .' she heard her mother whisper loudly from the kitchen. 'You know what she's like.'

'I'm doing it, Mum,' she said, reaching above the door frame for the new key. She saw her father shake his head.

She turned it in the door, and pushed it open.

It was the smell that hit her first. The smell of disuse. The odours of fresh paint and a new carpet, incarcerated for four years in this locked room. Forced to ripen into a chemical reek, now complimented by the sweet tang of fresh putty.

Shutting the door gently so Jack wouldn't hear, she walked to the window and pushed the curtains further apart to brighten the room. It had little effect. The room was naturally sombre. Like that gloomy parlour in the eighteenth-century cottage she and

Jonathan had rented in North Wales one Easter that felt as if bodies had once been laid out in it before funerals. Or perhaps it had just been a foreboding about the fate of their marriage.

She placed the tray gently on the long walnut Georgian table, one of the few beautiful pieces Kate had kept of Hugo's. How many times had she been in here? Once? Twice? In four years? The room was painted the same white Kate had chosen for the rest the house. Not the careful shade of off-white Hugo would have spent a month tracking down. This was Kate's white. An I-don't-care, this-will-do shade of white. The fresh putty used to fix the window broken by the burglar was lighter than the rest. She ran a finger over it. Dry.

Curious, Saskia looked round. There was nothing in here apart from a four-drawer oak sideboard with turned legs that she remembered from the Highgate house, too. Something Hugo had salvaged from one of his restoration projects.

She knelt down on the carpet and opened a door.

A silver Georgian-era epergne stared back at her, its delicate arms and tiny bowls, once ready to shine as the centre piece of a lavish dinner party, now tarnished and unloved.

Her hand shot out to touch its cold surface. She hadn't seen this for years.

A rush of memories came at Saskia, unexpected and pungent.

Dinner at Hugo and Kate's.

Opening the door further, she found the sets of gold-plated bone china that Hugo collected, his exquisite silver soup terrine, found in a cellar in a derelict property in Bath and polished to within an inch of its life, now blackened and dull once again.

She shut her eyes and saw it all for a moment. Friends seated along the Georgian table, silver cutlery, laughing, eyes shining under Hugo's prized candelabra. Hugo pouring the wine so generously that she'd find herself emptying half-drunk goblets into the sink at the end of the night, with Kate growling something about 'there goes our bloody pension down the drain'. Hugo the fabulous host. The spirit of Hugo.

Now all hidden away in a cupboard in a locked room.

She took out a modern taupe table runner that she recognized from their casual suppers around the kitchen table in the basement. A musty smell arose from it. She ran her fingers along it, then stopped.

There was a dark-grey stain on it, the size of a two-pence piece. Red wine, perhaps.

Why hadn't it been washed off?

A glint of glass below the china caught her attention. What was that? Kneeling down, Saskia pushed her hand into the back, trying not to knock over a set of cut-glass crystal. It was a bottle. Grimacing, she delicately placed her fingers around its neck and pulled it out.

As soon as she saw it, she knew what it was.

Saskia froze.

A dusty bottle of red wine, half-drunk, with a stopper in its top lay in her hands. Not a particularly good one. In fact, it was one she recognized as the high-end limit of the corner shop near where Hugo and Kate lived in Highgate. She had bought it in there enough times on the way to visit if she was late.

Kate had kept it. Hugo's last bottle of wine, from that night. The one he must have been drinking when those people came to his front door.

Now left to fester. Like all of them.

Saskia opened the wine and sniffed its faint, rotten tang. She surveyed its label, sad that her brother, the generous connoisseur, had been subjected to this bottle of crap as his last.

Just as it was unfair that the son who had inherited his father's

43

fun-loving spirit was having it squeezed out of him, drop by drop, by Kate.

'Hugs,' she whispered into the bottle. 'Don't be cross at me. I promise you, you wouldn't recognize her now.'

There was a noise to her right. The door was opening.

Saskia shoved the bottle back inside.

Jack appeared. His eyes were wide with surprise. He looked round the room and back at her.

'We're not supposed to eat in here.'

'Snores,' she said, standing up. 'Leave it to the grown-ups to worry about things like that. Anyway, you know that thing we were talking about?'

His expression changed.

'Yeah?'

'You know what? I've decided to let you do it. But if you tell anyone, I will seriously kill your head.'

CHAPTER FIVE

Oxford High Street was packed with people out enjoying the summer evening. Kate pushed her bike home over Magdalen Bridge, behind a young couple who had just bolted out of the hatch-door in the giant wooden gate of one of the university colleges on the High Street like rabbits from a secret burrow. Kate tried not to look at them but couldn't help herself.

Clearly they had just tumbled out of bed. They stalked along on long, skinny-jean-clad legs, their arms roaming from waist to shoulder then back again, fluidly, as if they were so high on each other they couldn't stop touching. The girl's hair was long and expertly teased into a perfect bed-head ponytail. The boy wore pointed Chelsea boots and had a black quiff. They spoke in loud confident voices. Oxford University–King's Road–Val d'Isère–Barbados, Kate thought. She knew that type of student.

Not her favourite.

She preferred the odds and sods. The girls in shapeless floral shirts and denim shorts, heavy legs self-consciously covered in dark tights, pointlessly long hair pulled back off spotty faces; the delicate-framed boys in glasses, dressed in white chinos and striped shirts, who looked as if their brains had developed so fast their bodies had never had time to catch up. The outsiders with their awkward physicality and brilliant intellects who looked as if they would spend a lifetime searching for like-minded souls.

That type were easier to bear right now.

Kate crossed the bridge and entered east Oxford. She pushed her bike up the relative peace of Iffley Road towards home, trying to shake off the humiliation of her aborted session with Sylvia.

She had been ready to talk, finally. After months of nearly ringing Sylvia, preparing what to say, she had gone there and it had all burst out at last. Now she had to shove it back inside, to be hidden away again. Her fear had been confirmed. Her problem was ludicrous. Laughable, even. No one could help her.

And if she couldn't help herself, how could she help Jack?

Kate looked ahead up Iffley Road. As if it weren't bad enough, Helen and Richard would be there when she got home, Helen plumping her cushions without being asked, Richard bellowing in his exhausting manner, asking how her fake client meeting had gone as if it was the most important job anyone had ever pitched for.

Kate walked wearily into Hubert Street a few minutes later and put down her bag.

Something was different. She listened. Voices drifted from the back of the house. A glance at the kitchen told her it was empty.

'Hello?' she said, taking off her helmet and peering into the sitting room.

'Hi, Mum!' she heard Jack shout.

She turned towards the dining room door.

Putting down her helmet, she turned the handle.

Unlocked.

She pushed the door open, with a growing sense of dread.

They wouldn't have dared?

She walked into the room to see Richard, Helen, Saskia and Jack sitting at the dining table.

Her dining room table.

The dining room table, where Kate and Hugo and her own

46

parents should have sat a hundred times, enjoying Christmas dinner and family weekend get-togethers and birthday and anniversary celebrations with Jack.

And now Richard and Helen, and Saskia, had forced their way in and taken their places.

Her eyes fell upon the table top. It was laid with plates and cutlery from the kitchen, along with Hugo's bone china serving dishes from the sideboard, and illuminated by his candelabra, the flames of the candles flickering above the old table runner from Highgate. Quickly, she searched out the stain. It was inches from Helen's hands.

There was a row of cards down the middle of the table. Jack was leaning close to Richard, hand on his chin.

Helen twitched nervously, her indented smile apparently stuck on her face, avoiding Kate's eyes.

Kate looked at her sister-in-law. Saskia glared back defiantly.

'We thought we'd sit in here tonight,' she said. 'Have a family meal.'

Kate ignored her. 'Jack, could you go up for your bath, please,' she said as calmly as she could.

'Mum – look at this trick Granddad showed me!' he exclaimed, jumping up, his green eyes flashing in the candlelight. He took her arm and tried to lead her to the cards. 'You've got to choose cards and put them into two piles, and at the end I can turn one pile into red and the other one into black. Really.'

Kate took his hand and held it firmly in hers.

'I said now, please, Jack. Bath.'

He checked with Saskia and his grandparents and dropped his head. He put the cards on the table and walked out, closing the door gently.

Kate stared at her in-laws. So Saskia had invited herself for dinner, too? Three against one now. Perfect. The dreaded triumvirate.

47

'Let me get you a drink, darling,' Richard said, grasping a bottle of rosé.

'No. I don't want a drink, Richard. Thank you.'

Helen nibbled a piece of bread.

'How did it go? Any good, do you think?' Richard continued, replacing the bottle. He pulled out a chair. 'Have a seat.'

Kate shook her head, as she sat down. 'I don't think so. When I explained the work placement situation she wasn't so keen.'

She surveyed the table. How could they do this?

'Not keen on having the local ruffians buffing up her floorboards, eh?' Richard was babbling now, filling the unpleasant silence around the room.

Kate shrugged. 'They're kids from deprived backgrounds, Richard,' she murmured. This wasn't the time for a sparring match with Richard about how she chose to use Hugo's money.

She slumped on the chair, her eyes taking in the sight of her and Hugo's private things. Ransacked. Displayed without permission.

She felt Saskia's eyes boring into her.

'It *is* the dining room, Kate,' Saskia said.

'Anyone else want a refill?' Richard exclaimed.

What was wrong with Saskia? Was she drunk? Her cheeks were pink like her mother's, and her eyes flashed dangerously in the candlelight. Kate tried to control her words. She and Sass might sprinkle their own conversations casually with swear words, but never in front of Richard and Helen.

'And very lovely it looks, too, doesn't it?' said Richard beaming. He waved his hand across the table. 'Hugo would always . . .' Without warning, his voice just cut away. His smile extinguished, like spit on a candle.

He coughed.

'Was this your idea, Sass?' Kate asked quietly.

Saskia sat up straight. 'I think we're the ones who should be asking questions, Kate.' She raised her eyes to the ceiling.

Kate sat, incredulous. Saskia hadn't even been invited this evening. Just turned up, as usual. And now she was questioning her in front of Richard and Helen, in her own house.

'Sass . . .?' she said, shocked.

Richard raised his eyebrows. 'OK, look.' He raised his finger in a stop signal to his daughter. 'Kate?' He turned to his daughter-in-law 'It's just that it is a little unexpected, darling. What you've done.'

Saskia's mouth fell open. 'Unexpected? It's complete bloody madness, Dad! At what point are you and Mum going to stop pussyfooting around her, and tell her this has to stop?'

'Sass!'

Kate and Richard glared at her.

But the volume of Saskia's voice kept rising.

'Or do you think she's going to stop you and Mum seeing Jack? Is that why you put up with it?'

'Sass! Enough!' Richard repeated, his jolliness long gone.

Kate sighed. After the trauma of Sylvia's, a fight between Hugo's family was the last thing she needed.

'Look, I did it in case they come back, Sass,' she said, trying to keep her voice calm.

'But you've just spent thousands on a new alarm!'

What the hell was her sister-in-law doing?

'Sass, I'm sorry, but this is none of your blood—' Kate stopped herself. '. . . Your business. You *know* the old alarm was unreliable, always going off. And even if the new one goes off, it still gives them a few minutes to get upstairs. And what if me and Jack are here? What if none of the neighbours takes any notice because they're so used to the old one going off by accident?'

'Oh for God's sake. This is BLOODY RIDICULOUS!' Saskia yelled, half-standing up.

Kate sat, open-mouthed.

'What about all that money you just spent on putting in the internal locks downstairs? And now this bloody thing,' Saskia exclaimed, pointing upwards. 'I mean, Jesus, Kate? How much did it cost? What the hell would Hugo say?'

Oh no.

Kate gulped hard. 'Sass . . . don't even . . .'

'And then tonight Snores tells us you're not letting him go to the secondary with his friends because you're scared he's going to be stabbed or something; you're thinking of sending him to some private school on his own? I mean, for God's sake, Kate, what is *wrong* with you?'

Kate blinked. 'He's called JACK,' she said, her voice rising to match her sister-in-law's.

Saskia stood facing her, furious.

Richard and Helen sat quietly. Why were they not stopping this?

Without planning it, Kate stood up, too.

'Actually, Sass,' she said, her voice icy, 'if you must know, though I don't think it's any of *your* bloody business, someone from that school was threatened with a knife. A sixth-former. At a party last weekend in Cowley.'

Richard tutted. He shook his head at his daughter.

'Listen, Sass. This isn't helping. Sit down, darling.'

He waited until she begrudgingly obeyed, then turned to Kate. She also sat down.

'Look, Kate, the thing is, these things happen,' he said, taking her hand. His hand was large and warm and comforting, like her own father's used to be. At what point did men's hands become that shape? Hugo's had never reached that stage. They had been too strong and busy and vital at his stage of life. Quick hands, energetic.

'I know you're just trying to protect him, darling, we all understand that. And you know I'd be absolutely delighted if you wanted to send the boy private . . .' Kate bit her fingernail crossly. Richard had never stopped bloody going on about it since she and Hugo had announced they were sending Jack to the local primary school in London. 'But I think what Sass is trying to say is –' he glared at his daughter – 'and perhaps not in the best way, Sass, is that perhaps things are going a little far. You have to prepare the boy for life, not hide him from it.'

Kate shook her head. It was all too much: the session with Sylvia, and now this.

'I'm sorry,' she said, holding up her hands. 'Richard, Sass, Helen – I appreciate everything you have done for me, I really do. And I know not everything is right in my life right now. But Jack is my child and, really, I'm sorry, but this is no one else's business.'

The room fell silent. She picked out the stain on the runner.

Tears began to form again. Exhausted with the effort, she swallowed hard to keep them at bay.

Saskia shook her head, angrily, her cheeks reddening. Richard lifted his palms as if offering peace.

'OK, darling, listen, everyone's getting upset.' He turned to Helen. 'Why doesn't Mum make us some coffee – we'll discuss this some other time, when everyone is more up to it.'

Helen cleared her throat.

'Actually, Kate. I think it is our business.'

Everyone looked at Helen in surprise. In fourteen years, Kate had never heard Helen speak with that firmness in her voice.

'It's gone too far, Kate. You've gone too far.' Her mother-in-law's voice quavered. 'We've stood by for years now watching this . . . this . . . behaviour, but this?' She pointed upwards. 'It's, it's . . . *lunacy*.'

Kate froze.

'And, for your information, Sass,' Helen continued. 'I have already spoken to Social Services anonymously about what is happening in this house and my rights as a grandparent, and, no, I am not worried about Kate not letting me see Jack.'

They all stared at Helen, shocked. Kate fought back more tears. 'No,' she muttered. 'Helen. How could you?'

Helen dabbed at her pink cheeks with a napkin. 'Because I won't let you do this to my grandson any more, Kate. After the terrible thing that has happened to him, this little boy deserves love and reassurance and happiness. But instead you've turned him into a nervous wreck. Do you know he tried three times tonight to stop us eating in here? He was so anxious about what you would say. I mean, for goodness sake, it's a *dining room*.'

Kate kept fighting back the tears, bewildered. What on earth was Helen doing? She waited for her mother-in-law to return to her benign, fragrant self. To apologize. To keep the peace.

But Helen continued, her voice cold.

'In fact, if you want the truth, Kate, I think he needs to come and live with me and Richard for a while.'

'No!' Kate cried, horrified.

'Richard can run him into town to school and pick him up.'

'Richard?' Kate said desperately, turning to her father-in-law.

Richard sighed. 'Darling, you haven't been yourself for a while. Helen's just upset.'

'I am NOT upset,' Helen barked. 'I am simply doing what we should have done a long time ago.'

Kate saw Sass flinch, too, at her mother's unfamiliar tone. She sat back and picked at a long, French-polished fingernail.

Richard regarded his wife. 'OK. Let me reword that. Darling, the thing is, Helen and I feel a strong responsibility to you, but we also need to think about what Hugo would want us to do.'

'You think Hugo would want you to take Jack from me?' Kate spluttered. 'Jesus. Have you been planning this, Helen?'

Richard shook his head. 'No. No. That's not what we're doing, darling. We're just offering to take him for a while to give you a chance to start thinking about how to improve things . . .'

'And if I say no?'

'My next call to Social Services will not be anonymous,' Helen said.

A stunned silence descended on the table.

Kate glanced frantically at her father-in-law. He shook his head sadly.

'Helen,' Kate gasped. 'How could you say that?'

Helen sat upright. 'I've never interfered, Kate. Not once, with all the alarms and hospital visits and the irrational rules and this obsession with . . .' She stopped. 'Because Richard said we needed to give you time after what happened. But you don't even seem aware of your behaviour. You lie to Jack constantly. You told him last week that you were in London seeing a friend, but we know you were at the hospital because you left the letter in the drawer where the clothes pegs are. And this business tonight of frightening him by saying someone had been here, stealing your casserole.'

No. No. This couldn't be happening. Kate clutched her seat.

'Some of it had gone out the dish . . .' she whispered.

'It had NOT GONE!' Helen exclaimed, dropping her delicate, pale hand on the table. 'You imagine these things, Kate! Constantly! And now he's copying you, for goodness sake!' Helen shook her head. 'I mean, this stuff about hearing noises in his wardrobe. Richard had to check inside three times the other night when you were in London. Jack was terribly anxious.'

Kate looked at her mother-in-law in horror. What was she talking about?

'I mean, he's nearly eleven, Kate! When are you going to let him go to the shop or walk to school on his own? What do his friends say? Nearly eleven, thinking there are bad men hiding in his wardrobe?' Kate saw Helen spot her confused expression, then blink with comprehension before Kate could turn away.

Helen sighed deeply. 'Oh, you don't even know, do you? The boy hasn't even told her, Richard.'

Richard shifted in his chair and grunted.

Kate felt the tears pushing and pushing, her resolve to fight them weakened by the shame of Helen's exposure of her lack of communication with Jack.

Helen wrung her hands together. 'I mean, can you even see what's going on here any more, Kate? You're his mother. Some opportunist, probably a drug addict, smashed a window, came in and snatched your laptop. It happens. You need to reassure Jack that's all it was. Not talk constantly about crime and accident and burglary statistics! The poor little chap's lying there in the dark, terrified that sinister figures are hiding in his wardrobe because of this constant anxiety of yours, and he can't even tell you because he knows it will make you worse!' Her face broke into a horrified laugh. 'I mean, this is intolerable! You should be fixing this for the boy. Reassuring him that it will never happen, not making it worse, Kate! Not after what he's been through.'

Desperately, Kate tried to think.

Helen continued. 'And that's why I feel it's time for Jack to—'

Kate held up a hand. 'No, Helen. No. Please. Don't say any more.'

Helen stopped mid-sentence.

'You're right. I know I'm anxious. But I am trying to fix it. I just didn't want to tell you,' she said.

'What, darling?' Richard asked.

Helen and Saskia sat expectantly.

The lie tasted bitter in her mouth. 'I've started therapy.'

'What did you say?'

'I've started therapy.'

'When?' Saskia asked, cynically.

'Tonight. That's where I was. A woman in Summertown. She's called Sylvia.'

'That's convenient,' Saskia murmured.

'She's at No. 15 Hemingway Avenue. Look her up if you like. My GP recommended her. And she said she can help me,' Kate continued.

'When?'

'Next week onwards. I'm going once a week, on Tuesdays, indefinitely. At seven-thirty. She says that it's all a reaction to the trauma of losing my parents, then Hugo. It's just anxiety. She says it's pretty normal. And that she can help me.'

The three of them sat, Richard nodding, Helen now a shade of fuchsia, Saskia, her eyes darting between them, checking their reactions.

'And I can talk to her about Jack, too. Find ways to help him, too.'

'Well – that's fantastic,' Richard said, using the overly jovial voice he always used to gee everyone up. 'Well done, darling.'

Saskia tapped her finger on the table. 'OK then. I'll babysit for you. When you go.' There was a challenge in her voice.

Kate nodded.

'So, that's every Tuesday, at seven-thirty? I'll be here,' Saskia added.

'Helen?' Richard said.

Helen began to rub at the stain on the runner with her finger. Kate watched her mother-in-law, her jaw slack, her eyes sad and serious, and she knew, in that moment, that Helen, like Kate, knew that the faded red mark was not wine.

'If this is true, Kate, then I am glad. But I have to tell you, there will be no going back for me now. Perhaps I should have spoken before. But the situation is that I have lost one son, and I won't allow my grandson to be lost, too. If you don't allow him to start having the happy childhood he deserves, Kate, I will do exactly what I have said. He is not your parent. You are his. If you are unable to start behaving as a present, engaged mother and control your constant anxiety around Jack, I will interfere as I see fit. So, let's call it a start. Let's see how it goes.'

Kate nodded.

'And now I would like you to go and get me the key.'

'The key?' Kate stuttered.

'To that thing.' Helen held out her hand.

Humiliation washed over Kate for the second time that evening. She felt her shoulders sink in defeat. Richard and Saskia averted their gaze. Helen raised her watery pale eyes to meet Kate's, and Kate knew in that minute that Helen, her sweet, chirpy mother-in-law, was now a serious foe.

Her cheeks burning hot, she stood up and walked out of the room and began to climb the stairs.

At the top, she walked through the door of the new ceiling-high steel cage that ran fifteen feet along the length of the upstairs landing, took the key from the door that locked her and Jack safely behind it at night, and brought it slowly back downstairs.

The child crept outside the house after breakfast. It was easy to do. Father had been distracted in the kitchen. He had asked about school, but his mind was clearly elsewhere as he cut bread in large, uneven chunks with a sharp knife, narrowly missing his knuckles. His face was still unshaven and he smelled yeasty as he leaned over to place the toast on the table.

Mother was still sleeping, her door firmly shut.

At one point the child thought of telling Father about the snake on the wall. But would that make it better or worse?

Better to check if anyone else had seen it first.

The child pulled on a jumper against the cold and tiptoed around the side of the house, disappearing behind the stilts that supported the front balcony. A morning frost hung on the trees on the hill opposite; the sky looked like a pane of glass that someone had breathed on. The miniature shape of a distant car moved along the top of the hill, where the woods met the road.

The child turned the corner of the house, looked up, and gasped.

The snake was so big. There was no chance Mother wouldn't see it.

It was slithering right across the wall, its body thick and grey.

Gripped by foreboding, the child looked around for the ladder and placed it against the wall.

The feet of the ladder did not feel particularly safe, wobbling on the rubble below, but the child persevered, climbing gingerly up six or seven rungs.

There was a crunching noise behind.

'What the hell are you doing?'

The child turned. Father was standing crossly, hands on hips.

His eyes moved up to the snake.

There was sound. A moan. Followed by a word that children shouldn't hear.

The child turned back to the snake, hypnotized by its writhing grey body.

'Get down,' Father whispered sternly. 'Go on.' The bones of his face looked like they were about to burst through the skin.

'You do not say a word to her,' he said, as the child reached the bottom.

His breath smelt metallic. 'Do you understand?'

The child nodded as Father spun around and ran for the car, glancing fearfully up at the windows of the house.

CHAPTER SIX

It was Monday morning, a school day. Normally, Jack would be tucked up under the duvet, buried in the deep hormonal slumber of a pre-teenager.

But things weren't normal. For an hour now, he had lain awake, ignoring the growing pressure in his bladder.

He rolled over to face the wall and picked at the Blu-tack behind his Arsenal poster. Rows of red-shirted players stood shoulder to shoulder, the goalkeepers in yellow perched above them. Thoughtfully, he stretched his feet towards the bottom of the bed, pushing his arms in the other direction. Nana had said he was 'about the same' height as Dad when he was ten and three-quarters, but that wasn't strictly true. On the back of the airing cupboard door at her house, he'd discovered the names 'Hugo' and 'Saskia' written against little black marks measured in inches that climbed up the door like a ladder. He had run his finger along a faded date in 1984 to his father's name. Dad had already been three inches taller.

Jack rested a hand on his stomach. The warmth helped with the cramps.

His eyes drifted to the old fitted wardrobe beside the fireplace. The doors were still firmly closed, as he had left it last night. His electric guitar was still propped up against it to hold the doors in place, now that the metal catch had stopped working properly. The bright red instrument leaned a little to the left, like a drunken sentry. 'What would his friends say about him being scared of sinister men in his wardrobe?' he'd heard Nana say last night through the stripped floorboards, as he'd lain flat, wondering why she was talking in a strange voice. As if he was ever going to tell Gabe and Damon that?

His stomach cramped extra hard.

He reached up and took down the little snowdome from his shelf and shook it. Glitter exploded above a miniature plastic mountain. He waited, then shook it again.

Finally, he heard the noise he had been dreading since seven o'clock this morning.

His mother's bedroom door opening. A pad of bare feet towards the stairs.

He rolled onto his back, stuffing his fingers in his ears.

'Jack,' she called gently. 'Are you up? We've slept in.'

'Hmm,' he replied, removing his fingers a fraction.

'You'll have to get dressed quickly. What do you want for breakfast?'

His stomach gurgled.

'Nothing. I'm not hungry.'

'You need something. Do you want a bagel?'

There was a click. He stuck his fingers back in his ears so hard, his nails scraped the skin inside. But it was too late. He had heard it.

'OK,' he shouted, willing her to go away.

She was opening the gate. Trying to do it so he wouldn't hear. Trying to pretend she hadn't locked it again with that padlock he'd seen in her shopping bag on Saturday. Even though he'd heard Nana tell her not to on Friday night.

Jack looked up at the plastic stars Aunt Sass had stuck on his ceiling when they moved here from London when he was six. Blood thumped inside his barricaded ears. *Boom, boom, boom.* He shut his eyes and imagined he was swimming under the ocean among those shoals of baby rays he'd seen at the aquarium in London with Nana and Granddad, the muscles in his stomach stretched out and eased by the warm water.

When the biggest cramp came, he focused hard on the poster and imagined saving a penalty shoot-out for Arsenal in the FA Cup. Six foot two, Dad had been. Still smallish for a professional goalie but possible. He needed to eat more to try to catch Dad up.

The faint aroma of toasted bagel floated into his bedroom.

With a grunt, Jack pulled himself out of bed and swept his hair out of his face. He took off his pyjamas, found his school uniform things in his drawers, and pulled them on. He removed the guitar and opened the wardrobe hesitantly.

A rail of clothes appeared, above two shelves that Granddad had built. Checking quickly that Mum wasn't behind him, Jack swept a hand behind the clothes, touching the wall to check no one was there. He went to pick up his trainers for PE from the bottom shelf, then stopped.

They had moved again.

He was sure of it.

He had chucked them in the other day, and now they sat neatly, pointing outwards.

Jack grabbed them by the laces and stood up. Had Mum tidied them up when she was putting away his clean laundry?

He rubbed his stomach hard, hunched his shoulders and went to open his bedroom door, knowing he couldn't ask her. She'd just start going on again about someone eating the casserole and look even more worried.

The bars of the cage glinted in the morning sun. They were as flat and wide as his school ruler, embedded into a long bracket on the ceiling above. The door had been pushed back quietly into its hook in the wall, leaving the entrance open to the top of the stairs.

Jack ran to the bathroom, peed and washed, then walked through the open gate quickly, trying not to look at it.

'What do you want on it?' his mother shouted, as he came downstairs.

'Peanut butter, please,' he replied, walking towards the kitchen. He would make himself eat it. Perhaps, when he measured himself again secretly on Nana's door this Saturday, there would be a difference. Sometimes he measured himself two or three times on the same day, just to be sure.

Kate turned, unsmiling, to butter Jack's bagel, as he sat at the table and watched her. Her shoulder blades were showing even more clearly than before through the worn cream silk of the nightie Dad had given her, like two L-shapes, back to back. He looked down at her legs. White string with knots in.

Jack sipped the tea she'd made for him and tried to think about something else.

'When's the new laptop getting delivered, Mum?'

She groaned as she placed his bagel on the table. 'This week, I hope. They tried to say they'd delivered it on Tuesday when I was in London – you know, when I went up to see Patricia, our old neighbour in Highgate,' she added swiftly. Her eyes slid off to the left again, Jack noted. 'I knew it was coming,' his mum continued, 'but I didn't have time to rearrange the delivery, so I thought they'd just take it back to the depot and I could get it the next day. Anyway, they're saying they did deliver it on Tuesday, but obviously they didn't. So it's their fault, and now they're sending another laptop on Friday.' His mum shook her head. 'I should have just gone to the bloody shop. I've got to get some figures off to David in London by next weekend for a sealed bid auction.'

She frowned and returned to the sink. Jack took a reluctant bite of his bagel, thinking. If he got Gabe to invite him round after school, they could use his mum's computer and see if Aunt Sass had done what she'd promised.

He looked up and saw Kate watching him from the sink.

'Jack, you're not getting one. Please don't ask again. There are reasons that ten is too early.'

He shrugged. 'I know. There are weird people looking at the internet. They told us at school.'

'Good.' She came over and sat down with a cup and no food. He could smell the hot raspberry from her tea. He saw her take an uncertain pause.

'I like your hair like that,' she said. 'Bet the girls do, too.'

'No,' he said, awkwardly. 'They like Gabe. He's taller than me.'

Her forehead immediately creased again with worry. He sighed inwardly.

'It doesn't matter. Don't worry about it, Mum.'

Jack took another bite of the bagel, pushing his teeth hard through the tough dough. Just chewing it made his stomach tighten painfully again.

Why was *she* frowning? Being small was his problem, not hers.

He chewed even harder.

Out of nowhere, Jack suddenly felt very, very cross.

She had locked that stupid, embarrassing gate again last night, even though Nana had told her not to. She had completely lied to Nana. Done the opposite of what she'd promised. And now he knew that she'd lied, and Nana didn't, and if Nana asked him when he went to stay this weekend, and he told her the truth, Mum would be cross.

He glanced at his mum, but her eyes were lost again, somewhere off in her secret place.

Why did she always have to make everybody so worried?

Why could he never tell her he was scared of the strange noises he heard in the wardrobe at night? Or of the cramps in his stomach, which he suspected might be caused by the same disease that boy had on Children in Need? Or of the Year Eight boys who were making him and Gabe a bit nervous?

Why could he not tell Mum any of this without her stealing his worries and turning them into her own, making it worse, not better?

Jack sat back.

A second wave of anger engulfed him.

A thought took him by surprise. Right now, this minute, he *hated* her. He wasn't just cross. He actually hated her.

Jack leaned forwards at the table, chewing harder, savouring this new, strange feeling, glancing at Kate as she stared out of the kitchen window into the garden, sipping her tea with a little hissing noise.

Thoughts began to pile into his head, one after the other. Yes – he *hated* her. Hated her stupid nightie that she wore all the time even though it had little holes in it like wounds. Hated the way she never listened to him and always made his worries her worries. Hated the way she kept talking about people breaking into their house and other bad things that made him lie awake at night, seeing shadows and hearing creaks. Hated the way she lied to Nana and was allowed to make their house grey and quiet all the time, just because she was the adult.

Jack put down his bagel and watched his mother chewing her lip.

The hate suddenly made him feel brave.

'Mum?'

'Hmm?'

'I want to go to secondary school with Gabe and everyone else.'

Kate stirred her tea even though she hadn't put any sugar in it. The bags under her eyes were even darker than usual, he noticed.

'I don't want to go to that private school.'

He waited for her reaction.

Kate sighed. 'Well, you don't have to.'

'Really?' He bit his bagel again, his appetite returning a little.

'No.' She took a sip of tea. 'Jack, listen, I made a decision this weekend. You know we moved to Oxford so Nana and Granddad could help me after Daddy?'

He nodded.

'Well, I think we're better now.'

He stopped mid-chew. 'What do you mean?'

'I mean, I think it might be a good time for us to go back to London.'

Jack tried to swallow the lumpen, soggy dough but it seemed to swell up and lodge in his throat. He tried again, but it stuck there, refusing to move forwards or backwards. In a panic, he took a mouthful of tea and gulped as hard as he could. The hot liquid forced the soggy mass down his throat, hurting it.

Perhaps it was because he was gasping to clear his mouth, that when he spoke it came out in a panicked rush.

'NO!' he yelled.

The sides of his mother's face drew back like curtains.

'Jack?'

His voice came out so loud it shocked him, too. But there was something about the shout that felt good. Before he could help it, he knew he wanted to do it again.

He jumped up. 'NO!' he cried.

'Jack?' There was a bewildered expression on her face. 'Why are you shouting?'

He didn't know. He just knew it felt good. He tried the new voice again.

'Because I'm sick of you always making me do what you want to do!'

Her eyes were round and wide, cold amber glass. Jack realized that he wanted to smash that glass, and make her eyes move. Make them move like Nana's. Make them *do something*.

'Jack!' She sounded scared. 'What's got into you? Why are you speaking like this? Has Nana said something?'

Tears were seeping into her eyes.

Oh, not *again*.

The little boy slammed both his hands down.

'NO!' he yelled. 'Don't cry. You always do that! I'm not looking at you any more!'

His mother opened her eyes wide. 'Jack. I'm not crying! I try very hard not to cry.'

He spun round, with no idea where he was going. He just knew he wasn't doing this. Clenching his fists, he stalked out of the kitchen into the hallway. He sat on the stairs, pulled on his school shoes without undoing them and grabbed his bookbag.

'Where are you going?' Kate asked, following him. She was gulping hard, like she was swallowing horrible medicine.

'SCHOOL!'

'But it's only eight o'clock. Gabe won't be ready to walk to school with you yet.'

He could hear the panic in her voice. 'I don't care. I'm going on my own. Everyone else does. Everyone else's mum doesn't think they're going to get KILLED BY A CAR OR A MURDERER!'

She looked dismayed. He didn't care. His voice was gaining

new volume with every sentence. Every time he did it, it felt like he was blowing things up.

Pow! Pow!

The power was exhilarating.

There was a loud sniff from his mother's direction. He glowered, looking for his trainers. He didn't care if she was upset. She never helped him. The truth was sometimes he felt a bit scared about the idea of walking to school on his own, but she should be making him feel *better* about it, not more worried. Helping him.

Jack saw his PE trainers by the stairs and grabbed them.

'Jack. Please. You haven't even done your teeth,' she said. She was trying to say calm grown-up things in a voice that was all wobbly and confused and hurt.

As he took his blazer off the banister, he looked up and saw the stupid cage gate.

He was sick of it. Everyone feeling sorry for him. For his Dad. For having a weird mum, and now a stupid house.

He turned and scowled at Kate.

'YOU go to London!' he shouted, unbolting the door. 'I'm not staying in this stupid house any more. I want to live with Nana. She said I could. I heard her. Nana's kind.' And, then, before he could stop himself, 'AND, she lets me go to the shop on my own.'

He heard Kate gasp. 'She WHAT?'

'She LETS ME GO!' he yelled defiantly. 'EVERY Saturday at twelve o'clock when the baker in the village opens to get bread for lunch!'

His mum opened her mouth wide, eyes furious. 'Bloody Nana,' she spat. 'How DARE she? I KNEW this had something to do with her. What else has she done? What has she said?'

He shook his head furiously. 'It's NOT Nana. It's YOU. You're

. . . you're . . . just the worst mother EVER! I just . . . HATE YOU!'

Turning to find the Chubb key for the lock, he saw his mother's face. It looked as if it had dried on to her bones.

At that moment, the little boy realized with a strange curiosity that she was not in control after all. The power had always been his to take. He could blow her up whenever he wanted.

He turned and shoved the Chubb key in the lock and tried to turn it.

Behind him came a low moan. It sounded like the cat from across the back when it went into a coma in their garden.

He stopped.

He had seen her worried, seen her eyes furiously blinking back tears, but he had never heard that noise before. A picture came into his mind of that terrible earthquake he had watched with Granddad on the news, where everything was blown up and broken, and the people on the news said that nothing would ever be the same again.

A cramp tightened in his stomach so painfully that he bent over and grunted.

What had he done? He'd told her about Nana letting him go to the baker's in the village. And now they'd fight about that, too.

To his shame, Jack felt tears coming into his own eyes. Desperately, he tried to grab the door knob and get out before she said anything else.

'Jack!' his mother gasped. 'No!'

He turned the Chubb key and a piercing sound exploded into the air.

Jack jumped back, shocked.

The burglar alarm.

She hadn't turned it off this morning.

The ear-splitting din filled his head, and he lifted his hands instinctively to cover his ears. At the same time he felt his mum grab the shoulder of his school shirt, pulling him back from the door. He jerked away from her.

'No, Jack!' she yelped.

His movement threw him off-balance. His body swung around in her grasp and veered sideways. He felt her try to grab him tighter to stop him falling, but he twisted loose out of her fingers.

Jack saw the hall radiator coming towards him out the corner of his eye. Before he could put out a hand, his forehead glanced off the side of it. It was sharp, and it hurt.

'Oh my God – Jack!'

He landed on his knees, and stayed there for a second, jolted. He touched his forehead and felt something wet. There was blood on his finger.

The house alarm was squealing at full pitch now, stabbing inside his ears.

It all felt too much. All this blood and power and noise and destruction.

Jack sat stunned, as Kate jumped up, ran to the alarm box under the stairs and punched in a number.

Silence abruptly descended on the hall again.

Jack leaned back against the radiator.

Kate rushed back and grabbed his face, looking at the cut.

'Jack. I'm so sorry,' she said. 'I was trying to stop you setting off the alarm.'

She wiped blood from his cut with her fingers. It smeared across her skin. Nana would do it with a tissue, Jack thought, jerking his head away. Nana always had a clean tissue. Nana would put a gentle arm round him that smelt of flowers, and talk calmly, not swipe at the blood with bare fingers as if it were attacking her, and look at him in terror. 'I didn't mean to pull you so hard,' Mum was gabbling. 'Is your head sore? Do you feel dizzy?'

He shook it.

She stopped speaking and let her hand drop. He saw her rub his blood between her fingers. She had retreated again. Lost in her head.

'Stay there. I'll get a plaster.'

She went in the kitchen, with her hand over her mouth. Jack sat in the hallway, fighting the tears that threatened to come properly now.

All of a sudden, he felt ashamed. He was sitting on the floor, trying not to cry like a baby, with a scratch on his head. He looked up and saw himself in the hall mirror. What if Dad was watching him? Acting like a baby? Granddad had told him that he, Jack, was supposed to be the man of the house now Dad was gone.

And just like that, Jack's hate for Kate disappeared as quickly as it had come.

As she hurried around looking in cupboards, her lips were forming words as if she were having a conversation with someone invisible.

It took him a moment to work it out.

'You have to stop this,' she was mouthing. 'You have to stop this.'

What had he done?

As she began to walk towards him, Jack dropped his eyes.

'Jack?'

He stayed still.

'Jack? Darling.'

Eventually, he looked at her.

'Let me . . . do this . . .' She knelt down and dabbed at his cut with an antiseptic cream that stung a little, and then placed a plaster over the cut. It was strange being this close to her. He could smell raspberry tea on her breath. He could see how the pale purple circles under her eyes grew deeper in tone under her dark eyelashes.

'Are you sure you feel OK?' She made him follow her finger with his eyes to be sure.

'OK. Oh, Jack.'

She sat back and surveyed his face. He saw her eyes working hard, as if she was thinking.

She went to speak, then stopped – then tried again. 'Jack. Listen. This is so bad. I don't know how to say this to you, but . . .' She looked him in the eye. 'If anyone asks you how you got the scratch, I need you not to tell them that you hit your head on the radiator.'

He waited.

'The thing is, they might not understand that it was an accident. Nana, for instance. Or your teacher. So, if it's OK, you could just say you fell off your skateboard. Is that OK?'

There was such a pleading tone in her voice that Jack shrugged.

She leaped towards him and threw her arms around him. He was too surprised to resist. Her body pushed into his face and he smelt her anxious sweat through the silk nightie.

'Jack. I'm so sorry. I don't know what is happening to me, but I will make this right,' she murmured. 'I just . . .' She sniffed. 'I just want you and me to be safe.' It was such an unfamiliar sensation, being in her arms again, that Jack let his face press against the protruding bone of his mother's shoulder and watched, curious, as a trickle of watery pink blood from his forehead seeped into the pores of her shoulder strap. He found himself hoping the stain would finally force her to throw it away.

He stayed there, even though he knew the embrace was to make her feel better, and not him. Knowing that she was trying.

The thing was, if he kept being angry like this, and destroyed her, he would also destroy any chance that his old warm funny mum, whom he was starting to forget, would return from behind those amber glass eyes. He had to do it for Dad, in case Dad was watching, counting on him to look after Mum, counting on him to be there waiting if she ever came back.

So Jack stayed there, still, inside Kate's embrace, trying to stay hopeful that she was still somewhere inside.

It was after nine by the time Kate had cleaned Jack up and she could drop him at primary school, nervously gauging his Year Six teacher's expression through the window as he entered the classroom. Kate left before Ms Corrigan could call her back. She knew that, under scrutiny, her eyes would expose the lie about the skateboard.

She drove home and ran upstairs to her office, sat at her desk and looked out at the rich green leaves of the magnolia tree that had months before shed its pink flowers onto the lawn. She sat there for an hour, doodling tight-knit webs and teetering towers onto white paper, then for another hour.

Jack's face haunted her vision. Blood dripping from his forehead. The angry voice that sounded as if it had emerged from a long tunnel, thickened by echoes. His glance of disgust when she asked him not to tell Nana what had happened.

Social Services. That was what Helen had said on Friday.

Kate bit her thumbnail. The skin around it was raw and wet.

From nowhere, a forgotten memory of her mother-in-law returned. A memory from fourteen years ago that Kate thought she had long put to rest. It had been the first time, she had met Richard and Helen. She and Hugo had arrived at their house for

Sunday lunch, trying to shake off the hangover from a student party in London the night before. Helen had come behind Richard down the hallway, drying her hands on a tea towel. Kate had smiled nervously as she went to hold out a hand.

'Ah, my precious boy,' Helen had said, ignoring her, instead reaching up to Hugo's face. She touched his cheeks tenderly, while Kate stood to the side, feeling awkward. Hugo had given her a flutter of a wink over his mother's head.

'How are you, my darling?' Helen asked.

Hugo took her hands in his own, physically turning her to the left. 'Good! Mum! This is Kate.'

Kate knew from the emphasis he placed on her name that he was introducing her to Helen as someone significant. Someone he and his mother had already discussed. But, as Helen turned her pale watery green eyes on Kate, Kate suspected, already, that she'd failed. Right there, hungover, in her studenty jeans and scuffed boots, with her Shropshire accent and her state school education, she knew that everything Helen, in her grand riverside house, had been hoping for had not appeared this morning.

'Hi,' Kate said, holding out a hand. 'Nice to meet you.'

'Hello, Kate,' Helen said, taking it. She displayed a modest smile. The smile stretched as she turned back to Hugo, only to find him watching Kate, mesmerized.

Later, Kate would wonder if that was when Helen decided that whatever concerns she had about Kate's suitability for her 'precious boy' were to be packed away immediately. That the glow in her son's eyes as he looked at Kate told her that this was deadly serious. There was no going back for him.

Certainly, Helen had never treated her like that again, to the point where Kate had convinced herself that she had imagined that first encounter. Blamed it on her hangover.

Till now.

She looked out of the window as the sun disappeared around the back of the garden. What if that malevolent undercurrent she'd glimpsed in Helen on their first meeting *did* exist? Had *always* existed, but been hidden for Hugo's sake, then Jack's?

On impulse, Kate sat back and opened a drawer in her desk, to take out a photo.

She hesitated, her fingers outstretched in mid-air.

The photo was turned on its front, not face-up as she had left it on top of her work diary.

Her heart pounding, Kate glanced round her office. Had she been burgled again?

Helen's irritated words flew back to her about the casserole. 'It had *not gone*.'

Kate stopped.

'Must have been Jack,' she reassured herself out loud.

She removed the photo, propped it on the desk, then lifted her eyes to meet Hugo's. It was a good photo. Saskia had taken it secretly through the kitchen window of their Highgate house five years ago. Unaware, Kate was lying back on Hugo's chest, his hand casually lying across the breast of her shirt. She was wearing a headscarf from painting Jack's room. Her face was tilted up, laughing. He was trying not to smile at her bad joke. Behind them was the magnolia tree, just a baby then, in a pot, its first pink blossoms yet to burst through.

Kate shook her head, the irony of it, painful.

'Don't laugh at me,' Hugo had been saying, putting on his hurt voice.

His fingers played on her rib below her bra, slowly, with no intent, while he used his other hand to write on a pad placed on the garden table.

'But how can I help it? You're so funny. See? I can't stop

laughing at you . . .' Kate opened her mouth as if to laugh – then froze. 'Oh wait – yes I can.'

'Fuck off.' He pinched her skin through her top, and carried on writing.

She lay back on the garden bench, looking at the baby magnolia tree.

'What are you writing?' she asked.

'Instructions for your assassination.'

'No, really.'

'Instructions for your assassination.'

'That's a nice thing to say to your poor wife whose parents were killed,' she said in a whiny voice, screwing up her eyes and laughing silently at her own mean joke. They both knew he was cornered.

He sighed loudly, and she grinned with satisfaction, feeling his chest reverberate under her.

'Some notes for the refurb on Algon Terrace,' he grunted.

She sat up sideways to see one of his neat sketches of a room dominated by a Georgian fireplace.

She lay back again, wondering where to plant the magnolia. If they put it just to the right, it would grow under Jack's bedroom. By the time he was eight or nine, the blooms would reach his window.

'It's not that I think you shouldn't do it . . .' Hugo started.

'But . . .'

'Well, I just don't want you to do it.'

'Hugo,' she groaned, hitting his chest. 'Honestly. Don't start. It's what I want for my thirtieth. You can't say no.'

'What about Jack?' he said, grabbing her hand and playing with it.

'What do you think's going to happen?' she asked, running his fingers through her own. 'I thought you wanted me to get back to normal again. Have some fun?'

'You are back to normal.' He dropped his voice to a stage whisper. 'Normal for a weirdo, anyway.'

She dug her elbow into his rib.

He shifted his weight to release it. 'Really. I just don't think it's a good idea.'

Kate tried to sit up. 'You're not serious?' she asked.

He shrugged, sipping his beer and continuing to write. 'I've just got a bad feeling about it.'

She threw her hands up. 'Says the man who's bought a car that looks like a penis.'

He pinched her harder, and carried on sketching.

'What do you think about all this, Sass?' she said, as her sister-in-law wandered outside to the garden from the kitchen, waving a camera.

Saskia settled herself on Kate's thighs gently, and leaned back. 'Don't know, don't care. Look. . .'

Hugo and Kate peered forward to see the image of themselves, with Kate laughing at her own joke, and Hugo trying to hide his grin.

'*You were laugh-ing!*' Kate sang childishly.

'Right. That's it. Both of you, off,' Hugo grunted, pushing off the combined weight of his wife and sister. 'I'm not sitting here being harassed. What time is your film?'

'Half eight?' Kate and Saskia said in unison, checking with each other.

'Right. I'm going for a quick drive in my penis car then.'

That had been the summer, five years into their marriage, when she had finally emerged from the darkness of her parents' deaths. The year she knew who she was again without their solid mooring on the planet. She was turning thirty, finding renewed strength in the idea of a new decade. Even broaching the idea of another baby, now Jack was starting primary school. Hugo had stopped tiptoeing about her, trying to make something better that could not be made better. With unspoken relief on both sides, they had found their way back to the easy rudeness of old. She had even made a risqué joke about the way she'd been after her parents' death, knowing her parents would not have minded. Knowing they would have just been overjoyed that she was starting to heal. It was over, the joke said to Hugo. He and Kate could finally move on.

Kate looked at the photo closely. The contours of her body and Hugo's ran into each other, without borders. What had it felt like to be that physically intimate with another person?

Her eyes drifted to the baby magnolia tree. They had never planted it, of course. Four hours later, Hugo had been dead.

'I don't know what to do,' she said to the photo. But the low resolution of the camera had blurred the sharpness of Hugo's pupils, robbing her of the chance to interpret some peace and understanding in his eyes.

What would he say, anyway? Tell his mother to keep her nose out of Kate and Jack's business? Or would he stand beside Helen as her ally? Would his face say that he now realized his mother had been right in that brief moment in her hallway all those years ago, when she first met Kate? She had been correct to be disappointed: Kate had proved to be a failure after all. Fallen apart in a crisis. A terrible mother to Hugo's son.

At one time, Kate would have known, of course. Years' worth of Hugo's reactions and opinions, she had discovered after his death, had been safely wired into her head, ready to draw upon in his absence. It had been a comfort. But that was from another time; already he was five years younger in this photo than she was now. Those reactions and opinions belonged to then, not now. Hugo had never seen an iPad or a Twitter page. He had belonged to a different time. He was disappearing from her view, like a man overboard in the wake of a ship.

Kate dropped the photo on the desk and looked at the clock. Nearly eleven.

Jesus.

Biting her lip, she glanced at her work schedule on the wall. David needed her funding proposal for his new renovation project in Islington by next week. She had to get out of here or she would never start work.

Kate jumped up. Flinging back her chair, she grabbed some papers and walked downstairs, pausing to lock the gate with the new padlock. Checking that all the windows, and then the inner doors, were locked manually downstairs, she grabbed her bag, turned on the alarm and left, double locking the front door.

Without meaning to, she glanced up at the strong sun that had now moved to the front of the house. Should she drive or cycle? Statistics about road accidents began to swarm around her head. Mixed up in them were half-remembered percentages to do with air quality and skin cancer.

- **90% of skin cancers are caused by direct sunlight.**

She caught herself, and pinched her palm hard with her other hand.

'Shut up!' she growled, bringing Jack's shocked, bloodied face from this morning into her mind.

Forcing herself to ignore the numbers, she marched down Hubert Street, towards the hub of east Oxford.

Helen's words returned to her. 'The next time I ring Social Services it will not be anonymous.'

Nobody could help her. She had to do this by herself, and it had to start now.

Magnus heard the front door bang next door. He looked down into Hubert Street from his upstairs window. The skinny woman, Kate, was going out again.

He picked up his camera and took a quick shot of her from behind.

Skinny, but not bad-looking. Dark hair, thick and lustrous. She even had the upturned nose like the girls from home.

It was her face that was a put off. Miserable. In need of a good cheering-up.

He shut up the laptop that had been delivered to Kate's house last Tuesday and turned it off. It hadn't been difficult. He'd just accessed her emails, noted when the new laptop was due, then lurked outside her gate in a baseball hat without his glasses, till the delivery van came, then pretended he was coming out of Kate's house when the man asked for someone to sign for it, and used an indecipherable signature.

It was a good computer, this one. Better than the one he'd stolen two weeks ago from her house, along with the email password she'd so 'cleverly' stuck on a sticky note beside it on her desk. She'd upgraded. He might even keep this one, instead of trying to sell it.

Talking of which . . . better check she was really going out and not just popping in to see a neighbour. He watched out of the window till the woman reached the end of Hubert Street, counted fifty, then bounced down the worn stair carpet, pulling on his black T-shirt from yesterday, enjoying being reacquainted with his own pungent smell. The kitchen was empty. It smelt slightly of damp – not that that bothered him.

'Hello?' His shout echoed around the cheap units and into the hall, where piles of post for former student tenants lay in messy heaps.

No one replied.

Luckily, the other students were out. Not that they spoke to him anyway. The short one with the sharp face had complained just last night about him singing drinking songs when he arrived home at 2 a.m. No one knew how to have a good time in this bloody town.

Magnus went out of the front door and walked up to Kate's house to check it was empty. He rang the doorbell, twice, ready with a fake question about the rubbish collection day. No answer.

Good. Quickly, he returned home and lumbered up to his bedroom.

He shut the door and locked it, just to be sure, then went to the heavy wardrobe that stood against the wall he shared with Kate's house, and moved it, grunting, a shoulder against the edge.

It travelled with a deep scraping noise across the laminate floor, leaving a fresh new grey skid mark on top of a previous faded one.

In front of Magnus was a hole in the wall, just above the skirting board, a metre wide by half a metre high. A scouting trip to steal the first laptop five months ago had told him the best place to do it.

It had taken him three days to create, chipping away the mortar with a rock hammer when both households were out, and taking out the bricks carefully one by one. As always, before entering the hole, he double-checked with a prod the metre-long, ten-centimetre-square piece of wood that he'd inserted under the top of it, which in turn rested on two more vertical wooden lintels that sat either side of it. The support didn't budge, still solidly supporting the weight of the bricks above it. He nodded, pleased.

In front of Magnus, on the other side of the hole, was a piece of MDF. He had painted it white to blend in with the wall next door and inserted across the hole with two clips. Carefully, he unclipped it and pushed it into the empty space beyond, then turned it diagonally and pulled it back through the hole.

In front of him now lay a gap into the bottom of a fitted wardrobe, which was presently covered in shoes and boots. There was a shelf just above his head.

Magnus pulled the shoes out of his way, lay on the floor, put his long arms into the hole and pushed the wardrobe doors ahead of him open. As usual, there was a thud on the carpet in front of him. Then he put his head through the hole and pulled his body after him, into the wardrobe, then out through the open doors on the other side. There was just enough room, with a few centimetres either side.

It was a tight squeeze but he did it.

Magnus pulled his big body into all fours, then stood upright, dusting off a scattering of mortar dust from his shoulder.

He stood the electric guitar upright again from where it had fallen, and surveyed Jack's bedroom.

CHAPTER SEVEN

Kate was trying. She really was, as she stomped across the backstreets of east Oxford towards Cowley Road. But the numbers wouldn't leave her alone. They buzzed inside her ears, their collective high pitch almost as unbearable as the house alarm this morning, as they screamed one of her most commonly used statistics at her: the one she reminded Jack of all the time when they crossed roads together:

- **You have a 45% chance of dying if you are hit by a car at 30 miles per hour.**

At every kerb. At every road crossing.

Listen to the figures, a voice said in Kate's head. It'll make you feel better. Let them in, and everything will be OK. You'll be back in control. Safe. Calm.

Clenching her fists, Kate double-checked at each junction, till she emerged from a side street into the bustle of Cowley Road.

At least there were people here, sights to distract her.

She lifted her eyes to the shimmering minarets of the mosque and the inert mothers in front of it in the playpark, grabbing a few seconds' rest on benches as their toddlers ran around. She stared hard at the O2 Academy announcing a gig by a band she vaguely recognized from long ago. She dodged the crowds with their carrier bags from Tesco and stared in the windows of a guddle of restaurants offering everything from South American to Indian to Thai.

Concentrate, she thought. Concentrate on the menus. Chicken masala, pimientos piquillo, steamed mussels with chilli. Don't think about numbers. Be normal. Be normal like those two girls walking along in vest tops, hands flying as they exchange stories of the night before. Like the man in the jester's hat cycling down the pavement, whistling, hands not touching the handlebars. Like the elderly lady remonstrating with her Jack Russell for peeing on a bin.

Kate blinked hard, her eyes feeling the strain of all this staring and glaring in their vain attempt to distract her brain from the numbers. The sun was raw on her face, burning her pale skin, blinding her.

A terrible desert-thirst grabbed her throat.

Kate coughed. She felt a flutter in her chest.

And then, without warning, she simply came to a stop.

She just stopped.

Right on the pavement, with no warning.

Her feet were stuck. Rooted. Refusing to move.

Kate put out a hand, frightened, and grabbed a doorframe. She leaned into the wood.

Her eyes settled on a small patch of dirt by the doorway.

She looked around and saw that it was alone on the swept pavement. The patch looked like road dust mixed with mud from shoes and old chewing gum. It was ground-in year-old grime, jammed into a corner, where doorframe met window frame. Too hidden to be cleaned by the owner or swept away by the street cleaner.

Nasty and stuck and horrible.

The perfect place for her.

As Kate stared at the patch of dirt, a nagging thought entered her mind. Just a whisper.

What if she could never get a grip on the anxiety? What if she could never shake off this sense of impending danger for her and Jack? Of being cursed? What if Richard and Helen really took Jack from her?

Kate shook her head in despair. They would give him everything; there was no doubt of that. Love, reassurance and fun. But Jack would never be able to stand up to Richard like Hugo did. He would never escape. He would become like Saskia, trapped forever in the gravitational force of Richard Parker's world.

The thought of losing Jack filled Kate with such grief that she clutched her stomach and bent over further.

What if she couldn't stop it, though? Was it just inevitable that she would lose him now: Hugo, her parents, Jack . . .

Kate stood there, head hanging, exhausted with trying to ward off a monster she could never see.

'Are you all right there?'

Kate jerked her head up.

A girl looked at her, concerned.

Kate realized the girl's head was peering out from behind the doorframe on which Kate was leaning. She saw a sign. It was a cafe she didn't recognize.

'Can I get you some water?'

Kate shook her head. 'No, I'm fine, thanks.' Beyond the glass door was a simple, white-walled room, with wooden tables.

'Do you do coffee?'

'It's a juice bar, I'm afraid.'

The girl's skin was make-up free and flawless, apart from a few freckles. She had long legs under a black mini-skirt and a white blouse. Her shiny auburn hair was twisted into a thick ponytail that hung down one side of her chest. Her smile was so friendly that Kate wanted to follow the girl inside. She wanted to leave behind the patch of dirt and the thoughts of losing Jack.

The cafe smelt fresh and sharp inside, like citrus fruit. Only one table was occupied, by a man with a pierced nose holding hands with a girl with pink hair. Pop music played over the speakers. A blackboard menu announced a variety of juices with names such as Superfruiter and Detox-alula.

'We've just opened so there's a special of 50 per cent off a juice of the day,' the girl said brightly.

The urge to sit down was overwhelming.

'Thank you.' Kate nodded.

'It's strawberries, peach . . .'

'That sounds fine,' Kate said, holding up a hand.

As the girl piled fruit into a giant liquidizer, Kate sat at the long counter along the front window and tried to gather her thoughts. A half-remembered number came at her.

- **40% of catering staff don't wash their hands after going to the toilet.**

Exhausted, she grabbed the printouts of her funding proposal for David from her bag, hoping it would help. Working often calmed the numbers. God knew why, but it did. She stared hard at the property details of the house David wanted to buy at a sealed bid auction and the estimates from each member of the renovation team, noting which ones she still had to chase up.

The house was a dilapidated Georgian terrace in Islington that was being sold by a housing association to fund a brand new block of fourteen flats elsewhere. She looked at the exterior,

85

knowing Hugo would have loved it. Three original fireplaces remained, as did the original wooden floors beneath stained brown carpets and cheap laminate. There was a major damp problem coming from the basement, a fairly serious crack in the back bedroom and a suspicion of woodworm in the floors, but nothing David and the team hadn't seen before.

She stared at the house, realizing what it reminded her of.

'You've what?' Kate had exclaimed, spinning round to look at Hugo. Hugo was leaning on his car bonnet on the pavement in front of the four-storey Georgian house in a tiny square in High-gate, opposite a pretty little garden with a bench in it. He'd told her they were going for a walk on Hampstead Heath to talk about their travel plans for the summer, then unexpectedly pulled off the road.

'I've bought it.' He laughed, with the mischievous smile he used when he knew he was pushing her to the limit of her patience. 'Or I've put an offer in, anyway.'

'But how . . .?'

He leaned over, grabbed her arm, then pulled her to lean against him, facing the house. She looked up. The house was in serious need of renovation. Grey paint peeled from its facade. Its front door had been replaced with a cheap wooden one with DIY-store stained glass. Terrible double glazing had been put in, presumably without planning permission. She could tell from here, that the roof was in serious need of attention.

'Dad came through with the start-up loan.'

Kate's eyes opened wide. 'No way? He gave in?'

Hugo nodded at the house, pleased. 'Yup.'

'Seriously? He's accepted you're not going to join his business?' She stroked his arm. 'Oh God, Hugo. Well done!'

Hugo squeezed her tightly. 'Anyway, it's enough to get it with an interest-only mortgage. Then the plan is, if me and David do a good job on it, we'll use it as a show-house for new clients. You and I could live in it after the wedding. The idea is to remortgage it and use the equity to get the business up and running. You can get stuck in when you get back.'

Kate had spun round. 'You're not coming?'

'No. I want you to go and have some fun without me. This is my fun. Trust me, if this takes off, me and David will need you flat-out when you get back to set up the next project.'

Hugo was beaming. He looked exactly like he did, Kate noted with a flush of love, when he'd announced to all their parents last month at Richard's favourite London restaurant – a choice Hugo didn't win, but as he'd now explained to Kate, the trick with Richard was choosing your battles – that he and Kate were getting engaged. He sighed. 'So, do you like it? Can we do it?'

She wrapped her arms round his arms, which were across her chest, forming a tight, double embrace. 'It's amazing. I love it. You're an arse for not telling me but you're very clever, too.'

He'd squeezed her tight. 'God. It's happening, Kate. Finally . . .' He kissed her ear, and she dipped her head to the side to let him nuzzle her neck. 'I tell you what, I feel lucky. Too bloody lucky, sometimes.'

Kate shut the property details and took a sip of her juice. Hugo and David had increased the value of the Highgate house so rapidly that the business had been racing ahead of them within two years, Richard's loan repaid. Their passion for, and expert knowledge of, the Georgian period, and their decision to use only the most skilled craftspeople to restore original detail had quickly gained them a reputation with discerning – and wealthy – buyers.

'I feel lucky.'

Hugo's words repeated in her head. Lucky, yes. Richard had

helped at the start, but it was Hugo's and David's passion and hard work that made their business work. Kate looked at the Islington house again. As a silent partner, she would benefit financially from this project, too, as she had from all the others, because of Hugo's hard work. Yet Hugo would never be there to enjoy it with her and Jack. Flinging down the details with frustration at the unfairness of it all, Kate picked up her juice again and glanced around.

Her eyes scanned the counter beside her and carried on around the almost empty juice bar.

Then they came back.

That was odd.

Where had that come from?

A paperback lay three seats away from her on the counter, beside the cafe door. Upside down and half read, it sat beside a half-empty juice glass.

Kate looked again. It was still just her and the New Age couple, and the cheerful waitress, who was wiping down the liquidizer, humming along to Dusty Springfield.

Kate was about to return to her proposal, when a word jumped out from the book's upside-down cover.

'. . . Odds.'

Odds?

Intrigued, Kate lowered her head at an angle until she could read the rest of the title: . . . Odds . . . Change . . . *Beat the Odds and Change your Life*.

Kate blinked. Was this a joke? Or had she actually started to hallucinate?

Intrigued, she leaned over and lifted up the paperback where it was open. 'How to Choose Which Airline To Fly With', the chapter heading said.

Oh my God. What was this?

Kate moved closer and flicked quickly through the book, checking no one was watching. It appeared to have odds grouped together about the safety of flying, and how to work out which airline was safest.

As she looked through, she felt her mind hungrily trying to digest all the statistics. This was incredible. There were so many. And that wasn't all. She thumbed through more chapters. 'How to Improve your Chances of Avoiding a Road Accident', 'How to Improve your Chances of Avoiding Dying Prematurely'.

It was all here.

Kate gripped the cover.

She wanted rip this book open, like a lion on antelope flesh.

'You OK there?'

Kate jerked upright, and in the window saw the reflection of a man. She spun round. He was walking towards her from the back of the cafe. The toilet door by the counter swung shut behind him.

Kate shoved the book away.

'Oh. Sorry, I was just . . .' she said, trailing off.

The man smiled. He was tall, with light brown hair cut short into a crewcut, and wearing a T-shirt with jeans. There was a faint stubble around his jaw and his eyes were such an intense blue she had to stop herself staring.

'No. Go ahead,' he said, gesturing towards the book, picking up the half-empty juice glass without sitting down, to finish it. His accent was Scottish.

'Um . . .'

'It's fine. Here,' he said, passing it to her.

'Oh. Thanks,' Kate said shyly. 'I'll just copy down the title, if that's OK?'

'Absolutely.'

She grabbed her pen and began to write. In her peripheral

vision, she saw the man finish his juice and take a mobile from a leather bag he had slung over his body. He stared at the screen of his mobile, reading something.

'*Beat the Odds and Change your Life* by Jago Martin . . .' she wrote, forcing herself not to start flicking through this compulsive book in front of its owner.

She saw the Scottish man tap a number into his phone.

'Hi, Liam,' she heard him say. 'It's Jago. Did you just text me?'

Kate's eyes flew to the book cover. Jago Martin. While the Scottish man talked on the phone, on impulse, Kate opened the back flap. Staring back at her was a photograph of the man in the juice bar. 'Professor Jago Martin of the University of Edinburgh', the caption read.

Kate looked up, astonished.

The Scottish man was ending his call. He looked back with slightly surprised eyes.

'You OK there?'

She nodded, embarrassed. 'Yes. Thanks.'

'Done?' He pointed to the book.

'Yes. Thanks,' Kate repeated, wishing she could think of something else to say. The man took the book from her, smiled and turned to walk out.

As she watched him go, an irrational, overwhelming need overcame her to stop him. Why, she wasn't really sure. She just knew she had to.

'Sorry . . . can I just ask . . . um, you wrote the book?' she called out in what she realized too late was a slightly hysterical-sounding voice above the husky tones of Dusty Springfield.

The man turned back amused. 'Uh. Yes. I did.'

Kate shrank back. 'Sorry. It's just . . . I saw your photo . . .'

'That's fine,' he smiled.

She waved vaguely at the book. 'It's just, do you mind if I ask you something? If you're an expert in this kind of thing?'

'Sure.' He turned back.

'I just wondered, that section on how to improve your chances of not being in an aircrash?'

'Uhuh.'

'How do you work that out?'

'The chances?' The Scottish man wrinkled his brow. He appraised her with his blue eyes, as if he hadn't really seen her properly the first time, then leaned back against a stool. Inwardly, she cringed. She must sound mad.

'Well,' he started, 'we'd check airline safety records. Maintenance levels. Pilot training. Weather conditions where the airline flies. That kind of thing. Actuaries do it all the time in the City as part of their research to calculate insurance premiums for airlines.'

She found herself fixated by his eyes. They were unusually bright blue, maybe because of his tan, she thought. The skin around them crinkled easily when he smiled, making her wonder if he'd lived somewhere hot.

'But doesn't that make you scared. Of flying? If you've seen all those records?'

'Me?'

Immediately she regretted her question. The crewcut and easy way he held his body gave him the look of a lean boxer, a man who wouldn't be scared by much.

'Sorry. I didn't mean to . . .'

'No, don't worry.' He waved his hand. 'I'm just wondering. Is this a professional interest?'

Kate shook her head. 'No. It's just, I just never know who to fly with. The one who's crashed recently because then you think the chances are they won't again. Or the one who's never crashed, in case a crash is due.'

The man frowned, as if thinking. 'You know what? I'm maybe not the best person to ask.'

She spotted a thin leather band just below the collar of his T-shirt. It sat on a tanned neck, reinforcing the impression that he travelled. She looked up and saw him watching her, and flicked her eyes away, embarrassed. 'But you wrote the book . . .' Her voice sounded more abrupt that she meant it to.

He hesitated. 'Ah, but you see, with my work, I travel all over the world for conferences. The kind of airlines I fly with are sometimes the ones with the less favourable safety records.'

Kate stared. 'Even though you know they have a high chance of crashing?'

'Well, higher, yes. Not high.'

She blinked. 'How do you do that?'

Just as she said it, the Dusty Springfield song that was playing finished. Kate's question blasted into the silence left in its wake. Her tone was so pleading that the man, the New Age couple and the waitress all glanced at her, warily.

'Sorry,' she said, lowering her voice, 'I just meant that . . .'

The man held up his hand. There was a glimmer of concern on his face. 'No, it's fine.' He opened his palms in a gesture of explanation. 'I just don't think about it.'

Kate stared.

The man's words reached out and wrapped themselves around her.

She couldn't explain it.

They reached out and pulled her in like safe, warm arms.

A stranger had opened his mouth and said something so profound, she knew, irrationally, that for a reason she couldn't explain, that it might hold the key to her survival.

'So, does that help? Have you got what you need?' the man said, standing up.

'Uh. Yes. Thanks.' Damn. Where was he going? Her mind darted around trying to find an excuse to stall him.

'Actually, can I just . . .' she started desperately, not even knowing what she was going to say.

But just as the man looked back, his eyebrows raised in question, his phone rang. He smiled apologetically at Kate and started a conversation with someone called Mike about a seminar he was teaching at the university that afternoon. Kate waved him on, even though she didn't want to. He waved back. 'Nice to meet you,' he called, walking out of the door. Kate craned her neck to see him unlocking a bike with one hand, as he spoke on his phone.

'Cor . . .' The waitress giggled, coming up, and lifting the man's glass.

'Sorry?' said Kate, jerking back. The waitress watched Jago, twisting her long auburn plait in her fingers. Kate looked at her, surprised. The man must be fifteen years older than the waitress.

Kate hesitated, then realized she had no choice. 'You didn't hear him say what college he taught at, did you?' she said, as casually as she could.

She saw the waitress's expression.

'It's a work thing.'

The girl grinned. 'No, but let me know if you find out! Mmm, that accent . . .' She fanned herself dramatically.

Kate watched the waitress uncertainly. She looked back out of the window and saw the man speeding off down Cowley Road precariously, still with a phone at his ear. For a second, she wished she had brought her bike so she could have followed him into the traffic.

The thought took her completely by surprise.

Kate never cycled in traffic.

CHAPTER EIGHT

The presentation was going well. Much better than she'd expected.

Saskia watched the suave man from the London marketing agency that she had hired for today's presentation to Dad and his partners fixing his smile firmly on Dad, just as she'd suggested. She'd chosen a marketing agency that specialized in design businesses, and the man certainly knew his stuff. It was important, he reiterated, that an agency such as Richard's quickly prioritized marketing to head off the effects of the current economic downturn. The Richard Parker Agency needed to concentrate on winning new, younger clients with a viral campaign that relied more on a multifaceted social media campaign.

Saskia tapped her feet under the table, watching her father's face, waiting for him to react. She'd seen him do this so many times with his own staff, keeping his expression completely impassive as an employee spoke, so that by the end you could almost see the sweat break out on their brow as they waited to see which way his face would break: the beaming grin of approval, or the eyes suddenly darting away, robbing them of eye contact, that told them he was not impressed with their efforts.

This time, however, Richard's face broke the right way. He

clapped loudly, the rest of his staff joining in on cue, relieved. 'Well done, sir! Impressive stuff,' he said, then, turning to Saskia. 'Good job, darling.'

Saskia smiled demurely as Richard's staff gave her another round of applause, as if they had any choice. She was Richard Parker's daughter, after all.

'Well done, Sass,' Richard repeated, as he picked up his car keys from his desk. 'Right. I'm off to work at home. Playing golf with Jeremy after lunch, if you're looking for me. Can you talk to the chap about fees and contract conditions?'

'No problem,' replied Saskia, patting his arm, then weaved through tables of computers and design drawing desks into her own office, shutting the door and sitting down.

She had done a good job. She knew she had. Another success to chalk up. As Dad often told his friends and clients, usually loudly and embarrassingly in front of her: 'Don't know what we'd do without our Sass. Bloody place would fall apart!'

Saskia sighed as she opened up her laptop. Not exactly true. And, anyway, with the salary her father paid her, there would be nowhere to go to. She must be the best-paid office manager in Britain.

Saskia looked at the screen and saw a note to herself: 'Snores'. Right.

Checking that Dad was gone, she summoned Facebook and started the process of creating an account for Jack. Ignoring the age-limit warning, she created an account linked to her own email address under her nephew's name, adding three years to his age and a photo of him wearing dark glasses, where he could easily have been thirteen.

When the nagging doubts surfaced, she pushed them away. If her sister-in-law was really going to dump poor Jack in a new school, it was the least Saskia could do to help him keep in touch with his old friends. She and Hugo had moved schools enough times as Richard built his bloody business empire to know how it felt.

Her finger hovered over the 'submit' button for a second. Saskia exhaled and pushed the button. Jack's Facebook page went live.

She opened up an email message to the marketing agency to request agreements in writing, her mind still on Jack. He was sensible. He wouldn't do anything silly, would he?

Saskia started typing, blinking hard.

Oh well. Too late now, anyway.

The minute the Scottish man left the cafe, Kate felt the urge to run straight to Blackwell's to buy his book.

She went to bite her thumbnail and stopped herself.

No.

She made herself summon Jack's pale, bloodied face again from this morning.

And now she'd made a fool of herself again, talking to a complete stranger about bloody numbers.

The book was a test of her resolve, and she was going to pass it. Buying it would completely contradict what she'd set out to do this morning. If she didn't get a grip on her anxiety, she was going to lose Jack. What was more useful was to think about what the Scottish man had said.

'I just don't think about it.'

How the hell did you do that? She put David's proposal in her bag. Well, work was the best way to start.

Waving to the waitress, she left the cafe and headed down Cowley Road, crossing Magdalen Bridge above students and tourists punting in the river below, into central Oxford. The elegant greenhouses of the Botanic Gardens appeared on her left.

She swiftly turned into the entrance, before she could change her mind and rush to Blackwell's on Broad Street.

As she entered the cool walled garden, a welcome element of calm descended on her again, as she knew it would. As Helen had once said, it was like a private park in here. No dog poo or footballs flying around. Just a lush lawn among the thick boughs of centuries-old exotic trees. Unless there was some rare disease communicated by a mulberry white or a honey locust tree that she didn't know about, the odds of something bad happening were instantly slashed. The numbers rarely followed her in here.

Kate settled on the grass between fallen pine cones, under the thick, gnarled branches of the 200-year-old *pinus nigra* that had been J.R.R. Tolkien's favourite, and pulled out her proposal. Her bottom lip held firmly between her teeth, she made herself concentrate on the various cost breakdowns and lists of planning submissions they'd require because the Islington house was in a conservation area. It was difficult to do without her laptop and the internet, but she managed, enjoying the change of pace of working outside with a pen.

After she'd done that, she pulled out a list of teenage applicants for work placements through the charitable foundation she and David had set up in his name after his death. Only David, Hugo's former partner, knew how much doing this had helped her, being able to carry out Hugo's dream, to give financial assistance and support to young adults who shared his passion for historical architecture, yet might not have the means to study or find work.

The first girl caught her eye immediately. Aged sixteen, close to the end of a difficult childhood in and out of foster care, she had been nominated by an eagle-eyed art teacher who'd spotted the girl sitting quietly on a day trip to the Tate Modern, doing beautifully detailed drawings of St Paul's Cathedral across the Millennium Bridge while her schoolfriends ate their packed lunches and messed around by the river. Kate smiled. Hugo would have loved this girl. Her words were unconfident on the application, despite the teacher's obvious help, but her interest in historic architecture shone through clearly, with some of her exquisitely detailed drawings included.

Kate marked her application for David to consider. Perhaps a summer work placement at the Islington property would be a good start.

She smiled mischievously, thinking of Richard and how much he hated her helping what he termed 'bloody no-hopers' with Hugo's money. And how much Hugo would have loved her for it. Their own little rebellion against Richard's conservative, money-obsessed ways.

A pang of hunger made Kate look up at ten to four. Her eyes settled on the bone of her ankle, which stuck out like a round white knob. She shifted weight, and placed one ankle over the other till she couldn't see it any more.

It was only a second, but the break allowed the Scottish man's book to infiltrate her mind again. It slipped in as if it had been by the door all afternoon, waiting for the opportunity.

She checked her watch again.

Jack had cricket practice until five, then had said something as she left him this morning, white-faced and quiet, about going to Gabe's after school. She hadn't even bothered to argue. How could she?

She put down her proposal and laid back on the lawn. A plane breezed across the summer sky.

The chapter on airline safety moved into her thoughts. David had offered her and Jack his house in Mallorca this summer. It had been the third year he'd offered, and the third year she'd turned him down. But, with that book, she could find out the safety records of the airlines who flew there. Make a calculated decision about the risk of flying.

Would it really matter if she bought the book? Just to help her do that? Three weeks away in Mallorca, without Richard and Helen's constant interference, might just be what she and Jack needed to find their way back to each other.

Kate's mind flicked through the other chapter headings she had spotted.

Hang on.

She tore at the grass.

If she had the book, with all its research on statistics, all the facts she'd need to feel in control of her and Jack's safety would at least be in one place. If she proved too weak to keep her addiction at bay completely, the book would at least stop her endlessly scouring newspaper websites and insurance sites for figures. It would help her break the habit. Like a smoker using nicotine patches.

She sat up abruptly.

Perhaps it wasn't realistic to try to stop this by herself immediately.

She could just cut down.

Yes. The book would help her cut down, and at the same time concentrate more on fixing things with Jack.

At the thought, Kate's limbs twitched with excitement at what was about to happen. Before she could stop herself, she jumped up, rubbing away the grass that was ingrained in dark red ridges in her calves, packed up her proposal and ran out of the Botanic Gardens. At the traffic lights, she marched right up Longwall Street, then left along Holywell Street towards Blackwell's bookshop on Broad Street.

She could have that book in her hands in *ten minutes*.

Kate's strides quickened. She half ran into the grand double-width of Broad Street, then, when she reached the circular grandeur of the Sheldonian Theatre, crossed over the road to

Blackwell's. So fixated was she on wondering whether the book would be in stock or if she'd have to order it and suffer an agonizing wait, that everything in front of her became a blur of faces, of pastel summer dresses and bare calves and rucksacks and sunglasses and . . .

. . . Then one close-cropped head came into focus.

Kate stopped.

The man.

The Scottish man from the cafe.

Jago Martin.

Right in front of her.

He was crouched down outside the gates of Trinity College further up Broad Street, talking to a young male student.

Kate stopped at the window of Blackwell's and pretended to look at a display of science books, keeping him in her peripheral vision.

The Scottish man and the student were looking at the tyre of his bike. He was using his finger and thumb to wiggle it. He stood up and looked at his watch, with a slight shake of his head, and said something. The student took back the pump from Jago Martin that he had clearly offered. They waved at each other as the student climbed onto his own bike and set off down Broad Street. As Kate watched, Jago looked back at the tyre.

From here she could see it was completely flat. Burst.

Without warning, Jago stood up and looked around him.

Kate gulped.

His eyes were scanning the street. Kate stood still. She felt his eyes pass over her, and willed herself to be invisible. His eyes kept going – then something seemed to register in his head. They stopped mid-track and returned to her. He gave her a long look and then nodded.

'Hello again.' She waved nervously, walking towards him.

'Oh, hello. What are the chances of this, eh?' He grinned.

Kate smiled. 'Have you got a flat?'

He surveyed the tyre. 'Hmm. I have. I'm wondering if it's the little bastard whose paper I just failed.'

'Seriously?' Kate said, aghast.

'Nah. Hope not, anyway. Think I went over some glass on Cowley Road.'

'Oh.'

'I don't suppose you know any bike shops around here?'

'Oh.' Kate looked round her. 'I don't. I know there's one back on Iffley Road, the one parallel to Cowley Road. That's the one me and my son use, anyway.'

Kate kicked herself. My son – why did she say that?

The man turned through 180 degrees and pointed towards the High Street with a questioning look on his face.

'Ah. No. Actually, it's quicker this way. Through the back streets,' she replied, pointing in the opposite direction.

'Seriously?' he exclaimed, banging his forehead with the flat of his hand. 'I've been going that way all term.'

'Well, I'm going back to Iffley Road in a minute, if you like – I can show you the short cut.'

Immediately she bit her tongue. Oh God. He'd think she was flirting with him.

She froze.

Or worse, that she'd followed him from the cafe.

What was happening to her today?

'I mean, you don't have to, I just . . .' she stuttered.

'No. That would be great,' the man said, standing up and hoisting his bag on his back. Self-consciously, she pushed her hair behind her ears.

'So, where are you off to?' he asked.

Kate pointed at Blackwell's.

'I was just going to . . .' She blushed, trying to think of a lie and failing. 'Actually, I was just about to go and buy your book.'

'Were you?' The Scottish man looked incredulous. He rubbed a hand over his close-cropped head, revealing a tanned bicep. 'God, well, that's nice of you, but I'm afraid it's only out in the States at the moment – the British version's not out till August. But, hang on . . .' He put his hand into his bag and pulled out the copy from the café. 'Here you go. Have this one.'

Kate gawped, as he held it out. 'Really?'

'Absolutely. I got some free ones from my American publisher that I lend to my students. This one was for the little bastard who may or may not have slashed my tyre. But, as his family apparently owns half of Wiltshire, you're very welcome. Let him get his own.'

He frowned. 'Hang on. Your family don't own the other half, do they?'

Kate laughed and shook her head.

'Good.' He raised his eyebrows. 'I tell you what: I'm going to get myself into trouble round here. My prole roots coming out. Anyway, here you go. Call it a thanks for stopping me going in the wrong direction for the rest of the summer.'

Kate took the book from his hands gratefully. Just feeling its pages sent a thrill through her. It was all she could do not to rip it open and consume the figures in great gulps.

'Thanks.' She nodded, taking it and gesturing him towards the end of Broad Street. 'It's this way.'

The man took his bike by the handlebar, and pushed it alongside her.

'I'm Kate, by the way,' she said, holding out her hand.

'Pleased to meet you, Kate,' he said, taking it. She liked his voice. It was relaxed and friendly, each word confidently

102

enunciated, as if he were in no rush to finish it off before heading to the next one.

She looked at him shyly. 'So, what *are* the chances of this? How would an expert in probability explain this, then? Meeting a stranger twice in one day?'

They crossed back into Holywell Street, past a row of seven-teenth-century terraced cottages with heavy, studded oak doors and fairytale windows.

'Ah – well, let's see,' Jago said. 'Where do you live?'

She pointed ahead of her. 'Where we're going. East Oxford?'

'OK. And I'm staying here at Balliol, back there.' He pointed behind him to the college next to Trinity. 'So we work and live and shop within, what, a mile or two of each other? I've been here for eight weeks. We probably pass within twenty yards of each other every few days. It's just today, we recognize each other's faces.' He paused as if he'd had a thought. 'Now – that's actually a good project for one of my lazy undergraduates. Pick a stranger in the centre of town, and see how many times you see them again in a fixed period of time. I should make them do it just to get them out of their bloody beds in the morning.'

Kate smiled. 'Do you mind if I ask why you are in Oxford? If you teach at Edinburgh?' They turned into the long curve of Longwall Street, back towards Magdalen Bridge.

He shot her an appraising look. 'Good question. Actually, I'm on a one-term guest lectureship. Because of the book.'

'Really?'

'Uhuh, well, you know, there's a trend at the moment for popular books about science and maths, written by academics. Brian Cox on the universe, that kind of thing?'

She nodded. 'My son Jack loves them.'

'How old is he?'

'Nearly eleven.'

'Good for him. Well, there you go. This idea about chance and probability is big news right now, especially in the States – I taught there for a while, by the way, in North Carolina.' Kate nodded. 'Anyway, it gives the university a bit of kudos when you write a bestseller. Suddenly everyone wants a bit of you. So here I am, enjoying my fifteen minutes of fame.'

Kate smiled. It was so long since she'd walked along chatting to someone like this. A stranger. Desperately, she stumbled around for something else to say. 'And do you like it? Or do you miss Edinburgh?'

'I do. I particularly miss the rain.'

'Really?'

'No.'

She glanced sideways at him, confused. She shook her head. 'Sorry.'

'No – don't apologize. I'm being an arse. Seriously? I like the students here. They keep you on your toes. What about you – what do you do?'

Kate went to speak, but Jago held up his hand. 'Hang on. Let me guess . . .'

She shut her mouth again and waited.

He screwed up his eyes as if thinking. 'OK . . . The person who injects new ink into recycled ink cartridges?'

His question took her by such surprise that Kate laughed out loud. She couldn't believe the sound. It was so unfamiliar. It sounded like a shriek.

'No?' he continued, as she tried to gather herself. 'Let me think. Detective superintendent?'

Kate giggled again, unable to stop herself.

'OK. Greek Orthodox wedding planner?'

'No!'

He winked. 'You see, eventually if I go on, I'll get it. That's probability for you.'

'Ah, I see. Well, actually, I do some project managing for a historical renovation company,' she said, checking for cyclists in the bike lane before they crossed at the end of Magdalen Bridge. 'And I run a foundation attached to it to help kids from deprived backgrounds get into architectural studies and renovation work.'

'Do you, now?' Jago said, looking impressed. 'Good for you. I should tell my sister about that. She teaches in a big inner-city school.' He mimed a muscleman. 'You should see her. Five foot, and feisty as shit. But she's always saying it's hard for some of the kids to get a break.'

Kate nodded. She liked the way he spoke about his sister. It reminded her of Hugo.

They stopped at the end of the bridge, and she looked ahead.

Damn.

They would be across the roundabout in a minute, then into Iffley Road. The bike shop was just beyond the junction. They were nearly there, and then he would be gone.

'Jago,' she blurted out. 'Do you mind? Can I ask you something? About the book again?'

'Uhuh.'

'You know what you said earlier, about flying with dodgy airlines? That you put it out of your mind. Can I ask you how do you do that?'

He stopped outside an Indian restaurant just before the bike shop, and scratched the stubble on his chin. She looked up at him. He was different physically to Hugo. A few inches shorter, at around six foot, and lean and muscular, where Hugo had been broad like Richard, with the first softness around his stomach thanks to all that good red wine. As Kate looked at Jago, her eyes fell behind him to their reflection in the window of the restaurant. If you were driving past right now, this is what you would see, she thought. They looked like a couple. The image of her with a man again was so strange, she couldn't stop glancing at it.

She saw his face become more serious.

'Well, what I meant is that you can't control these things. You can make an educated guess that might lower or increase your chances of something happening, but in the end, you can't control everything. Nothing in life is certain apart from the fact that we're all going to die. You can spend all day trying to work out which is the safest airline, then choke on a peanut in the departure lounge. And, personally, I feel life's too short. Don't know about you, but I'd rather be lying on a beach somewhere.'

He regarded her with his intense blue eyes.

There was a spark of interest in them she hadn't seen earlier. She lowered her eyes self-consciously.

'Well, this is me,' he said, stopping outside the bike shop. 'It was nice to meet you, Kate, and I hope you enjoy the book. But don't take it too seriously. Remember, it is meant to be a bit of fun.'

'I won't,' she lied, knowing that the minute she left him she would go straight to the juice bar and rip it open.

'Anyway, as we've now established, I expect I'll bump into you again.' He touched her on the arm pleasantly, and walked off. Kate felt alarm rising, as he went to go into the shop.

She wasn't ready to let him go. Not yet.

'Jago?' she called, not even knowing what was coming next.

He turned.

She searched in her head frantically. 'Listen, if you're new to Oxford . . . you know, I'd be happy to show you round. Jack and I only moved here a few years ago ourselves, so I know what it's like.'

She saw him hesitate. Glance at her wedding ring.

She cringed inwardly. What was she thinking? He was probably planning to drop off his bike and head off to ask out the gorgeous young auburn-haired waitress in the juice bar. Not some worn-out, thirty-five-year-old mum with – she noticed, to her embarrassment – a rip in the knee of her jeans.

'Uh. Well,' he said carefully. 'To be honest, the students at Balliol were ordered to take me on enough tours of Oxford when I arrived to last me a lifetime. It's all very nice but . . . I don't know, maybe a drink one evening? That would be good. You could tell me a bit more about your work with the kids.'

Kate almost stepped back in surprise. 'Um. Yes.'

'OK. Well, what about tomorrow tonight?'

Tomorrow was Tuesday. The night Saskia was booked to babysit so that Kate could go to her manufactured therapy session with Sylvia. She appraised Jago. He had already given her more to think about in five minutes than that woman probably would in three months.

'Would it be OK to make it quite early – about half past seven? I've only got a babysitter till about nine.'

'Yup. Absolutely.' Gratefully, she noticed he didn't even flinch at the mention of Jack. 'I'll leave it to you where we meet.'

Kate blanched. She couldn't possibly decide that quickly. She'd need time to work out the safest place to meet and the safest way to get there.

Jago watched her expression. 'Right – tell you what, here's my number,' he said, taking out a pen and scribbling on a piece of paper. 'Just text me where you want to meet.'

'Perfect,' she said, relieved.

'OK – see you,' Jago said, pushing his bike inside.

'Good luck.' Kate smiled.

As she was about to walk away she heard him call her name.

'Actually, Kate. Sorry to be a pain, but if we're meeting tomorrow, can I keep that copy? I was going to go to the library straight after this to finish my notes. I'm using it in a seminar tomorrow for a bit of fun, and it's so long since I wrote the bloody thing,

I've been having to remind myself today what I actually said.' He made an apologetic face. 'I'll dig out another one from my room tomorrow for you.'

She held the book tightly in her hand.

'Sure,' she said, fighting to control her impulse to cling to it.

'I won't forget, promise.' He smiled.

She waved and walked up Iffley Road fighting the urge to beg him for it back.

Maybe it was better. A test.

All of a sudden, a thought hit her.

Her mind hadn't summoned up a single statistic about arriving home safely since she met Jago Martin in Broad Street.

Not one.

And, for the first time in a long time, she'd actually enjoyed a conversation with someone, too.

She looked up Iffley Road.

What if she could get home without thinking about any numbers?

Steeling her jaw, Kate picked up speed, summoning up Jack's anxious face to spur her on, trying to forget about Jago Martin's book.

CHAPTER NINE

The clock on Gabe's computer in his bedroom said 5.45 p.m. Jack looked at his new Facebook account on the screen, eyes glowing. With Gabe's help, he already had eleven friends: ten from school, and Aunt Sass, who had insisted that if she was going to go behind his mum's back she was at least going to see what he was up to. Gabe's mum had made him do the same, so at least Jack wasn't the only one with a smiling grown-up on his friends list, with watchful eyes. As long as Sid at school didn't start writing rude things. Aunt Sass was cool, but even she'd be shocked at some of the stuff Sid showed them on his phone at playtime.

'Mum says you can stay for tea, J!' Gabe shouted from downstairs.

'But you've got to phone your mum and tell her, Jack,' came Gabe's mum's voice from the kitchen. Her voice always sounded relaxed, as if it was lazing on a beach. 'You know what she's like, yeah?'

'OK,' Jack called. He frowned. He knew Gabe and his mum would be making faces at each other about his mum. He picked up his mobile, thinking. He wasn't ready to speak to her yet. He felt too guilty. She'd only be at home, worrying again, more probably because of what he'd said this morning. No – he knew what he would do.

hi mum, he texted. He sat for a moment, listening to Gabe fighting with his brother downstairs, and Gabe's mum shouting, 'You two!' and 'Enough!' Jack swept a curve of fine blond hair away from his face. It would be nice to have a brother so it wasn't always just him and Mum. He supposed he wouldn't get one now.

He lifted his fingers, wondering what to say.

Kate's phone buzzed as she walked in the house.

hi mum. gabes mum says i can stay for tea. can i?

hi jack, of course, have fun, she made herself text back, fighting the urge to tell him to ensure Gabe walked him home afterwards. She sighed, imagining Jack in the loud, happy chaos of Gabe's house, wishing he never had to come home. She was just about to turn off her phone, when a new text arrived.

are you ok mum?

Kate gasped. 'Oh,' she whispered. The unfamiliar intimacy of his words took her by surprise.

yes of course! she typed.

But just as she was about to send it, she stopped.

She sat down at the kitchen table and stared at the screen, looking at his question.

are you ok mum?

He was asking her. After their awful fight this morning, and the lie she made him tell his teacher, the least she could do was answer truthfully.

She thought for a moment, then tapped in a different reply.

honestly jack? no. not really. but it has NOTHING to do with you. it's me, and i promise i am trying to fix it. really, really sorry about your head

110

She pressed the 'send' button, and grimaced. Was it too much? She sat nervously biting her fingernails. His message pinged back.

i'm sorry 2

'Oh!' she whispered. He was trying to talk to her. After all this time, he was *trying to talk to her*.

Sitting upright, Kate tried to think fast.

no jack. you've done nothing wrong. it's me, and i know some things have gone wrong and i promise that i'm doing everything i can now to make it better

She waited, gritting her teeth. This was excruciating. Like digging a pencil in a raw wound. If she felt like this, how must he be feeling?

Nothing happened.

She sat upright, waiting for his reply.

She waited another minute.

Damn, she'd scared him. She couldn't expect him to go from never talking about the terrible thing that had torn their lives apart to an open, frank discussion, just because she had decided it would be good for them. She bit her lip and decided to take a risk.

maybe you can help me?

This time the reply was almost immediate.

i dont know what 2 do

'Oh Jack,' she said sadly. *u cd tell me what i'm doing wrong*

She waited.

but then you get upset

She sniffed. *sorry. jack – i didn't realize*

She thought for a minute, then typed again. *you know, it's so good to talk about this with you. could we talk about it more when you get home?*

She waited and waited.

His message pinged back.

gabes coming, bye.

Kate put her phone down, reeling at what had just happened.

This was good. This was a start. The fight she'd had with Jack this morning had been awful, but maybe they'd needed something like that to start talking again.

And then there was Jago Martin. She didn't know why, but somehow, ever since she'd met that man this morning, something had felt different. Better. A tiny bit hopeful.

Just don't think about it, he'd said.

And she hadn't. Not about a single statistic. She'd fought it all the way home.

Out of nowhere, an impulse overtook her. She ran upstairs, unlocked the padlock to the gate, grabbed it, and marched into the study. Without stopping to think, she unlocked and flung open the window.

It was time. Things had to change. Today.

With a grunt, Kate threw the padlock as far as she could into the garden. It landed on the trampoline and bounced up, knocking Jack's football sideways.

'Fuck off!' she called out.

There was a sound to her left. A throat being cleared. She looked to see a man sitting in the garden next door, holding a beer bottle, looking up at her. He had very long legs splayed out in front of him, and was dressed in black with deathly pale skin and bad glasses. One of the students, presumably.

'Oh. Sorry,' she said. 'Not you.'

'OK then! Everybody's happy!' he said, raising his bottle. His accent was musical, each word sounding as if it were formed carefully to incorporate unfamiliar vowels. His top half was swaying a little as if he were drunk. He kept looking at her, as if he were trying to get into focus. Even from this distance she could

112

see his eyes were an odd shade, a silvery pale blue. The colour of a husky's.

'Well. Bye,' she said, withdrawing and shutting the window.

She locked it again and went to run a bath.

She lay in the bath for a while, using her hands to create waves of warm water to wash over her body, thinking about Jago Martin.

Jesus Christ. She was going for a drink with a man.

A man with interesting blue eyes who had awakened something in her today she couldn't even begin to describe.

As she lay back in the bath, her eyes settled on her vanilla hand lotion that sat on the bathroom windowsill.

She blinked.

It was a quarter empty.

She had only bought it on Saturday yet it was almost a quarter empty. Surely she hadn't used that much? Kate looked around the bathroom. Was it an old one she'd forgotten about? The familiar sense of unease settled on her.

Helen's words came back to her about the casserole. 'It had *not gone*.'

'For God's sake! *Stop this*,' Kate muttered to herself. What was wrong with her? She had obviously just used more than she'd realized.

A door slammed downstairs, making her jump.

'Mum?'

Jack was back.

'I'm in the bath. Are you OK?' she called out nervously, sitting up. She fought the urge to ask if Gabe had walked him home.

'Yeah,' he shouted up. 'Can I watch *The Simpsons*?'

'Got any homework?'

'No.'

'OK. See you in a while.'

There was a pause.

'Gabe walked back with me, by the way,' he called.

She berated herself in the mirror. 'Oh, OK.'

Ten minutes later, she went downstairs to see Jack lying on the sofa, the plaster still on his head. She waited to see if the intimacy from the texting earlier was still there but he just glanced up at her like normal, and back at the telly.

Probably too much to ask.

'Hi.'

'Hi.'

'How's your head?'

'OK, thanks.'

'Anyone ask?'

'Ms Corrigan. I said it was my skateboard.'

'Oh. Sorry,' Kate said, ashamed.

'It's OK.'

The barrier was back up. She could see him tensing again. She sat uncertainly on the arm of the sofa, pretending to watch the television. Helen's words came back to her: 'You are his parent, not the other way round.'

Whatever she suspected now about the depth of Helen's negative feelings towards her, on that point Helen had been right. Which is why Kate had lain in bed this morning, forcing herself to do what she never did: delve painfully into the bank of memories of their life before Hugo died. Trying to find something she could try. One flashback from the kitchen in their old house in Highgate had given her an idea.

Would he go for it, or was he too old now?

'Jack?'

'Hmm?' he replied, grinning as Bart showed his bum to Principal Skinner.

'I was thinking of making some flapjacks for Nana and Granddad for you to take this weekend. You don't fancy helping, do you?'

He turned, unsure, and she saw him trying to judge whether she meant it or not.

'Now?'

'Hmm.'

'Have we got stuff to make flapjacks?'

Kate shrugged uncertainly. It was so long since those Highgate days when Jack stood on a stool to reach the counter, the pair of them chatting as they baked cakes for Hugo's lunchbox. 'Isn't it just butter and porridge and honey or something?' she said.

Jack scratched his nose. 'Golden syrup, I think, we used at school. We could get it from the corner shop.'

He stood up and she realized he was trying to hide a pleased smile forcing its way onto his face.

And then, to Kate's delight, there he was, finally. In Jack's expression, just for a second, as he went to turn off the television. The hidden grin. Just like in the photograph Saskia had taken on the terrace in Highgate as he tried not to laugh at her joke.

Hugo.

CHAPTER TEN

It was six-thirty the following evening by the time Saskia finished work in central Oxford and made her way slowly to Hubert Street.

She walked along, blinking, thinking crossly about work.

The contracts had come through from the marketing agency this morning, and she'd spent the day setting up an official Twitter account, relieved that Dad and the partners were finally listening to sense about needing to move with the times and promote the agency through social media. By lunchtime she had thirty-nine followers.

'Look at that!' Dad had exclaimed in the office, summoning a few others to look at Saskia's screen, to her embarrassment. 'Don't know how you get the hang of these technical things so quickly, Sass.'

Saskia stomped towards Kate's house. It was not that difficult. Dad could have done it himself, in no time. He wasn't an idiot. She reached Hubert Street and looked up apprehensively.

At least Kate would be going out to her therapy session in north Oxford, but first they had to face each other.

They hadn't spoken since Gate-gate, as Saskia was now calling Friday's showdown. She hadn't spoken to Mum about it, either.

Just spent the weekend having a drink with her book group in the village and going through her divorce papers from Jonathan, desperately trying not to ring and beg him to reconsider.

Nervously, she rang the bell.

Kate opened the door. 'Hi.'

'Hi,' Saskia said, meeting her eyes awkwardly – then did a double take.

Kate had transformed. She was wearing new dark skinny jeans that actually fitted her instead of the old size tens that hung from her loosely, and a tailored white summer shirt Saskia hadn't seen before. She was wearing make-up, too. Just a touch, but it was there. Soft blush on her cheeks, a touch of eyeliner and mascara. Perhaps that was what had put a new light in her eyes. The start-ling little flecks of gold that had been tarnished for so long were sparkling again, as if given a good polish.

'Come in,' Kate said. Sass followed, taken aback. Kate's dark hair had been blown dry and sat silkily just below her shoulders. From the back, the jeans reminded her what long legs Kate had. The shirt was doing wonders, too, to cover up her corset-thin waist, and the bony protuberances of her shoulders and arms. Saskia blinked. She hadn't seen Kate look like this in years.

The old sense of insecurity awakened.

It had been difficult when Hugo arrived back from university all those years ago, enthralled with the self-assured girl from Shropshire he brought with him. Those first times the five of them went out together, Dad sweeping them into a restaurant or on a birthday visit to the theatre, Saskia had realized that it was now Kate who people – men and women – looked at before her.

Then after Hugo died, one day, it just stopped.

On the street, men had started to glance at Saskia first. Some-times they didn't look at Kate at all. It was as if Kate's beauty had died with Hugo. Water drained from the flower.

Saskia followed Kate into the kitchen, uncertainly, and sat at the table.

'So . . .?' she said tentatively, watching Kate pull a bottle of white wine from the fridge.

'What?'

'Well . . .'

'I don't want to talk about it, Sass.'

Saskia sat back.

'Look,' she started awkwardly, 'for the record, I was really cross with you about that fucking gate. I mean, for God's sake, Kate. But I had no idea Mum was going to turn into Ninja Helen . . .' She lifted her arm in a karate chop and crossed her eyes.

'I don't want to talk about it,' Kate repeated.

Saskia blinked hard and poured them each a glass of wine. Kate worked around her, clearing up the mess from tea and putting out a plate of pasta with pesto for Saskia that she'd kept warm in the oven. Saskia tried to gauge her mood.

'Right – so how angry are you with me? On a scale to one to ten?'

'To be honest, I don't know what I feel.' Kate sighed, sitting down and gulping her wine. 'I just know I can't talk about it with you right now.'

'OK, but you're going to see this woman. Tonight?'

Kate took another sip, put down her glass. 'I'm getting help, yes.'

They surveyed each other.

Perhaps it was seeing her dressed like this, but Saskia found herself wanting the old Kate back in a way she hadn't done for a long time.

She ran a finger down her wine glass, imagining telling Kate that she'd sat outside Jonathan's office at lunchtime in a cafe just to catch a glimpse of him. Imagining telling Kate the truth about the mess of her marriage, and about how fed up she was working for Dad but could see no way out. For an agonizing second, she pictured curling up with Kate on the sofa, like in the old days, and talking till their honking laughter woke Hugo and he came downstairs, crumpled and cross, and told them to shut up.

But the chill emanating from Kate told her not even to think about it.

'Is it all right to stay tonight?' Saskia said in the end, motioning to her wine. 'I left the car at the village station.'

Kate nodded. 'Of course.'

'Can I borrow some knickers tomorrow?'

Kate stood up and shut the dishwasher. 'Help yourself – you know where they are.'

Saskia saw her pause. Kate swivelled round. 'Actually, if you're staying over, do you mind if I stay out for a while afterwards? One of the school mums is having a birthday drink at a bar on Cowley Road later?'

'Yeah. Of course.' Saskia tried to keep the surprise from her voice. Kate was going out? Well, at least that was something positive she could tell Mum. Kate seeing friends and going to therapy. It might defrost the situation before Helen had any more earth-shattering notions about taking Jack away.

Kate hung a cloth over the tap.

'Right. I'd better go. I have to be there at half seven. Oh, and I'm not expecting anybody tonight, so can you not . . .'

Kate stopped mid-sentence, the words teetering on the end of her tongue.

'. . . answer the front door when it's dark,' Saskia finished for her. 'Don't worry. I know the house rules.'

Kate turned away. 'It's not a house rule,' she retorted over her shoulder.

Saskia shrugged. There was no point inflaming the situation.

Kate picked up her bag. 'And can you make sure Jack's in bed by nine?'

'Yup. Will do.'

The mention of Jack made Saskia flick her eyes away from Kate guiltily. She had checked his Facebook before she'd left the office and seen how quickly he'd been swamped with friends. She'd also seen a quiz posted by someone called Sid entitled 'Is Jack a dick – yes or no?' with his friends, including Gabe, all apparently 'jokingly' agreeing that Jack was.

'Thanks – see you later,' said Kate, grabbing her jacket and finishing her wine in one gulp. She headed out of the kitchen and shouted, 'Bye, Jack!' into the sitting room before stopping by the front door to grab her bike helmet.

Saskia sipped from her own glass and turned.

Kate was checking her reflection in the hall mirror. It was so long since Saskia had seen her sister-in-law pay the slightest attention to her appearance that she couldn't stop staring.

Tonight men would be glancing at Kate again, she realized. With a pang of sorrow, Saskia thought of Hugo. One day his self-assured girl from Shropshire would not be his any more. She would belong to another man.

She blinked, and turned away.

No. She had to be positive. Think of Jack and keep trying to support Kate – not wind her up. And the good thing was, it looked like the therapy was already helping.

It had not been an easy choice, but in the end Kate had picked the Hanley Arms, just a quarter of a mile from Hubert Street. Far enough away that Saskia wouldn't spot her go in there and realize she was lying about the therapy, and close enough to home to be able to cycle back along the quiet pavements later tonight, and avoid thinking about traffic accident statistics.

of personal stuff to tie up in North Carolina
ng and doing research, then I'm heading over
ls to do some mountain-biking.'
looking at the men again. 'So, where did you
xford?'
at Balliol.'
y? Is it nice?'
bottom of his pint. 'It is nice. All stone steps
where I can stand and smoke a pipe. If I actu-
'
stracted. 'So is your room nice?' she repeated
cing back over at the football fans.
't reply, she turned back to see him watching

l.
bing on?'

eally choose this table?'

near those guys?'
They're quite noisy – don't you think?'
she felt a little drunk. A little out of control.
g since she'd drunk two glasses of wine.
vard onto his elbows. 'I hope you don't mind
look really nervous.'
Horrified, she felt the tears back again, trying
she swallowed hard to make them go away.
ese guys? Because you look terrified of them.'
eyes, defeated.

hey just seem a little aggressive.'

She arrived to find Jago locking his newly fixed bike to a lamp post outside. 'Good timing,' he called. He looked up at the pub. 'Your local?'

'Kind of,' she lied, locking her own bike to a railing. She had been in here once with Saskia. You had to know people in a pub for it to be your local. 'New tyre, then?' she ventured pointlessly.

'Yup. Thanks for the recommendation.' Jago smiled, opening the pub door open for her. She passed through with her own nervous 'thanks'.

He was wearing jeans and a slim navy shirt over it that made his eyes look even bluer, and properly exposed the thin leather band around his neck. Suddenly, Kate felt completely tongue-tied. Her mind went blank. What had she been thinking? She couldn't think of one word to say to this man. This was awful.

It didn't help when she heard jeers coming from inside the pub.

'What do you want to drink, Kate?' Jago said, walking up to the bar.

'Um, white wine, thanks,' she muttered, glancing to the source of the noise. It was a group of five or so men in football shirts, their bodies and faces moving jerkily, en masse, as they swore and bantered with each other, and threw back pints and laughed in ferocious, loud cackles.

She was so occupied with the men that she didn't realize what she had done at first. It was only when Jago turned and asked 'Ah – Chardonnay or Sauvignon Blanc?' that she realized she was about to order her second glass of white wine tonight. Which would push her daily limit over three units and increase her chances of cancer.

'Sorry. Actually, could I change that, could I have a soda and . . .' she started to say, then saw Jago's face. His intelligent eyes watched her earnestly.

Just don't think about it. That's what he had said. Don't even think about it.

'A what?' he asked.

She summoned up Jack's anxious face. 'No, actually, either's fine,' Kate muttered. 'I'll get a table.'

Quickly, she moved as far away as she could from the men, who were watching a raised television near the bar. She wound her way through ten empty tables till she could go no further, and stopped at the toilets.

She saw Jago turn to place the drinks on a nearby table, then look up to see her miles away. He shot her a playful look.

'Is this a special table?' he asked, wandering over.

'No . . . Sorry. I just thought it was quieter.'

He sat down and looked around. 'No. It's fine. Excellent for the toilet, and –' he pointed at the wall – 'the fire extinguisher.'

She smiled, despite herself. 'Have you been teaching this afternoon?'

He nodded and regaled her with a story about a super-smart but cocky student of his who he had noticed banging his knee up and down, then discovered was wearing earphones under his beanie during a lecture.

'And, to cap it all, when I question him about it, he says he's listening to a recording of my lecture from last week, cheeky little bastard. Anyway, tell me about the project you're working on.'

Kate tried to gather her thoughts. But they kept slipping to the other side of the bar. 'Get in there!' one of the football fans growled, standing up and throwing one arm at the television screen, as his mates yelled behind him, then clapped.

'It's a house in Islington that the developer I work with, David, is going to turn back from three flats into a house . . .' she started, forcing herself to recall details about plans they had to

'Do they?' He looked over. 'So, you're worried about what they *might* do, rather than what they have done.'

Kate glanced up, surprised.

'Yes.'

She dropped her eyes again, ashamed. It was time to go. She was a disgrace, a mess. She couldn't even have a quiet drink in a pub without this bloody nonsense ruining everything.

'Kate. Here.' She looked up to see Jago standing up. He was holding out his hand. She took it. It was dry and warm.

She stood up, trying to hold herself together. He understood, she realized with gratitude. He was taking her out of here to another pub.

Jago led her through to bar towards the front door. However, as they reached it, to her bewilderment, he kept going towards the men.

Kate's heart skipped a painful beat, and she began to fall back. But Jago kept leading her firmly.

With her hand in his grasp, Jago approached the largest of the group. Kate struggled but he wouldn't let go. The man was so big that his cheeks were as wide as a pig. His eyes were lost between folds of skin, his head shaved round the back, with black hair gelled into spikes on top. Forearms the size of Kate's thighs burst out of the sleeves of his football shirt.

'Don't,' she whispered.

To her horror, Jago walked straight up to the man and slapped him on the back.

'How's it going, lads?' Jago said, pointing at the screen. 'What's the score?'

Kate's legs began to shake.

The man put down his pint and surveyed Jago belligerently with his tiny eyes. Jago met his stare face on. The man's mates watched, beers suspended in mid-air in thick-fingered hands.

He opened his mouth.

'Two–nil, mate – fucking beauty, that last one.' He lifted up his arm as the crowd on the screen cheered the opposition's run towards goal. 'Mark him, you fucking wanker!'

Jago smiled, as he took Kate's hand again and led her past towards the door. 'Thanks, lads.'

'See you, mate,' the man called, raising his pint. His tiny eyes turned to Kate, who was now pale with fright. 'Night, love.'

She walked outside, her heart hammering so hard in her chest that it was difficult to breathe properly. Her legs felt as if the muscles and bones had been removed inside and they were about to collapse.

She put out a hand to touch the wall.

Jago turned.

'Kate! What the fuck? You're shaking,' he exclaimed.

She tried to speak and it came out as a stammer. 'Why . . . did you . . . do that?'

He took her shoulders. 'They're just lads out for a drink. It's the end of the season; they're hyped up. But they're harmless. Kate? What's going on?'

To her horror, she couldn't hold the tears back. They flooded into her eyes.

'Oh, shit. Are you sick?' Jago sounded concerned.

'No.'

'Then . . .?'

She wiped away the tears, ashamed.

'Kate! Seriously. What did you think they were going to do?'

She shook her head, hating herself. He reached out and took her shoulders gently. Self-consciously, she pulled back, disconcerted at being so physically close to a man after all these years. She shook her head. 'I don't know. I know they seem OK to you, but to me . . .'

'What?'

He watched her carefully.

'I can't explain it, OK?' she said. Her voice sounded strident and ugly. She threw up her arms, banging into his. 'I'm a freak.' She felt him flinch. Pulling out of his grip, she turned away. 'That's all I can tell you, Jago. I'm sorry I suggested a drink. It was a really bad idea.'

She started to put her helmet on but, in her rush, dropped it on the pavement with a crack.

'Fuck!' she cried, throwing her hands up in the air. She had to get out of here.

'Kate!' Jago repeated calmly. He leaned over before she could, and picked up her helmet, but didn't give it back to her. 'What do you mean, you're a freak?'

She shook her head. This was dreadful. 'Jago, I'm sorry. I just don't want to talk about it. I've got to go.'

But he wouldn't move out of her way. 'Oh no. Not till you tell me.'

A pit of disappointment opened up inside her. Now he was starting to see what she was really like, he was going to cycle off in a second, and that would be it. In all the bloody years she'd lived in Oxford, he was the first person she'd felt any type of real connection with. Tiny, but real. And it had given her hope. For whatever reason, he was the first person she felt able to talk to since losing Hugo.

And she was going to make him disappear, thanks to her *fucking* anxiety.

Fighting back fresh tears, Kate knew she had ruined whatever chance she'd had of getting to know this man. 'Look. I'm sorry. I didn't mean to be like this. I just can't be around other people right now. It's complicated. It's my fault. Not yours. I'd better go.'

She reached out to take her helmet from him, but Jago put it behind his back. 'No. Not until you tell me.'

What was he doing? 'You don't want to know.'

'Why don't you let me decide that?'

She looked at him defiantly. He held her gaze. What the hell? She'd never see him again anyway.

'OK. Well, if you really want to know . . . It's hard for me to be around people like that . . . Because of my husband . . .'

Jago glanced quickly at her wedding ring. 'Oh right. I'd assumed that you . . .'

'No. My husband – he died.'

Jago brought down his hand with her helmet to his side. 'Oh God. I'm sorry.'

'No, it is not your fault. You wouldn't have known. I just . . . I shouldn't have come. I'm sorry. I just – when we spoke. It seemed to help.'

'With what?' Jago dipped his head to the side. It was such an understanding gesture, one she had seen Sylvia make in their session, that she felt a lump in her throat. She shook her head. 'It'll sound crazy.' The second time she'd said that in the past week.

He touched her arm. 'Come on. Trust me. I'm a doctor. Of mathematics, but it's still worth a try.'

She gave a reluctant smile. The fading light was throwing their faces into shadow. Jago waited patiently for her to speak. What did she have to lose?

'OK. It helped because I spend a lot of time doing this. A huge amount of time, actually. Worrying about what might happen to me and Jack. I have this constant obsession about the chances of bad things happening to us.'

'What do you mean, "chances"?'

She rolled her eyes, anticipating his surprise – or, worse, amusement – at how crazy it was going to sound. 'Chance, odds, statistics. You know, "You have a 15 per cent chance of having a bike accident if you cycle on a weekday compared to 10 per cent at the weekend". That kind of thing.'

Jago looked shocked. 'Is that why you wanted the book?'

She nodded and her voice dropped to a miserable whisper. 'And if you want to know the truth, it's ruining my life in so many ways I can't begin to tell you.'

'Are you serious?'

She regarded him, curious at the tone in his voice. He wasn't laughing at her, or suddenly remembering he had to be somewhere else.

Jago turned and sat on the pub wall. 'Bloody hell. You poor thing. Do you know, Kate, I was just talking to my publisher in the States about this last week. There's a psychologist working on a book about exactly this.'

Why hadn't Sylvia known that?

'It's an emerging phenomenon, apparently: people trying to gain a sense of control over their lives by using statistics to do with safety or health. Living with a constant fear of imagined danger. The closest my publisher could compare it to was a kind of obsessive compulsive disorder.' He stuck out his lip like a naughty boy. 'Kate, I'm sorry. Now I feel bad. Is that why you were asking me about how you put these things out of your head?'

She looked away, embarrassed.

'That's hard. Sorry.'

'No, really. It's really not your fault,' she said more calmly, knowing it was time to end this embarrassing encounter before she humiliated herself any more. 'But, listen, I think it's better if I just go . . .' She held her hand out for her helmet.

'Go? No!' Jago said. 'No way. I feel a bit responsible now. Right. Just give me a second to think.' He turned one way, then another.

'Right. I know.'

'What?'

'Get on your bike,' he said, giving her the helmet.

'What?'

'Come on.'

Before she could stop him, he jumped on his – without a helmet, she noticed queasily – and set off to the end of the street, where the road turned into an alley that she knew led to the river.

'Where are you . . .?' Kate called out.

'Come on!' he shouted back.

Before she could reply, Jago disappeared. Kate looked around her. Damn. If she didn't follow him, she might lose him altogether and he'd think she'd gone off without saying goodbye. Shakily, she unlocked her bike, put on her helmet, checking it quickly for cracks, and rode down the pavement towards the alley.

CHAPTER ELEVEN

The evening light was fading as Kate emerged onto the riverbank. The sky was the colour of a light bruise. Two fishermen were packing up for the evening. Kate turned right, then left, and saw Jago waiting for her fifty yards up ahead on his bike.

'Where are you . . .?' she repeated, but he just turned and started cycling again, with a gesture for her to follow.

What was he doing?

Filled with apprehension, Kate went after him, pushing hard on the pedals to negotiate the bumpy towpath. Going away from Oxford, the path was quieter. She cycled past a dog walker; two students jogging together with swinging ponytails under baseball caps; and a lone rower on the river heading for home, his oars creating rippling silver pyramids in the water.

She kept expecting Jago to stop, but he didn't. Kate panted with the exertion of cycling so fast. This was ridiculous. She looked behind her. They must be a mile from the pub now. What was he doing? In a minute they'd be outside Oxford, in the countryside.

'Stop, please,' she mouthed at his back, but Jago was already disappearing around a bend.

It was too far to go back now alone. So she turned on her lights and pushed on, hoping he'd be waiting.

Eventually they stopped passing anyone. Just three solitary canal boats moored for the evening, smoke drifting from their chimneys; a heron on the bank. She cycled on, taking in the unfamiliar sights. She never came out here on her bike. After her embarrassing hysteria on the pavement tonight, she had to admit that the ride through the still evening felt oddly calming. It was beautiful out here on the river at this time. She turned behind her to see a disappearing sun cracked orange along the horizon, turning the ferns and ducks black against it. A meditative pace took over in the motions in her legs. An unusual lightness filled her body.

She was leaving Oxford behind, for whatever reason she wasn't sure yet, but she was leaving it. And in doing so, she became aware of it falling away from her, even for a short time, the trouble with Richard, and Helen, Jack and Saskia caught up in the opposite direction of the river's current. For a few exhilarating seconds, Kate realized she wanted to cycle like this all night.

In the end, it was another five minutes before Jago started to slow down. She saw him up ahead, in the dying light, coming to a stop.

'Here!' he shouted, and disappeared. She arrived thirty seconds later to find a gate off the towpath. She dismounted and pushed her bike through, onto what appeared to be a single-track country road, overhung with branches, with a few gated houses set discreetly back from the road, a forest behind them.

Jago was already back on his bike, cycling ahead.

Kate jumped on hers again. Right. Now she could catch him. Tell him to stop.

She pedalled fast, only to see Jago turn right again, this time down an even narrower lane with a rough, unserviced surface. He pulled over after fifty yards.

Kate came up behind him in the dark.

'What are you doing? I had no idea you were going . . .' She panted. 'Where are we?'

Jago put his finger to his lips as he dismounted.

'What?' she whispered.

'There.' He pointed at the ditch. He put his bike in it and walked off before she could protest. There was only one street-light back at the top of the lane, so she could hardly see his face, just the curve of his cheek from behind, as he walked towards a gate.

'This way,' he said quietly, pointing up at the ten-foot-high arched bars.

'No!' she gasped. 'No way!'

But Jago completely ignored her, put his foot on the first iron railing of the gate and hoisted himself up.

'What the . . .' Kate grunted, throwing down her bike beside his and following him. By the time she reached him, he was half-way up the gate. She peered. Through the iron railings lay a sprawling country hall, Gothic peaks silhouetted in the sky.

'Jago. What are you DOING?'

'Ssh,' he replied, again holding his finger over his lips. He reached the top of the gate, put his leg over, and headed down the other side. 'Come on,' he said, as he reached her at eye level through the railings. His eyes dared her.

'Absolutely not,' she mouthed furiously.

'OK. Stay there, then.'

'Jago!' But he had already begun to melt into the darkness beyond.

What was he doing?

Kate peered behind her at the lane, and then at the forest. She wasn't bloody staying here by herself or cycling back down that empty dark towpath alone. Crossly, she reached up to the bars and pulled herself up and over. As she scrambled down the other side unsteadily, she saw Jago emerge out of the shadows to take her waist gently and help her dismount.

'Quick,' he whispered, grabbing her hand again. 'Before anyone sees us.'

'Who?'

He didn't reply. Her heart thumping, she allowed her hand to settle into his, despite feeling self-conscious at the touch of his skin. Pulling her firmly, as he had done in the pub, Jago skirted the boundary hedge, staying in the shadows, away from the gentle light cast from the ground-floor windows of the grand hall on to a manicured lawn.

Kate inhaled deeply. The air was fresh and warm, filled with the scent of blossom and cut grass.

'I think it's round the back,' Jago said.

He led her along the hedge till they cleared the illuminated patch of lawn, then bent down and scurried like a soldier on manoeuvres towards some stone steps. She copied him, entering a network of vegetable and flower beds.

'There it is.' She heard him exclaim quietly.

In front of them appeared a square pond surrounded by an old stone wall. Lilies floated in black, silky water.

'Glow worms!' Kate pointed in delight at tiny green lights glowing in the gaps of the wall.

Jago smiled. He let go of her hand and pulled out a jumper from his bag, and laid it on the grass. He motioned her to sit on it, then sat down beside her. He sighed contentedly then lay back on the grass.

'What is this place?' she whispered. 'It's beautiful.'

'It's cool, isn't it? Someone at Balliol told me about it.'

'But what is it?'

He winked. 'Now that, I'm not going to tell you.'

'Why?'

'Because I've taken you somewhere you know nothing about, so you can't calculate anything that's going to happen.'

Kate tried to make out his expression in the dark to see what he meant.

'I've decided to do a guerrilla experiment on you – the kind of thing my department head keeps threatening to sack me for.' He threw her a look. 'He thinks I'm "unorthodox", by the way. We're going to sit here without you knowing anything.'

She blinked. 'I don't understand.'

'Kate?' Jago said, sitting up on his elbows. 'You're sitting in a strange garden with a guy you know nothing about, miles from anywhere. No one knows you're here.'

She glanced at him warily. 'And . . .'

'Are you scared?'

She watched the reflection of the moon in his pupils and waited for the fear to come. She shook her head slowly. 'No.'

'And why do you think that is?'

She paused. 'Because I haven't had time to think about it.'

'And there you go.'

He sighed and lay back down.

Neither of them spoke for a while.

Kate let her eyes adjust to the dark. She scanned the garden, making out the trailing branches of a weeping willow and a statue that lay behind it in the shadows.

'Well, it is beautiful. Whatever it is.'

'"Nothing can cure the soul but the senses, just as nothing can cure the senses but the soul",' Jago murmured.

'Hmm?'

A rustle told her that he was turning to face her.

'Nothing. Kate, can I ask what happened? To your husband.'

She sat forward and picked up a twig.

'Or should I not ask?'

The glow worms shone like fairies on the pond wall. She dug the twig into the grooves on the sole of her shoe, dislodging dried mud. She imagined trying to tell him, but knew she couldn't. She shook her head.

'Sorry,' Jago said. 'I'm being nosy.'

'It's fine. I just don't really talk about it.'

'Why?'

She glanced at him sideways. He still wasn't giving up.

She continue to pick at her shoe.

'Well, I used to. I just found it didn't help. People would say the wrong thing. Not on purpose, but they just did. They'd say: "How do you feel?", really kindly. And after a while I realized that, yes, they did care about me, but underneath they were actually more terrified by what had happened to me. What they actually wanted to know was not "How do you feel?" but "How bad do you feel? How bad is it? Will I be able to endure it if it happens to me?"'

She paused. Jago said nothing. His silence was like Sylvia's, relaxed and unhurried. It made her want to talk more.

'Then,' she continued, 'after an hour of me talking, you'd see them thinking, "God, get me out of here. This is depressing." Not that I could blame them. I'd see them five minutes later chatting on the pavement to a friend about getting their highlights done. Back in the real world.' She glanced back at Jago. 'Where I felt I couldn't go any more. And it was difficult. So I stopped.'

Kate turned her attention to the mud at the bottom of her other shoe, digging the twig into the grooves, waiting for him to change the subject.

Jago, however, stayed silent. They sat two feet apart, side by side on the damp grass, listening to the trickle of water from the pond, and a splash of fish jumping.

He plucked a piece of grass and put it in his mouth. 'OK, but can I ask if that's when it happened? This obsession with numbers. Because of your husband dying?'

Inside, Kate felt all the words she'd prepared so carefully for Sylvia pushing hard to escape from her again, desperate for release now that someone was finally willing to listen. Even if it were to a man she'd only just met.

Jago was lying, chewing grass, like a chilled-out student at a festival. If he had worries of his own, they didn't show. What would it be like to be like that? What would it be like to spend time with someone like that, with an easy, boyish laugh?

She leaned forwards and dug methodically back along each groove of her trainer again. 'I feel like I'm in a therapy session.'

Jago grunted. 'Really? My ex-girlfriend would think that was hilarious. Apparently I am officially "the worst fucking listener in the world".'

Kate glanced over curiously. Ex-girlfriend. 'Ha. Well, trust me, you're better than the so-called therapist I saw this week.'

'Oh, really? So what's the answer . . .?'

Awkwardly, she rested back on the grass beside him, aware of how strange it felt to lie beside a man again, even two feet apart. How long had it been since she had done this, just been with someone, just talking?

'No. I think I'd already started obsessing about this stuff before then.'

'Oh. How come?'

She looked ruefully at the dark sky. 'Oh, because my parents were killed in a weird accident.'

Jago hesitated. 'Seriously?'

'Uhuh. About five years before Hugo died.'

'And is that difficult to talk about too or . . .'

'No. It was a long time ago. On the night of our wedding, actually.'

Jago turned, his face astonished. 'Are you making this up?'

'Wish I was.'

'And that's when it started?'

'Well, I do remember obsessing about the accident.'

'What happened?'

She shrugged. 'That was the thing. It was just really bad luck. My parents were in a taxi coming back from the reception. They were travelling up the mountain road to our house in Shropshire and they came round a bend and drove straight into the body of this big stag that had been shot by a poacher. It must have escaped, then collapsed on the road. And I remember wondering what the chances were of the stag dying right on that road. I mean, why not by the side of the road, or not on a bend? Why at night, and not during the day when the driver might have seen it? Why on the night of my wedding? I mean, I found out afterwards that fifteen people die each year in Britain in traffic accidents caused by deer. Fifteen out of sixty million. So why *my* parents?'

Jago shifted. 'And, what? They hit it . . .?'

Kate nodded. 'They were going about fifty miles per hour. Probably too fast. The taxi swung sideways across the road and overturned down the hill into the river. The taxi driver, Stan, from our village, was in his sixties, and I remember a doctor telling me that reaction times slow with age. That if he had been in his fifties, like my dad, his reaction time would have been 50 per cent quicker. And I kept wondering, if my dad had been driving, if that millisecond of difference would have changed everything. I was angry at Stan for a long time. I had been at school with his granddaughter, and I couldn't speak to her again.'

Jago whistled. 'Wow. I don't know what to say.'

Kate pushed her hair behind her ears. She wanted to talk more. It was good to talk like this. 'Don't worry. Really. There's nothing to say.'

'God, you've had some bad luck, Kate.'

She faced him, resting on her elbow. 'Ah, now there's a question. So tell me, do statisticians believe in luck?'

She watched his silhouette in the moonlight. He had a neat-shaped head and sharp cheekbones that suited a crewcut.

'What? In a mathematical sense? No. I mean, you will always have people at either end of statistical calculations. The one who gets struck by lightning seven times. The person who wins the lottery four times. But, no. It's totally random. There is no formula for luck.'

'Well, I'm not convinced about that,' she said. 'Don't laugh, but sometimes I think I'm cursed. I think I am that person at the end of the statistical calculations. I am the person who gets struck by lightning seven times. I mean, it has to be someone, doesn't it?'

'You?'

She knew how crazy her words sounded.

He made a *pff* noise then put out a hand and touched her arm fleetingly. 'Well, I'll tell you, that's nonsense, Kate. Being cursed is for fairytales. Not for kind souls, which I know you are.'

There was a note of paternal kindness in his voice that reminded her of a Scottish dentist she had seen as a child. Unexpectedly, it brought a bittersweet tug of memory of her father.

'Thank you,' she whispered.

There was a long pause. The branches of the willow danced in the breeze. After a while, Jago cleared his throat. 'Kate, I'm just wondering.'

'Hmm?'

'Well, obviously I was joking about this being a guerrilla experiment. But, seriously, I'm curious . . .'

'What?'

He frowned. 'I just wonder . . .'

She sat up. 'What?'

He ripped some more grass away. 'Would you mind if I spoke to my publisher about what you've told me? See what the psychologist he told me about is doing in the States on this kind of anxiety?'

He was offering to *help*. 'I suppose it would be interesting. But why would you do that?'

'I don't know yet. I'm interested from an academic perspective, I suppose. That's my thing, doing interdisciplinary work with other departments. So, partly because of the involvement of probability, but also because I . . .'

There was a rustling past Kate's ear. She sat up. A rabbit lolloped past the pond and up onto the unlit lawn beside the house.

'Fuck,' she heard Jago mutter.

There was a sharp *click* and a huge sensor light abruptly illuminated the whole lawn and the pond. Kate and Jago's faces were caught blinking in its beam.

'Go!' called Jago, jumping up and grabbing her hand.

There was no time to think. Kate let him pull her blindly across the lawn and back towards the hedge. Somewhere behind her she heard a door opening, spreading a slice of light onto the hedge.

'Quickly,' Kate gasped as Jago reached the gate and stood back to let her go first. He put a strong hand on the small of her back to help her climb up. To her amazement, she heard a chuckle behind her.

'I can't believe you're laughing,' she spat as she hauled herself up over the gates, her legs trembling, and waited for him to follow.

'Go!' he shouted, pointing at the bikes.

Kate grabbed her head. 'My helmet!' she yelped. 'I've left it on the lawn.'

'No time – go!'

Gritting her teeth, she jumped on her bike and waited for Jago to get over the gate and grab his, then followed him up the dark lane, wobbling so much she nearly tumbled in a pothole. She could hear him up ahead, as he crossed back through the gate, still laughing. Despite her heart pounding at the fear of being caught, she couldn't stop a reluctant grin breaking on her own face.

When they hit the towpath, Jago didn't stop, but sped back to Oxford, checking occasionally that she was behind him. She pedalled hard, trying to keep up with him, feeling her thighs protesting at being asked to work so hard when the adrenalin was still pumping through her body.

Without the helmet, her hair flew away from her face and flicked around her eyes. It made her feel as if she were cycling at seventy miles an hour; that the ground was disappearing beneath her in the dark.

In fact, she thought, it didn't even feel as if she was cycling. Perhaps it was the two glasses of wine, but she felt as if she'd lifted off the ground and was speeding above it.

Like she was flying.

Kate lifted her chin into the wind, spitting bugs from her mouth. A real swarm, not a number swarm. The night-time breeze caressed her skin. An image popped into her head of the man with the jester's hat on Cowley Road yesterday. Was this how he felt? She imagined her features set like his, bemused eyes, whistling lips.

And before she could help it, Kate did something extra-ordinary.

She lifted her hands off the handlebars. Just for a second, ignoring the water beside her. The bike sailed, just for a moment, effortlessly onwards.

'Oh!' she gasped, as the bike began to wobble.

'Woo-hoo!' came a shout.

She looked ahead to see Jago looking back, pedalling slowly, waiting for her to catch up. Seconds later she reached him, and he sped up again. She fell in behind him, into his slipstream. Their legs began to move in tandem, in a shared rhythm.

They were flying together through the dark.

Together. She was together, with someone. Connected. Talking. Not just physically sharing the same space with another adult, like Saskia or her Oxford neighbours or the parents of Jack's friend's, yet feeling a million miles away from them. She had forgotten what it felt like.

Kate shut her eyes, just for a second. Another sensation flooded back to her as she cycled along, from long ago. Of falling, and falling, and falling. Of floating into nothing, her body relaxed completely, not tense and rigid like it was now. Of tumbling at speed into a beautiful void but not being scared. Free from worry and physical restraint. Of having no choice but to let everything letting go and . . .

Crack!

Kate's front tyre hit a stone, sending her bike to the left an inch.

She yelped. Her eyes jerked open, and she pulled hard on the handlebars to remain upright.

The bike wobbled, then steadied. Alarmed, Kate peered around.

How had that happened? They were nearly back at the pub.

Houses and lights emerged on their right. She saw Jago duck

under the bridge, and followed him. Seconds later, they swerved back up the alleyway. Jago stopped at the pub. Kate pulled up beside him, panting.

He got off his saddle, straddling his bike frame, and grinned. 'OK?'

Kate spluttered to a stop. 'Just about. I can't believe you made me do that,' she gasped. 'What was that place?'

He touched his nose. 'Ahah. The less you know, the less you'll try to predict.'

She tried to draw breath. 'No. It was fun.'

She blinked, surprised at her own words. But it was true. Unbelievably, she'd actually had fun.

Jago sat back on his saddle. 'Thank God. I was starting to think the extent of my social life in Oxford was going to be talking to Gunther from Austria about algorithms in the bar.' He wiped an insect from his brow. 'Right, are you all right from here, Kate, or do you want me to cycle you home?'

Kate shook her head, touched by the gesture. It was the type of thing Hugo had offered to do when they first met at university in London, even though she'd lived north of the river, and he'd lived south.

'Listen,' Jago said, checking his new tyre. 'Thanks for telling me what was going on. It wouldn't be the first time a woman's run off on me half an hour into the evening.'

Somehow Kate didn't believe it.

Then Jago slapped his forehead. He opened his bag and searched inside it. 'Shit, I forgot to bring you that book.'

Kate wavered, remembering Jago's promise. She tried not to show her disappointment.

'You know what, though,' Jago said. 'Perhaps we could call this Step Two of our guerrilla experiment. Step Two: *Binning the Numbers*. See if you can do without it.'

Kate stood there uncertainly, thinking of the airline statistics she needed desperately if she was going to book tickets for Mallorca. 'What was Step One?' she asked.

Jago put his finger on his lip, as if thinking. 'Step One: *Not Thinking about it: Riding off into the Night with a Weird Scottish Bloke and Doing a Bit of Breaking and Entering*.' He watched her closely. 'Could you do it? Cope without the book?'

'Um, OK . . .' She knew her struggle to agree was etched on her face.

Jago shot her a sympathetic look. 'OK, well, what if I promise to keep one for you in my bag at all times in case you change your mind?'

She nodded, grateful at his understanding.

'Brilliant.' Jago gave her a grin. 'Kate, listen. This was the most fun I've had in, well, a while. Can we do this again?'

'I'd like that.'

'Good. I'll give you a ring? Tomorrow?'

Then, without warning, Jago leaned forward and kissed her cheek. 'Right . . .' The warmth of his skin on hers stunned her. 'Better go. OK.'

'OK.'

'See you,' Jago called. He stood up on his pedals and cycled to the junction, turning left towards central Oxford.

Kate stood paralysed, waiting for him to disappear. She lifted a finger to touch her hot cheek, which was stinging slightly from the brush of faint stubble on his chin. It had been so long since she'd felt the touch of a man's face against hers. The smell of soap from his skin mixed with the damp saltiness of his T-shirt lingered for a second.

She shook herself. What was she thinking? It was dark and she needed to get home. She cycled to the junction, and looked. Iffley Road lay in front of her. The turn for Hubert Street was a few hundred yards away on the right.

The brief sense of elation she had from riding along the river-bank lingered. Could she do it, while she was on a roll?

On the road? No helmet?

She looked left, then right. When she was confident there was no traffic in either direction, she stood up on her pedals and pushed hard out into the empty road, gripping the handlebars.

As soon as she did it she knew it was a mistake. Out of nowhere a car came speeding round a bend and up behind her.

'Oh no,' Kate groaned, starting to wobble. A bassline thumped through open windows as the car swerved around her.

What was she doing? Idiot! Cycling on a main road without a helmet! Kate waited for the impact. The number she'd read on a website about bike accidents flew into her head.

- **85% of bike casualties are not wearing helmets.**

The car shot past her, leaving three feet of room – but it was enough to force her, gasping, onto the pavement. She pushed her bike over the kerb.

'I just don't think about it,' Jago had said.

Just don't think about it.

Desperately, she tried to push the numbers away but they wouldn't leave her. No. She wasn't quite ready for this yet.

But tonight something had changed.

She had taken a step forward. Tiny, but still a step.

She'd had *fun*.

By the time she reached home, five minutes later, the lights were out. Saskia and Jack must be in bed. Kate crept in, feeling guilty.

She locked the inner doors downstairs, turned on the alarm and tiptoed upstairs. At the top, she saw the cage door. It stood wide open. She walked through it, ignoring the impulse to run to the garden and find the padlock.

Again, she heard Jago's voice in her head.

Just don't think about it.

She passed the front spare room where Saskia slept and then Jack's room, to reach the bathroom.

She was about to turn off the upper hall light when a noise stopped her. It was a heavy scraping noise that seemed to be coming from Jack's room.

That was odd.

His door was half open. Kate peeked in and tried to focus in the dark. A heavy breathing from the bed told her that Jack was asleep.

The noise started again, like something substantial being pushed along the floor.

It was coming from his wardrobe.

Kate's stomach did a somersault. Jack was right. This was not imagined.

Nervously, she crept towards the wardrobe door, and carefully picked up Jack's guitar. She grasped its neck with her right hand like a bat, and with her heart thumping hard, ready to scream out to wake up Saskia, began to open the door . . .

'What are you doing?'

Kate jumped.

Jack was sitting up in bed, staring at his guitar in the shaft of light from the hall outside.

'Oh, hi! Nothing,' she barked, sharper than she intended. 'I was just . . . um . . . putting away your washing. Sorry.'

She opened both wardrobe doors wide, hoping Jack wouldn't spot the absence of laundry, and surreptitiously swept the back of the wardrobe to check no one was there.

'Did you hear that funny noise?' Jack asked.

Kate berated herself. What was she doing? Exactly what Helen had warned her about: transferring her anxiety to Jack.

'Uhuh, and it's nothing to worry about,' she replied brightly. 'It's just someone next door moving something around in their room. The walls in this house are so thin. I hear noises sometimes, too – from the bedroom next to me.'

Not as loud as that weird scraping, she could have added, but didn't.

His voice came back uncertain in the dark. 'Oh, OK.'

'You OK? Sure?' She tried to sound reassuring.

'Yeah.' He turned over in his bed. 'Night, Mum.'

'Night, Jack.'

Kate tiptoed to the bathroom, trying to ignore the uneasy feeling that had crept back over her. She brushed her teeth and washed, replaying each scene from the cycle ride in her head to distract herself. Soon lost in thought, she crossed quietly to her bedroom, turning off the hall light. She shut the door, turned on her beside lamp, and took off her T-shirt. It smelt of the grass from the walled garden. She picked up her moisturizer, and did a double take in the mirror. Her cheeks were flushed, her eyes bright. She sat on the bed and smoothed the cream onto her skin.

What the hell had she just done? With a complete stranger?

She lay on the bed, running the evening's events back through her head.

That feeling she'd had, as she'd climbed the gate. That tension in her stomach. What was it? It hadn't been fear. She knew that. It was different. It had arrived as she climbed up to the top of the gate, and saw the dark garden beyond. A kind of tension she hadn't felt for a very long time. A kind of . . .

And then she knew.

Excitement.

Intrigued, Kate changed for bed. She climbed in between the sheets, and looked at the pile of unread books Saskia kept giving her from her village book club. Poor Sass. She was only trying to help. Her nervous blink had been back tonight. It wasn't as if her little sister-in-law's life had turned out the way she'd planned it, either.

Kate turned out the light. She felt the cool sheets on her body. And, as she did, a thought about Jago Martin and his blue eyes passed through her mind. The touch of his hand on her arm and . . .

There was a clicking noise.

Kate jerked upright and saw a strip of light appear under her door. Jack had turned on the hall light again.

He was still scared.

Kate lay back, cross with herself. If ever she needed evidence of the harm she was doing to Jack, there it was. Right under her door.

'You have to stop this,' she whispered. Jack had seen her anxious face by the wardrobe. Seen her holding the guitar as a weapon. Knew that she, too, feared there were bad men in his wardrobe.

She had to *get a grip*.

Normal adults didn't check their wardrobes at night.

She thought back to the garden. What did Jago say? Just because she'd had some bad luck, it didn't mean she was cursed. Just because her parents and Hugo had been killed, it didn't mean it was more likely to happen to her or Jack. She was *not* fated to be struck by lightning seven times.

How did that American professor put it? People living with a constant fear of imagined danger, convinced their instincts are trying to warn them.

No, she reassured herself, she and Jack had no more chance of being killed than anyone else. They were normal, too. Not cursed; just unlucky.

She lay back on the pillow, feeling new hope again. Jago was going to help her – was *already* helping her – stop worrying about threats that were completely imagined.

She was *not* cursed.

Mother woke around 10 a.m. The child stood in the hall, watching her emerge from her bedroom in a long T-shirt, pulling a belted woollen cardigan around her waist. She was scratching her head. Make-up was smudged under her eyes. Her dull brown hair was hanging around her face, streaked with metal grey, her fringe pushed back angrily.

Once Mother would have said, 'Do you want some breakfast, sweetheart?'

But not any more. The child had learned to make breakfast alone.

The child watched as Mother began to walk into the kitchen.

From behind the child there was a faint squeaking noise.

Mother stopped.

With a silent gasp, the child dropped back into the shadows, waiting to see if Mother was going to stop and come back.

But, after a second, Mother carried on, marching into the kitchen. She slammed the door.

The child turned quickly and ran back to the bedroom where the rocking horse was.

The squeaking was much louder in here. The child lay flat on the floor as quietly as possible and pressed an eye against the gap in the floorboards.

It took a moment to come into focus, but finally it did.

Father's head, a few feet below. He was turning a metal handle in his hand, trying to be as quiet as possible.

Planning to kill the snake.

But this time the child wasn't so sure that Father could stop it. It was bigger than the other one. The child was starting to think that it was going to wrap around this house and squeeze them all to death.

CHAPTER TWELVE

Why hadn't Jago rung?

Three days after her night in the secret walled garden, Kate looked out of the kitchen window at the magnolia tree, trying not to feel disappointed.

The irony was that, at first, she'd hoped that he wouldn't call her.

On Wednesday morning she'd woken in a panic, wondering what on earth she'd said the night before. About the numbers. About her parents. Jack? She had let her guard down with a man she hardly knew. Let his intense blue eyes into places where no one was supposed to go. Kate had sat up alarmed, and turned off her phone.

By Wednesday evening, however, when she turned it back on to find he hadn't rung as promised, she'd been slightly perplexed. By Thursday, she was checking every ten minutes.

Now, on Friday, she was sitting here, fighting the urge to ring Jago.

She looked back at her new laptop, which had arrived this morning. She closed down her proposal for David, which she'd transferred onto a spreadsheet, and Googled Jago for the sixth time that day. His own website had turned out to be the best: a small photo of him smiling on a mountain bike, listing his education (Stirling University, MSc; University of Edinburgh, PhD; University of North Carolina, post-doc research) and interests (travel, music, hiking, mountain biking). There was even a sweet little biog with details about his mum (a GP) and dad (a maths teacher), who lived in Stirling, and his two (teacher) sisters. She followed the links, too, to his department at Edinburgh, which had a more official photo, and a few American newspapers that had reviewed his book, and a list of his publications. His specialty, she noted with interest, was applying probability theory to economic models set up by new governments recovering from civil war. That must be why he flew to developing countries so much.

Professor Jago Martin was even more impressive than he had let on.

To her consternation, she realized she really did want to see him again.

A man she hadn't even known a week ago.

Grabbing a pile of fresh laundry, Kate headed up to Jack's room. She looked at Hugo's shoes on Jack's shelves, and turned guiltily away. Putting Jack's pyjamas in his bag, she realized she would miss him this weekend. They had baked twice more this week. Nothing much had been said. Just chatter about ingredients and who was stirring the pot, or rubbing in the butter, but it was something. A breakthrough. Again, tiny, but something. And now he was off to Helen's again and . . .

Kate's hand flew to her mouth.

A memory detonated in her mind.

She had *completely forgotten*, in all the upset about Jack hitting his head on the radiator.

What had he said to her in the hallway, just before it happened?

'Nana lets me walk to the shop alone.'

Kate's eyes flew to Jack's calendar. Tomorrow was Saturday.

Oh God. He'd be walking along the river path with other people's dogs running around off the lead.

She shut her eyes, knowing the numbers were coming for her.

• Hospital admissions for dog attacks have risen 5% this year.

In her mind, she saw Jack walking on his own along the river path from Helen's house a quarter of a mile to the shop in the village. A horrible dog running round the corner, attacking Helen's Labrador Rosie, and Jack trying to save her.

She smacked her hand down on her bed.

How *dare* Helen overrule her like this? It was almost as if she were trying to make her more anxious, not better.

Kate tried to remember. At what point had she given them this blatant co-ownership of her son? At first it had been necessary – that first year after Hugo when she couldn't lift her head from the pillow. And moving to Oxford to allow them to fill in for Hugo's absence with Jack in practical ways had seemed sensible. Yet now, it had become so much more: the fortnightly weekend sleepovers, the constant 'popping in', the up-coming trip with Jack to Dorset at half-term, the bloody house key to let themselves in, the decisions about Jack's safety with no regard for her feelings . . .

They were taking over her son.

Kate looked over at Jack's wardrobe. The guitar was back against the doors. He was still trying to lock in the bad men.

A sense of helplessness came over her. If she tried to cut down contact with them right now and cancelled tomorrow's sleepover, Helen might really blow up. Carry out her threat to tell Social Services about Kate's anxiety, and give them examples of the detrimental effect it had on Jack.

No, she couldn't risk it.

There was only one way out of this.

She would just *have* to learn to control it.

Then, in August, she would find a way to get Jack to David's house in Mallorca, away from Helen and Richard's interference, and give their relationship a real chance to start afresh.

Kate stood up, determined, and headed back downstairs to the laptop, remembering that David needed her proposal for the Islington house by six. She could ask him about the Mallorca house in the email.

Then she just needed to work out how to get on a bloody plane. Jago's book with its reassuring pages of airline statistics came into her mind.

Followed by an image of Jago.

Disappointment coursed back through Kate. She had been so convinced this Scottish man with his kind voice and searching blue eyes had the answer.

Richard arrived at Hubert Street to collect Jack at 5.30 p.m.

'Hello, young man!' he called cheerily as Jack appeared with his bag. Fighting every instinct she had, Kate stood on the step with the most relaxed smile she could muster, and said nothing.

Helen's absence on the doorstep said it all. The threat was clear. The years of pretending to be fond of her for Hugo, and then Jack's sake, were over. If Helen could take Jack, she would.

Richard kept beaming, as if protesting his innocence in all this, but Kate knew better. His eyes still moved busily, as they had done the first time she met him, analysing the situation. By now, however, Kate knew why. Richard looked for ways to maximize every situation – work or social – to his own benefit. Luckily, Hugo had taught her to ignore the ebullience and not trust him an inch.

'We'll have him back by five on Sunday, Mum,' said Richard, arm round Jack's shoulder. 'Good golly!' he exclaimed, when Jack proudly handed him a box of flapjacks and brownies. 'Are those for us? Fan-tastic!' Kate winced. 'So – Sunday at five, Mum!' he repeated, as he left, as if Kate suspected he was in the middle of a child-snatching operation organized by Helen.

'Bye, Mum,' Jack said, waving.

As she watched him go, Kate couldn't help it. 'Jack?' He turned. She pulled him into an awkward hug, aware of Richard watching as he opened the car door.

'Please be careful,' she whispered in his ear. From this angle she saw the faded scratch on his head. Could she really trust him not to tell Helen about the radiator? she thought shamefacedly. It was so much to ask of him.

Jack nodded and pulled away. Kate wrapped her arms around herself and walked back to her front door. As she waved Jack off with a raised hand, a movement of curtain from next door caught her eye. She looked up and saw the student with the strange-coloured eyes watching Richard's car as it reversed out of the driveway.

For a second, Kate's mind flickered somewhere uncertainly, as if trying to focus on something.

And then her phone buzzed in her hand.

are you there? jx, the text said.

And she forgot.

Jago!

Kate shut the front door, and rushed to the kitchen. After various attempts to type funny, clever replies, she deleted them.

yes . . .

i'm in the juice bar – can you pop down?

She read the message again. Now?

She looked at her laptop screen. She still hadn't finished the proposal. If she went now, the spreadsheet would be late for David. He'd waited patiently for her laptop to be delivered all week, on the condition that he got the figures by six o'clock tonight to give him time to calculate his sealed bid for the Islington house tomorrow.

But if she didn't go, Jago might not be there later.

Chewing her pen, Kate stood up. The proposal would be late by only half an hour or so. She'd still get it to David by 6.30 p.m.

This was more important.

Pausing to think, Kate picked up her coat, texted Jago to say she was on her way, and flew out of the door, hoping David would forgive her.

CHAPTER THIRTEEN

She arrived ten minutes later, trying not to look as if she'd been running. Jago was sitting at the same place by the window, reading a *Guardian*. He looked up and waved as she passed the window.

Her stomach fluttered.

'Hi, Kate,' he said, standing up. Before she knew it, he had leaned over and kissed her on the cheek. 'How're you doing?'

'Good, thanks.' To her dismay, she blushed. She placed her jacket on the back of the chair next to him, trying to hide her face.

'I wasn't sure if you'd be on your own,' he said, as she sat up at the counter.

'No. Jack's at his grandparents for the weekend.'

'Oh. Does he get on well with them?'

She kept her hands self-consciously over her hot cheeks, nodding. 'They've got a huge garden and a dog, so he's in heaven.' An image of Jack beside the river alone forced itself back into her mind, and she pushed it away.

The waitress with the auburn plait came over and did a double-take. 'Oh, hello again.' She grinned at Jago. 'You managed to track him down, then?'

To her annoyance, Kate's cheeks burned even hotter. 'Ah, it was just about buying your book . . .' she stuttered at Jago, avoiding his eye. She gave the waitress what she hoped was a dismissive look. 'Juice of the day, please.'

'Oh. Sure,' the girl said, raising her eyebrows.

'So, am I keeping you from work?' Jago said, turning to her. It was good to see him again. He was wearing a navy T-shirt emblazoned with the name of a band that she didn't recognize.

'No. Not at all. As long as I get it over tonight,' she lied.

'OK. Well, look,' he said, leaning on the counter. 'Anyway . . .'

'Yes.' She smiled.

'I've been thinking.'

'Uhuh?'

'About the other night.'

She took a sip of juice, knowing she had to say it. 'Jago. I'm a bit embarrassed about that, actually. I think I probably sounded a bit weird and . . .'

'No.' He touched her arm. His voice was reassuring. 'You didn't, Kate. At all. And, actually, I am hoping I might be able to help you, with this obsessional data anxiety stuff.'

Kate glanced around the cafe. It was fuller this time, the tables occupied by students. Jago dropped his voice. 'Sorry.'

'No. It's OK. Well. That's nice of you, but what do you . . .?'

Jago sipped his juice. 'Well, I rang the psychologist in the States who's writing a book about it.'

He had done that for her? It had been so long since anyone had done anything kind for her. A lump came into her throat.

'I won't bore you with it all,' Jago continued, 'but I thought you'd find some of what he said interesting. I did.'

Kate nodded, curious. 'Go on.' She tried to stop herself looking at the arc of his bicep in her peripheral vision.

'Well, part of his theory is that this anxiety disorder has developed because of the de-programming of our fight-or-flight instinct.'

He laughed. She tried to make the expression on her face a little less vacant.

'OK. Well, as I'm sure you know, human instinct is wired for survival. To fight the wild bear or run away from it.'

'Yes. I get that bit.'

'But most of us in the developed world don't require that primal instinct any more.'

She shifted in her seat, remembering she had no make-up on.

'I don't quite . . .'

'OK. Think of it this way.' He paused, as if thinking. 'If there are no wild bears to escape from, or invading marauders to fight, what do we do? We switch off our fight-or-flight programme. We stop relying on our wits to survive.'

'And . . .?'

Jago took another drink of his juice. The music changed and 'Love Me Do' by The Beatles started. Kate slipped a sideways glance at the waitress.

'Well, why don't we have to protect ourselves any more?' he asked.

Kate shrugged. 'Because others do it for us.'

'That's right. They do. They keep our borders safe and create laws to protect us. Provide us with clean food and safe shelter. But if we entrust others to protect us all the time, and stop using our own instincts to survive, how do we know we're really safe?'

'They tell us we are?'

'How?'

Kate thought for a moment. 'Through information. They give us statistics.'

Jago banged his hand gently on the counter. 'Very good. And there you go. The people who protect us constantly quantify that protection. "A recent test showed that your family will be bla-bla percentage safer in this car than that car," and so on.'

Kate turned to face him more fully, intrigued.

Jago continued. 'But there are hundreds of statistics. Thousands. So what do you do? If you're me, you just get on with life. Accept that nothing is 100 per cent certain apart from that we'll all die. Use a bit of common sense mixed with a few statistics and your own experience. So, for instance, I might fly to an important conference in a country whose airline has a less good safety record because I know that airlines usually don't crash so I'll probably be fine. But I won't go without, say, taking my malaria tablets. Common sense tells me that's a risk not worth taking.'

'Whereas I . . .'

'You don't fly at all. You miss the important conference. You stay at home convinced that by manipulating statistics you are controlling your own fate by keeping yourself safe. Do you see?'

'I think so,' Kate said. Some of this did actually make sense.

Jago continued. 'And that, according to the experts, is why our reliance on statistics is spilling over into an obsessional disorder for some people. For someone already suffering from anxiety – and I'm assuming after what's happened to you, Kate – it appears to offer choices that relieve that anxiety. Scared of being ill? Arm yourself with statistics. Buy this cycle helmet and you'll be 22 per cent safer than with that one. But, of course, all statistics are just an average of something that's already happened. A guesstimate of what might happen next, not of what *will* happen. You can't predict the future with certainty. You might set off in your shiny new cycle helmet and a lorry rolls down a hill because the driver was stuck in traffic for three hours due to a freak accident, and is so tired he forgot to put on the handbrake, and it squashes you flat. You can't avoid danger altogether. But you can spend time convincing yourself that you can, by manipulating the figures – and not living much of a life in the process.'

He gave a dramatic gasp as if he'd just finished a sprint.

'Sorry. Going on there.'

They both smiled.

Kate held out her hands. 'I could choke on a peanut in the departure lounge.'

'Exactly. It's no wonder that when people start trying to work all this out they become . . .'

'. . . Neurotic. Like me.'

Jago winced. 'I didn't say that.'

'No. It's OK,' she said quietly. 'It's interesting. I'm just thinking about it.'

Jago finished his juice, then turned round to face her.

'So . . .' he said. 'What do you think?'

'I think . . . it certainly explains some things, but I'm not quite sure how it changes it.'

'Ah, well, this is where I bring in my, what we will very roughly call an experiment. I'm interested to know if it's possible for you to counteract this dependency on statistics . . .'

She demurred. 'And you would want to do this because . . .'

'Who knows. It might lead to an interdisciplinary research paper with the psychology department at Edinburgh somewhere down the line. So . . .'

Kate felt a glow on her face. He was offering to spend more time with her, to do things together. She felt a bubble of hope. A glimpse into a future that a week ago did not exist.

'OK. And if I did agree to be your guinea pig – what would that entail?'

Jago frowned. 'Well. That's the thing, Kate. That's what I wanted to talk to you about. What I'm planning is not orthodox. But sometimes, in the early stages, you have to throw ideas out there and see what comes back. The trouble is . . .'

162

'Hmm,' Kate said, sensing a 'but' coming.

He grimaced. 'OK. Honestly? I'm concerned that you might not be up to this.'

Disappointment crashed over her. She dropped her eyes. Was Jago actually here today, trying to tell her he didn't want to see her again, in the gentlest possible way? Finding some round-about excuse to extract himself while pointing her in the direction of help?

'What do you mean?' she asked, trying to stop her voice wavering.

He crinkled his eyes. 'The thing is, I'd need to try to kick-start your instincts, so you react rather than think. I'm just concerned that maybe that's just asking too much of you at the moment. If you're feeling a little fragile. You know, to be spontaneous. I don't want to mess with . . .'

Kate held up a hand. Right now, all she knew was that she wanted nothing more in the world than Jago's help.

'Jago,' she said more firmly than she meant to. 'I want to try.'

'Really?'

Their eyes met. He looked into hers closely and, for the first time since they'd met, she let him.

'OK, well, let's see . . .' he said. He glanced out of the window and fixed his eyes on a woman with a white retriever. The woman was in her sixties, tall, with a silver bob, glasses and a Barbour waistcoat. She tied the dog to a lamp post, then disappeared into the health food shop next door. The dog gave a half-hearted bark, whined and settled on the pavement.

Jago turned to Kate. 'So, OK. If, for instance, I asked you to untie that dog and lead it away, could you?'

Kate looked at the dog. 'Er, no.'

'You couldn't?'

Oh, God, he looked serious. 'You want me to steal a dog?'

Kate laughed, waiting for Jago to say it was a joke. But his gaze remained steady. Kate glanced back at the dog uneasily.

He really did not seem to be kidding. Could she do it?

She had one chance here.

'Um, OK, I suppose so.'

'Great,' Jago said, slapping the counter. 'So, that's what I want you to do. Go out there, untie the dog, walk down to the pedestrian crossing near Tesco and wait for me.'

Kate shifted on her stool. 'You really are serious?'

'I am.'

'Jago. That's a bit crazy.'

Jago shrugged. 'As I said, Kate, what I'm planning isn't orthodox.'

Kate sighed. She stood up reluctantly and hesitated. When he still didn't stop her, she moved towards the door – slowly. Jago watched her go, saying nothing.

She waited for him again. He did nothing.

She opened the door next, praying Jago would call her back and say she'd passed the test. That she called his bluff.

But still he didn't.

Before Kate knew it, she was outside on the pavement. As she shut the door, she looked down and saw the patch of grime from the other day, still stuck in the doorway.

And then she knew. She was *not* going back there.

If this is what he wanted her to do, she would do it.

Kate turned to look at Jago through the window. He was paying the waitress for their drinks. As she counted out the change, he gave Kate a tiny encouraging nod.

Resigned to her fate, Kate turned to the dog. Close up, it was younger than she'd realized. It gazed up with hopeful brown eyes. Kate peeked into the health food shop. The owner was talking to a girl behind the counter.

This was silly.

Jago had better know what he was talking about.

'Jesus,' she murmured, kneeling down as if tying her shoe, feeling her heart starting to thump. She reached out a finger and touched the dog's lead. What would she say if the woman caught her? She thought for a second, then she knew. She'd pretend she thought it had been abandoned and was taking it to the police.

Feeling a little reassured at her own lie, Kate undid the lead, checked again that the owner still had her back turned, and led the dog away.

'Come on,' she said, not even stopping to see if it was following. To her relief, she felt its weight on the lead. Kate half shut her eyes, as if that would make her invisible, and began to run towards the traffic lights up ahead, cursing Jago as she went.

'Quick,' a voice said behind her. She turned to see Jago pacing up behind her, putting his change in his pocket, looking ridiculously relaxed. He pushed the button for the pedestrian crossing.

'I can't believe I'm doing this!' she hissed. 'I can't believe you've made me steal a bloody dog! What are we going to do with it?'

Jago chuckled. 'Go,' he said calmly as the green man lit up on the signal. She crossed the road, the lead turning damp in her sweaty palm.

At the other side, she glanced, panicked at the health food shop. The dog's owner was coming to the door, her head turned back towards the counter, still talking.

'What now?' she yelled at Jago.

He motioned with his head. 'That lamp post. Quick.'

'Where?'

'There.'

Following his eyes, Kate dropped down, and threw the lead

165

frantically around the lamp post, as if it were burning her fingers. The dog sniffed at her, then sat down again on the pavement.

'Go!' Jago said, grabbing Kate's hand and pulling her back up the Cowley Road. Kate exhaled with relief as if she'd dropped a burning pot.

As they passed the health food shop, there was a tinkle as the dog's owner came out, shouting back a cheerful goodbye. Jago stopped and pulled Kate down with him beside a railing, and began to unlock what she now realized was his bike.

'Ginny?' Kate heard a well-spoken voice call out across the road. 'Ginny!'

There was a bark from further down the road. Kate peered through the railings.

'Ginny?' She saw the woman stare across the road, astonished. 'Gosh. How did you get over there, girl?'

There was such a note of surprise in her well-spoken voice, that to her embarrassment, Kate felt the corners of her mouth turn up. Jago saw it, and grinned at her.

'Don't. That was mean.'

'*Gin-ay?*' Jago whispered in a falsetto posh English voice. '*What the jolly-roger-dodger are you doing over there, gel?*'

Kate couldn't help it. A bubble of laughter exited her mouth in an unladylike snort. Jago threw back his head and laughed in his laid-back boyish way that she realized she was starting to love hearing.

'Oi, you,' she said. 'I better have bloody passed your bloody test.'

'You already had,' Jago said, standing up with his lock. 'I just fancied a laugh.'

'Jago!' Kate opened her eyes wide, and went to bang his arm. To her surprise he caught her hand in his, and pulled her into a half-hug.

'So, madam. Are you free tomorrow night?' he said cheerily.

Kate jerked away, panicked. This was Cowley Road. Someone might see her. Saskia. Jack's friends.

'Uh, yes. Sorry,' she said.

'Excellent.' Jago beamed, seemingly unperturbed. He grabbed his bike from the railing. 'So, say, the Hanley Arms, 8 p.m., OK?'

'OK, great.'

Jago winked, as he pulled into the road. 'You did well. OK, listen, we'll have some fun tomorrow. And don't worry about it.'

Kate watched him go, then spun around to double check that the woman had indeed been reunited with her dog. There had been no harm done, she reassured herself. The dog was safe.

Then, she noticed someone watching her.

The waitress in the juice bar.

Their eyes met through the window. The waitress, who Kate suspected fancied Jago, was not smiling any more. Her eyes were watchful and wary. Kate baulked. Had she seen them take the dog?

Throwing the girl a brief smile to pacify her, Kate turned on her heel and set off back home. But there was a rap on the window.

Kate's stomach lurched. Had she been caught?

Without Jago, she didn't feel so brave.

She looked over and saw the girl beckoning her.

Apprehensively, Kate crossed the road. The girl came out holding a bag.

'The Scottish guy – he left this,' she said.

'Oh. Thanks,' Kate said, taking it from her, trying to turn and head off before the waitress mentioned the dog.

'You kind of rushed off there,' the girl said.

Kate lowered her eyes. 'Thanks. I'll give it to him.'

'Interesting guy,' the waitress said, her own eyes burning into Kate.

Kate shifted uncomfortably. 'He is. Anyway, thanks for this.'

And, before the girl could make her feel any more awkward, Kate set off back to Hubert Street, not quite believing that a beautiful twenty-something girl was a little jealous of her.

As she marched away, she saw the dog and its owner climbing into a car. She smiled inwardly. What would Jack say if he knew what his mum had just done? It had been like a student prank – silly but also a little fun. How long was it since she had been silly?

As she walked along, Kate opened Jago's bag. His book was inside.

Touched, she realized he'd done what he promised, kept the book for her if she ever needed it.

Well, did she?

She took it out and felt the weight of it in her hands.

It was all here. Everything she needed to satisfy her – if she wanted to carry on being a complete lunatic with no life and no son.

Shutting it determinedly, Kate put it back in Jago's bag. No. This was going straight in the shed. She was locking it away.

This obsession with numbers had to end.

Kate marched on, knowing that however crazy Jago's methods were, they were the answer to her imaginary fears.

CHAPTER FOURTEEN

The football still sat in the middle of the trampoline, waiting for the blond boy to come home and kick it.

Spoilt brat, Magnus thought, looking out of the window onto the gardens at the back of Hubert Street. All these toys, in the garden and in the bedroom. And a scooter too.

He rubbed the red, open pores of his nose, and clicked one more button on the laptop in front of him. 'Installation five minutes', said a message popping up. Magnus glanced at the clock.

He sat back on Kate's swivel chair and pushed his long legs against the wall of the study under her desk.

It had been thirty-five minutes since he'd seen her race off towards Cowley Road, and two minutes less than that since he'd squeezed himself through the ragged brick hole behind her son's wardrobe. Five more minutes was all he needed.

Magnus looked around Kate's study, inhaling the faint leftover fragrance of her vanilla hand lotion. He liked it. So much, in fact, that he'd taken some in a little saucer to keep in his room. 'Brrr, brrr, brrr,' he parped like a trumpet, clicking his fingers on the table as the installation symbol on her new laptop in front of him read 'Four minutes and thirty-nine seconds.' He opened the drawer and took out the photo of her and a man. He'd seen that one before.

'Brr, brr, brr,' he sang through his closed lips. Four minutes and three seconds. He stood up and wandered out of the study into the hall, noting that the cage at the far end, across the stairs was open for the first time. That was interesting. He smirked. Silly woman.

Trying to stay one step ahead of him with her new alarm and this cage.

The cage he was right inside.

He turned right and entered Kate's bedroom.

It wasn't as tidy as usual today. The bed was made more roughly, a duvet chucked on top, its four corners sprawled randomly, like the limbs of a gunshot victim. Her nightclothes lay strewn on the pillow. Not the usual flimsy nightie with the holes, he noted with interest, but a new long grey T-shirt. He lifted it and pushed his nose into it, inhaling. It didn't have the same soft silkiness of the other nightie against his bristles, but still. Interesting.

'Brrr, brrr, brrr,' he sang, rolling the 'r' with his tongue. The fitted wardrobe door was open, with two pairs of jeans hanging over them. Idly, he took a pair down and held them up to his crotch at the mirror. Yup. Too skinny. He placed one hand inside the top of the jeans, and pushed his arm all the way down one leg. Nearly fitted his arm.

As he put them back, the photo by the bed caught his eye. That was new. A black-and-white image of a man and a woman in their fifties looked back at him. The man was handsome, not unlike Magnus, with dark blond hair and glasses, and a small nose. The woman not so much. Her nose was sharp, and she was almost as skinny as Kate. Magnus took out his camera and photographed it. Then he snapped the grey T-shirt on the pillow.

Sighing, he sat on the bed and pulled his long legs up onto the duvet, turning his head to sniff the pillow. He pushed his buttocks and thighs into the duvet and wriggled a little. 'Brr, brr, brr' he sang, the tone of his voice becoming falsetto.

Suddenly, there was a click of a key in a lock downstairs.

He sat up abruptly.

No way. The skinny woman was back? That quick?

Standing up quickly, trying to stop his weight creaking the floorboards, Magnus paused to listen. He heard her go to the hall cupboard. *Beep beep beep* the alarm went as she turned it off.

Have to be quick now.

Walking swiftly, he re-entered the study. 'Thirty-nine seconds', the message on the screen said. 'No problem,' he murmured in English.

He heard the woman unlocking the door into the kitchen at the back of the house. That meant she'd be walking right under his feet in a second, so he'd have to be careful not to creak the floorboards.

Calmly, he counted down with the computer: 'three, two, one . . .', then ejected the disk he had put in the side of her computer. He tiptoed heavily to the door and peered out of the study.

Damn. She had come back out of the kitchen and was running up the stairs.

It was too late now. He wouldn't make it back to the boy's room.

Before she reached the top of the stairs, Magnus slipped into Kate's room. Checking he'd put the photograph back on the table, he laid himself down on the floor, put his hands under her bed frame and pulled himself carefully under Kate's bed.

A pair of ankle boots with worn-down heels got in his way. He shoved them and pulled his big feet in, away from the edges.

The air was different under here. Warmer, and stale.

Never mind. It wasn't a big deal. He'd done it before, twice. He'd just stay for a while. He heard her reach the top of the stairs then walk up the corridor. Her humming was interrupted by a mobile phone ringing in her hand.

'Hello . . . Oh, hi, David. . . I'm so sorry. Give me another twenty minutes. I've had a difficult week with Richard and Helen. I'll tell you when I see you.'

Magnus listened, interested. He didn't get to hear the skinny woman's voice that often.

'When I see you,' Magnus mouthed under the bed, trying to copy her vowel sounds.

Magnus lay back on the carpet under the bed and stretched out among dusty boxes, and relaxed, holding his nose tight so he didn't sneeze. It was only twenty minutes.

Of course, ultimately, it was his choice. He could pop out right now and give her a right old fright.

But no.

It wasn't time for that yet. There was a lot more to do first.

CHAPTER FIFTEEN

Kate sat down at the computer, typed in the last few figures and sent David the document twenty minutes later. Relieved it was done, she wandered back out of the study to go downstairs.

A whiff of something drifted into her nostrils. A male smell. Hormonal. Cloying and unfresh. It wasn't the first time she'd smelt it, but Jack wasn't here right now. She poked her head inside the boy's bedroom. His deodorant was lying on the shelf as normal.

She looked around for discarded sports clothes to see if that was what was causing the smell, but there was nothing there. Compared to most boys his age, Jack was tidy, she guessed. Bed made, toys in boxes. The only thing that was out of place was his wardrobe door, which had fallen open again, pushing the guitar to the floor. She walked over and closed the door, resting the guitar against the handle this time, to keep it shut. She picked up the deodorant and shook it. No. Still some in there. Maybe his teenage hormones were just going into overdrive right now. She sighed. If only Hugo was here to guide him through the secrets of male puberty.

A pang of guilt stopped her. If she started something with

Jago, how or when would she even begin to broach it with Jack? How would it affect her efforts to bring them closer again?

But without Jago, would it even happen?

She rubbed her lips together. They were dry from biting them in concentration as she wrote the proposal earlier. It was too early to think about all that. She'd only just met him. Briskly, she walked out of Jack's bedroom, and entered her own to find some lip salve.

She paused mid-step. That was strange. The smell was in here, too. Kate wandered to the dressing table and slicked some salve across her lips, looking round for the source again.

As she turned to go out, something caught her eye. The ankle boots she'd meant to have re-heeled ages ago, were sticking out of the bottom of the bed.

Humming, Kate leaned over and picked them up.

As she headed back downstairs to place them by the front door, she realized there was a new bounce in her step. And then she knew why. For the first time in a long time, she was looking forward to something. Eight o'clock tomorrow night at the Hanley Arms.

Back in the kitchen, she saw Jago's bag on the floor, and felt a new resolve take over. Before she could change her mind, she marched out of the back door and locked the bag in the shed. Back in the kitchen, she grabbed the kettle, pleased with herself. As she waited for the water to fill it, her eyes focused on the magnolia tree outside, the only plant she had brought from their Highgate home. The tree was so much taller than when Hugo had last seen it. Its trunk and branches were thickened and matured. They had grown up and away, in different directions.

A band of pain tightened around her chest so fiercely, so unexpectedly, Kate gasped.

Hugo.

Oh God.

Tears welled in her eyes.

Was this it?

After five years, was she going finally to leave him behind and move on?

'I'm sorry,' she whispered. 'But I think this man will help me. Please, don't be cross. It's for Jack, too.'

Just at that minute a bird flew off a branch, the bounce shedding two dark green leaves onto the soil below.

Kate watched, startled. Was Hugo watching her? Trying to tell her not to do it?

Resolutely, she turned and plugged the kettle in. No. It was time to stop exhausting herself looking for imagined signs. There had been a time when she thought she would never let Hugo go. She would die old and lonely, holding onto the shirt he wore that night, splattered with the blood that spilled onto the floorboards, covered the table, the half-eaten food, the table runner. Now, she knew she would go insane if she didn't let him go, and take Jack with her into the future. Whatever this thing with Jago was, it was time to at least try . . .

A thud from upstairs made Kate recoil.

She stood stock-still. The sound had come from the front of the house. From Jack's room.

Ice entered her veins.

Her mind shot back to the break-in of two weeks ago. The sickening terror of seeing the dining room lying open, shattered glass on the floor. Was there someone in here again?

She glanced terrified at the alarm box in the hall. It had definitely been on when she came home. How could they have broken through this one?

Then common sense returned.

Kate felt colour return to her face.

Jack's wardrobe door. The guitar must have fallen over.

Calm, she thought. Calm. She shut her eyes and tried to summon the sensation she'd had on the riverbank on Tuesday night.

She inhaled deeply.

One thousand, two thousand, three thousand, four thousand . . .

Tumbling down, into a never-ending void.

Her arms and legs free, with nothing to fight against.

Everything falling away.

Kate opened her eyes, and felt better.

Pleased, she realized she had done it again. Wrestled back a little control.

Pouring boiling water into a cup, she wondered what Jago had planned for tomorrow night. As she did, an impulse came to reach out and take a flapjack from a plate on the worktop. She bit into it, surprised at how sweet it was. The sticky oats felt chewy between her teeth. The sugar exploded into her mouth, into each crevice, making her jaw ache for more.

She looked at the flapjack with surprise. That was *delicious*. She chewed, thinking.

This thing Jago kept saying – that the statistics were just exacerbating her anxiety – was interesting. That they were making her feel even more unsafe than she did already.

She took another bite, and nibbled it, a touch of optimism flushing through her.

Things were going to get better.

Then she remembered about Jack going to the shop in Richard and Helen's village tomorrow morning.

She looked up at the kitchen clock.

'Don't panic,' she whispered to herself. There were still ten more hours to decide what to do.

The sun appeared through the clouds at lunchtime, caressing the house, trailing its golden fingers from room to room. The child sat on the bedroom floor at the far end of the house, fitting pieces into a jigsaw of a seascape, tensing each time Mother came near, to the bathroom or to empty the laundry basket outside in the hall. If there was a creak of floorboard or a heavy sigh that sounded perilously close, the child gently knocked on the floor to alert Father to be quiet down below. At least Mother was doing the laundry now, far up at the other end of the house in the kitchen. You could tell by the slam of the washing machine door, then the metallic clank and hiss of the iron, slammed across shirts and trousers, back and forwards.

Father grunted. Through the tiny crack the child could see he was still turning the metal pole. His face was red. Sweat drops were pouring down his face.

The child crawled to the door to check Mother was still in the kitchen down the hall, then turned back to the pile of jigsaw pieces to look for the puffin's beak. If Father killed the snake, then maybe that would be it. The house would be quiet again, maybe even forever this time.

The child saw the puffin's beak in the pile of jigsaw pieces and grabbed it, distracted.

Then there was a thud.

A door was flung open.

The child jumped up and peeked out of the bedroom door.

Mother was emerging from the kitchen with a basket of wet washing under her arm. Her face was the colour of a week-old potato.

The child jumped back, dropping the puffin's beak on the floor, and whispering loudly.

'She's coming!'

Father made a loud sound. It was not a groan of effort, like before. It was painful, like the yowl made by the farmer's dog on the other side of the hill, chained to a post in the yard.

The child stopped breathing, peering out of the door.

Mother was coming towards the bedroom.

At the last minute, she turned and headed down the stairs of the house and went outside the front door to hang the washing on the line in the hillside. 'Never get clothes fresher smelling than hung outside,' she had said once, in the old house that they had rented down in the town. The small, dark, cosy house with its nice neighbours, where no one had ever screamed. Where Father used to lay his arm on Mother's shoulder in the kitchen after work, when she was cooking, and she didn't pull away as if he had burned her.

The child jumped up and checked through the picture window in the hallway, then returned, ears hot, to whisper through the floorboards.

'She's going to the washing line. She's going to see it!'

Father groaned heavily, and shook his head. There was something wrong.

The child ran to the rocking horse, and pulled away the dressing gown, then gasped in horror.

A new snake had arrived. A huge snake. Twice the size, maybe three times the size of the first one. And it was writhing down towards the floor.

178

CHAPTER SIXTEEN

It was Saturday lunchtime, and the river was busy with boats.

Rosie pulled hard on the lead, panting, as Jack followed her back to Richard and Helen's house, the paper bag of warm bread from the village baker and Granddad's newspaper under his arm.

He looked at the river on his left, wondering if any of the boats motoring past were Granddad's. Everyone knew that Saturday morning was Granddad's time on his own. He had been out on his for an hour already, and had said he was looking forward to the chicken and vegetable soup that Jack and Nana had made together this morning.

A small feeling of dread grew in Jack's stomach as he looked ahead at the bend.

Rosie pulled on the lead, chasing an interesting smell in the reeds.

'No, girl,' Jack said, pulling her back, aware of his responsibility.

He didn't have many memories of Dad, but the few he did have were becoming brighter all the time. The clearest one was Dad telling him about his dog Pip who'd drowned in a river when Dad was fourteen. Jack remembered because Dad had said that he had cried for two days. He remembered feeling stunned, that big men like Dad ever cried.

Jack came around the bend and saw what he had been dreading.

Up ahead, the narrow path disappeared into a canopy of trees. Together they created a tunnel that lasted for two or three minutes' walk, cutting off the view of the river.

Not that Jack would ever tell Granddad, whom he suspected had never cried even about a dog or anything, or Mum, who was already too worried about him walking on his own, but sometimes, under this long tunnel of trees, Jack felt scared.

He felt that someone was watching him.

'Come, girl,' he said nervously. Often, he was lucky and managed to cross through behind some dog walkers or a family, but today the path was quiet. The only other pedestrians had passed in the other direction.

Jack dropped his head and quickened his pace as he entered the tunnel. He'd just have to be brave and do it.

The smell changed instantly, as it always did. Musty and earthy, the ground slightly damp. The sun was left outside, the light in here a sinister grey.

Jack pulled Rosie's lead lightly to tell her they were going faster, and kept his eyes on the gravel of the path, glancing up occasionally to check how close they were to the other end.

It was no good.

As usual, the sensation of being watched descended on him slowly. And, as it did, the distance to the patch of sunlight at the other end stretched further ahead.

If anyone had asked him, he would have found it hard to describe it. There was nothing real. No more than a sense of a blurred shadow that melted into the foliage and bark. Yet Jack knew that, if it wanted to, the thing behind the trees watching him could travel quicker than a car. If it wanted to catch him, it would.

Jack quickened his pace, till the muscles inside his legs were stretched as far as they could go.

'Come on, girl,' he repeated, jerking Rosie's lead harder than he meant to.

She looked up at him with timid soft eyes and did as he asked.

Then, behind him, there was a noise.

Jack heard a *noise*.

It was a sound he had never heard inside this tunnel before, but had always feared.

A padding sound.

Feet.

Like heavy feet breaking into a trot, right behind him.

A gigantic, painful cramp shot through Jack's stomach so abruptly, it forced a small moan from his mouth.

'Quick, Rosie,' he gasped, too scared to look back.

Something had come out of the bushes, just like he'd always feared it would.

It was coming to get him.

Jack fixed his eyes on the end of the tunnel, making his legs go even faster till he thought the muscles might snap inside them.

'Don't run,' he told himself, remembering what Mum had told him to do if he ever came across an aggressive dog: 'If you run it really will go for you.'

But as Jack quickened his walking pace, the padding behind him became faster too.

And then . . .

RUFF! RUFF! RUFF! RUFF!

The barking came out of nowhere, making Jack skip upwards with fright as he paced to the end of the tunnel. A second cramp shot through him, nearly making him double up in pain.

It was only when he felt the vibration in his hand that he realized. The barking was coming from his mobile – the ringtone he and Gabe had put on it yesterday for a laugh.

Someone was phoning him.

'Hello?' he shouted, racing on along the path, praying the thing behind him would be put off by the presence of the person on the phone. The end of the tunnel lay ahead, only fifty metres to go.

'Jack, it's Mum,' came a voice.

'Hi, Mum.' The sound of her voice in this dark, scary tunnel made Jack feel so relieved as he marched forwards, waiting for the thing's hand on his shoulder at any second, that he wanted to cry.

'Jack, I just wondered where your PE kit was,' she said. She was trying to sound casual, he could tell. 'I was going to wash it. Did you take it to Nana's or have you left it at school?'

Forty metres, thirty metres. Jack raced on desperately, willing his legs to stretch more. He knew what Mum was doing. He'd told her he went to the village shop at twelve o'clock, and she was checking on him, but pretending she was ringing about something else.

Right now, though, he didn't care.

He was relieved.

'I put them in the wash basket,' he said, ready to shout in case the thing grabbed him. Only twenty metres to go. 'Oh, and Mum,' he said, trying to keep her on the phone till the end, 'Nana says, can you pack my raincoat for going to Dorset at half-term because it might rain.'

'Oh. OK. You've got your navy one for school. That'll do, won't it?'

He heard the skip in the rhythm of her voice. As if she sensed the strange tone in his voice and didn't understand it.

'Oh, OK.'

'OK. Well, listen, we'll talk about what you're taking to Dorset when you get home,' she said. 'I just wanted to check where your PE kit was.'

She was going to ring off. And he would be left in here with the thing.

There were ten metres to go. Jack couldn't help it. The padding was so loud now behind him, he broke into a run, even though he knew Mum could hear his panting on the phone. As he reached the opening in the trees, he dived through it, as if he was crossing the finish line on sports day.

'Jack! What's going on?' his mum called. 'Are you all right?'

A boat appeared on Jack's left, an elderly couple reading newspapers on its deck. The woman looked up and smiled at him.

Jack stopped and twirled round. 'Yes . . .' he panted. 'Um, Rosie was running towards the river in Nana's garden. I chased after her.'

He heard her pause. Heard her try to work out if she could trust him. 'Jack? Are you sure everything is OK?'

'Yes. But thanks for ringing, Mum.'

She paused again. 'Oh, OK. You're welcome. Look forward to seeing you tomorrow. Perhaps we can do some more baking.'

'OK. Bye,' Jack said, ending the call.

He stood gathering himself, humiliated at the shaking he felt in his legs, hoping Granddad wouldn't sail past right now and see him looking like this.

Then Jack stopped. He could *still* hear the padding.

Swinging round, he looked inside the canopy. It was long, grey and full of shadows – and completely empty.

And then Jack realized the sound was his own blood, pounding in his ears.

*

183

That Saturday evening, Kate was ready at 7.45 p.m. sharp, showered and wearing her new jeans again, this time with a white T-shirt, a new thin navy cashmere jumper she had bought in a shop in the High Street this afternoon and socks and hiking boots, in case they were going to climb over any more gates. She had applied some make-up and blow-dried her hair again.

Today had been surprisingly relaxed. She was still pleased with herself at the way she'd managed to check Jack was all right without making him suspicious, or causing another conflict with Helen, while putting her own mind at rest. Once she had got to grips with this anxiety, maybe she'd even be able to let Jack walk to the shop herself.

As she walked out of her bedroom, the laptop caught her eye through the open door of the study. A little thrill of anticipation ran through her. Of course! She hadn't done that yet.

She paused for a moment, biting her lip, then, feeling like a teenager, wrote Jago's name with 'wife' and 'girlfriend' beside it.

A small, grainy photo came up in Google Images of someone else's Facebook page of Jago laughing beside a pretty, petite girl with white-blonde hair piled on her head and dark eyebrows. 'Jago Martin and Marla Van Doorsten at Thomas and Julia's wedding', said the caption. Kate stared. Was that the ex-girlfriend?

She felt a tiny pang of jealousy. Where had that come from? She was as bad as the young student waitress in the juice bar.

As she stood up, a number flew at her. It was one that had haunted her for five years.

- **70% of all homicides are committed by someone you already know.**

'Kate, shut up!' she said out loud. But as she began to walk quickly to escape, she stopped.

184

Hang on. Was it really that stupid to be careful? After all, she'd met Jago in the street.

A tiny window was opening up in the gloom of her consciousness, she realized. Something new was happening. Her mind was trying to tell the difference between irrational fear and reasonable caution.

She was a single mother. She should be cautious of strangers, for Jack's sake, as well as her own.

Nobody who knew her, knew Jago. Nobody would know where she'd gone.

Instinctively, she knew it was a sensible precaution, and that she had to follow it. So she grabbed a pen and a Post-it note and scribbled on it.

'Dear all, I've gone out with Jago Martin, a visiting professor at Balliol. This is his phone number . . . I should be back by midnight, Saturday. Kate.'

She re-read the note.

Was that mad?

No, she thought firmly, grabbing her bag and walking back to the door of the study.

It was sensible. Probably the first sensible decision she'd made in a long time.

Next door, Magnus walked back into his bedroom, carrying a bowl of cereal and a bottle of Coke. A flicker of movement on the screen caught his eye. He sat down in front of Kate's laptop he'd stolen last week from the delivery courier. He put down his bowl of cereal and walked quickly to the table.

An image of Kate walking away from him appeared on his screen.

'Yes!' he hissed, clicking on a button to magnify it.

The surveillance software hadn't worked on her last laptop, but this new, upgraded one was better.

Magnus sat stuffing cornflakes in his mouth, watching Kate through the in-built camera of her own laptop, walking down the corridor, and then disappearing left, down the stairs.

And then there was nothing. Just the open door of the study behind the computer, and the empty hallway beyond.

Magnus grinned and high-fived himself with both hands.

CHAPTER SEVENTEEN

Kate arrived at the Hanley Arms five minutes early. The pub was busy. Saturday night crowds spilled into the little beer garden at the back. She stood nervously, in a small space between the front door and the garden gate, moving from side to side, to let people come and go through the two entrances.

What on earth did Jago have planned for tonight?

A few men glanced at her, a couple behind their girlfriends' backs. She diverted her eyes to the road, unused to the attention.

By eight o'clock, Jago was not there. At five past, Kate was checking her phone every few seconds, with a growing sense of unease.

Had she misunderstood?

It was when she was checking her phone again, that she became aware of someone waving at her from a car.

It was a woman in an old white saloon, parked up on the pavement, its engine running. She was stretching across to wind down the window manually.

'Kate?' the woman rasped through the gap.

The woman had short bleached-blonde hair striped with dark roots and she had bags under her eyes. Her stomach strained at her navy T-shirt.

'Sorry?'

'ARE YOU KATE?' The woman's voice was not unfriendly, just firm and good natured.

Kate nodded, confused.

'Taxi, darling. Out to the Warwick Arms at Chumsley Norton?'

Kate shook her head, bewildered.

'No. Sorry. That's not me. Must be someone else.'

The woman glanced at a piece of paper on her lap. 'I think it is you, darling. Your bloke ordered it. Jay-boy or something?' the woman asked.

Kate baulked. 'Jago?'

'Something like that,' the woman said, glancing back at the note, then giving Kate an expectant smile.

'Um,' said Kate, flustered. 'But I don't think that can be right. He's not even here.'

'So do you want it or not, love? Makes no difference to me. He's already paid. You'll have to hurry up, though, I've got another pick-up back in Cowley at nine, so . . .'

Kate stared at the car.

He was trying to get her to go in a taxi?

After what she'd told him, about her parents being killed in one?

To face her fear?

She felt panic rising. No, that was too much. She was not getting in that car. There was rust on the back door and there was a growling noise coming from the bonnet. Absolutely no chance.

'No, I think there's been a mistake,' she said, shaking her head. 'Sorry.'

The woman shrugged. 'OK, darling. No problem.' She put the car into gear. With a heavy bump, it jerked off the pavement and down towards the alleyway. Desperately, Kate looked around, hoping that Jago would appear and explain. Instead she felt a buzz in her palm. It was a text.

Kate! Get in the taxi, it said.

What? She glanced up.

Where was he?

The woman had reached the end of the cul-de-sac and was doing a clumsy three-point turn.

She was talking to someone, on a radio.

A number buzzed around Kate's head. It was the one that had stopped her going in taxis ever since her parents' accident.

- **People who drive for business purposes have a 40% higher chance of road accidents.**

She tried to focus.

The car looked even worse from the front, with a cracked number plate.

Kate brain scrambled. All taxis would have to have MOTs and licences, wouldn't they?

The woman gave Kate a nod as she went to drive past.

There was another buzz. Kate looked down.

Kate. You said you could do this!

Where the hell was he? She looked around helplessly.

What should she do? She visualized the alternative: sloping home because she was too scared to get in a taxi. Spending the evening at Hubert Street alone again.

Jago's words crept into her mind: 'You wouldn't fly to the developing country. You wouldn't go to the important conference. You'd stay at home trying to be safe.'

What was the alternative? Sitting with Sylvia in her sombre sitting room for years, talking about her feelings?

Or take a leap of faith and put her trust in Jago.

The taxi picked up speed as it headed past Kate to the T-junction.

Before Kate could stop herself, she raised her hand. It braked abruptly.

'Changed your mind?' the woman called out.

Kate nodded.

She opened the rear door.

They didn't talk at all on the way to Chumsley Norton. The woman was too involved in a conversation with her sister on her headset, about their mother's sciatica. Another of Kate's regular traffic accident statistics flew at her.

- **In 80% of car crashes, the driver is distracted.**

Kate tried to ignore the anxiety it immediately provoked in her, gripping the seat, pushing her body against it, as if she could control the car's speed with her thighs. She was sweating inside her new jumper, subsumed with the effort of 'not thinking about' what was happening, as they sped through traffic lights on the ring road, the engine roaring grumpily, and then took an A road under a bridge.

'Nine miles,' 'eight miles,' Kate mouthed, trying to forget about a local news story she'd once read about teenagers dropping bricks off a bridge on this road, as they passed signposts for this mystery village, her eyes fixed on a box of man-size tissues, glancing behind every so often to check if Jago was following.

Soon, they turned off the A road and took rural lanes, the names on the signposts becoming increasingly old English in their eccentricity. Pog Norton. Sprogget Corner. Hedges rose higher, verges widened, and the road narrowed, so that by the time Kate's driver and her sister had decided to see if they could tempt their mother out of the house with a trip to Bicester Village shopping outlet centre, the chance of becoming stuck if they met another car seemed a certainty.

But they didn't.

The woman took a series of twists and turns, then cut off her conversation with her sister.

'That's you, darling,' she said, pointing up at a battered sign with pellet shots in it which said Chumsley Norton.

Kate blew through her cheeks like an athlete finishing a sprint. She'd done it.

'Here you are,' the woman called, pulling up.

'Thanks,' said Kate. She lunged out of the taxi onto the verge, dumbfounded at what she'd just achieved. Her first time in a taxi in *eleven years*.

She looked around. Chumsley Norton had sounded like a pretty, chocolate-box village. Instead, it looked more like an unremarkable scatter of houses that the country road stopped at momentarily before travelling on to somewhere more interesting. There were about ten pairs of them, semi-detached and red brick, with the look of 1950s council houses. On the bend before the houses stood an ancient thatched pub.

As she turned to shut the door, the quietness of the village hit her.

She popped her head back in the taxi.

'Excuse me. Did he definitely say here?'

'He did.'

'OK . . .' Kate said uncertainly, still holding the door. 'And he said he'd meet me here?'

'Back in Cowley in twenty minutes, Control,' the woman barked into her radio. 'Don't know, darling.' Her expression told Kate that she needed to go.

Not wanting to, Kate shut the door.

The taxi headed on to a layby in front of the pub. Kate stood at the car park entrance. The pub looked deserted.

Hang on. This didn't feel right.

Suddenly, she knew what she should do. Wait for the taxi to turn around in the layby, then ask the driver to wait so she could check Jago was here. Resolutely, Kate stuck out her hand. But to her shock, the taxi accelerated round the bend, past the pub and down past the houses, presumably taking an alternative route back.

'No! Wait!' Kate shouted, throwing up a hand. The taxi disappeared into the distance.

As the noise of the engine faded, it was replaced by an expansive quietness. Not the idyllic rural tranquillity of a meadow; more a creepy absence of human life.

Holly hedges down either side of the road obscured the front gardens of the red-brick houses. There was a smell of silage in the air.

Kate dropped her head and hurried into the car park to find Jago.

From a distance, it had looked like an advertisement for English tourism, but as she neared the pub, its neglect became apparent. White distemper flaked off chubby cottage walls; dark ridges of rot streaked the window frames.

Kate glanced up the empty road. If Jago had been watching her back at the Hanley Arms, where was he now? She looked up at the approaching dusk, and then at her watch. It was 8.40 p.m.

Jago must have somehow got ahead of her, she reassured herself, or come on the alternative route the taxi had taken home. Kate walked up to a studded door and swung it open to reveal a small bar. A large man with rolled-up shirtsleeves under a waistcoat, stood wiping glasses. His hair was pulled back into a greasy black ponytail. He surveyed her without expression.

'Evening.' His voice was gruff.

'Hi,' she said shyly.

She saw him glance to the right, and raise his eyebrows. Three men sat huddled at the bar, backs to her, like wolves around a kill. They stared with unfriendly curiosity.

Kate glanced round. Scuffed chairs and tables sat on a flagstone floor.

Oh God. Jago was *not* here.

The barman nodded his chin upwards in a 'what can I get you?' gesture.

'Um, orange juice, please,' Kate said, looking out of the window back at the darkening road. Where was he? She jammed her hand in her bag and yanked her phone out so abruptly that tissues flew with it. Bending to pick them up, Kate lifted a finger to dial and . . .

There was no signal.

Kate waited, praying, as her phone searched . . .

The barman smacked the orange juice down on the bar, making Kate jerk her head up. She stood up and approached, aware of the wolf pack's eyes on her.

She checked her phone again. Still no signal. Oh God.

'I'm actually looking for someone,' she said quietly, aware they were listening. 'A Scottish bloke with a crewcut?'

'A Scottish bloke, eh?' the barman repeated loudly.

Kate shrank back, wishing he would lower his voice. Grins split the wolves' mean faces.

'I could do you a Welsh bloke with a fat arse,' the oldest one, with a long nose and purplish lips, said, pointing at his mate, a rotund man in a dirty red jumper.

There was a group snigger.

Memories of the Hanley Arms and the football fans came back to Kate with unpleasant clarity. She glanced outside again. There was, however, no escape from them here. No bike outside. No pavement to run back along to Hubert Street.

Where the *hell* was Jago?

An approaching engine noise made Kate swing around hopefully. Through the window, she saw five or six scooters pull into the car park, ridden by young lads, gesticulating and swearing at each other as they stopped their bikes. The old familiar band of stress tightened around her chest. Were they coming in here too?

Trying to hide the anxiety in her voice, Kate handed over her money, gesturing to her phone. 'Sorry, I can't get a signal. Have you got a payphone?'

The barman regarded her with eyes as hard as a rockface. He jerked his head backwards. 'One up the road,' he said, turning back to the wolves.

Up the road? What did that mean? Kate felt her cheeks smart at his rudeness. She took her drink uncertainly to a table by the window. Peering out she could see a dim light in a layby, fifty yards beyond the houses in the dark. Was that it? Was he joking? She couldn't walk up there alone in the dark! The wolf pack talked under their breaths. The word 'tart' floated out.

The door banged open and she turned, hoping again for Jago. Instead, a teenager walked in. He had a ratty face and short hair gelled carefully onto his forehead in fine lines.

'Evening,' he said with a sly grin.

Outside, Kate saw the rest of the group sit at a table with a broken umbrella in an empty beer garden. She sat forwards, to relieve the stress tightening around her chest.

Where was Jago? How would she get back to Oxford without him?

She tried to control her anxiety and to think calmly. Was this a test? To see if she could take a taxi to this village, then walk into a pub full of belligerent men on her own. And then what? Phone a taxi from the pub back to Oxford?

But would Jago even know there was no phone signal out here? Kate glanced out at the phonebox again.

What if she ordered a taxi and an old man like Stan who'd killed her parents turned up? At least back at the Hanley Arms, she could see the woman. She'd had a choice whether to get in the car.

The urge to get out of this horrible pub was overwhelming. Almost on reflex, Kate stood up, knowing she couldn't do it. She'd have to ring Jago and ask him to come and pick her up instead. Or Saskia, although God knows what questions that would lead to later.

But first she needed a phone.

Kate looked apprehensively at the barman, who was pulling pints for the teenager. She walked up casually and put her hands on the bar.

He ignored her, continuing his work.

She waited half a minute, sensing the wolves' eyes on her again.

And another.

When she could take no more of the sneering looks and muttered grunts, she forced her to lift her hand. 'Uh. Excuse me.'

The barman stopped, a tray for the teenagers in mid-air.

'I'm sorry. I was supposed to meet someone who hasn't turned up. And I can't get a signal. Would you mind if I used your phone?'

Her voice sounded tinny and posh among the gruff, spat-out words of the men.

The barman shook his head in astonishment. 'Am I talking to myself here?' he exclaimed without warning. 'I haven't got a BLOODY payphone! Up the ROAD!'

Kate stood in the middle of the pub in shock. Why was he being like this to her? 'No. Your phone,' she tried to say miserably. 'I mean your own phone. I could pay you.'

The wolves howled in delight. The teenager shook his head, sniggering, as he loaded his tray with six pint glasses.

'The phone in my house?' the barman said, sounding incredulous.

Kate shrugged. What had she done to him?

The barman banged down the tray. He walked to a door behind the bar, and opened it. Kate saw rickety stairs leading to somewhere dark. 'Go on, then,' he said.

Five pairs of mean eyes burned into Kate.

'Um,' she muttered, stepping back. 'No, actually. It's fine. I'll use the phonebox.'

Face burning, she ran to the door, and rushed outside, letting it slam back into the wave of male laughter.

What had Jago done?

Why had he sent her to this shithole of a village?

This was not funny.

This was not silly.

This was *horrible*.

Kate marched up the dark country road towards the phonebox, bewildered. What did he want her to do? She didn't understand.

'Idiot,' she muttered to herself. She should *never* have stolen that dog to impress him. Clearly, he now thought she was much more relaxed and tough than she actually was, which had landed her here, on a remote road at night, completely out of her depth.

As the lights from the pub faded, the intense blackness of the countryside fell over Kate like a blanket. She tried not to think about what could happen to her out here, hugging her arms around her for protection, despite the warm air. The aggressive squawks of the teenagers back in the beer garden floated behind her, and she marched faster to escape the whole horrible scenario.

And then, as if things couldn't get any worse, something happened.

As Kate reached the second-last house in the row, she realized the teenagers' noise had changed. It was becoming louder.

Somewhere inside her head, an alarm went off.

Without making a conscious decision to do so, Kate dived off the road and into the shadow of the holly hedge. Swivelling round, she saw the teenagers climbing on their bikes. They'd just ordered pints. Why would they do that?

Holly leaves spiked Kate's skin through the wool of the new jumper that she'd so carefully chosen for her date. Right now, however, she didn't care. Nervously, she watched the gang put on their helmets. Rat-boy had heard her say she was walking to this phonebox.

They knew she was out here, alone.

Kate stared at the boys as they revved up their engines.

She knew then that she had done something very stupid.

She should have never have got in that bloody taxi.

She should never have left the pub before she'd found a way to speak to Jago.

The holly ripped into her jumper again, and she let it, knowing that if she was right, she was in trouble.

CHAPTER EIGHTEEN

Saskia glanced up from her laptop to the clock on the other side of her mother's vast country kitchen – 9.40 p.m.

'Snores!' she shouted.

She shut down the webpage she'd been reading while no one else was in the kitchen.

'What're you doing?' said Jack, wandering in from the sitting room in the dressing gown he kept at his grandparents' house.

'Nothing,' she lied. He walked over the flagstone kitchen floor towards the oak table where she sat. Rosie ran in behind him and dropped her head into Saskia's lap, looking up with soft brown eyes. 'Just catching up on work. Right. Time for bed.' She smiled, stroking Rosie's head. 'Want some juice or something?'

He nodded. His face had relaxed again, she noticed, like it always did when he stayed with his grandparents. The little lines that prematurely etched his forehead dropped away, and his cheeks looked softer.

Saskia stood up. Jack pulled Rosie towards him. She licked his face and lay down on the floor.

Saskia returned with the drink.

'Thanks.'

She looked at him sideways as she sat back down. She dropped her voice.

'Snores, what's wrong? You've been quiet all day.'

He shook his head. Too quickly, Saskia thought.

'Is something wrong?'

'No.'

'So what really happened to your head?'

He hesitated. 'My skateboard, I told you,' he said, gulping juice.

'Well,' she said, lowering her voice. 'I don't think it was your skateboard. I know when you're lying. You're rubbish at it.'

He dropped his eyes.

She reached out and rubbed his arm. 'Come on. This is me.'

He shrugged. 'She didn't mean it.'

Saskia blinked, realizing he was telling her something important. 'What, someone at school? A girl?'

'No.'

Saskia frowned. 'So who . . .' She looked at him, startled. 'You mean your mum?'

He glanced behind him.

'Hang on,' Saskia said, getting up. She closed the kitchen door and came back. 'Right – come on. What happened.'

'Don't tell Nana.' She could see the worry in his eyes.

'I won't.'

Jack put down his juice half-finished. 'She was trying to stop me going out of the front door when the alarm was on, and we were arguing.'

'You and Mum?'

'And I was shouting.'

Saskia's mouth dropped open. 'That's not like you. What about?'

'Lots of things. She locked the gate again.'

'But Nana has the key.'

'Mum got a new one. With a padlock.'

Bloody, bloody Kate, Saskia fumed. Not that she was surprised. She rubbed his arm gently. 'Oh, Snores.'

He pushed the glass away, and dropped one hand to his stomach. The lines appeared back on his forehead like skin on hot milk.

'What's wrong with your stomach? Did you fall there too?'

'Nothing. No.'

She tried to think, knowing he was trying to tell her something. 'Is that why you said it was your skateboard?'

He shrugged again.

'Snores? And Mum told you to say that?'

'It was an accident. She didn't mean to do it.'

Saskia blinked. Oh God. This was all they needed. If Mum found out what Kate had done, all hell would break loose. She tried to sound reassuring. 'Oh, OK. Listen, mate, you mustn't worry. This is adult stuff. It's between Nana and your mum. And it'll all get sorted, I promise.'

'But Nana says I've got to come and live here, and it's making Mum cry.'

Saskia wanted to hug him but he looked so angry she suspected he'd shove her away. 'Do you want to live with Nana?'

'Sometimes.' There was a tiny fissure in his voice. 'But I don't want to leave Mum on her own.' The fissure widened, and his voice cracked. 'And anyway, she says we're moving back to London.'

Saskia regarded him with disbelief. 'She said what?'

'That's why I shouted.'

Saskia glanced up at the door again, double-checking her parents couldn't hear.

'Oh God. OK.' Right. That was going to send Helen completely off the scale. Saskia thought for a second, then took Jack's hand. 'Snores, listen. Right now, I want you to go to bed and not to worry about this. Me and Mum, and Nana and Granddad, all love you more than anything. And the rest of it, we adults will all sort out together, OK?'

Jack nodded. 'But don't tell Nana.'

'I won't. But don't you tell her either – or about London. Not till I've spoken to your mum about it.'

The door opened and they both glanced up nervously. Richard walked in, holding an empty crystal tumbler. Rosie jumped up and ran to him.

'What on earth are you two up to!' He beamed. 'Do you want a drink, darling?' he said, without waiting for an answer, walking to an array of spirits on the worktop.

'No, thanks, Dad. I'm going to head home. Snores is off, too, aren't you, mate?' She caught her nephew's eye and winked. He nodded.

Jack stood up and gave his granddad an awkward hug, and then Saskia.

'Good night, young man. Sleep well. Don't let the bedbugs bite.'

'Not everyone gets bedbug bites, Granddad,' Jack replied. 'Some people are immune. It was the news last night when they were talking about all the bedbugs in New York.'

'Smartybum,' Saskia said, as Richard chortled.

'Seems OK?' Richard said, turning to Saskia as Jack left the kitchen to say goodnight to Helen. 'Darling? You think?'

'Um.' She hesitated, lifting the laptop lid to shut it down, hating Kate for putting her in this position. 'Yes. I think so.'

'Sure you don't want to stay, darling?' Her dad was pouring himself another Saturday-night gin and tonic, and a brandy for her mother.

Yes, she wanted to say. Anything not to spend another night in an empty bed opposite the space where Jonathan slept for four years, but she knew she couldn't. 'No. I should get home.'

As her finger hovered over the 'off' button, she looked at the page she'd been researching earlier, and at her father's back. Then she looked up at the photo on the wall. The photo Hugo had taken of Jack. For a second, Saskia nearly opened her mouth. Nearly started to tell Richard about her dreams, to leave the agency and sort out the mess she had made of her life.

But she didn't.

No, she thought, closing the laptop and standing up. Right now, Jack needed her more. That would have to happen another time.

Right now she had a battle to fight with Kate.

CHAPTER NINETEEN

Kate dived into the small garden of one of the semi-detached houses and crouched on the ground, her heart banging like a pneumatic drill. The garden was unlit, as was the house. She listened to the scooter engines burst into life in the pub car park. If she was right about this, there was no way the teenagers could see this far up the dark country road. If they started looking, they'd be simply guessing where she'd gone.

Kate crawled along the holly hedge till she reached the fence that divided this semi from the one next door. A dustbin stood in the corner. Its unpleasant fishy smell mixed with the stink of silage drifting off the fields. Kate pushed the bin firmly, slipped into the gap behind it, then put it back in front of her.

She tried to think calmly. The boys wouldn't have a clue where she was. For all they knew, she'd had her own car outside, or entered one of these houses, or run off into a field.

She sat, hugging her knees, trying to stop them shaking.

So why was she so certain they were coming for her?

Her mind flew to Hugo, to those men in the courthouse, and then she knew.

The noise of the scooters grew into a harmonized whine. Kate peeked through the hedge. Her stomach lurched.

She was right.

Once you have encountered evil, you recognize it, she knew. It makes a different sound to everything else. A splintered, clashing commotion that causes heads to rise in alarm. It has an energy that blurs all around it, forcing you to look.

The gang was searching for her.

Accelerating out of the pub, they spread out across the road like an airshow formation, their headlights on full beam creating a spotlight effect.

Moving forward slowly.

Hunting her.

Kate held herself even tighter. They can't find you, she told herself. They can't search every part of twenty dark gardens, every surrounding acre of field, every ditch. It would take hours. One of the residents would hear them. Call the police. Do something.

'Where'd she go?' came a yell from beyond the hedge.

There was a shriek of out-of-control laughter.

Kate sucked in a lungful of air. Bring more oxygen into your body, she told herself. She'd seen it on a self-defence course on the telly once. It stopped you becoming paralysed with fear. Helped you run. She looked around the cramped front garden. But where would she run to?

'Go up to the phonebox, John! See if she's there,' a shout came. A second later a scooter roared past her up to the layby ahead. Now they were in front and behind her on the road.

'Shit,' she whispered. They were serious. This was not a prank.

She peeked through the hedge again, and saw the headlights separate off in different directions.

Kate kept trying to breathe away the tightness spreading across her chest.

'Coming to get you!' One of them yelled.

'Look in the gardens!'

They were doing exactly what she thought they wouldn't, entering each front garden.

Methodically.

One by one.

Kate turned, desperately hoping to see one of the residents looking out of a window, phone in hand to the police. Yet no curtains twitched. Presumably the people who lived in these isolated houses were also scared. They were choosing diplomatically to ignore the rural gang, presumably hoping they'd go away and not cause them any more trouble.

Kate was on her own.

Her mind returned to Hugo, with a sudden, awful clarity. And in that moment, she knew. This must have been what he'd felt like that night with those men. His heart pounding. Hunted.

Frantically, she stuck out a hand, searching for something. Anything. Nettles stung her fingers. She jerked them away, only for them to trail over a wet and spongy object, making her recoil even further. She tried the other hand and felt something hard. Holes and ridges, on a dry surface.

A brick. She grabbed it. She knew it was stupid, but somehow the hardness gave her strength.

There was a deafening roar to her right. In the tiny gap under the fence she saw a scooter enter the semi next door. Its light tickled her feet under the fence.

'Not here, mate!' a voice shouted close by.

Kate grasped tighter.

Another memory of Hugo detonated in her mind. Of finding him on the floor, a pool of blood soaking into the floorboards he'd so lovingly restored. Of her, screaming and screaming, as she watched all that passion and expertise and love disappear into nothing in front of her, as his brain and his heart shut down. Gone. Stolen. Wasted. For *nothing*.

And right then, Kate realized, perhaps because things had come to a head recently, that she'd had enough of being scared.

A seam of anger opened up inside her.

People like these boys had ruined her life. Their wilful, thoughtless violence had killed her husband, terrified Jack and damaged her relationship with her son to the point where his life would be ruined before it had even started, and she was at risk of losing him.

Kate scraped the tips of her fingers on the brick pores.

She was sick of it.

People like this, taking the power away from others because they could.

And in that moment, she knew that despite the shaking in her legs and arms, if a single one of these boys came near her, if they threatened to do any more harm to her and Jack, she would take this brick and she would fight him.

'Here, pussy, pussy!' a teenager shouted above the scooter engines. His friend laughed in encouragement.

'Come and try it,' Kate mouthed.

The scooter reversed out of next door, and travelled along the front hedge. The growl changed to a *put-put-put* as it finally turned into the garden she crouched in.

'Seriously,' Rat-boy shouted through the hedge, 'where the fuck is she?'

'I'll look in here, mate,' yelled his friend.

A scooter entered Kate's garden in an explosion of light. She could see the silhouette of the boy from here. He was small, not even her height. Skinny, too. His headlights lit up the shabby front door of the house, and part of the bay window. As the boy began to turn his handlebars to the right, towards the dustbin where she hid, Kate lifted her hand, knowing she had to take her chance before he did.

A plan formed. She would strike him as hard as she could, before running out into the dark field behind, where she hoped the gang could not follow on scooters.

Kate lifted the brick, her hand shaking, as the headlight moved towards her, ready to leap out and . . .

A new noise arrived out of nowhere. A car, speeding towards the scooters.

Kate froze.

'Oi, oi,' a teenager said. Someone whistled. Without warning, the scooter in front of her was backing out of the garden, draping darkness back over her.

All the boys were backing up now. Through the hedge she saw them gathering around a black hatchback, their engines whining together.

The car door opened. A new voice joined the melee. Deeper, bassier. One of the men from the pub?

Kate watched, trying to stay calm and think clearly. Was this her chance to sneak through the hedge next door and make for the fields without being seen?

Then, without warning, the scooters moved again. They turned full circle in a blaze of light, and with a roar started to accelerate. Like a swarm of vicious wasps, the six scooter boys buzzed past her, past the phonebox, and carried on out of the village.

'Woo-hoo!' they yelled.

Kate stood uncertainly, holding the brick, listening to the increasingly distant drone.

'Kate?' She heard a man shout in a Scottish accent.

'Jago?'

*

Her breath broke from her in painful gasps. She didn't even realize she'd been holding it again.

'Where are you?' he said. After all the ugly yelling and spat-out insults, his voice sounded kind and civilized, drifting over the hedge.

'Here,' she replied, still listening out for the boys. But the whine of the scooters was fading. The gang was gone, really gone. It was over. Kate bent over with relief, and rested her hands on her knees.

'Kate?' Jago called again. She wiped her face, guessing from the scraping on her skin, that she was just rubbing grit from the ground into the sweat.

It was *over*. She shouldered the bin away, her nose wrinkling at the smell of cat poo, coming, she suspected, from her shoe.

A gate scraped open. Jago's head appeared round it.

She contemplated him crossly, waiting for his face to register the state she was in, then break into an expression of abject apology.

But it didn't.

'Hi there,' he said breezily, surveying her. 'So, how did it go?'

Kate wiped mud off her hands, registering his tone and finding herself confused by it. 'Er, how did *what* go, exactly?'

'The experiment.'

Was she hearing right? Yet from what she could tell in the dark, his face looked untroubled. No, more than that – interested.

Like he was . . . *observing* her.

Jago seriously did not seem to have a clue.

'Er, Jago?' Kate said, trying not to sound as irate as she was starting to feel. 'Do you have any idea what's just happened here?'

'Tell me.'

'*Tell me?*' Kate repeated, waiting for him to sound even a little penitent. What did he think had gone on here? That she'd rung a taxi from the phonebox and was sitting in this scruffy little garden for fun, while a gang of rabid teenagers roamed the road outside?

'Uh, well. Everything went wrong. The guy – sorry, the *fuckwit* – in the pub had no payphone.' Her voice started to rise, but she didn't care. She pointed a muddy finger at herself and caught it on a holly leaf sticking to her chest. '*I* had no phone signal, so, I don't think you realize, but I've had to walk to down here in the dark, to this phonebox to ring you, and those –' she pointed to the road, and her voice rose even more – 'little WANKERS heard me talking about it in the pub, and followed me.'

She waited for him to analyse her meaning. To throw his hand across his mouth, as he registered the dangerous position he'd put her in. To beg forgiveness and offer to make it up to her.

But Jago stayed still.

Observing her.

'*Jago!*' Kate exclaimed. 'I don't think you quite understand. Those boys were CHASING me.'

He still didn't react.

'Er, you know your experiment?' she said, her voice rising further. 'The one where you sent me out to this shithole with no way of getting home – it went very horribly wrong. I was nearly really badly hurt.'

She took a big step back and waited for him finally to acknowledge his blame.

But to her astonishment . . . Jago *smiled*.

He must be *joking*.

'Kate,' he said, turning his hands palm up, as if he were explaining a point of mathematics to his students. 'It didn't go wrong. In fact, it went perfectly. You did brilliantly. Seriously.

The boys just told me they had absolutely no idea where you'd gone.'

Kate stood in the horrible little garden, repeating Jago's words in her head to check she'd heard them right.

'The "boys"?' she exclaimed. 'You mean the GANG who just chased me up a dark country road, shouting, "Here, pussy, pussy".'

'Did they?' Jago grimaced. He walked a step towards her. 'Listen. Kate. That's Liam, he's the porter's son, from Balliol. I told him and his little mates to chase you for ten minutes then call me. I was hiding in my car at the pub. I didn't realize they'd be quite so, er, imaginative, though.'

She scowled.

'Jago. Please tell me you are joking. You could not have set this up.'

'Well, it took me a bit of planning. I had to bung them fifty quid and buy them a round – they were quite specific about that, cheeky little bastards – but I thought it was worth it. You said you wanted to do this, Kate.' Jago reached out and picked a holly leaf off her jumper. 'You said you could be spontaneous.'

Kate pulled back from him. 'What? You PAID them? To do that?' She lifted her hands and put them on her head, unable to believe her ears. 'That's just . . . I'm sorry, that's just . . . CRAZY!' With a surge of anger, she marched right past him, desperate to get out of this horrible pit of a garden.

She flung open the gate and let it slam behind her, walking out into the dark road, not even caring where she was going. 'OK. Fine!' she shouted back, not knowing what else to say. Humiliated that he was seeing her like this, out of control; that he'd made her behave like this. 'Brilliant. Well done, you. Now could you just please get me out this fucking place?'

But, on reaching the road, Kate felt the brick she still grasped in her sweaty hand, and realized she was not finished. She spun round to see Jago walking unhurriedly through the gate. His calm demeanour somehow just made her angrier. Angrier because he'd frightened her so much, on purpose, when she'd confessed so much to him about her anxiety, but also because, she suddenly realized, she'd had so much hope that he might be the answer. And instead he'd forced all the feelings outside. Betrayed that trust. Forced her to lose control. Humiliated her. Turned her into this screaming lunatic with twigs in her hair who couldn't stop shouting.

'Actually, it's really not OK!' she yelled, unable to hold back her fury. 'Because, do you know what I nearly did?' She raised the brick. 'I thought that boy was going to hurt me, and I was preparing to hit him. To defend myself. That's serious, Jago. That's a ridiculous position to put someone in, experiment or not.'

To her fury, Jago just shrugged.

'Jago! I am not a GAME,' Kate yelped, smacking the brick down on the ground with a crack. She walked to his car, her legs shaking harder as the adrenalin of the chase drained from her.

Jago continued behind her, looking bemused. 'Jago!' Why was he not reacting? 'You don't understand. You shouldn't have done this to me. For God's sake, my husband was . . . was . . . MURDERED!'

The word came from nowhere. The word she never said. Kate shouted it out into the country lane and heard it echo around the houses and gardens and fields.

For the first time since he'd arrived, Jago seem to come to life. He stepped forwards and put his hands on her shoulders.

'Kate, I know,' he said.

'No!' she said, flinging them off. 'You don't know. He was *murdered*, Jago. By a pack of men who came to our house in

London and pushed their way in the front door to get the key to his stupid sports car. And when he fought back,' she said, clutching her stomach, 'they stabbed him. Just like that. With Jack upstairs. And now you . . .' She pointed at him. '. . . send me out here and set a pack of feral teenagers on me!'

For the first time, Jago looked sorry.

Kate stopped, knowing she was really starting to get out of control. This was doing nobody any good. She put a hand on the car to steady herself, and counted, the way she'd been taught so long ago.

One thousand.

Two thousand.

Three thousand.

Four thousand . . . Her pulse slowed. Jago stood, saying nothing, letting her recover.

After a moment, she leaned back against Jago's car. She shook her head ruefully. 'I'm sorry, I know you're trying to help me, I really do, but you shouldn't have done this. You really don't know enough about me to make decisions like this.' She pushed off the car, and went to open the door. Her voice was calm now, the disappointment of all that Jago had seemed to offer fallen apart on this empty road. 'Can you take me back to Oxford, please,' she said, starting to feel very, very cold.

And then she felt Jago's hands on her shoulders from behind.

'Kate,' Jago said quietly. 'When I say, I know, I really do know. About Hugo.'

'You can't.'

'I know what happened,' Jago said. 'I went on the newspaper websites for Shropshire, and worked out from what you'd told me about your parents' accident, who they were, and what their names were, and from there, I worked out who Hugo was. I know everything.'

Hugo's name sounded so oddly wrong on his lips. As if he'd stolen it from her head. Kate lifted her eyes, baffled. 'You knew? And you did this to me?'

Jago turned her towards him. This time she was too stunned to fight him. Part of her, she realized, wanted this still to be OK. Still wanted to hang on to the hope he would help her. So when he then pulled her gently towards him, into his arms, she resisted but did not refuse.

'Listen, Kate,' he murmured above her head. 'I might look like a student but you have to trust me. I know what I'm doing. I read up on what psychologists are doing in the States before I set this up tonight. I got some advice from one on the phone, too. You were safe. The whole time this evening.'

She started to speak again, but even as she did, she felt his words soothe her. He was giving her an escape route from her fear. Telling her she had been fine the whole time.

'I don't understand.'

'Listen,' Jago continued, his chin on her head. 'I'll explain. We had one chance to kick-start your survival instincts. And we did. And you're fine,' he mumbled into her hair. 'A bit muddy, and slightly smelling of cat poo, but fine. I mean it, Kate, you were brilliant.'

She stayed in his arms, a warm refuge in this stinking hellhole of a village.

'The reason I did it is that you need to get faith back in yourself that you can deal with things. And you can. You lived in London, for God's sake. You have street sense. You know how to look after yourself. You hid. They'd have given up soon and fucked off. You'd have rung me to pick you up, and you'd have been fine. This was *real* danger, not imagined. And what did you do? You dealt with it. You survived.'

Kate listened to him. It was true. After all this time of being

213

scared of shadows and creaks in the dark, it had been a relief to fight back. To know she would have hurt them before they hurt her.

As Jago held her tight, calm slowly descended. She allowed herself to lean against him a little, partly because her legs were shaking so much and she was so cold. The anger subsided a little. She knew then that she wanted still to hope. She wanted Jago to be the answer. She hadn't lost him after all. Her body relaxed a little. He gave her a gentle squeeze, then laughed. 'I thought you were going to belt me with that bloody brick.'

'I might still,' she growled. 'Bloody hell, Jago. How could you do that to me?'

He blew something off her hair. 'You know why. Anyway, I'm impressed. *I* wouldn't mess with you.'

She couldn't help it. She reluctantly smiled into his T-shirt.

'So how do you feel?' he asked.

She shook her head, self-conscious. 'Don't ask.'

'I mean it, tell me,' he repeated, dropping his head down to meet hers. His lips brushed her cheek as he said it, and she closed her eyes, distracted by the singular sensation on her skin.

She couldn't say it.

'I don't know. Confused.'

Jago lifted her chin. 'Bollocks. You know exactly how you feel. Now say it.'

She looked past his eyes and up at the sky, hating herself. She had thought of Hugo tonight, of that terrible night that had torn them apart. If she said it, it would mean saying goodbye to that. To Hugo. She would be stepping back into the real world.

'Say it,' Jago murmured, his mouth getting closer to hers.

But she couldn't, so Kate did something else. She lifted her own mouth, not knowing what would happen, but to her relief, found Jago's lips waiting for her.

214

And to her shame, the kiss on that dark road, covered in mud and holly leaves and sweat, was unlike any kiss she and Hugo had had for a very long time.

It was a kiss from before they married.

From before Jack.

From before her parents died.

From a time when there was no anxiety or fear.

'Alive' was the word she wanted to say to Jago, but couldn't, as she let his kiss jolt her back to life.

CHAPTER TWENTY

After saying goodnight to Jack, it took Saskia twenty minutes to race to Kate's house in east Oxford. She pulled across the bottom of the driveway. Kate's car was there. Good.

The car clock said 10.15 p.m. Saskia blinked. It was late to burst in, but this couldn't wait. If Mum caught a whisper that Kate was planning to move back to London all hell was going to break loose.

Saskia glanced up at Kate's house and pulled on her handbrake crossly. How come she had been elected intermediary in all this? She had her own problems. Lights were on in the sitting room and upstairs. As Saskia turned off the engine, she saw a shadow cross past the curtain in Jack's room.

Good. At least Kate wasn't in bed.

Exiting her car, she looked around. Hubert Street always felt so quiet at night, despite its closeness to the bars and restaurants of Cowley Road.

'Right,' Saskia muttered, marching up to Kate's front door. A security light burst into life as she rang the bell. What was the option? The last thing any of them, including Jack, needed was Social Services accusing Kate of emotional neglect or asking for a mental health assessment.

The upstairs hall light shone dimly through the glass of the front door. She waited, tapping her foot, for Kate to arrive.

Nothing happened.

Saskia pressed the bell again, then followed it with a rap of knuckles on the glass.

Seconds passed. 'Kate?' she called, irritated, through the letter-box. 'It's me – Sass.'

Saskia opened the letterbox wide, only to find that Kate had fixed a plastic cowl on the other side to stop people reaching in to take keys.

'Kate!' she shouted, aggravated.

Saskia walked backwards and took another look up.

The light in Jack's room had gone off.

What was Kate playing at?

Scowling, Saskia fumbled in her bag, took out her phone and rang the house number. A second later, she heard Kate's phone ring out in the hallway. Five times, before the faint rumble of the answer machine reached her ears beyond the front door.

Either Kate was ignoring her or something had happened. Had she accidentally locked herself in behind that stupid gate?

'You OK there?' a man's voice said, right behind her.

Saskia jumped about two feet in the air. She whipped round, and found the weirdo from next door standing in Kate's drive-way.

'Yes,' she said abruptly, her heart hammering. 'I'm fine.'

He was so tall close up. Towering above her, with his weird pale eyes staring through greasy glasses.

'I thought you were maybe a burglar,' he said, grinning. 'Lot of burglars in this street, you know? I keep an . . .' He pointed his fingers at his eyes, then at Kate's house. 'For her. You know?'

Saskia could smell beer. She looked out again at the silent street.

'Er. I'm not a burglar, but thanks,' she said, turning her back on him and rummaging desperately in her bag for Kate's spare keys.

'It's nice to help people, you know?' the man said, a tone of defensiveness creeping into his voice. He put out a hand and leaned against the doorway as if to steady himself. The action brought him a couple of inches closer to Saskia.

'Yes, well, thanks, but, as I said, I'm fine,' she said coldly.

'Hey.' A jokey tone entered his voice. 'Hang on. How do I know you're not a burglar, huh?'

'Listen,' said Saskia, employing her finest public school accent. 'I'm her sister-in-law. But thank you. Goodbye.'

To her horror, the man didn't move. Mouthing a swear word to herself, she turned and jammed the key into the door, blinking. Thankfully, it slipped in on the first attempt, and Saskia shoved the door open with relief.

Beep beep beep.

Saskia jumped again. The alarm was on!

Shit. Now she was going to have to leave the front door open while she turned it off, with him outside. Pulling the door as close as she could behind her, and shouting 'Kate! I'm here!' She dashed to the hall cupboard, desperately trying to remember the code. What was the fucking number? Hugo's birthday. Third of March. 0303? Or was it the month and the year. 0375? She turned on the cupboard light and battered at the box with fluttering fingers, then pressed 'reset'.

The alarm stopped.

Quickly, she turned around.

The weirdo was standing right behind her in the hall.

'What are you doing?' she gasped. 'Can you get out, please?'

'You want me to look around?' he said, pointing upstairs.

'No, I don't,' she said firmly, trying to hold her nerve as she herded him out of the house with a hand held in front of her. 'Really. I'm fine. I'd like you to go, please.'

'OK. Bye,' he called.

'OK, fuck off,' she whispered as she slammed the door behind him.

Her heart was thumping. What a freak.

Now, where the hell was Kate? Saskia turned and saw that all the inner doors were closed.

'KATE?' she called crossly up the stairs.

Tentatively, Saskia switched on all the lights and climbed the stairs.

The cage door lay wide open at the top.

'Kate?' she called more quietly. 'Answer me. You're creeping me out.'

She crept into the spare front room first, but there was just an empty single bed and chair, lit by a lamp on a timer switch. Next, Jack's room, which was still dark. She switched the main light on and looked around. Nothing. Ten seconds later, it was clear that there was no one in Kate's bedroom or the study, either.

Saskia crept back downstairs.

'Kate?' she said more timidly, nervously scanning the downstairs hall.

Had she fallen? Saskia reached up above the doorframe of the dining room and used the key to unlock each inner door, one by one, checking behind sofas and tables.

Finally, Saskia opened the kitchen door.

Another lamp on a timer switch was on in here, too.

Saskia's eyes roamed the room until they settled on the kitchen table.

There was a note.

She read it, then lifted her eyes angrily to the back door.

*

219

The journey back to Oxford was quick, the roads quiet at this time of night. They drove back from Chumsley Norton to the dual carriageway, and then when they reached the city centre, Kate guided Jago over Magdalen Bridge and back through east Oxford. Gratefully, she noted that Jago had switched on a device that heated her seat. She stretched back against it, drained. The heat felt good on her bones. She watched students in evening dress, running through the streets.

Tonight she didn't feel so different from them.

She'd had an adventure too.

She rubbed her lips together, fascinated by the musky taste of Jago's lips that still lingered there.

'Better?' Jago asked.

She nodded, and curled up further into the seat. 'I still can't believe you did that.'

'Sorry. I just felt we had to take the risk.'

She sighed. 'So you know about Hugo?'

'I'm really sorry, Kate. I'm not surprised it's left you with this kind of anxiety. It would do that to any of us.'

Kate shook her head sadly. 'You know, the irony was that Hugo wasn't bothered about money, not like his dad. Richard's a businessman, totally money and power obsessed. Hugo just wanted to do something he loved. But, probably because he did love it, he was good at it and, this one time, he made a lot of money unexpectedly just when the property boom happened. And he'd grown up with Richard having all these nice cars, and I think it was just a whim left over from his childhood.'

Kate's hand moved automatically to below her ribcage for the thousandth time.

Jago tapped the wheel. 'And they tried to steal it?'

She nodded.

'I'm sorry. That's shit, Kate. For you and your little boy. The newspaper said they got the guys?'

'Yeah, but the trial was horrible. Their DNA was at the scene so they couldn't deny the car theft – but they wouldn't plead guilty to Hugo's murder, and when they were found guilty, they shouted these awful things at us in court. Honestly, Jago, I can't tell you how awful it was for me and Hugo's family. They were evil. It was terrifying.'

Jago turned into Iffley Road, nodding. 'Well, I'm not surprised it left you feeling scared. Not many people ever see real evil. You hear about it, but you don't see it.'

The kindness in his tone belied his boxer's looks. She liked watching him drive. He was a confident driver. She felt safe with him.

'How did you know to choose that pub, by the way?'

He shifted gear as they accelerated up the long stretch of road. 'Ah, well, that was a bit of luck. One of the visiting American professors made me go there one night with him. He'd seen it on a website with a thatched roof and had some romantic idea of English villages. Of course, we turned up and met the tosser who runs it. I remembered I couldn't get a phone signal and there was no payphone, so it seemed perfect.'

Kate pointed ahead to Hubert Street. Jago indicated and pulled in right, parking in an empty space.

'That's weird,' he said, looking around. 'This looks like my road in Edinburgh. So . . .'

'So . . .' she said. Her limbs felt as if they were made of cloth. She waited, wondering what she would do if he asked if he could come in.

'So,' Jago said, leaning over towards her and taking her hand. 'Seriously, are you OK?'

'I think so. No. I am.'

He pushed away a damp strand of her hair from her face. 'Listen. Kate. I promise, you were never in any danger.'

She sat, mesmerized at the touch of his fingers on her skin, the sensation familiar from old in some ways, brand new in others. 'I know. I do actually believe you.'

'Good. Out of interest, what did it feel like when it was happening? What you saw, what you smelled, saw . . .?'

Kate looked out at her house. 'It's funny you say that. I smelt things so strongly I almost gagged. Like the holly bush and the silage. And sounds, too. Even though I was behind the hedge, I could sort of tell where each of the scooters was by sound.'

'Like all your senses were on alert. Hypersensitive?'

She nodded.

'Like an animal under attack.'

'I suppose so.'

'That's interesting.'

His hand was resting on the gear stick. He saw her look at it, and raised his fingers up. Tentatively, she brought her own hand to meet his. Their fingers entwined for a second, before he sighed a little and leaned over, and she lifted her lips to meet his again.

Inside the car, it was a longer kiss. Kate didn't know where she wanted it to go, she just knew she didn't want it to stop. Jago pulled her into him as her breathing deepened.

Suddenly, however, he broke free from her lips.

'Kate,' he whispered into her ear.

'Hmm?'

'I'm going to go.'

She hesitated, not sure if she was relieved or disappointed. 'Is it the cat poo?'

'Maybe a little.' He smiled. 'But, seriously, you've had a fright tonight, it wouldn't be fair of me to, well, *not* to go.' He grimaced. 'If you know what I mean? I don't want you to think I'm, well . . .'

She nodded, gratefully. 'No, you're right.'

'Sorry. Didn't say that very well.' He lifted her hand with his.

'This is a bit weird for me, too, you know.' On an impulse, she lifted her other hand and hesitantly touched the side of his head, letting the stubble of his crewcut run lightly under her fingertips. He leaned his head into it like a cat. 'That's nice.'

'Did you and your girlfriend go out for a long time?' Kate said, doing it again, remembering the photo of the girl on the internet.

'Felt like it, sometimes,' Jago replied. 'No. I'm joking. About five years.'

'When did you split up?'

'About three months ago. We were . . .'

She saw his eyes drift over her shoulder, in the direction of her house. He leaned his head to the side, a curious expression on his face.

'Is that someone looking for you?'

Kate turned swiftly and, with a start, saw Saskia peering out of the curtains in Jack's bedroom.

'Oh, my God.' She pushed Jago away abruptly. 'Oh, God. Jago. You've got to go. Sorry.' Kate grabbed the door handle, panicked. 'Jago. She can't see you.' She saw an uncertain look on his face. 'It's Hugo's sister, my sister-in-law. It's complicated. But listen, ring me, OK?'

He placed a hand on her shoulder. 'OK. But wait till she goes back inside. She'll see you when you open the car door and the light comes on.'

Kate waited till Saskia disappeared behind the curtains.

'OK. I'm going. So, thanks for going to all that effort to completely petrify me,' she said sarcastically, leaning back to kiss him briefly.

'You're very welcome,' he grinned. 'I'll ring you tomorrow to check you're OK. But you did well. Stick with it. We'll get there. I'm convinced this will help you.'

223

'Thank you,' she repeated, this time without the sarcasm, because she meant it. And with that, Kate jumped out and ran to find out what her bloody sister-in-law was doing in her bloody house.

CHAPTER TWENTY-ONE

Saskia was already at the door when Kate arrived.

They stood face to face, glowering at each other.

'What the hell are you playing at?' Saskia exclaimed, leaning forward to pick a holly leaf off Kate's jumper.

'What am I playing at?' Kate said, walking past Saskia. To her annoyance, she realized she was lowering her head in case Saskia could tell from the glow in her eyes what she'd been doing in the car. It was her house! She was thirty-five bloody years old. This was ridiculous!

'What are you doing here?' she barked. 'Where's Jack?'

'At Mum's, he's fine. Come in. Before that bloody weirdo comes back,' Saskia said, shutting the door.

Kate dumped her bag in front of the hall mirror. 'Who?' She checked her reflection. Jago was right. Her face was smeared with streaks of mud.

'That weirdo next door. The student. With the weird eyes and glasses. What's that smell?' Kate saw Saskia look suspiciously at her shoes. Kate ignored her, taking them off. 'Which one?'

'The tall one. Student. With glasses.'

'They've all got glasses. I mean it, Sass,' she said, spinning round. 'What are you doing here? Why are you in my house?'

Saskia glared back at her. Kate tried to remember. When had Saskia turned from her sweet, shy little sister-in-law into this morally superior woman who seemed to think she had some ownership over Kate's life? Saskia pursed her lips and lifted up a note.

Kate cringed as she saw her own words upside down. 'I have gone out with visiting professor Jago Martin . . .'

'Sass!' She exclaimed, grabbing it. She felt like a teenager, her secret stash of cigarettes discovered by Mum under the bed. 'For God's sake. That's private.'

'Well, I can't believe you did THAT!' Sass said, pointing at the back door.

'What?'

'Ran out of the back door. If you had a man here, you should have just answered the front door, told me it wasn't convenient and I'd have come back tomorrow. Not sneaked out and hidden in the bushes. Look at you!' She pointed at Kate's muddy face. 'Where is he? Still out there?' Saskia waved her hand.

'What are you talking about? I've just got home.'

Saskia did an exaggerated expression of disbelief. 'I saw you, Kate! Or him,' she said, pointing at the note. 'Upstairs in Jack's room.'

What was she talking about? 'Sass! No. You didn't.'

'I fucking did, Kate. Walking across the curtain. I can't believe you. And the reason, by the way, that I let myself in is that I thought you'd fallen and hurt yourself.'

Kate felt a shiver pass through her. 'Sass. Seriously. I'm not lying. I've been out. Since eight. I've just got back.' She looked up the stairs. 'Have you been up there?'

'Yes, I've been right round the bloody house. There's no one here, Kate. And the alarm was on too.'

Damn Saskia! The unnerving sense of unease Kate kept having

in the house crept over her again. Kate felt it eating away at the new sense of empowerment Jago had given her this evening, like paint stripper. Throwing up her hands in frustration, she stomped off into the kitchen.

'Sass! One minute you're all telling me off for being overly anxious, the next you're winding me up!'

Saskia's cheeks turned as pink as her mother's. For a second, Kate prayed poor Jack had not inherited the same skin.

'Kate. I saw someone at the window. And then the light went out in Jack's room.'

Kate tried not to let her nerves seep back in. 'Maybe you were looking at the bedroom next door.'

Sass hesitated.

'What?' Kate growled. 'You look like you're dying to say something.'

'Well, I was just thinking . . . that it sounds like we're both imagining things at the moment. Doesn't it, Kate? You know, like Jack falling off his skateboard, for instance.'

Kate tried to meet the challenge in Saskia's eyes, but was floored by a wave of shame.

'He told Mum he fell off his skateboard. And then he told ME that you told him to say that.'

'Jesus, Sass, are you spying on me?' Kate tried to exclaim, but her voice was already weakened by Sass's revelation. 'For your parents? Is that what it's come to? You record every mistake I make with Jack, and what? Helen writes it in her report.' She spun round. 'You and I used to be friends. What's happened to you?'

She saw Saskia blinking hard, trying her best to hold her ground. 'But is it true?' Saskia demanded.

Kate threw up her hands. 'What do you expect me to say, with your mum ranting about calling Social Services. It was an accident, Sass, and if Helen wasn't causing all this upset in the first place, it wouldn't have happened.'

Kate walked across the kitchen and switched on the kettle. In the reflection of the window, she saw Sass put her note on the table, and berated herself for ever writing it.

'And who is he, this Jago Martin? This visiting professor? Where's he visiting from – London? Is he the reason you're moving back there?'

'Oh, for God's sake!' Kate said. 'What do you do to my son! Sit him down in a bright room and interrogate him the minute he gets to Helen's? Honestly, keep this up, Sass, and I'll be ringing Social Services!'

She and Saskia scowled at each other again.

They held each other's furious stare for five long seconds.

Sass looked down. Kate heard her sister-in-law's voice crack a little.

'What if Hugs could see us now, Kate? He wouldn't believe it.'

Kate pulled down two cups from a shelf, tasting her betrayal of Hugo on her lips as she did it.

A twinge of sadness passed through her.

For all their problems, she and Saskia had trudged together, side by side, for five years, struggling together through their grief for Hugo. Yet this week Jago had given her a glimpse of the future, and if she knew anything, it was that she needed to keep going now, even if that meant leaving Saskia behind.

Jago had reminded her tonight what it felt like to feel alive. And she wasn't going back.

'Sass,' Kate said. 'Hugo can't see us. He's gone.'

Exhaustion coursed through her. Her shoulders slumped.

'God. I need a cup of tea. Sit down.'

*

Kate looked distracted, Saskia thought, putting coasters out on the kitchen table. There was a dangerous light in her eye, and three more holly leaves on her jumper. What the hell had she been doing? Saskia bit her lip. She needed to calm down. She'd already said more than she meant to. Any more and Kate might tell her to leave.

Already, she wished she had broached the subject differently. Made peace with Kate, not poured more petrol on the fire, as she had the other night when Mum had threatened to take Jack away. She hated getting angry. She'd always been so rubbish at it, Hugo had laughed out loud on the rare occasions she lost her temper.

Saskia leaned over and picked off another leaf as Kate put down two mugs of tea and a plate of flapjacks. 'So, is it true? About London?' she tried, in what she hoped was a more reasonable voice.

Kate was avoiding her eye, as if she didn't want Saskia to look too deeply inside them and see something. 'No. I don't know. I've been thinking about it. Oxford's not home for me, Sass. It never has been.'

Saskia blinked, three times. Kate coming to Oxford was supposed to keep the family together after Hugo. How had it ripped it further apart?

'And him?' she said, trying to keep the hurt for Hugo out of her voice. 'Does he live in London?'

She stopped, astonished.

Kate was eating a flapjack.

It was so long since Saskia had seen her sister-in-law eat casually, and not push her food to the side of her plate as if it were contaminated, she couldn't tear her eyes away. Tonight she looked like the old Kate, stirring those giant dinner-party pots in Highgate, beating eggs and flour, adding stock and saffron and spices with deep concentration, dancing around the kitchen

229

as she tasted recipes, the look of the deeply contented cook on her face.

And now, just for a second, with fascination, Saskia glimpsed her again. She was just nibbling a flapjack, but it was the way she ate it. With pleasure, picking up stray crumbs with her fingertips, checking what was coming next after each bite.

Kate shook her head. 'No.'

Saskia couldn't help herself. 'So, who is he?'

Kate rolled her eyes, and Saskia immediately told herself to take a step back. If Kate had really met someone, the last thing Saskia needed was to alienate him with her disapproval, perhaps creating a new ally for Kate; someone who might later encourage her to take Jack away from her and her parents altogether. 'No one. Just someone I met.'

'Nice name,' Saskia tried, fumbling about. 'Like a cross between Jack and Hugo.'

Kate glanced up.

'Like it's meant to be, or something.' Saskia heard a bitterness enter her voice.

Kate sighed. 'Sass, nothing has happened.'

She couldn't help it. She had to know if this was the end. 'But it will?'

Kate pushed her hair behind her ears. 'I don't know. I've just met him. It's been five years. I have to start again somewhere.'

Tears welled in Saskia's eyes. Before she could help it, a big fat one ran down her face. 'Sorry.' She sniffed. Tonight's unexpected glimpse of old Kate – Hugo's Kate, not this moody, strange, Oxford Kate – had exposed old wounds.

Old Kate would have reached out and rubbed her arm, with a kind look on her face. This one held her tea tightly in both hands. 'Oh, Sass, don't,' she said.

But Saskia couldn't stop the tear. 'It just feels scary, Kate,'

Saskia continued. 'That if you meet someone, you'll stop being our family. That you'll join someone else's. You'll won't be my sister-in-law any more, you'll be theirs.'

There. She had said it.

There was a silence at the table.

Kate rolled her eyes. 'Don't be a pillock, Sass.'

A gulp of air caught in Saskia's throat. They both burst out laughing. Sass sniffed and sat back, feeling better. 'Well, I've got to admit, he's doing something right. You look happier. And you're going out again. I wish I was.'

Kate chewed her flapjack. 'What's happening with Jonathan?'

Saskia reached out and took one, too. They never talked like this any more. What would she give to tell Kate everything right now?

'He just sent the divorce papers,' she said carefully.

Kate looked genuinely surprised. 'Yes,' Saskia would love to have said, 'things go on in other people's lives too, Kate. You're not the only one with problems.'

'Wow. Sorry, I didn't realize.'

Saskia shrugged and bit her flapjack.

'Sass. I still don't really understand – what happened there? It all seemed so sudden.'

Saskia heard the old kind sympathy in Kate's voice. Wanted it back so desperately. Could she trust Kate with the truth, these days, though, or would she just blurt it out in front of Richard and Helen next time there was a big argument?

Saskia thought about the way Kate had blatantly lied to her about not being home this evening, when she so clearly had been with this new man – and decided not.

The old Kate never lied.

'Um, I don't know. He just got bored with me. He got bored of me moaning about working for Dad all the time, and not doing anything about it.' She shrugged. 'He said that when he met me at college, I seemed like someone who was going places and it turned out that I wasn't. He was fed up of me not standing up to Dad. So now he is going places on his own.' She sighed. 'He's right, though, Kate. I know it. I'm a bit of a failure who makes coffee for Dad for a living.'

Kate frowned. 'That seems a bit unfair, Sass. Not exactly grounds for divorce. And what about the Charlbury lot? You don't seem to see them much at the moment.'

'They've all sided with Jonathan. Actually, Marianne's having a party for her thirtieth tonight. A sixties thing. And I'm not even invited. Jonathan is, of course. *And* I've got a fabulous beehive wig I look great in.'

It was a feeble attempt at a joke, and she knew it.

Kate sipped her tea. 'Well, you know, Sass. I remember at your wedding Jonathan told me that he'd had an Italian girlfriend for three years and never bothered to learn Italian. I always thought you deserved someone who would learn Italian for you.'

'Why didn't you say?'

'It was after Hugo. You needed Jonathan to look after you, and, to be honest, I didn't have the strength.'

Saskia remembered. Old Kate would have sat her down with a bottle of wine, and told her the truth, because she wanted only the best for her.

Saskia sat forward, wondering. There was one thing she could tell Kate. 'Well, if I tell you something, will you not tell anyone?'

'What?'

'I'm thinking of finishing my degree.'

Saskia did a double take as Kate picked up a second flapjack. 'Have you spoken to your dad about it?'

Saskia laughed bitterly. 'No.'

'You should.'

232

'You know, I was just looking at that amazing photo Hugo took of Jack this evening –' she pointed at the same photo, blown-up and framed on Kate's kitchen wall – 'that one, at Mum and Dad's today. Do you know that I took up photography before Hugs?'

'No.'

'Well, I did. And my art teacher said I had potential so Dad bought me a really nice Nikon. Anyway, Hugo got interested and borrowed it and, well, you know how brilliant his eye was. And then Dad came to my coursework exhibition at school, and was saying how great my photos were . . .' Saskia sighed. 'And I said – as I always did, doing my self-deprecating thing – "Thanks, Dad, but you know, Hugo's already way ahead of me." And Dad said, "Well, he's just more imaginative, darling."'

'So what, Sass? He's your dad. He's not the bloody king of the world.'

'Easy for you to say, Kate. You stand up to him.'

Kate shook her head. 'No, Sass, that's not true. Standing up to Richard is exhausting. I step around him, just like Hugo taught me. I wish he'd taught you too.'

'Hmm.' Saskia tapped her fingers. 'I've missed this. Talking to you.'

'I'm always here, Sass.'

Sass felt the tears coming again, but rubbed them away, as she always did in front of Kate. It had never felt right to cry in her presence. As Hugo's widow, Kate's grief had taken priority over hers and everyone else's. 'But that's not true. You're not.'

Kate sighed. 'Don't start on me, Sass.'

Saskia pushed her hair away from her face. It was time to stop, while the going was good. 'So, can I meet him? This Jago?' she said.

Kate looked away. 'Sass. I've just met him.' She pushed back her chair. 'Anyway, listen, I'm exhausted. I need to go to bed. Are you staying over?'

'No, I'll go.'

Saskia stood up as Kate did, and picked up her coat. They walked into the hall. As she put her coat on, she looked up and remembered.

'Kate, I've got to tell you: Jack was upset tonight. He says you're still locking the gate upstairs. He's terrified that Mum's going to ask him about it.'

Kate threw her hands up. 'God. Not this as well, Sass! Look. I've thrown away the padlock. They're coming to take the bloody thing out next week. And that's the last thing I'm saying about it.'

'I didn't tell Mum, Kate,' Saskia said, allowing the hurt to come into her voice. 'It's not easy, you know. Being in the middle of you all like this.'

She saw Kate soften a little. 'I know.'

Saskia opened the front door, and jerked her head back up to the cage. 'Although, to be honest, after talking to that weirdo next door, maybe you've got a point. He's odd, Kate. He smells of drink and I saw him watching this woman in her house in Walter Street the other week.'

Kate walked behind her, locking the inner doors in the hall. 'Sass. Please,' she sighed. 'Don't do this to me. There's *no one in the house*. He's just a piss-head student – just like we were once. Really. Anyway, as you said yourself, there's no point having the gate if I've got the alarm on the windows and doors. What's he going to do? Climb through the attic skylight?'

Saskia picked up her bag. 'I know. I just want you to be OK.' She looked at Kate tearfully. 'I always have done.'

She saw a glimmer of sadness cross Kate's face, and she hoped it was regret for their old friendship. 'OK, but let's worry about things that are real, OK?' She gave Saskia a half-smile and shut the door behind her.

Sass walked to her car, wanting to cry. In the old days, they had never parted without a hug or a kiss.

In her heart, she knew now that there had been too much damage. It was never coming back.

The child sat frozen, looking at the new huge grey snake, knowing instinctively now that there was nothing Father could do.

The snakes were coming too quickly. Wrapping around their house.

They could not hide them any more from Mother.

A noise came from under the floorboards.

'Get out!' Father was yelling. Shrieking, almost.

The child looked through the floorboards to see Father running away from the basement wall, pointing outside.

The child turned, knowing there were only seconds to take something special.

The cuckoo clock that Aunt Nelly had brought back from Austria?

The rocking horse?

A book?

'GET OUT NOW!' Dad yelled.

And then the child knew.

The little snowdome sat on a shelf, the glitter snow inside settled calmly at the foot of the plastic mountain.

The child grabbed it and ran as fast as possible from the snakes, the motion sending up a cloud of glitter above the plastic snow.

By the time it settled on the ground, the child knew that something bad was going to happen.

Something that would change everything for ever.

CHAPTER TWENTY-TWO

It was Tuesday, 6 p.m. Cricket practice was over, and Jack arrived back at Hubert Street with a lot on his mind.

Gabe wasn't helping.

'Go *on*, J,' Gabe hissed, sitting on his bike. 'Ask her now! I'll wait.'

Jack typed in the combination to the sidegate lock and opened it.

'No. Later,' he scowled, pushing his bike through to the side of the house. Gabe didn't understand. He didn't know what it was like to have a mum like his. Gabe's mum let him do anything he wanted.

'Aw,' Gabe said, frustrated. 'But before we go to the park tonight, yeah?'

Jack nodded, even though he knew that might be a lie.

'Bring the ball, J, yeah?'

'OK. Come and get me after tea.'

Jack shut the gate behind him and checked it was locked again, as Mum had taught him, and leaned his bike on the wall. He looked through the kitchen window.

She was walking around, licking a spoon.

His stomach cramped at the thought of asking her.

She turned and saw him.

She waved – and *smiled*.

Jack stared, bewildered at the sight. His mum was *smiling*. Not a fake version of Gabe's mum's, but her own. A smile that he recognized from long ago in a way he didn't understand. It lit up her eyes and made them shiny, and changed her face. It made her look pretty, and younger. A lot younger than Gabe's mum.

Jack waved back hesitantly. Why was she doing that?

Curious, he walked to fetch his ball from the trampoline, and stopped. It wasn't there.

He turned, and surveyed the garden. There weren't many places it could be. There wasn't much here. Just a lawn that looked as if it had been laid like a carpet, its edges meeting the fence on three sides. Granddad cut it sometimes, and was going to teach Jack to do it soon. There was a patio without any seats, a shed, the magnolia tree and a giant trampoline. Mum had bought one that was too big, as if she were trying to fill up the garden rather than look at it.

Jack crawled under the trampoline, thinking. Maybe if Mum was in a good mood, now would be the time to ask her.

He tried it out in his head: 'Mum? You know Gabe's sleepover for his birthday on Saturday? It's outside in the garden on the trampoline. Can I go?'

He imagined that cheerful expression he'd just seen disappearing, and the worry wrinkles coming back across Mum's face. Jack sighed. The thing was, he wasn't completely sure he even wanted to go to Gabe's sleepover.

His mind flew to the three Year Eight boys who'd befriended him, Gabe and Damon on Facebook. At first it had been exciting. Damon said the boys were cool. His brother Robbie knew them at secondary school, and one lived on Gabe's road. But then the

Year Eight boys read about Gabe's sleepover, and said they'd come after Gabe's mum was asleep, and bring cider and cigarettes and it would be a laugh.

Jack's stomach spasmed again.

He wanted to tell Mum. Get her to talk to Gabe's mum and make sure the sleepover was all safe, so he could not worry about it. How could he, though?

He stood back up again. The ball wasn't here. His eye wandered to the shed.

'Hi,' he said, wandering in the back door.

She looked up. 'Hi! How was cricket practice?'

He shrugged. 'Good, thanks.'

A smell took him by surprise. Rich and meaty with spices; his taste buds popped. It smelled like the cooking at Nana's house, but spicy.

'What are you making?' he asked, wandering to the cooker. A large red pot he recognized from a high-up cupboard sat inside the oven.

'I am making lamb tagine,' his mum said. 'Well, trying to. I used to make it for Dad. It's an experiment, though. I'm a bit out of practice. It might be rubbish.'

Jack gawped. The kitchen table was set, too. For the two of them. With knives and forks and glasses, and she'd lit a candle in the middle, even though it wasn't dark outside.

He leaned against the worktop, intrigued. The trays they used to eat in front of the telly remained stacked in their normal place.

He saw his mum pick up her mobile, look at the screen, then put it back down by the cooker.

'Who was that?' he said. Not many people rang his mum.

'No one. I thought I might have a message. Do you want to help?' she said. 'Dad always used to do the couscous for me. It was all he could do, mind you.'

Jack ears pricked up. Not only had she smiled in a new way, she was talking about Dad in a brand-new way that he hadn't heard before, either. Not in the sad way that made him feel she was dragging him under a murky river.

She pulled out a packet and handed it to him. Her face was more of a normal colour today, too. Like pale cake dough that was starting to cook. Jack watched her, fascinated. What was happening to her?

It was almost as if she was . . . He stopped himself, knowing it was too much to hope.

'You need to put that in a bowl, then pour on the boiling water. Then, when it's soaked in, rub some olive oil in – then fluff it up.' She winked. 'I'm sure you'll do it better than your dad. You've got my hands.' Kate reached out a hand, and picked up his fingers, which were slim like hers. 'Dad had great big fingers, like Granddad. You know, I used to call him Mr Sausage Fingers.'

Jack regarded her, astonished. 'Mr Sausage Fingers!'

She nodded. 'And you could put in those almonds in the packet over there, and chop that mint for it, too.'

'What did he call you?'

Kate stopped, searching her thoughts. Then she smiled. 'You know what? He called me Mrs Mad.'

Jack opened his mouth and howled with laughter. 'Mr Sausage Fingers and Mrs Mad?'

Kate threw back her head and joined in.

The kitchen was filled with the explosion of his and Mum's laughter. It flew into the spaces round the vacant chairs at the too-big table and the half-empty cupboards on either side of the fireplace and the shelves of dusty rows of Mum and Dad's CDs that no one ever played. It flew past the photo on the wall that Dad took of him waving at an aeroplane when he was five. Dad had lain on the ground to take it, so that Jack's arms looked as long as a giant's, flung up into a china-blue sky where a tiny yellow plane sailed by.

Then the laughter finished its circuit and came to an abrupt stop.

Nothing was left in the room but the echo of it.

Mum picked up her phone again and looked at it. Then she dropped her head and carried on washing a bowl in the sink.

A new much more painful cramp came out of nowhere and stabbed Jack hard in the stomach. He dropped a hand to cover it. 'OK. I'll do it in a minute. Can I have the key to the shed first, please? I can't find my ball.'

'Wasn't it on the trampoline?' Kate asked more quietly than before, reaching up and taking the key.

'Thanks,' he said, walking out. He unlocked the shed, and went inside. It smelt of cut grass and chemicals. Things from their old house in London were stacked on the shelves, things that were never used. Gardening equipment. His old inflatable paddling pool that he couldn't remember using but had a photo of with him in when he was two. A giant suitcase he'd never seen Mum use. Dad's skis.

Jack pushed a spade away and sat on a box, running one hand over the metal catches of the skis, the other on his stomach, thinking about what had just happened in the kitchen. Those men in London had been put in prison for stealing Dad and stealing Dad's car, but they'd stolen lots of other things from Mum, and from him, too. Things that were difficult to put in boxes and measure.

A half smile broke onto his face at Mum's joke about Dad. Mr Sausage Fingers and Mrs Mad. That was funny.

She had *really laughed*.

Jack measured his feet against the bindings. Granddad had

said Dad had been planning to take him skiing when he was six, and that he could have Dad's skis when he was older, so it would be like he was skiing with Dad after all. As usual, his foot sat in the middle, with space at both ends. Dad had had big feet. He knew that because he tried on his shoes sometimes, wondering if his toes would ever reach the end.

It was while he was sitting there that Jack's eye was drawn to a book sitting underneath the table.

'*Beat the Odds and Change your Life* by Jago Martin'

Jack picked it up. What was this?

The cover fell open. 'To Kate. What are the chances? Jago Martin,' it said inside.

His eyes flicked back to the name. Who was Jago Martin? How did she know the man who wrote this book?

He started to flick through. This was the mad stuff that Mum talked about. Numbers. Things that might happen to you. He glanced through the aeroplane figures, then the traffic figures. Did she hide this in the shed and come and read it in private?

Jack looked at the book. He didn't want Mum to talk about these weird numbers any more. He wanted her to laugh more, just like she had in the kitchen.

Carefully, he hid the book under his jumper and stood up. Maybe she'd just think it had got lost. Locking the shed behind him, he walked through the kitchen, realizing to his surprise that there was music playing. A CD cover lay beside the dusty old CD player in the corner, and Mum was swaying a little as she stirred a pot.

Jack did a double take to check he was right. He was. Mum was *dancing*.

'Five minutes till tea, Jack,' she said.

'OK,' he replied, astonished, running off upstairs to get rid of the book under his mattress.

She was playing music. Smiling and dancing.

He *couldn't* ask her about Gabe's sleepover. Not today. He didn't want to spoil it.

He had seen a peek of his old mum through the glass amber eyes and he didn't want to scare her away.

CHAPTER TWENTY-THREE

An hour later, Kate walked around the kitchen, clearing plates and checking the clock.

Seven o'clock, and still no text from Jago.

Where was he?

She had actually enjoyed today, and wanted it to continue. Sitting at the table with Jack to eat had been a revelation. For the first time that she could remember, they'd both had second helpings. They talked about his cricket practice, and Jack had mentioned a film he wanted to see, which had given her an idea.

She blew out the candle.

And now, if only Jago would text, this might be the closest she'd had to a normal day in a very long time. This idea of having something to look forward to again was becoming addictive.

She put her and Jack's dirty dinner plates into the dishwasher. She hadn't been able to stop thinking about Jago all week, and the crazy night in Chumsley Norton. The episode came back to her in waves. Disbelief at what he had done, how she had reacted, and then a guilty thrill at what had happened afterwards. Yet now it looked as if he wasn't going to text her after all. She wiped her hands. She had a bloody good mind to go to the shed and read his book.

That was funny, she considered, hesitating by the recycling bin. Jago hadn't mentioned his lost bag, and she'd completely forgotten to tell him the waitress had found it.

Wrapped in thought, Kate threw the cardboard packet from the couscous into the kitchen recycling box, on top of an empty tin of tomatoes, and porridge and nut packets they'd used for the flapjacks and brownies, noting with surprise that the box was already full. She lifted it and felt its weight. That was unusual. They normally only half filled one box a week. She carried it out of the kitchen, vaguely aware of a new strength in her muscles, as if someone had changed her batteries.

Her stomach gurgled at the presence of paprika and turmeric. The food had been so much richer than they usually ate. In fact, Kate thought, opening the front door, she really should have kept Jack at home longer to digest his food before . . .

Pow!

The number came out of nowhere. The one she had every time Jack went to the park with Gabe and Damon.

• A third of sexual crimes are committed against children under 16.

'Shit,' Kate murmured, slamming the door and dropping the recycling box in the hall. Where the hell had that come from? She stood against the wall. There had been so few numbers today. Only three major ones instead of the usual ten or twelve.

'Don't think about it,' Kate said to herself. She sat down on the stairs. 'It's nonsense. An average of what has happened doesn't guarantee it *will* or *won't* happen to me or Jack. And if you don't give him some independence, he'll never grow up.'

She forced herself to her feet, opened the door and . . .

245

. . . The swarm inside her head had gone.

She stood on the doorstep, checking cautiously.

No. Really. It was gone. That quickly. Pleased, she stepped forwards to empty the kitchen box into the green recycling bin quickly, before turning to shut the front door behind her.

This was really working, she smiled. Just thinking about Jago and his advice improved things instantly.

And she was thinking about him.

Constantly.

Especially about the kiss on the dark country road, and then in the car.

Kate walked to the mirror. She ran a hand down over the flat front of her new T-shirt, stopping it on her hipbones. She had woken at 3 a.m., in the dark, and found herself imagining Jago lying next to her on the opposite pillow, watching. In the dim light of the moon coming through her curtains, she had thrown back her covers, lain sideways and slipped a hand under her nightshirt, allowing it to rest on the dip in her waist, as if the hand were his. She had explored her body, to see what he would find. What she discovered was a mountain range of jutting hip and clavicle bones, and sharp ribs that made bridges across her chest above the hollow valley of her stomach. Two quiet little mounds of breast in the middle that no longer filled the old bras she couldn't be bothered to replace. The rough terrain of dry skin on neglected knees and elbows.

What would she see in his eyes if he ever saw all this, she thought again, looking in the mirror? Disgust? Pity?

Hugo had loved it. All of it. Pregnant, ill, stretched, shrunken. From the start, and to the end.

Last night, Kate had turned over onto her stomach and pulled the covers close. She had only kissed Jago. He had made it clear he was not going to expect more unless she wanted to. She still had a choice. She did not need to let him see her this way, so there was no point anticipating her own self-consciousness or his disappointment.

Yet, as she looked now in the hall mirror, she knew that wasn't really true. Her body was rebelling. She was wearing earrings for the first time in years, bought before she knew what she was doing, this afternoon in Oxford. The small silver hoops hung under her hair, in reopened holes stinging slightly, emphasizing the cut of her cheekbones. A newly fitted lace bra sat under a pretty charcoal top that set off the blackness of her hair and the amber of her eyes. The choice was slipping away from her. Jago's kisses had jump-started her body out of a five-year slumber, whether she liked it or not.

And now her body was staging its own private coup, waking her up at 3 a.m. to think about him lying opposite her on the pillow, when her mind was telling her to proceed slowly.

You have a child, it said. If this man can help you, fine; if he can bring you and Jack back together, fantastic; but your priority must always be fixing your relationship with Jack not what *you* want. You need to get to know this man before you think of doing anything serious with him because . . .

Drriiiiinggg.

Kate jumped.

Sass. Please, be Sass.

She walked to the front door and opened it.

'Oh! Hey!' said a tall man with glasses standing there, very close to the doorway. His head jerked back as if he were surprised to see her.

'Oh,' Kate said, startled, moving back. 'Hi.'

'Magnus!' he said, holding out his hand. 'Your neighbour.'

'Oh, hello,' Kate replied, giving him hers automatically. The

247

man took her hand in large, damp fingers. He grasped it hard. Too hard. He grasped it till the bones squeezed it together and it began to hurt. It was all she could do not to say 'ow'. She pulled it back off him, and stepped back into the house to give herself more space.

This must be the one Sass was talking about.

'You know maybe when the bin men come?' he asked, waving an arm towards the dustbins outside his own house.

'Oh. Tomorrow,' she said, putting her hand under her arm to stop him grasping it again. 'Wednesday.' How could the students not know that? No wonder there were bloody binbags all over the front of their garden.

He still wasn't moving back. She felt herself withdrawing further. Didn't they have personal space where he came from?

'Tomorrow? Hey, great. Thank you.' He paused and looked at her for a long second. The look made her want to pull even further inside her house. But before she could, the student walked off.

Kate nodded uneasily. 'You're welcome.'

Relieved, she shut the door. She walked quickly to the kitchen and washed her hands. Saskia was right. A little strange.

Her phone buzzed on the kitchen table. She dried her hands and grabbed it, praying.

'Yes!' she hissed, when she saw Jago's number.

Blackwell's at 7.45 pm

Kate's face broke back into a happy grin. 'Bit close to the bone there, mate,' she said.

She walked around, tidying the kitchen, imagining telling Jago about the weird student.

'Kate, he's just a student with a nervous handshake who turns into a tosser around women,' she imagined him saying. 'Trust me, I have six of him in every class. You've got to tell the difference between real danger and imagined danger.'

She looked at the clock. Only half an hour till she saw him.

'Please, Sass,' she muttered, before running upstairs to clean her teeth, her thoughts about the odd student next door left downstairs, her mind now fixed on a challenge she'd been planning to set herself all day.

Saskia came just before 7.30 p.m., full of apologies, her fine pale hair even flatter than normal, as if she had spent the day pushing it back. To Kate's relief, Jack arrived back at the same time, with Gabe and Damon in tow to drop him off, their cheeks all flushed from playing football. Inwardly, Kate congratulated herself for the second time this week. She had managed not to phone Jack in the park to check up on him, and he looked as if he'd had fun.

This was all going even better than she'd hoped. And now she was going to try something she hadn't done in years. She was going to try to cycle to Broad Street on the road.

Determined, Kate pulled on her denim jacket and, at the last minute, remembered to grab the bag with her ankle boots. She buckled up her new bike helmet firmly, checking the straps twice, and went outside. 'Jack, show Sass where the dinner is, will you?' she called, taking her bike out of the sidegate.

Then she saw Jack and the other two boys mumbling at each other, scowling at her under their skater-boy fringes.

'Jack's mum?'

The call came from Gabe. She turned as she walked down the drive, to see Jack hitting Gabe's arm crossly.

She stopped reluctantly, anxious to face the challenge she'd set herself. 'Hi, Gabe.'

'Can Jack come to my sleepover on Saturday? My mum's says he's got to ask you, and he keeps not asking you because it's in the garden and he thinks you'll say no. And if you say no, I'm going to ask Sid. So can he?'

The smile slid off Kate's face.

In the garden? What was he talking about?

'Oh, what? Like camping, Gabe, in a tent?'

'No – on the trampoline. In the sleeping bags.'

He was joking? Three ten- and eleven-year-olds, lying outside at night, alone in a city, with city foxes, and burglars and . . .

The numbers began to buzz annoyingly in her head.

Kate realized everyone was looking at her: Saskia, Jack and his friends. She tried to pull herself together.

Gabe stared curiously at her freshly blow-dried hair, and she lowered her made-up eyes.

'It's just my mum thinks you might worry about it . . .'

'Shut up, Gabe,' Jack glowered.

'*My* mum said yes,' Damon piped up.

Kate saw Saskia start to open her mouth, probably to tell some irritating story about how her and 'Hugs' used to camp in their garden, and shot her a dirty look.

Don't dare, it said.

Then, to her sorrow, Kate saw Jack jut his jaw tensely as he had in the car the day she'd gone to Sylvia's. He was embarrassed. In front of his friends.

The buzz of numbers grew louder in Kate's head. She tried to ignore them, cursing Gill, Gabe's mum, for putting her in this position.

'Um, listen, I'm in a hurry, Gabe,' she said, trying to keep her tone bright. 'Can you tell your mum I'll ring her tomorrow? And, Sass, don't wait up, I might be a bit later tonight,' she continued, pushing off on her bike before Saskia could interrogate her.

Kate waved at Jack, and pulled into the road, aware of the murmur of astonishment passing between Jack and Saskia as they realized that she was not riding on the pavement. Trying to concentrate, she cycled to the junction and regarded Iffley Road nervously, and the long stretch of it that ran right into Oxford.

But it was no good.

Gabe's request had rattled her. Rattled her good intentions.

She looked up and down Iffley Road. This afternoon, on the way back from Tesco to buy ingredients for the tagine, she'd managed half on the road, the rest on the pavement. Yet now she felt less brave. Kate gripped the handlebars, waiting for a long break in the traffic, then pedalled hard across the road, trying not to think about it. She cycled down Iffley Road as fast as she could, desperate to get this over with.

But the idea of Jack sleeping outside with no adult to protect him was starting to make her feel sick. The other numbers she knew by heart began to bombard her.

- **A third of children do not report sexual offences to an adult.**

'Don't think about it,' she whispered. A lorry went past, making her swear out loud.

The numbers caught her up again.

- **Two-thirds of road accidents happen on 30 mile per hour or less roads.**

She tried to ignore it.

- **More crime takes place at night than at any other time.**

It was no good. Panting, Kate pulled in by the ivy-strewn school on the corner of Magdalen Bridge.

Bloody Gill, and her bloody laid-back, hippy ways.

And this bloody, bloody road.

Kate leaned against a wall, raging at herself. The figures were flying at her so thick and fast now that she suspected she might have to push her bike all the way to Blackwell's, which would make her late for Jago.

'Get a grip,' she told herself. 'Lots of stats are made up by people to sell things. Jack wouldn't be on his own in the garden. The others would be there. If you don't do it, he'll be left out of the group.

One thousand.

Two thousand.

Three thousand.

Four . . .

Seconds later, she started to relax. A minute later, she was back to normal. Tentatively, she climbed back on her bike and headed shakily across Magdalen Bridge.

Almost immediately, she found herself in a pack of city cyclists. Mostly students, and a mother, to her alarm, with a toddler in a child's seat. Kate stayed firmly in the middle, as if the pack would protect her, gritting her teeth. The toddler was laughing, as his mother cheerfully sang 'The Wheels on the Bike Go Round and Round'. Kate gripped her handlebars as if she was hanging from a trapeze as the road dipped round to Longwall Street, to the quieter turn-off to Hollywell Street.

Eventually, the welcome width of Broad Street loomed ahead.

'Come on,' she muttered.

However, her rhythm started to escape her. Her legs felt as if they were jamming down randomly on the pedals now, at risk of slipping off with each push.

Finally, the Sheldonian Theatre came into view, and Blackwell's.

She was nearly there.

She had done it!

Kate drew up in the central parking area and dismounted. Her hands were trembling, and she shook them.

She looked behind her, amazed. For the first time in five years, she'd cycled the whole journey on the road. It had been horrible, panic-inducing. But she had *done it*.

All thanks to Jago.

She looked across the road, with a shiver of anticipation. Broad Street was busy, packed with pedestrians on this summer evening. She couldn't see him. She pushed her bike through a group of Japanese tourists, to the bike rack by Blackwell's, conscious of a tremor in her leg muscles, too. Locking her bike, she looked around. A 'ghost walk' tourist group was gathering on the pavement. A boy cycled past her in college robes, a carrier bag of wine balanced on each handle.

Kate stood by a wall, glancing intermittently towards Balliol. She was a little early. She wandered to Blackwell's arched windows and peered in at a display. She checked her watch for the fifth time: 7.52 p.m. Oh God, this wasn't going to be another of Jago's taxi rides was it? Because . . .

'Hey. Good timing.'

She turned, to see Jago walking towards her, holding a rucksack. He was wearing a white T-shirt and darker jeans, and looked really pleased to see her.

'Hi,' she said demurely, panicking at how to greet him. Jago had no such reservations. He leaned down, smiling, and kissed her confidently on the mouth, the smell and touch of him making her blush a little – then he stepped back and hit himself on the forehead.

'Shit.' He held out his rucksack. 'Can you take this, Kate – my bike's just there.' He pointed. 'I've left my jacket in my room.'

Kate nodded, trying to hide her flushed cheeks.

'You look nice.' He winked, walking back towards Balliol. Kate pushed her hair behind her ears awkwardly, trying to remember how to behave in this situation. She had met Hugo when she was twenty-one. It hadn't felt awkward then, but normal. He was the last in a steady succession of teenage and college boyfriends, so she was well practised. She took the rucksack to Jago's bike, noticing a clinking noise inside.

As she went to put it down, a piercing sound made her jump. It was high pitched and sounded like the rape alarm Dad had made her take to university that had gone off on the coach to London. It came from Jago's bag.

The tourists from the ghost walk looked over.

Squeallll!!

Leaning down, Kate ran her hand along the front of the bag. She felt a hard lump in the front pocket.

The noise stopped suddenly.

She hesitated, about to stand up . . .

Then it started again.

'Ooh, shut up,' she muttered. Customers inside Blackwell's were coming to the window now. Not knowing what else to do, Kate unzipped the pocket. A phone sat on top of Jago's wallet.

A phone?

'Marla ringing', the screen said.

Kate paused.

Marla?

The siren noise was increasingly desperate with each ring.

What should she do?

She hovered her finger over the answer button.

Then, as quickly as it had started, the noise stopped.

'You missed a call from Marla.' A message popped up.

'Right,' Jago said, coming up behind her, his jacket over his arm. 'Let's go.'

'Oh,' Kate exclaimed, jumping up. She glanced at the open zip of his bag.

'I'm sorry, I was just . . .'

'Was it going off?' Jago said, bending down. 'Sorry. I turned the alarm ring tone full up so I could hear it from the shower. My publisher in London was supposed to ring about the launch. Was that him?' He picked up the phone.

Kate said nothing.

Jago looked at the screen. A shadow passed over his face as he saw the caller's name.

He looked at Kate. 'Did you answer?'

'No!' she stuttered. 'No. I wouldn't . . . I just . . . I . . . it was just ringing and ringing and . . .'

'No, don't worry. I'd better just listen to this, though.' He pressed the message, and held the mobile to his ear. When it had finished, he changed the ring tone back to the one she'd heard before, an acoustic guitar strumming, lost in thought.

'Oh. OK then.' He made a face. 'Well, that's unexpected.' He stood up, zipping up his bag. 'Marla, my ex-girlfriend. I'm supposed to be seeing her in August in the States, but she's at a conference in Paris, apparently, and wants to stop off in London some time this week.'

Kate tried to keep her expression unassuming.

Jago looked a little stunned. 'Sorry. That's thrown me a bit. We haven't spoken for three months.'

Kate hesitated. 'Well, do you need to go and ring her? I mean, we can do this another . . .' She prayed he wouldn't accept her offer. 'I mean, I can go.'

Jago stood up. He punched her gently on the arm. 'Oi, you're not getting out of this that easily, mate. No. I'll ring her back later.' He leaned over and unlocked his bike. 'Come on.'

'But if you two have stuff to . . .'

'Kate, let's go,' he said, climbing on his bike. 'If I'm not mistaken, you and me have business,' he added, looking back with

255

a heavy-lidded look laden with an ambiguity that sent a shiver through her.

'OK,' said Kate, climbing back on her bike. The plastic bag on her handlebars swung against her. 'Though, Jago. Just a sec. I need to hand this in to that heel bar on the corner first.' She pointed to the end of Broad Street. 'It's open till eight.'

Jago pointed where she now saw steel shutters across the door. 'It's five past. You've just missed it.' He put out a hand without hesitation. 'Give them to me – I'll drop them in tomorrow.'

'Oh . . .' she said, surprised, holding onto them. 'No, you don't have to, I mean, I . . .'

Jago kept his hand outstretched. 'It's no problem. Really. It'll take me two seconds in the morning.'

Yet Kate couldn't let go of her grip on the bag. It was so long since anyone had done anything kind or thoughtful for her, she realized she didn't know how to respond. A painful rush of memories flashed through her mind: of Hugo, bringing her a coffee when she was working, without her asking. Of sticking her running clothes in the washing machine when she was out, because he knew she'd need them later for the gym, and had forgotten to do them herself.

Kate looked up at Jago and saw him examining her with his blue eyes. In his expression she saw understanding, as if he had guessed what she was thinking.

'Come on,' he said gently, prising the bag from her fingers. 'Let me do this for you. I'd like to help.'

Their fingers touched as he took the bag, sending a tiny thrill through her. He hung it on his handlebars and headed off Broad Street towards town, waving a hand behind him for her to follow. Kate pulled uneasily back out into Broad Street.

'Hey. Look at you. You're cycling on the road,' he called back, picking up speed.

Her mouth twisted into a pleased smile.

Jago went in front, turning right at the top of Broad Street, then on up Woodstock Road. Kate followed, feeling like a new colt, skinny, unsure legs, pushing awkwardly against the pedals as two lorries thundered past her.

- **Lorries are involved in nearly a third of all road accidents where people are injured or killed.**

Kate shook her head to force the number away. Luckily, a minute later Jago turned left and free-wheeled past rows of mews houses in Jericho. As the traffic died away, he beckoned Kate forwards to cycle side by side.

'So how've you been after Saturday? No after-effects.'

'No. How are you? You looked a bit surprised back there.'

He shrugged. 'Sorry. I didn't expect to hear from her again. I'm only going back to North Carolina to pick up my stuff. The last time we spoke she slammed the phone down on me shortly after calling me a "mother-fucking piece of shit", if I remember correctly.'

Kate sat back a little more comfortably on her saddle.

'So, why do you think she's coming over to London?'

'I really don't know. Anyway, it's not important. What is important . . .' he said, turning onto a bridge across the river, 'is this. Right. So Step Three: *Jump-Start Kate's Survival Instincts by Completely Terrifying her in an Oxfordshire Village and Nearly Get Brick on Head for Trouble*,' he said. 'And tonight . . . Step Four: *Kate Fucks with the Statistics and Shows them who's Boss.*'

'Oh God,' Kate muttered as Jago sped ahead of her with a grin. She picked up her speed to stay with him. At the point in the path where she had veered right towards Sylvia's last week, Jago forked left. Quickly, the path emptied of joggers and pedestrians. It was narrower, darker, overshadowed by the hanging branches of willow trees.

They passed a fisherman packing down a small red tent as he finished up for the day. With a start, she remembered Jack's sleepover in Gabe's garden. Kate's chest tightened again, and she tried to breathe it away. She could deal with that tomorrow. Now, she needed to concentrate on tonight.

The lights of the last houses started to disappear behind her. It was amazing how in Oxford, just a few hundred yards from the High Street, you could feel you were in the countryside. As the sun began to set, Kate fixed her eye on the reflective spot on Jago's rear mudguard. They cycled for five more minutes.

Then Jago stopped.

Kate braked and put her feet down. Jago held up a hand as if listening to something. He turned, put his finger over his mouth and climbed off his bike.

'What?'

He jerked his head towards an opening in a hedge. They pushed their bikes into it, laid them down and emerged on the other side in a meadow. Kate heard her feet squelch and looked down. This was wetland. Her nostrils filled with the potent smell of wild grasses and water mint.

'OK?' Jago whispered.

'Er, no, but go on,' she replied, glancing around nervously. He took her hand without asking. 'Come on.' They set off across the soggy grass, Kate feeling her fingers stiffening in his grip. He was so unselfconscious about these things. Why couldn't she be? With Hugo, she supposed, there had been no boundaries between their bodies, but this was a new country with Jago. A new hand, a new size, a new grip. Strange and foreign.

Two minutes later they arrived at a gap further along the hedge. Jago peered through it back onto the towpath.

'Come here.'

He put a hand around her waist and guided her forwards, so she was nestled between his arms, with her back against his chest. She tried to concentrate on what he was showing her.

A small canal boat sat alone, chained to the path. She could just make out its name – *Honeydew* – in faded yellow paint. Piles of logs sat on its deck. Plant pots were scattered across the top, some of them cracked, full of herbs and flowers. A dim light shone inside.

'What?'

Jago lifted his finger to his lips. A figure passed the window. Kate drew back.

'Someone's in there.'

'Sssssh . . .'

He was a man in his sixties, wearing a navy cowl-neck potter's top. He had waist-length grey hair matted into dreadlocks, streaked with nicotine, and a crumpled, round, red face.

Kate watched the man walk along his boat, shutting each pair of curtains. A murmur of a radio started up from within.

'What are we doing?' she mouthed.

'You are going to steal his boat,' he said, with the same deadly serious voice he'd used when he told her to steal the dog.

Kate pulled away, shaking her head.

'Sssssh.' Jago laughed, pulling her tight against him. He pointed. A rowing boat with a small outboard engine sat bobbing on the river. One end was tied to the canal boat, the other to a hook on the riverbank.

'No way,' she whispered. 'The dog was bad enough, Jago.'

He squeezed her tight, his breath ticking her cheek. 'It's just an exercise.'

She turned her mouth to his ear, feeling his bristle brush her cheek. 'In robbery?'

'No. About you taking control of the numbers. You let these stats bully you. If you steal this boat, you change the crime statistics for Oxford tonight. I want you to fuck with them, like they're fucking with you. See what it feels like.'

His breath tickled her ear.

Kate tried not to be distracted. She shook her head again.

He continued. 'Kate. Have you felt any different since the other night? You're on the road. That has to be good, yes? Trusting your instincts to keep you safe?'

She shrugged. The small physical action pushed her body back into his chest a tiny bit. In response, he hugged her closer. It was all she could do not to turn round and lift her lips to his again.

Jago kept talking in her ear. 'So, come on. Let's do it. If he sees you, we'll run back to the bikes behind the hedge. But, honestly, he looks so stoned, we could probably take his canal boat and he wouldn't notice.'

It was a funny joke, but she didn't feel like smiling.

'Kate. Do it. We're on the right track here.'

He stroked his hand down the side of her arm, easily, comfortably. She stood watching the boat through the gap.

To her surprise she found herself, just for a second, intrigued at the unpredictability of the situation. At what might happen.

'Just do it, don't think about it,' Jago said.

They waited until darkness began to fall. The man was whistling. Kate could hear him, walking around inside, clattering some pans. She crouched down in the hedge. Checking that Jago was watching, she crawled out onto the path as the dim light from the canal boat, diffused through red curtains, reached her body.

The rowing boat bobbed on the current. Painstakingly, Kate

moved one hand and one knee together at a time in tandem, till she reached the metal rope cleat on the bank.

This was crazy.

She fumbled her fingers, undoing the rope, trying not to think how deep the water was. The first knot came undone easily and she dropped the rope into the rowing boat. The freed end of the boat gave a buck of excitement, and glided away.

It was too late now. Kate sized up the other knot, at the canal boat end. She crawled forwards, wanting to get this over and done with as quickly as possible. But when she reached it, she saw it was a different type of knot. Tighter.

'Halfway,' Jago whispered.

Kate glanced up at the canal boat, to check. It was a such strange concept. That the owner had no idea she was out here. That *she* was the bad person in the shadows.

She began to unpick the second knot, using one finger and thumb on each hand. Luckily, it came away more easily than she expected and . . .

A loud bang exploded above her. A light burst onto the deck.

Kate's heart began to pound so heavily that it felt it had dropped into her stomach.

The man with the grey dreadlocks walked onto the deck. He coughed, and the faint smell of something curried mixed with incense drifted towards her.

Kate crouched, holding the loose rope. The urge to run overwhelmed her. But if she stood up, he'd see her. He'd be able to leap off the canal boat and grab her.

She lowered herself as flat as possible into the shadows, glancing in panic to her right, convinced her heart was pounding so loudly that the man would hear it. 'Stay there,' Jago mouthed.

The man doesn't know you're here, she tried to tell herself to calm her growing panic. Just like the teenagers in the village.

You are in control. If you jump up now, he'd be more scared than you.

Kate began to count to calm herself.

One thousand. Two thousand. Three thousand . . .

She listened to the man picking wood off the woodpile, praying for him to finish and go back inside. Radio Four blared from somewhere.

Then there was a movement. Kate peeked up and saw, to her dismay, that the freed end of the rowing boat was moving further away from the bank, like a toddler pulling wilfully from its mother.

She shrank back down. If the boat owner looked up and focused his eyes in the dark, he would see it. He would . . .

'Oi!'

The man's yell burst into the night.

'What the fuck are you doing?'

Kate's heart jumped inside her chest so hard it felt as if someone had defibrillated her.

'What are you doing to my fucking boat?'

'I . . . I . . .' she began to stutter.

But before he could say another word, a dark figure came out of the hedge and ran straight up to the man.

'What the . . . get off . . .' She heard the man growl.

She saw Jago reach the side of the little fibreglass canal boat and shove it hard. It moved about a foot away from the riverbank, but enough to catch the man off balance. He staggered one way, then the other, then flew over the side with a splash.

'Get in the rowing boat,' Jago yelled to Kate.

'What? No! He's in the water!'

'It's shallow. Get in the fucking boat,' Jago said, running towards her.

Shakily, she did what he asked, putting in one foot, and gasping as the boat rocked underneath her.

'Fuck,' Jago hissed, jumping in beside her. He grabbed her waist to steady her, sat her firmly on the bench, then reached for the outboard engine cord, still standing up. 'That went a bit tits-up.'

'Jago. Stop . . .' she hissed, as the boat roared into life.

'Get off my fucking boat!' the man shouted from the water.

Jago leaned over expertly, and shoved them off the side. Quickly, he manoeuvred the boat into the middle of the river, ignoring the impassioned yells.

Kate looked around frantically. 'Jago. There's no life jackets.'

'Kate?' he shouted above the engine. 'Can you swim?'

Kate rolled her eyes.

'Well, there you go, then,' he shouted. He sat down and accelerated the boat back up the river towards Oxford. Frantically, Kate looked back. The boat owner was pulling himself up onto the bank, his dreadlocks flattened around his ruddy face.

He looked like a tree monster.

She turned and saw Jago watching the man. He transferred his eyes to Kate and made the face of a child who'd done something very naughty.

To her horror, a snort of laughter burst from Kate's mouth. Appalled with herself, she tried to stifle it with a hand, but it was too late. Jago had seen it.

'I knew this innocent nice girl thing was all a front,' he called out, kicking her leg.

She shook her head, fighting back the smile but failing, and guiltily checked back again to ensure the poor canal boat man had made it out of the water safely.

It was an odd sensation, though, she thought, to be fighting back a smile, instead of tears.

They turned a bend, and the boat carried on, its cheap engine spitting and growling into the night. At a safe distance, Jago pulled into the bank to retrieve their bikes, then carried on, the bikes balanced in the middle of the boat.

When they were further away from the canal boat, he cut the noisy engine and pulled out the oars.

'Er, OK. Sorry about that,' he deadpanned.

'I can't believe you, Jago,' Kate exclaimed, checking behind them. 'We're going to get arrested.'

'No, we're not,' he said, pulling back on the oars. 'I could smell his bong from behind the hedge. He won't call the police. Lie back and enjoy it. He'll be fine. He'll think we're drunk students and go looking for his boat in the morning.'

Kate made an unconvinced face at him; then, having no choice, stuck in the middle of the river, did what she was told, resting her head back and watching the thin blood-red stripe across the horizon to the west, as the last of the day's sky collapsed into embers. Jago rowed on.

She'd never met anyone like him, Kate thought. While her conscience was telling her that stealing this boat was wrong, for some reason she trusted him. There was something maverick about him that fascinated her. Maverick but fun. Kind at heart. After all, he'd only run at the man with the dreadlocks to protect her, and he hadn't hurt him.

As Jago turned to check the man wasn't following on the bank, she cast her eyes surreptitiously over the neat shape of his close-cropped skull and the sharp cheekbones that always softened when he smiled, surprising her. She didn't know why, but instinctively she knew that being around someone who was not scared of boundaries and rules was exactly what she needed.

The ebb and flow of the oars through the reeds rocked her gently.

The boat moved on under the arriving moonlight. The hard knot in her chest, as she thought about the man with the dreadlocks, started to relax. There was no point dwelling on it, or she would ruin the point of this evening. The man had climbed out of the river. He'd be shaken but not hurt. She made herself concentrate instead on the sky above and the rich smell of foliage. It was so unusual for her to be out at night, she'd forgotten how water and trees shape-shifted and became charged with new meaning and atmosphere in the dark, displayed a different type of beauty.

She realized she had no idea where they were going and, for the first time since she could remember, that was OK.

As they passed the spot where she'd seen the fisherman's tent, the thought of Jack and his night-time sleepover pushed its way uneasily into her mind again.

So she tried something different. She concentrated on seeing Jack's sleepover from the perspective of tonight. Jago rowed them to a fork in the river. They took the right turn, down a lane of water she didn't recognize. Kate told herself that if she denied Jack the chance to go to Gabe's and to do something exciting and different, he would never have what she had now.

An adventure under the stars.

Jago rowed them for another five minutes. The air was lush with wet plants.

'Do you know why night smells different to day?' he murmured.

Kate held up her hand. 'Jago, I'm still mad at you for pushing that man in the water.'

'But do you?'

'No.'

'Well, it's to do with convection. Heat moves molecules

around in fluid. So when the sun's shining it stirs it all up, and the smells are diluted in the air. Then when night comes, the heat goes, and things stop moving. Smells becomes more intense.'

'Really?' She nodded, impressed. 'It's a shame.'

'What?'

'That when we stop this boat how much useful stuff's going to be lost when we get on to dry land and I kill you for making me do this.'

Jago snorted. She threw her head back, pleased that she had made him laugh.

She opened her mouth to speak, then stopped.

'What?' Jago asked.

'I was just wondering, how did you get into academia?'

Jago carried on rowing steadily. She glanced at his arms, as they tensed with each stroke. Her hand moved to her own upper arm, and she rested it there, trying to remember how different the texture and density of a man's arms were.

'Well, my dad says that my brain just seemed to understand numbers from early on. I made him set me sums all the time. And I suppose I get the teaching thing from him – he teaches English, so do my sisters – and the maths stuff is probably from my mum's side. They're all doctors.'

She tried not to give away that she already knew this. 'And you didn't want to be a doctor?'

He shook his head. 'No. I like working in a university. You get the freedom to explore areas you're interested in. Paid to go abroad. Long holidays. I'm sure that sounds very selfish, compared to my mum. She's amazing. She works with geriatric patients.'

'No. But you do work for new governments in post-war countries – that's not selfish.'

266

Jago shot her a curious look.

Damn. Kate kicked herself. What had she just said?

'Did I tell you that?'

She pretended to look back at something in the water. 'I don't know. Didn't you say you flew to developing countries, or something. I just thought that . . .?'

'Oh. Yes. No, you're right. So I did,' he nodded.

Silence descended on the boat.

'And you Googled me, didn't you?' he said after a second.

'No!'

'Yeah, you bloody did. Don't worry. I'd probably Google me too. Scottish skin-head with a penchant for dog-rustling.' He wiped a fly from his face. 'I'm going to do you later. Find embarrassing photos of you at school.'

'Fuck off,' Kate giggled, savouring the word. It felt good to swear at some one in a bantering way again without it holding any menace.

There was a small lane of water up to the right.

'That's it, I think,' Jago said.

Kate saw a white jetty in the moonlight, up ahead of them. It sat at the bottom of the garden of an Oxford college whose name she couldn't remember.

'Come on.' Jago took the boat in, tied it up loosely, and climbed out. 'We can hide out here for a while just in case he decides to come looking tonight.'

She passed out the bikes and the rucksack to him, then he held out a hand. She took it, glad to be back on dry land.

Jago took a rug out his rucksack and laid it down, then pulled out a bottle of red wine and two plastic glasses. Kate glanced at the wine, surprised. It was a good one. A French one that she and Hugo used to buy in the old days. She glanced at him, registering something she had only vaguely noticed before, that Jago's

267

T-shirt and jeans were always good makes. Expensive brands. Book deals in America and Britain, she suspected, sipping her wine, probably meant that he was far from being an impoverished lecturer. Relieved, she realized that would make things simpler.

'You really think he might be looking for us?' she said, sitting down.

'Nah. Probably still drying his hair.'

'Don't,' she said, feeling mean as she smiled.

'So,' he said. 'You did well. How do you feel?'

How did she feel? 'Er . . . I'm not sure.'

'Like a terrible person?'

'Would it be bad to say, Not really?'

'Not at all,' Jago said, looking at the bottle with appreciation. She liked the way he did that; it was what Hugo would have done. She sipped her own wine, watching him. He was so like Hugo in some ways. They were both people who created fun out of the most mundane moment. But Jago had an edge – an edge of adventure that Hugo had never had. Hugo would not have stolen someone's boat. He would have bought them a boat if they needed it.

Jago put down the bottle. 'No. I think it's interesting,' he said.

'Why?'

'Because I think normally you'd feel bad about doing something like that. You'd worry about the old guy, because you're a kind person, but, in the context of what we're trying to do . . .'

Kate interrupted him, blurting out: 'It feels . . .'

She stopped.

Jago waited.

She tried again. 'I do feel bad for him. I really do, and I'm worrying about him right now. But I do kind of understand what you're getting at – why we did this. And I suppose, just for once, it feels comforting. For it not to be me who the bad thing is happening to.' She picked up a flat stone and turned it in her hand. She hesitated, then knew she would. 'Can I tell you something?'

'Hmm,' Jago said. He sat closer to her, then lay back so they were touching side by side, looking at the stars.

'All evening, I've been worrying about Jack going on a sleepover in someone's garden. Worrying about the bad things that might happen to him outside at night.'

She cringed as she heard her inner fears voiced for someone else to hear.

But Jago looked genuinely interested. 'Ahah! And now you *are* that bad thing, outside at night? For someone else?'

She nodded and took another sip. It followed the last one to the back of her throat and gave her a little flame of courage. She turned the stone, over and over.

'And how does that feel?'

'Empowering, I suppose. In a very weird way.'

'Did you ever feel like this before your parents died, too – anxious about things?' He rubbed his hand over his head, and she remembered the feel of it, the soft stubble under her fingers, and wanted to do it again.

'Oh God, no. No. I didn't worry about anything then. Who does when they're a teenager?'

'Like?'

'Well, I don't know. We lived in the countryside. I rode horses – jumped five-bar gates, that kind of thing. Went on school skiing trips. Spent my teenage years bombing around country roads in Minis at ninety miles per hour with drunk farmer boys, feeling invincible.'

'Seriously?' Jago sat up to check her glass. There was a gentlemanly politeness about him that reminded her of her own dad.

'Yeah. And that's just the start of it,' she said. 'Me and Hugo were going to go travelling after uni but he stayed in London to set up the business and I went with some friends. I did all sorts of stuff I can't even imagine now. Hitched through Vietnam. Bungee jumped in Thailand. I even worked at a parachute centre in New Zealand for three months as a receptionist. Learned how to skydive on my days off.'

Jago's mouth fell open. 'You're fucking joking?'

She giggled at his face. 'No, I'm a qualified skydiver – got my international licence and everything, believe it or not.'

Jago's mouth dropped open. 'I've always wanted to do that. Kate, I'm impressed. So you weren't always such a wimp.'

'Oi.' She sat up and sipped her wine. 'It's funny. I've been thinking a lot about that recently. How it felt.'

'You haven't done it since?'

She shook her head. 'I nearly did. For my thirtieth birthday – a sort of symbolic re-entry into the world after losing my parents – but it didn't happen.'

'Why?' Jago shifted towards her so that his leg brushed against hers.

She tried to make hers relax against it, unfamiliar with the physical contact. 'Well, I did a refresher course and went up in the plane. But the weather changed, and we couldn't jump. Hugo was watching me down below. Jack was with him. I think something rattled Hugo. The day he died, he was trying to persuade me not to rearrange the jump.' She lay back. 'I sometimes think he'd had a premonition of death when I was up there. Only it wasn't mine. It was his.'

A crack came into her voice. She bit the soft part of her cheek, cross with herself.

That time was over now.

Tears were not allowed in the future.

Jago gave her a moment, then banged her gently on the leg, as if he sensed that she was struggling.

'What's it like?'

'What?'

'Jumping out a plane.'

How long was it since she'd spoken about normal things? About times before? Like tonight with Jack about Hugo, and Mr Sausage Fingers.

'Oh, it's unbelievable. Like nothing else. There's all this noise of the plane engine, and you're sitting at the edge, feeling more scared than you ever will in your life. Then you step out and throw yourself into this vast open space. You count slowly, and your parachute opens, and you've survived. You're flying. And then there's this sense of total euphoria.' She shook her head wryly. 'Honestly, I can't even get on a bloody aeroplane to go to Spain now. Feels as if it was someone else.'

Jago rubbed her arm. 'No, it was you.'

'One in a million.'

'Hmm?'

Kate looked up at the sky. 'Your chances of both your chutes not opening. Well, actually one in ten thousand of each chute not opening, so one in a million of both chutes not opening. And knowing my luck, Mrs Seven Times Hit by Lightning. Well, it has to be someone, doesn't it. . .?'

Jago sighed. 'Your luck is more or less the same as anyone else's, Kate, I keep telling you. The same as that old guy on his canal boat right now, thinking, "Why me? Why my rowing boat and no one else's?" You and I both know that our decision was random. It wasn't about him, in particular. But tonight you fucked with the crime statistics. Thefts in Oxford have just gone up, reported or not. It's that simple.'

Jago lay back.

Kate realized she didn't want to talk any more.

They lay there for a while, side by side, as they had done in the secret garden a week ago, but this time touching. Gradually, she became aware of a small patch of warmth on her skin. Glancing down, she saw that Jago's hand, which was resting on her stomach, was located just where her jumper had ridden up, exposing an inch of skin.

She shut her eyes, listening to the distant sounds of traffic and chatter in the nearby High Street, savouring the sensation.

Willing his finger to move.

She wasn't even sure how it happened, when it did. Whether he moved his finger or she breathed deeply, pushing it slightly with the motion.

But there was friction.

A tiny movement of skin on skin.

Kate heard her own breathing deepen into the warm night.

And this time, when his finger moved, there was no confusion about its intention. Kate kept her eyes closed as Jago, slowly and quietly, trailed the edge of his nail across her side. She heard his weight shift. Knew he was now watching her.

His finger moved further, tracing tiny distances back and forward under her jumper, his own breathing becoming louder close to her ear. This is strange for him, too, she reminded herself. His first time, possibly, with someone new since Marla. Tracing new maps on a new body. Exploring.

Either way, he wasn't in a hurry. As if he sensed her self-consciousness at being touched after so long, he trailed his fingernail lightly and slowly across her stomach, giving her a chance to stop him at each border, his breathing gentle beside her ear. Higher and higher his finger moved, circling her belly button, tracing across the mild stretch marks left by Jack, up the sides of her torso, making her shiver, till she felt it find its way across the bottom of her bra strap and wait there a while.

He kept her gaze, watching, as he slowly lifted the cup of her new bra with his finger, pulled it down. He waited for her to stop him. When she didn't, it moved inside.

Where his fingertip came, gently, to rest.

Kate inhaled deeply and lifted her head, seeking out his lips with hers. His lips met hers and . . .

Suddenly, a guitar began to play right beside them. They both opened their eyes and looked at each other confused.

'Phone.' Jago sat up, scrabbling around, letting Kate go.

'Quick, in case that bloke hears it,' Kate whispered, looking behind her into the meadow.

'Shit. Fuck,' Jago swore, pressing buttons in the dark.

The screen went bright. 'Fuck,' he mouthed at Kate, holding up a hand. Jago jumped to his feet.

'Hello?' There was a pause. 'Oh, hi. How are you? . . .'

Kate sat up, straightening up her bra and jumper. He rolled his eyes at her. 'No, I did get it. I'm just . . . busy . . .'

Kate felt her heart sink. Marla.

'Well, what do you mean, you're going to . . .?' Jago's voice took on a stern tone. 'That's not what we said . . . I mean. Look. Marla. Can I call you back in half an hour? I'm in the . . . library.'

He shrugged a 'sorry' at Kate.

'OK. Ring me then.'

He put the phone down and sighed.

'Shit, shit, shit. Sorry!' he groaned. 'I didn't mean to answer it. I pressed the wrong button.' He looked at Kate apologetically, leaned down with a small groan and hugged her tightly in her arms. He looked around at the bikes. 'I'm going to have to go and sort this out. She's a bit . . .'

Kate waved a hand. 'Look. Don't worry. It sounds complicated.'

'Trust me, it was. We spent last year flying back and forwards across the Atlantic for the weekends to sort it out, then just

273

arguing when we got there. But, listen, I do need to sort this out, Kate.' He dropped his hand onto her cheek. 'She wants to come to London tomorrow. There's no rush here, is there? We have plenty of time, yes?'

Tomorrow? Kate tried not to show her disquiet at the news.

Instead, she made herself nod and he pulled her up, and hugged her again. 'She's not going to let this go, so I need to sort it, so you and I can get on with what we're doing, OK?' She nodded against his chest, realizing she was becoming more familiar with the shape, the wide, neat boxer's shoulders, the flat muscular wall of his chest.

She had to trust him.

Both their lives were complicated. Jago's eyes drifted. 'Hey, look,' he murmured, jerking his head.

The rowing boat was drifting in the current.

'We can still take it back. Do you want to?'

She thought of the poor man with his wet dreadlocks, and the truth was that she really did want to take it back. But this exercise was about making a leap of faith. And Jago had taken a risk himself to help her, however mad it might seem, by stealing the boat. The least she could do was to try to let him help her.

So she shook her head, realizing she didn't want to laugh any more.

'OK, then, well done,' Jago said, packing up quickly and climbing on his bike. She followed. He leaned over and looked at her intently.

'You have amazing eyes, you know?' he said. 'I know it sounds cheesy, but I have to say it. I was trying to think what they remind me of. It was this lake I saw in India once in a sunset. Looked like the water was made of liquid gold.'

He hugged her again. Kate stayed in his embrace for a second, her anxiety about lifejackets and being arrested and drowning and lorries and sleepovers all put away for a little while. Replaced by one single thought.

Marla.

CHAPTER TWENTY-FOUR

Saskia switched Kate's dishwasher on, turned out the light and shut the kitchen door into the hallway, checking the clock as she went.

Kate was late tonight.

Had she gone out with this Jago character after her therapy?

Pausing in the hall to check there was no sound coming from Jack's bedroom upstairs, she walked into the sitting room and put her cup down. Turning on a late-night arts panel programme for company, she sat on the sofa and pulled Kate's laptop onto her lap.

Her face was burning with embarrassment.

Images of what had happened after work in town tonight kept coming back to her, turning her cheeks as pink as Mum's.

If she'd walked out of the office five seconds later it wouldn't have happened.

But she hadn't. And there, in front of her, on the High Street, was her old flatmate from Oxford Brookes, Marianne, carrying a dry-cleaning bag, her brunette bob gleaming in the sunlight. Probably, Saskia thought bitterly, containing her dress from the thirtieth birthday party that Saskia had not been invited to on Saturday night in Charlbury.

'Oh,' they both uttered awkwardly. 'Hi.'

Marianne glanced about nervously, as if seeking an escape route. 'How are you, Sass?' There was a chill to her voice.

'Good, thanks. How was your, um, birthday?' Saskia asked, before she could help it. Back at college, it would've been unthinkable that they would not have been present at each other's thirtieth.

'Good,' Marianne replied quietly. 'I'm sorry I didn't . . . it's just, with Jonathan and Christian being friends, and . . .'

Saskia couldn't help herself. 'It's OK, Marianne. How is he?'

Marianne pulled a face. 'Um, OK, considering.'

Saskia felt a flush of hope. 'Considering? You mean, considering the divorce?' she asked. Was it possible Jonathan was having second thoughts?

Marianne shook her head sharply. A shadow of anger passed across her face. 'No, Sass – considering what you did to him.'

Their eyes met for a second. Then Marianne glanced up the road. 'Listen, I'm sorry, but I've got to get the six o'clock train back.' She lifted an arm awkwardly. 'I'd better go.'

'Bye.'

Saskia nodded, stunned. Jonathan had *told* Marianne? He'd sworn he'd never tell anyone! What, now the divorce papers were signed and the money was amicably divided – including the deposit Richard had given them for their house – he was breaking his side of the promise?

Saskia watched Marianne marching down the road, terror creeping over her. Marianne and her husband Christian used the same contractors as Dad. If they knew what she'd done, it wouldn't be long before Dad did, too.

Saskia took a sip of tea, and sat back on Kate's sofa, blinking even harder than normal. Her eyes felt dry and sore. She imagined Richard's face when he received the news. Jonathan had been a coup for him. Bright, well-connected and successful on his own terms, yet never a threat to Dad. Everything Richard had wanted in a son-in-law. A perfect marriage to boast about at the golf club. Divorce had most certainly not been in Dad's plans.

Saskia glanced at the laptop. If ever she needed to get away from Richard, it was now. Pulling up an application form, she read through what would be required of her.

Hugo had escaped. Now it was her turn.

It took Saskia half an hour to complete the first part of the application. As she stood up to fetch more tea, she heard a movement above her.

'Where's my mum?' a voice said.

She looked up. Jack was leaning over the banister in his pyjamas.

'Snores – you've got to get to sleep! It's half ten on a school night. Your mum will be cross with me if she finds you up.'

'Why's she so late, though?'

Saskia sighed. Why did Kate always have to lie to him? 'She's just out with some friends.'

He gave her a look that said they both knew that wasn't true.

'Or one friend. I'm not sure, really. Maybe someone she works with.'

'Mum works at home. By herself.'

Saskia exhaled and sat on the bottom step. Bloody Kate. Leaving this to her again. She tried to keep her voice reassuring.

'Listen, Snores. Don't worry too much about it. If you want to know where she is, just ask her. Going out is a normal thing for an adult to do. You're just not used to her doing it, that's all.'

He shrugged.

'What's that you're reading?' she said, trying to distract him.

'Found it in the shed. It's about maths and stuff.'

'Is it, now, smartybum? Your dad was good at maths too. You get it from him. Well, it's time for lights out, so see you later.'

But he stood there stubbornly.

'Jack, what's the matter? Are you hearing noises again? Want me to check in your wardrobe'

He shook his head. 'But who's she gone out with?'

Saskia stood up, tired of being the go-between. Kate needed to sort this out. 'Listen, your mum will be back soon. Ask her tomorrow, OK? Now, listen, I have work to do. I'll come and check you in a minute.'

She waited till he disappeared, then went to switch the kettle back on. She checked the oven clock, irritated with Kate. Nearly 10.45 p.m.

Where was her sister-in-law?

Magnus sat on the other side of the wall, upstairs, reading through Saskia's application on his link to Kate's laptop.

Interesting.

With luck, she'd come back soon. He liked this blonde one. Liked watching her close up on the screen. Those big green eyes and that little worried face that you just wanted to squeeze into a smile.

He stopped and picked up Jack's football from the floor of his bedroom and twirled it on his finger.

'Brr, brr, brr,' he sang.

Next, he flicked on to Jack's Facebook page, and then onto Jack's friends' pages.

His pale eyes widened behind his glasses as he looked at one belonging to 'Gabe'. What was this? Sleeping on a trampoline on Saturday night. Out in the garden?

Magnus whooped loudly. The whoop of a man driving huskies across ice.

A bedroom door slammed down the hallway from his.

He made a face at the wall. These students weren't being very friendly to him. One of them kept asking him suspiciously which course he was doing at Oxford Brookes because they never saw him there. He'd made up something that sounded real: integrated visual computer studies. 'The smell comes right into my room,' he heard the bony one whine in the kitchen last night.

Never mind. This would all be over soon.

The child burst out of the bedroom, ran down to the front door and exited, racing to the side of the house.

Father was emerging from the basement door. His face was the colour of dried clay. Dust had turned his hair grey.

'Go there!' he yelled, pointing far from the house.

But the child froze on the spot, looking up.

There were more snakes on the wall. They were everywhere. They were writhing and spitting and squeezing the house to death. Large chunks of brick were starting to crumble off the wall as their tails smashed into it. They were not even chunks, like pieces of cake, but like what was left when you pulled a Lego tower apart, no discernible shape, just oblongs sticking out of squares, rectangles with sloped ends, where they'd taken the trim of the next brick with them.

Father ran back, and picked up and spun the child away onto the grass. He stood there, his hands by his sides, making strange sobbing noises.

The child watched, transfixed. The chunks, coated with white plaster, were smashing into the path below. Mortar dust puffed into the air like smoke signals.

Then, as the child realized that life would never be the same again, a whole block of wall cracked, then slipped downwards, before picking up speed and landing with an enormous crash.

Eyes wide, the child watched the rocking horse come into view through the hole.

A scream came from behind them, so piercing that both father and child put their hands to their ears, and spun round.

Mother was standing there, a half-empty basket of laundry held in a semicircle from her stomach.

The basket dropped to the floor as her hands flew to her own face.

The child saw a tiny vein burst in Mother's left eye, like red paint hitting water.

CHAPTER TWENTY-FIVE

Friday afternoon, and the traffic was light.

Kate free-wheeled down Headington Hill so fast that the wind pushed back the hair below her helmet like curtains in a tornado. A supermarket delivery lorry overtook her, only feet away, but she hardly noticed.

Her mind was elsewhere.

It was three days since she'd seen Jago by the river the night they'd stolen the rowing boat.

Three days without a word.

Kate checked behind her shoulder, then pulled out past a rotund man in a T-shirt and an ill-fitting suit on an old bike who was putting his brakes on every few seconds.

She pulled back in, and carried on sailing down the hill.

No, not a word from Jago since they'd ridden back along the river path to Blackwell's on Tuesday night. Not even a suggestion of when they'd meet again. Just one more kiss as he tied up his bike, and a distracted 'You did well, safe home' before he went off to Balliol, clearly impatient to ring Marla.

Kate free-wheeled through the green light at the bottom of Headington Hill, cycled in a steady rhythm towards Magdalen roundabout, flew around it and headed over the bridge and up the High Street. Three minutes later she stopped at Carfax cross-roads, waited for the traffic to break, pulled over at the corner of Cornmarket and Queen Street and dismounted.

She looked around.

The centre was packed today. The tidal pattern of the city was changing again. Tourists were starting to outnumber students, signalling the start of June. It was unusually warm, and legs were making their first nervous outings of the year in a variety of shorts. Kate took off her helmet and looked around, hoping for a glimpse of that cropped head or a reassuring snatch of Scottish accent. She allowed herself a little internal cheer of self-congratu-lation. Two and a half miles today. The furthest she'd cycled for five years on the road non-stop. And the fourth time she'd man-aged to cycle in traffic without stopping since stealing the rowing boat on Tuesday night.

Kate chained up her bike to a rack. The numbers were quiet, too. Present, but less insistent.

All thanks to Jago.

Who'd bloody disappeared, to London, presumably, with Marla.

Kate yanked the chain harder than she needed to, to check the bike was secured properly, then stood up and walked off down Cornmarket, trying to put Marla out of her mind, at least for the next ten minutes.

Winding her way through the tour groups and parents with buggies and boys on skateboards, she reconsidered the revelation she'd had only fifteen minutes ago, as she'd stood in a queue to buy a chicken from the organic butcher in Headington to roast for Jack tonight, before announcing that she was introducing a new weekly movie night at home for the two of them, and had bought the film he wanted to see.

There was a clue.

A clue that, for a moment, at least, would give Kate a break from the film that had been running in a loop in her own head for three days. 'Based on a true story', it could have been billed. It started with the facts. The scene where Jago disengaged from her on the jetty that Tuesday night, as the significance of Marla's second call finally registered on his face.

His ex-girlfriend desperately wanted to see him after three months.

The next scene had him waving Kate off before heading into Balliol to ring Marla to find out what was going on. 'I'm pregnant,' Marla said, in Kate's best American accent. 'From our last night together. I need to see you.' In Kate's imaginary narrative, Marla had then jumped on the red-eye from Paris, while Jago had driven straight to Heathrow. He had arrived to see Marla standing wanly at a distance. Not tall, dark and skinny, like Kate, but petite and curvaceous, with white-blonde hair, dark eyebrows and a cute little nose. They had run to each other, tears spilling down their faces, as Marla declared that she wanted to give it another try for the sake of the baby. She missed him. She'd move to Oxford, Edinburgh, anywhere, to be with him. It didn't matter how darn cold and damp it was.

And that was it.

THE END.

Kate moved sideways to avoid a man drawing a famous painting on Cornmarket's pavement in chalk.

But then, in the butcher's today, as Kate had looked down at the Doc Martens of the student in front of her, she remembered.

Her ankle boots.

Jago had put her ankle boots in his bag that Tuesday night to take to the heel bar for her the next day, because it had been closed.

So, if she were right, if he had driven off to London on

Tuesday night and been lying blissfully in Marla's arms ever since, Kate's boots would still be in his rucksack, lying abandoned in haste in his college room.

Or . . .

Kate prayed.

The little heel bar loomed ahead of her at the end of Cornmarket, its window half the width of the neighbouring French children's boutique and organic cafe.

Kate turned into the scruffy entrance, shuffling sideways to avoid hitting a rack of umbrellas and shoe polish right inside the door. The shop was gloomy and cramped. It appeared empty at first. Then a movement behind the counter told her she was wrong. A tiny ancient man with grey hair slicked into a sculpted wave on his head stood behind the counter, peering down at something. With great effort, like a tortoise from its shell, he lifted up his head to peer at her through his glasses.

'Oh. Hi,' Kate exclaimed. 'I was just wondering if my boots were ready. Black ankle boots, should be under the name "Kate"?'

The old man stopped. He wiped his hands on his apron and turned slowly, a deep bend in his back, to a shelf. He rummaged through a pile of plastic bags, then pulled out one.

Kate's heart leaped.

'Sorry,' she said to the elderly man as he handed them to her. 'Do you know what day these were brought in?'

The old man's whole body looked like it was sighing. He peered at the ticket.

'Wednesday,' he muttered.

'Really?' she smiled. So Jago hadn't gone straight to London the night of the canal boat. She could, at least, erase that particular awful scene from the film.

'How much do I owe you?' she said brightly.

'Ten pounds,' the old man said weakly, as if he were too exhausted to add 'please'. She handed him a note, took the boots with a cheerful 'thanks', and headed out of the shop, lost in thought.

Jago had still been thinking about her – on Wednesday, at least – regardless of Marla's intentions.

Kate returned up Cornmarket, cheered up, and retrieved her bike. She was about to turn back to Headington to rejoin the queue in the butcher's that she'd abandoned twenty minutes ago, when another thought occurred to her.

Perhaps Jago had never gone to London at all.

Perhaps he'd said 'no' to Marla on the phone that night, that he didn't want to see her. That he'd moved on. Met someone new? Perhaps he was sitting in his room right now, working. Thinking about Kate. Planning their next night out.

She looked over her shoulder.

If she went back down Cornmarket, she could take the route past Balliol back to Headington.

What harm would it do?

Kate turned, a flutter of anticipation in her stomach, pushed her bike down to the junction and turned right. Balliol's entrance was just visible from here. She cycled over to the left side of the road and took her time approaching the porter's gate. The gate was open for visitors, half of its wooden arch pushed back, revealing manicured lawns beyond.

She glanced through cautiously.

The wooden gate was as impenetrable to casual passers-by as a castle keep. To gain entry, she'd either have to ask for Jago blatantly at the porter's lodge, or pose as a tourist and pay an entrance fee. Either way, if she did see Jago, they'd both know there was nothing 'casual' about it at all.

She cycled on past.

She'd just have to hope that he'd spring one of his last-minute calls on her when she was least expecting it. And pray that, in the meantime, she didn't spot him and Marla rocking around town like the young couple from the other week, all tousle-haired and freshly emerged from bed.

It was just as Kate was starting to accelerate up Broad Street back to Headington that she heard her phone ring.

She stopped abruptly, forcing the cyclist behind to swerve around her crossly.

She pulled the phone from her pocket so fast she nearly dropped it.

'Hello?' she said hopefully.

'Kate? It's Gill.'

Shit. Gabe's mum. They'd been swapping phone messages all week, and she'd forgotten to try her again today. 'Hi, Gill.'

'Hi-ya,' Gill answered in her lazy voice, tinged with its student-protest self-righteous edge that Kate suspected she kept firmly as a rebellion against ever growing up, despite being close to her forties.

'Calling about tomorrow night.' Gill's tone was both teasing and antagonistic. 'Kate. Listen. Before you say anything, they'll be fine, love.'

Kate paused to make herself calm the irritation Gill always provoked in her. 'I'm sure they will be, Gill. It's just Jack said they were sleeping outside. By themselves?'

Gill gave a little tinkle of laughter, her humour at Kate's concerns clearly being relayed with exaggerated facial expressions for whoever was in the room with her. She then turned on the slow, patronizing voice that she presumably used for the elderly people she cared for at the retirement home in Cowley – probably irritating the shit out of them, too, Kate suspected. 'Listen, love. They'll be right outside in the garden at the back? It's not exactly the middle of a warzone. They're really looking forward to it, Jack especially.'

Kate grimaced into the phone. She *hated* it when Gill did this. Implied that she knew Jack better than Kate. It was too painful to believe that Jack's guard might come down in Gill's noisy, messy, laid-back house, with its Indian throws and candles and general air of stoned inertia, in a way that it never did with Kate.

When Kate said nothing, Gill carried on. 'Honestly, Kate, love, I can hear you worrying. You worry too much.'

Kate felt her hackles rise. If she said no, Jack would never forgive her. He might even mention it to Helen, who would in turn accuse Kate of stopping him having fun at what Helen's would surely perceive as a 'harmless' sleepover. She sighed. 'OK. Well. OK, then.'

Gill hesitated dramatically, to illustrate her shock. 'You're all right, then?'

'I said, it's fine.'

'Ooh. Well, that's a first!' Gill exclaimed in what was supposed to be a playful voice. 'We'll send him back with Gabe on Sunday, yeah?'

'OK, bye.' Kate mouthed a swear word at the phone, then said, 'Thanks.'

She shut the phone, and stood at the side of the road, fuming. Why had she thanked her?

'Cheer up, darling!' a man shouted at her from a passing van, looking back with a grin. 'Can't be that bad!'

Kate stuck a finger up at him, eliciting a howl of laughter from inside the cab.

'It will be OK . . .' she whispered to herself, shaking away the tears that threatened to come.

You are *not* cursed. Let Jack have his adventure, like you had yours by the canal boat.

Just because he's outside does not mean he'll be attacked.

Yet the anxiety was pummelling at her in a way it hadn't done for days.

She shook her head as the numbers broke loose and came flying at her.

She couldn't slip backwards. She couldn't.

Jago. She needed to speak to Jago.

She put out a hesitant hand and rang Jago's number.

To her consternation, it went straight to message.

'Erm, Jago. It's Kate. I'm outside, just passing Balliol. Just wondered if you fancied a coffee or a drink or something.' She sighed, aware of the panicked tone of her message. 'But maybe you're not there so . . . don't worry.'

She pressed the red button, and was about to put it back in her pocket.

Her phone rang in her hand.

'Kate? Jago,' said a Scottish voice.

'Oh. Hi,' she said, relief flooding through her. 'Sorry, I just . . .'

'No, it's fine. It's great to hear from you. It's just that I'm in London at the moment. I'm not there.'

She paused, shocked. She was right. He'd gone to Marla.

'Oh, well, don't worry, I just . . .'

'No, it's fine. How are you? Not been arrested by the rowing boat police yet then?'

She forced a laugh. 'No.' She tried to think of something else to say but all she could think of was Marla sitting right beside him.

'Listen. I'm glad you rang. I was going to ring you later anyway. What are you doing tomorrow night?'

She moved to let another cyclist past. 'Um, I haven't decided yet. Interesting you ask – Jack might be going to that sleepover I told you about, but . . .'

'Brilliant,' Jago said. 'So you're going to let him go? Well done. Well, do you fancy coming up to London, then?'

She pushed her hair away. 'Uh, I don't know. What did you have in mind?'

'Ah! Step Five of the experiment, of course.'

The thought of seeing him tomorrow thrilled her so much she didn't allow herself to feel nervous about what that might consist of. 'Yes.'

'Excellent. Well, can you meet me at . . . hang on, let me just check this . . .' She heard a rustle of paper. 'Highgate Tube?'

Kate frowned. Highgate? Where she used to live.

Jago heard her hesitation. 'Or, if you don't fancy it we can wait till I get back to Oxford next Friday . . .'

He was in London for another week? Could she do this? Leave Jack outside on a trampoline at Gabe's, and go to Highgate?

'Yes. I can come,' she said weakly.

'Great. I don't know what time yet so I'll ring you tomorrow to let you know. And don't worry about getting home. I've got the car, so I'll run you back to Oxford afterwards.'

Kate nodded. At least then she would only be round the corner from Jack as he lay in Gabe's garden on Saturday night. 'Oh. OK. Great, see you then,' she said.

'See you then!'

She put her phone away thoughtfully.

Highgate.

She tried to remember. Had she told Jago that she and Hugo lived there, that night they were in the secret garden?

And why hadn't he mentioned Marla?

She mounted her bike again, and cycled home, arriving back just before Jack and Gabe.

'Did you talk to Gabe's mum?' Jack called out as he came in, taking off his blazer.

'I said yes. But, God, Jack, I'm trusting you. If there's any funny business with Gabe or Damon . . . I mean it, you stay on that trampoline and don't move.'

She watched his face, waiting for him to explode with delight. And he did smile, but a flicker of something else passed across his face.

'Jack?' Kate asked uncertainly. 'What? You do want to go?'

'Yeah,' he said, putting his bag down, and running upstairs.

Confused, she stood in the hall, trying to work out what she'd glimpsed in his expression, and couldn't. To her sorrow, Kate realized she'd lost so much precious time with Jack over the years that she couldn't read him. She couldn't read *her own son*.

She walked back into the kitchen, determined that would change now.

Magnus saw Kate arrive back on her bike, then the boy, in his school uniform with his friend. The boys waved briefly at each other, then Jack entered the house.

He sat back, fingering the silver necklace he'd taken this afternoon from that woman's house on Walter Street. The window had been open again, making it easy. Taken him two seconds to lean in and whip away her bag. He also had her phone, which had some interesting photos on it. Very interesting photos.

He sat on his unmade bed, flicking through it, eating a chicken dish he'd found in Kate's fridge while she'd been out on her bike. It was good. Like the stew back home. He'd taken five spoonfuls, then wiped around the top with his finger before he put it back in the fridge so that the previous tideline disappeared and didn't give him away.

Magnus was about to drop his eyes back to his bowl of stew, when a movement caught his eye on his computer. He sat up and saw the skinny woman Kate had opened her own laptop and was looking at him with wide eyes. He jumped back, covering his mouth with his hand, for a second thinking she could see him.

'Jack,' she shouted. 'Have you been eating over the laptop?'

'No,' he replied. 'You told me not to.'

'You're sure? There's a crumb stuck in the letter J.'

Magnus stopped mid-chew, looking down at his bedspread, at the skinny woman's flapjack, which he was having for pudding.

He chewed again.

He'd have to be more careful or all the planning would have been for nothing.

CHAPTER TWENTY-SIX

The next morning, Jack jumped out of bed, almost banging his head on his bookshelf in haste. Ten past nine, his Arsenal clock said. The earliest he'd been up for a long time on a Saturday morning.

He grabbed the curtain and looked outside, squinting.

Sunny.

He frowned.

Ever since the Year Eight boys had been on Gabe's Facebook again this week, saying they were definitely coming on Saturday night, he'd been hoping for two things: one, that Mum wouldn't let him go to Gabe's and he could blame it on her; or two, that it would rain today and they couldn't sleep on the trampoline.

Rubbing his stomach, Jack picked up the Dr Who books he'd bought for Gabe's birthday present. Beside them he noticed a paper bag Mum must have put there yesterday. He opened it and found a Dr Who birthday card. Nervously, he pulled out the wrapping paper. Also Dr Who. He sighed. At least she was trying. It was better than last year, when she'd made him give Gabe a card with a pink flower on it that she found in the kitchen drawer because she'd been too lost in her head to remember to buy one.

Jack stood up straight and stretched. He opened his wardrobe to find his jeans.

He stopped.

His trainers were lined up again on the bottom shelf, not how he'd left them. Had Mum been in here, rooting around in his things to see if he had any secrets?

With a gulp, Jack thought about his Facebook page. The last time he'd used it on her laptop when she'd been out, he'd forgotten to remove all traces of it with the laptop's 'clear history' button, and it was just luck she didn't find it. Jack bit his thumbnail. If she ever found out, he couldn't bear to think about the worry that would appear on her face. Now he'd glimpsed his old mum again in the kitchen, he wanted her back twice as much.

Feeling a little sick, Jack pulled on his T-shirt.

He padded to the door, and opened it quietly in case Mum was still asleep. Her door, however, was open, her bed already made. He stood there, relieved. The men had come to take away the gate yesterday when he was at school. He ran his eyes over the holes in the ceiling and floor that they had filled in with plaster. He and Mum hadn't even discussed it at dinner last night. The gate had just gone. There were other things to think about, anyway. The Year Eight boys, obviously, and the roast chicken and rhubarb crumble that Mum had made, which were so delicious that he'd had two portions of each. The film that she'd surprised him with was good too. Not that Mum had watched it properly. It was supposed to be movie night for the two of them, but he'd seen her eyes drift back into her secret place a few times. At least she was trying. Then they'd talked about the film when he was getting ready to go to bed.

Jack was starting to walk across the hall to the bathroom, when he heard Mum's mobile ring down below in the hall.

'Oh – hi, Jago,' she said in this happy voice.

Jack paused mid-step. The action forced him to put more weight back on the foot behind, making the floorboard creak heavily.

'Oh. Hang on,' Mum said, lowering her voice. He heard her pace across to the sitting room and shut the door.

Jack tiptoed back into his room. He crouched down, lifted his rug, and lay, his ear to the gap in the stripped floorboards.

'Uh, eight? That should be OK,' came a muffled voice from the room below. 'Should I bring anything?'

There was a pause. Then his mother laughed.

Jack put his hand flat on the floor.

A proper laugh. Like the one in the kitchen when they were talking about Mr Sausage Fingers.

But not with him, with this man called Jago on the phone.

Jack crawled to the bed, retrieved the book that he taken from the shed, and checked the name.

Him.

He flicked to the man's smiling photo.

Was this the 'friend' Mum was out with when Aunt Sass was here the other night?

He skimmed through the pages, reading some of the numbers.

He hesitated, and did a double-take.

That was interesting.

Picking up a red felt-tip that was beside his bed, he marked something in the margin.

'Jack!' his mum shouted up. 'I'm going to head up to London for the evening to see an old friend while you're at Gabe's. What time are you going?'

An old friend? Jago wasn't the name of any of her and dad's old friends who sent him birthday cards. Why didn't she just say 'friend'?

'Six.'

'Could we go slightly earlier?'

'Probably,' he replied, placing his hand on his stomach as the spasm gripped hard.

Before, he'd just been scared of the Year Eight boys, but now he was worried about this Jago man too.

Jack rubbed his stomach to soothe it, trying not to cry.

He didn't want Mum to go.

By the time five o'clock came round, the cramp in Jack's stomach was so bad that he had been to the bathroom three times and thought he might be sick.

Mum came downstairs, wearing black jeans and her old black leather jacket with a hoodie underneath. She had that black stuff on her eyes again, and her lips were, for once, not stuck inside her mouth, and had something shiny on them. She smiled that nice sparkly-eyed smile again.

'Do you need any help?' she asked, pointing at Gabe's books, which he was trying to wrap.

'No, thanks,' he muttered, even though he'd had to rip off the sticky tape twice because it kept wrinkling up.

'Right, we'd better get going,' she said, pulling on her ankle boots.

Jack surveyed her from under her fringe.

He wanted to tell her so badly about the Year Eight boys.

Yes, Gabe would be furious at him, but anything right now was better than knowing that the Year Eight boys were coming in the middle of the night, when all the adults were asleep.

Could he tell her? She had been better recently. Maybe she wouldn't panic. Maybe she'd just be calm and talk to Gabe's mum about it and it would be OK.

Jack opened his mouth.

'Mum?' he started.

'What the hell is this?' she exclaimed.

She was staring at her ankle boot, turning it sideways.

'What?'

'The heel's too short. Has he given me the wrong ones back?'

Kate whipped off the boot and looked inside. 'That's so weird. They're definitely my boots but that old man's chopped about an inch and a half off the heel. What the hell is going on?'

'What do you mean?' Jack said, starting to feel cross with her. He was trying to tell her something important and all she was thinking about was boots and dressing up to see Jago Martin.

'Nothing. It's just strange.'

'Can you still wear them?'

'Good question, Captain,' she winked at him, pulling on both boots. He hated it when she called him that. It was a stupid word that she used, he suspected, because she didn't know what else really to call him. His mum stood up, flexing her toes inside the black leather, and moved from foot to foot. 'They actually still work because the leather's so soft. It's odd, though. Maybe the old heel was so worn down he had to make them shorter. Never mind.'

She picked up her bag, and put her hand on the door.

'Right – sorry, Jack, what were you saying?'

Even though they had been shortened, the heels still made her taller. She looked pretty again, Jack thought. Damon's big brother Robbie had said she was 'hot' the other day, and he supposed that's what he meant too. Her eyes were not made of glass, today, anyway. They looked as if the sun had shone so hard into them that they had burst into flames.

Jack bit his fingernail. How come this man Jago could make her look happy like this, but he couldn't?

He tried to think. If he did tell her about the Year Eight boys now, her eyes might glaze over again. Her skin would go tight and white and her shiny lip would disappear back inside her mouth.

He realized she was regarding him closely. 'Jack? Are you OK? If you don't want me to go to London, I won't.'

He forced himself to smile. 'I'm fine.'

'Sure?'

'Uhuh.'

'OK. Got your stuff?'

She was really looking at him. Right into his eyes.

He nodded.

Then, without warning, she pulled him in for a hug. Not an anxious, sweaty hug, but the type of kind cuddle Nana gave him – soft and reassuring, where the adult was in charge of the hug. As he pulled away from her awkwardly, she caught him on the side of the face with an unexpected kiss.

He guessed she was trying to find the right words.

'Jack, please, tonight, be sensible. And if you're worried about anything – and I mean anything – call me, OK. I'll come straight back.'

He went to pick up his bag. She carried on talking as she opened the front door.

'You know what, Jack? After what's happened to you, I think it's amazing how well you do at so many things and you have good friends, too. Dad would be so proud of you. And when I get back I want to tell you about two more nice things I've got planned. I really enjoyed movie night last night. I think it's time we had a bit more fun. OK?'

He walked through, hiding his face, feeling tears spring back into his eyes. Desperate for her not to go.

CHAPTER TWENTY-SEVEN

Kate arrived at Paddington Station at six-thirty, having fought the urge twice to text Gill a complete lie, that Jack had a cold and ask if the boys could sleep inside tonight.

Don't think about it.

As always, after Oxford, London appeared to be in mid-tornado. Heels, suitcases, hands, words, blasted in all directions. Laughter, yelling, requests for directions to the start of a new life, maps, interview suits, couriers, squealing brakes and frustrated horns.

The mass purpose of intent of this huge city lifting her up and shooting her along, like flotsam on surf.

Kate stood still among the rush of people, feeling her energy levels instantly rising, her posture straightening.

One word echoed around her head, as it always did when she arrived here.

Home.

The Tube from Paddington to King's Cross was jam-packed: the Saturday shoppers and tourists working their way around central London like giant multi-legged creatures, carrying coffee, bags, maps, matinee programmes as they swayed from carriage handles and raced for seats.

The last time she'd been here, a few weeks ago for the hospital scan, she had ridden amid the throngs of the Tube, thinking London was where she and Jack needed to be again. Away from Helen and Richard's disapproving looks and endless excuses for 'popping in'. Back in a world where life raced on, not floated by.

But today, as Kate stood on the Northern Line platform at King's Cross, she felt less sure.

The Northern Line had been their Tube, their carriage to Highgate.

The journey home.

It had been four years since she had been on the Northern Line. Four years since she had been to Highgate.

The sensation of loss was so sudden that Kate stumbled back against the wall when the first train came.

She let that train go, and waited three minutes for the next, and then the next.

As a fourth train appeared and left she shook herself. If she was going to move on in her life, repair her relationship with Jack, start a relationship with Jago, she had to go and say good-bye to Hugo properly now.

So, when the fifth train came, she pushed herself away from the wall. She propelled herself through the doors before a compulsion to run away from the platform took over, and found a seat in the half-empty carriage.

The train kept stopping.

Each time, inside the dark tunnel, the window reflected back to Kate the reason why it had been four years.

The empty seat beside her, where Hugo used to sit.

Flashing at her as the train picked up speed again. Empty, empty, empty.

The seat of a ghost.

The hundred steep stairs from the bowels of Highgate Tube station up to the pavement teetered above her.

She leaned against the wall, sensing her heart putting up its shutters.

If she closed her eyes, she could feel Hugo's hand on her back, pushing her up the stairs after a night in town, his voice echoing along the tiled walls.

'Come on, you lazy cow, hurry up. I've recorded *Match of the Day*.'

'Can I just say that I am not lazy – I am drunk.'

'Lazy and drunk.'

She touched the handrail where she had bent over laughing, as he waited, that easy smile on his face.

'Come on, I mean it. Hurry up,' he had said, with a slap on her bum. 'Or I'll leave you here for the muggers.'

'No, you won't, because if you do that, then you won't be getting any later.'

Hugo had snorted. 'Yeah, well, I'm not going to get any later, anyway, am I? Five quid, you're asleep on the bed with your jeans on three minutes after we get in.'

And she had sniggered so hard, she'd bent up double, and he'd given this sort of roar, and wrapped her up under his arm and raced her up the stairs, squealing.

Today, she walked the stairs alone, each step a mile high.

And then up the steep lane alone, towards Highgate Village.

Some of the Edwardian house fronts looked familiar, owned by people she'd once known. Anouk, the Dutch mum, from NCT;

Jean from the Highgate History Society, who had told them so much about the history of their house; Hugo's old schoolfriend Frank, who had moved in with his wife Sarah just before Hugo was murdered, and joined their Tuesday night pub quiz team. Kate peered in and saw a child's bike. Were Frank and Sarah still there? Leading the life she and Hugo would have had?

She made her way to the top of the lane and the busy main street of Highgate Village. Nothing had changed. Beyond it, at the bottom of the steep drop of Highgate Hill, lay central London, miles in the distance, the skyscrapers like icebergs emerging from the Arctic mist of today's overcast sky. A couple in their thirties walked across the junction in front of her, both in well-cut black coats, the girl laughing with a flash of red lipstick.

They could have been her and Hugo, on their way back from pushing Jack's buggy around nearby Hampstead Heath, cheeks flushed, eyes bright, on their way to buy cake from the deli before going home. Or returning from a shopping trip to the farmers' market, Indian breads and Moroccan harissa in rucksacks on their backs, Hugo's arm around her shoulder, as they strolled along the cobbled narrow streets of this old London village, with its walled gardens and studded wooden gates, pleased with themselves that, after all that had happened to Kate, they had created this good life for their family.

'A fine, fun-loving, hard-working young couple, ready to walk through life shoulder to shoulder', as her dad had said in his speech, the night of their wedding, none of them realizing he would not be there to see it.

Just trying to make a good life for Jack.

The shutters were half open on the house.

It took her a minute to check, but they were the ones Hugo

had tracked down in the salvage yard in Enfield and pains-takingly stripped back to their natural pine in his workshop in the garden, one by one, then lovingly waxed.

The new owners had painted them white.

Kate walked around the square twice, fighting a new wave of nausea at the sight of it, peeking over at the four-storey house from different angles. The half-open shutters on the ground floor revealed a glimpse of the jaw-dropping view across London at the back of the house. There was a dining table, just where theirs used to be. The table they had sat at talking about their plans, looking over the Soviet-scale 1970s estate in the distance, with its ever-changing life stories played out on stacks of balconies and in rows of windows, imagining how the magnolia tree would look in spring when its branches came into their own.

She sat on a bench opposite and scanned the house further in stolen glances, trying to remember what it had looked like when those windows were full of chattering guests drinking champagne at Hugo and David's famous 'open house' parties, to celebrate their latest restoration project and act as show-house to prospective clients. It had been a different life. One she could no longer believe she'd been part of. Windows full of their friends and family, estate agents, their architect, work contractors, old clients, new clients, solicitors, bank people, Georgian Society friends; all of them drinking Hugo's fine wine, celebrating Hugo, David and Kate's latest project and toasting the next. She glanced up to the square black roof and small windows of the Georgian attic. Jack's playroom. The place she would sit rocking him after she and Hugo had argued – the pair of them exhausted from the sleepless nights – about who was doing their fair share of the childcare and cooking now Jack was born, why they never had sex any more. Rocking Jack, looking down at his tiny face, wondering secretly if it would be possible to love her and Hugo's next child as much as she loved this one.

Worrying about a child who would never now exist.

She wandered back through Highgate Village, listening to passing chatter about rugby scores and film reviews and property prices. The pinboard outside the public toilet was crammed with notices. Hundreds of leaflets, in eye-popping colours, fought for attention, fluttering off all sides of the board, offering sessions and lessons in tai chi, Japanese, meditation, singing, Brazilian dance, osteopathy, theatre, book groups, writing groups, mother and baby jogging, cranio-sacral therapy . . .

The endless promise of the city. A promise of an exciting race through life.

Kate suddenly felt exhausted.

A pang for gentle, calm Oxford came out of nowhere.

As Kate turned, she spied her old theatre actress neighbour Patricia, with her distinctive grey beehive, emerging from the delicatessen, chatting to a bespectacled man with a chihuahua. Desperate not to be seen, Kate dived into the nearest pub and ordered a bourbon from a barmaid she didn't recognize.

'No – I heard her. Jo definitely said peach juice!' The cosy, wooden walls echoed Kate's own words from long ago back at her as she sat down.

The infamous bellini quiz question moment. Crammed in here, with their Highgate gang every Tuesday for the pub quiz.

'I'm telling you, mate, she said peach schnapps. She's trying to get out of it because she cocked up!' Seb had yelled at Hugo, who threw down the pencil in mock-anger to show he was having none of their excuses about one teammate hearing another teammate's answer wrongly, and losing them the quiz.

'Seb. You're a wanker!' Jo had shouted.

'One bloody point – they're going to beat us now,' Hugo groaned. 'Use your bloody ears, Seb. . .'

Did Jo and Seb or any of the others even live here any more?

She had stopped answering their Christmas cards years ago, tired of their awkward messages and clear struggles on the envelope about how to address it to her and Jack without making Hugo's absence any more obvious than it already was.

Mrs H Parker and Family.

Kate and Jack Parker.

The Parker Family.

The Parker Family Minus Hugo, who Was Brutally Murdered.

The old familiar thick belt of grief tightened around her middle and squeezed hard.

Kate jumped up and chucked back her bourbon.

No.

She had to get out of here.

She slammed down her glass, grabbed her coat and ran out of the empty pub.

The sun had completely disappeared now behind the murky sky. Clouds gathered ominously above her, even though the June air was still thick and warm. She ran across the roundabout crossing, picking up speed as she hit the lane back down to the Tube again. Her newly heeled boots thumped on the pavement as she set off at a pace down the hill.

'Kate?' she heard Patricia shout, surprised, the well-enunciated, loud vowels of the actor reaching out down the street to catch her.

But she kept running.

Leaving Patricia behind.

Leaving Hugo behind.

Leaving it all behind.

She couldn't let herself feel that physical grief. Not any more.

It was time to move on.

This was not home.

London was not home. Not any more.

This was a place of ghosts, and memories that had rotted like old fruit.

She had to find her way to the future

She needed to see Jago.

Jago was the key.

CHAPTER TWENTY-EIGHT

Maybe it was the change in weather, but London looked mono-chrome today compared to the pale gold of summery Oxford. Archway Road roared unpleasantly with thick lines of traffic. Flowers that had burst forth in bright shades in the unusually early summer sat with their heads bowed in the still, fume-filled air.

Kate crossed back over Archway Road and started down the steps in the steep bank towards the Tube entrance.

'Please be here,' she whispered.

She reached the bottom step and peered around to the left.

Jago was standing, reading the *Guardian* just under the tunnel entrance, at the top of the stairs down to the platform.

Just seeing him gave her back a surge of the inner resolve she thought she'd lost today.

'Hi!' she had to stop herself saying too loudly, walking towards him.

'Hey!' He was wearing the fitted dark jacket again, and walking boots under dark khaki trousers. 'You look nice,' he said, putting his arm round her and kissing her. She wrapped her arms around him and stood there, against his chest, feeling the warmth of his body, refusing to pull back from the hug.

'You OK?' He squeezed her gently.

'Hmm,' she said, staying there. 'Just glad to see you. Strange day.'

'Ah,' he said rocking her gently. 'Shit. Of course – Highgate. I didn't think.'

She pulled back reluctantly. 'I thought that's why you'd chosen it.'

'No, not at all. It was actually Highgate Woods, I wanted to bring you to.' He pointed his finger in the opposite direction to Highgate Village. 'Sorry. I didn't even click that they were the same thing. I don't know London. Is it a bit close for comfort?'

She shook her head, relieved. 'No. No, it's fine. As long as we don't have to go into the village.'

His brow wrinkled. 'What – has it been a bit weird?'

'A little.'

'OK. Well then, I think a drink's definitely in order. I saw a pub on the main road.'

She nodded.

And, with that, he rolled up the newspaper and offered her his hand.

She took it, relieved that she did not have to worry about anyone seeing them here, and walked up the slope, trying not to think of the hundred times she had done it with Hugo.

The pub was not one she and Hugo had visited. It was large and anonymous, with rows of tables and a sports screen in the corner. She sat down as Jago went to the bar.

'What's that?' she asked, as Jago rested two shorts on the table.

'Whisky doubles. Give us courage.' He looked around approvingly. 'Nice. Good table. Not a toilet or fire extinguisher in sight.'

She made a face at him but was secretly pleased. He was right. She hadn't even thought about it. She waited for him to take off his jacket.

'Aren't you warm?' she said, taking a sip. The whisky followed the bourbon down, turning her insides to fire.

'Yes. But I can't take it off.'

'Why?'

He tapped the side of his nose.

'What? The jacket is part of the plan too, is it? Oh God.' She pointed at herself. 'Is that why you told me to wear a hoodie?'

'All will be revealed,' Jago said, drinking his whisky. 'So, how've you been? You let Jack go on his sleepover then?'

She made a face. 'I'm trying not to call the mum right now.'

'Really? Well, don't. He'll love it.'

'But I am feeling good. Better.'

Jago put down his glass. 'You look much brighter.' He looked at her appraisingly, then grinned and leaned forward and kissed her softly on the lips, before pulling back. 'Sorry. Been thinking about doing that all week.'

Kate blushed. If he'd been thinking of getting back with Marla he wouldn't have said that, surely? 'Don't be sorry. Well, I don't know what you've done, but I'm really not thinking so much about the numbers at all. Just a few times a day, and I can stop myself quickly.'

'Seriously? That's amazing, Kate. To be honest, after the canal boat debacle, I thought you might pull out . . .'

Kate took another sip of whisky. 'No, it's been a good week. The best I can remember for ages. Anyway, how are things with you?' She hesitated. 'With Marla. What happened?'

Jago sighed heavily. She scrutinized his face, searching for something that might say: 'Since I last saw you I have been in London making passionate love to my American ex-girlfriend, who has dropped the amazing news that I am about to be a father, so, after tonight, you won't see me any more – bye.'

But there was nothing.

'Or should I not ask,' she tried, desperate for some sort of idea of whether it was really over or not.

He put his glass down. 'I'll tell you later, I promise. Right now, however, we have my dastardly plan to carry out, so no distractions. I'm a bit nervous about this one myself.'

'You're nervous? What the hell are we doing?'

'Well, it's a bit risky, but as you've now foolishly revealed your rather impressive adventurous past to me, I think we should go for it.'

She grimaced. 'OK. But can we please not do something illegal this time. I have to think about Jack. And no more boats.'

Jago laughed. 'Ah. OK. Well, it's funny you should say that – what about bats?'

She thought she'd misheard. '*Bats?*'

'No bat phobias?'

She examined his expression. '*Bats?* No, but . . .'

'Good, because I'm taking you bat-watching in Highgate Woods. Have you done it before?'

She finished her whisky. 'No. I'm surprised you got tickets – don't you have to book months ahead?'

Jago winked. 'Ah. Now, I said I was taking you on a bat-watch. I didn't say I was taking you on the official bat-watch. And it may not end up being bats that we actually watch.'

'What do you mean?'

He took a final swig and put his glass down. 'Now, that would be spoiling the fun. Right, come on. Let's go.' Jago looked outside. He checked his watch, then looked back at her. He folded his arms on the table and leaned forwards on them until they were touching hers.

'Did I say, I've got the car? I can take you home afterwards.'

Their eyes met. Kate felt her cheeks flush again, remembering the gentle trail of his finger across her body. He beckoned her with his eyes, and she leaned forwards to meet his second, longer kiss.

They entered Highgate Woods ten minutes later, through Onslow Gate, standing back to allow the last of the day's buggies and joggers and dog-walkers out. A thick canopy of hornbeams and oak trees announced the start of the dense, ancient seventy-acre wood. Jago dropped his eyes as they walked onto the main path. He pulled up his hood, obscuring his face, and nodded to her to do the same. 'This way,' he muttered, taking her hand.

Kate did as she was asked, dipping her head down.

There was a noise behind her. She turned to see two small groups enter behind them. They were heading down the main path, which she knew led to the rangers' hut and cafe in the middle of the wood. One group consisted of two loud, well-spoken men in their late thirties, accompanied by – and happily ignoring – two boys a little younger than Jack, with fashionable long shaggy haircuts and expensive fleeces, who fought with sticks and yelled at each other in confident mini versions of their fathers' voices. A few steps behind was a separate group of two women in their early twenties, speaking to each other politely in heavy English, one with a Spanish accent, one possibly Polish. Lonely au pairs who've met through the school playground, Kate guessed.

'Oi,' Jago whispered, touching her arm.

'What?'

Keeping his head down, he motioned sideways. Checking there was no one else behind them, and that no one from either group was looking back, he pulled her abruptly off the main path onto a smaller one that forked to the left. He broke into a fast walk.

'Where are we going?' she whispered.

Jago held his finger to his lips. He led Kate down yet another path, then forked left again. Then, without warning, he pulled her off it.

A giant fallen oak lay on the ground. Jago motioned for her to crouch down with him behind it. How did Jago know where they were? she thought, looking around at the thicket of trees. She'd come to this wood at least twice a week for years with Jack till he was five, and she had still occasionally become lost due to the lack of landmarks. Had Jago memorized a map?

'OK?' he said, turning round.

'Oh, yes. Having a lovely time, thanks,' she deadpanned, picking an insect from her face.

He grinned. 'It won't be much longer. The rangers are going to lock the park gates in a minute. They'll come through looking for stragglers, so stay down.'

'They're going to lock us in? I didn't know they did that.'

'At night, yes.'

On cue, a distant roar of engines drifted across the woods.

'Ssh,' Jago hissed, putting his arm round her.

Kate crouched down into him.

The ranger's truck passed on the other side of the trunk.

Kate's stomach started to churn.

She looked around at the darkening wood and thought of Jack. Quickly, she whipped out her phone and texted:

are you all right?

She waited, but nothing came back. He was probably too embarrassed in front of his friends to reply, she thought, putting her phone away.

Jago leaned into her ear. 'The bat-watchers gather by the wildlife hut, for the ranger talk. Then they give them bat detectors and set off when it's properly dark.'

'Right. So what are we doing? Stealing the rangers' sandwiches from their hut?'

'No, but that's not a bad idea. I haven't had any tea.'

She snorted suddenly, and put her hand over her mouth as he poked her in the side. 'No. We're going to build on our canal boat escapade. Step Five: *Monster in the Dark*.' He pointed at her. 'That's you, by the way. The monster.'

'What do you mean?'

Jago pushed her hair away from her face, trailing a finger across her cheek as he did it. Any resistance she felt to tonight's experiment started to drain away.

'I'll tell you in a minute.' He looked back up. 'Right. They've gone. Scared?' he whispered.

'What do you think?' she said sarcastically.

She watched him take a black box out of his pocket. He shook it and it made a crackling sound.

'What's that?'

He gave her a mischievous grin. 'I got it off the internet. Are you ready?'

She shrugged.

'Good. Come on, then.' He grabbed her hand and headed off through the woods.

They crept along the lane towards the rangers' hut, staying among the trees. Gradually, a murmuring of voices reached them. The wildlife hut loomed ahead. Kate surveyed its familiar shape with a shock.

This place?

She'd completely forgotten about it.

A hundred potent recollections filled her mind. Jack had loved that hut. How many times had she taken him to see the wildlife exhibits, opening the nesting boxes and crouching down beside the stuffed fox.

314

As they crept along through the trees, more buried memories came back to her. Jack had been a *different child* then. A child who whined like normal children. Cried if she didn't let him stop to colour in the sheets the rangers left in the hut. Laughed if she chased him around the cricket field. Let her kiss his cheeks and ears again and again, when she caught him, then returned them to her, the kisses of a child; soft, wet, toddler lips hungry on her cheeks.

As Jago pulled her along, Kate looked back in the direction of Highgate Village.

And then those men had come to their house one night and . . .

For the first time in years, Kate felt that sickening hatred return.

Maybe it was being back in Highgate after four years, but with a painful clarity, she saw the long-term consequences of the men's actions. At the time, they'd just stolen Hugo. Now she realized how much else they'd taken. They'd ripped her and Jack from their home and friends, from Jack's school, and forced them to move far away. They'd given her no choice but to rely on Richard and Helen. They'd turned her into a nervous wreck. Turned Jack into a fragile, frightened boy who had to turn to Richard and Helen or his friends, even his friend's mother, because Kate was so damaged, so lost to him . . .

Jago put out a hand, making Kate jump. They stopped behind a thick trunk.

'OK. We'll wait here till they start moving across the field,' Jago said.

'I still don't get this.' She heard a tone of bitterness in her voice, and tried to eliminate it. It wasn't Jago's fault.

Jago took her hands.

'Kate,' he whispered. 'You're convinced you're cursed. That

you and Jack are fated to fall into the path of bad people. The burglars in Oxford. The poacher who shot the deer. The robbers who stabbed Hugo . . .' She winced. 'But you're not. You've just had some really bad luck. We all do at some point. You took control of the numbers at the canal boat. Now I want you to take control of those monsters that scare you.'

Kate shivered, despite the warm air.

'How?'

'I want you to become one. See how it feels.'

She shook her head, not understanding.

Jago ushered her forwards.

The sky was darkening now, but in the distance, crossing the wide open acres of the cricket field encased by forest, she could see the torchlight movements and shadowy outlines of a group of twenty bat-watchers. She could hear the boisterous boys with long hair shouting from here. Two rangers with torches walked beside the pack, talking.

'Them,' Jago said, pointing.

Kate followed his finger and saw the young au pairs at the edge of the group.

CHAPTER TWENTY-NINE

Jack sat on Gabe's bed, looking out of the window into the garden, the lacy outline of the tall trees waving against a dark sky. Gabe's house wasn't as big as theirs, but the garden went on forever, disappearing round a bend where Gabe's mum grew her vegetables, and down to the fence, where the trampoline lay out of sight of the house.

Gabe's mum hadn't been quite truthful with his mum about where it was situated. She'd made it sound on the phone as if it was outside her house, but Gabe's bedroom was next to hers, and you couldn't see it from there.

The clock said half-past nine. They'd had their pizza and watched a film. It was time for the sleepover.

Gabe's mum stared through his bedroom window.

Jack prayed, his hand on his stomach trying to calm the burning sensation inside.

'You know, I think it'll be fine, boys, yeah?' she said, scratching the blue scarf she often wore wrapped around her head. 'I thought it was going to rain earlier, but it's still warm. You still up for it?'

Jack looked at Gabe, hoping he'd be brave enough to say he was scared of the Year Eight boys, too, and call it off.

'Yeah!' Damon said, jumping off the bed.

'Yeah!' Gabe copied him.

Jack tried to smile but right now he wasn't sure he could stand up, his stomach was so sore from the spasms.

Gabe's mum turned. 'Right, you lot, grab your sleeping bags and let's go, yeah?'

Gabe jumped up.

'But what about . . .?' Jack whispered at Gabe. Gabe tried to look unconcerned, probably because Damon was there. 'It'll be cool, don't worry.'

Jack stood up uncertainly, and they all trooped downstairs. Suddenly he didn't like Gabe's mum as much. His mum did lots of things wrong but at least she tried to keep him safe. Jack gathered up his sleeping bag and felt his mobile in his pocket, remembering Mum's words that he could ring her.

Gabe's mum was right. It was hot and sticky outside. They tramped down the long lawn, till they reached the vegetable patch, the light from the kitchen disappearing behind them as they turned the bend. Damon was making silly faces with the torch.

Jack looked around, worried. Gabe's house was semi-detached, with an alleyway next to it, so the Year Eight boys could get down the side and climb over the fence.

'Right you lot, have fun!' Gill called. 'I'll leave the key under the mat at the back, Gabe, if you need to use the loo – no peeing on my carrots. See you in the morning!'

She walked off, leaving them to line up their sleeping bags on the surface of the trampoline. They put down their Deadly 60 cards and torches.

'This is fucking wicked,' Damon laughed, using the swear words they all used whenever adults weren't there.

'Yeah!' Jack said. In the light of the torch, Gabe was smiling, but Jack saw him look at the fence a couple of times, too.

Jack checked his watch. Only 9.40 p.m. Nine hours to go. He crawled inside his sleeping bag and put his hand his stomach to try to relieve the cramp, averting his eyes from the alleyway.

CHAPTER THIRTY

Kate watched the young au pairs on the cricket field.

A ranger was shining a torch in their direction, and it briefly illuminated them. The Spanish one was slightly heavy, wearing a light coat and had a bright smile. The other one had a long dark ponytail, and a square face, and was as skinny as Jack, and not much taller. Kate watched their awkward stances, knowing they were new to all this. Still finding out where they fitted in, in this enormous metropolis.

'Why them?' She turned to Jago.

'Why not?'

'Because they look like nice girls.'

'You've got to get out of this way of thinking, that how you behave controls your fate. Fate is fate. We all have bad luck sometimes.'

'But they're just young. That guy on the boat at least looked like he'd . . .'

'Kate. You're not going to murder them.'

She rolled her eyes.

'Please. We'll be out of here in half an hour and I won't let anything bad happen to you, or them, I promise. I just want you to follow them for a bit in the dark. See what it feels like. It'll be good for you. Now, listen, I'm going over to the field.'

'What?' she said alarmed.

Jago glanced up. If the moon was usually visible from here, it was now hidden deeply from sight behind charred clouds. Kate realized she could hardly see his face. She looked back in the direction of the cricket field, which was becoming difficult to make out. The torch had moved ahead of the au pairs, and the girls had disappeared into the dark cloak that fell over the cricket ground, inside this thick bowl of forest that sharply cut out the city lights behind it.

'It gets so dark inside the trees – you can't see twenty feet beyond your face. I'm hoping the rangers won't notice me now, as long as I keep inside the shadows. And while I'm doing that, I want you to head that way –' he pointed to the right – 'and take the path behind the trees. Follow it to end up near the cricket scoreboard. Wait behind it. Just make this noise –' he made a five-beat clicking noise, with his tongue, that could have been a bird pecking at a tree – 'and I'll find you.'

'But I . . .' she began to protest.

He squeezed her hand. 'Try it.'

Kate tried out the noise, shaking her head at the ridiculousness of it, and he gave her the thumbs-up. To her shock, he then finally unzipped his jacket, revealing underneath it a dark fleece with some sort of badge on the chest. With his khaki trousers and black bat detector, she realized what he could pass for.

A Highgate Woods park ranger.

Before she could open her mouth to exclaim, Jago pulled out the black box and slipped off into the dark.

She was on her own.

Half an hour, he said. And this would be over.

Nothing bad would happen. He promised.

She waited until she thought she could make out Jago's

shadow emerging from the trees. When rangers shone the torches, she could see a few of the people pointing black boxes at the sky, and hear the young boys yelling as a high-pitched tutting noise over the airwaves indicated a bat. All faces pointed upwards. Small groups started to scatter left and right in the darkness as bats were spotted, the two rangers accompanying some of them. It was then that she saw Jago do it. The dark outline of his head moved beside the two au pairs, who were standing nervously at the edge, presumably too polite to ask someone to share their bat detector with them.

She saw the shape of the Spanish girl's nose as she turned towards Jago, and Jago's cheekbones lift as he smiled and handed her his bat detector, checking the other rangers weren't looking over. The second au pair turned, and the three of them spoke.

Kate started to move as well as she could in the blackness of the woods. Uneasily, she crept to the rangers' hut, then down behind the cricket field.

She stole along the boundary, holding onto tree branches, deep in the shadows. The shouts of the bat-watchers drifted across the cricket field from different directions now, fifty yards apart. She could make out the young boys in the middle of the field with some sort of neon glowsticks snapped to their wrists, running around randomly, yelling and playfighting.

Kate felt her way to the scoreboard and settled herself behind it.

From here, she could make out the distant outline of the wildlife hut again. So many happy memories with Jack in this place destroyed.

The men who killed Hugo would not leave her mind.

She pictured them for the first time in years, leering and swearing at her in court.

Those angry fists they gestured with, the hands that had

ended Hugo's life so cruelly. All Hugo had ever done was be true to his heart, and loyal to his family. He had tried to lead a good life, and they had ripped it to shreds, like animals.

Curiously, Kate regarded the groups of bat-watchers.

It was an intriguing sensation, Jago was right.

None of them knew she was here.

She was the shape in the shadows, the noise in the wardrobe.

She was the one in the dark, waiting.

Just for a moment, she shut her eyes to see how it felt.

She opened them at the sound of Jago's voice drifting towards her.

'You're right, well done. I'm Irish.'

She realized the Spanish au pair was answering him in heavily accented English.

'Ah. From Dublin, maybe?'

'Very good!' she heard Jago exclaim. 'Not many people would get that first time.'

He was flattering the girl, Kate realized. Drawing her and her friend towards Kate. She peeked out from the scoreboard and saw Jago had taken them quite some distance from the crowd.

'I'm afraid we're not having much luck here,' he said pointing his bat detector at the sky. 'Probably the noise of the children in the field. I think we might take a few of you up this path and see if we have more luck.'

To Kate's amazement, Jago pulled his phone from his pocket.

'Janet. Robin here. I'm taking my group down Hazelnut Path. Do you want to bring a few others over here? See if we have better luck? . . . OK. See you in a minute.'

He turned to the au pairs. The Polish girl was still pointing the detector at the sky, giggling. The box emitted a crackling sound.

'Well done!' Jago said. 'There must be a bat up there. We're close,' he continued. 'Let's see what we can find.'

And with that he led the au pairs off the edge of the dark cricket field into a narrow path behind a row of hornbeams.

Kate paused, unsure of what she was supposed to do. So she followed them.

Jago kept talking to the girls, leading them onto an even narrower, blacker path. Soon, they were deep inside the woods with only Jago's torch for light. Kate noticed he kept it ahead of his body, trying not to let the rangers back on the field spot it.

'Up there,' Kate heard him exclaim. Then she heard him say into his fake phone, 'Janet. Are you on your way? We're on Oak Path now.'

She saw the au pairs' cheeks rise in the dim torchlight, as they presumably smiled innocently. 'The others are just coming,' Jago said. 'You keep pointing up there, and I'll just pop back and shine my torch to tell them we're here. You girls OK here for a minute?'

They nodded beaming.

Kate watched. It was a strange sensation of power, them not knowing she was here.

Jago walked down the path, and with the girls' backs to him, switched off his torch.

Kate saw Jago take a silent step into the trees off the path, about ten feet from where she stood.

She made a gentle clicking noise with her tongue.

Jago came over, leaned right into her ear and whispered, 'They're lost now. The bat-watch finishes in ten minutes. I'm going back to the field to fill out the numbers. That gives you ten minutes to follow them around a bit. Then come back to the field in case the rangers do a head count and we need to make up the numbers again.'

'But what do you want me to do?' Kate whispered, glancing round the tree trunk at the girls, who were still looking up at the sky.

Jago breathed heavily into her ear. 'Kate. A true predator has no morals. Those men who killed Hugo had no morals. If you really want to know what it feels like, you have to lose yours. Even just for a few seconds.'

A timid voice drifted towards them in the dark.

'Where is the man?'

The other one now: 'Eh. Hello?'

'Do it, Kate,' Jago murmured, before disappearing off into the woods.

Kate stood uncertainly, trying not to crack the twigs under her feet.

She crept forwards to the side of the tree trunk, and saw the girls glancing anxiously up and down the path, whispering to each other. The light from the fake radar sat under the Polish girl's chin. Her eyes were round and scared. The girls turned round once, then again, looking disoriented, then began to call out together.

'Excuse me!'

'Hello? Sir?'

'Are you there?'

Kate stepped back. Her heel pressed into a twig. It broke in two with an explosive crack.

The girls froze.

'Hello?' they whispered.

Kate watched, knowing they would be starting to feel like she had in Chumsley Norton. Their senses heightened. They would hear every sound magnified.

One of the girls spoke breathlessly. The other took her hand, and they began tentatively to walk down the path, away from the

325

noise Kate had made, presumably trying to take themselves back to the cricket field.

But they were going the wrong way.

Further and further into the woods.

Kate looked on, knowing again how they were feeling. Their hearts would be thumping, their palms sweating, their bodies covered in goosebumps, waiting for evil to jump from the shadows. Just like she felt when she got home to Hubert Street every day. Walking round the house, shoulders hunched, anticipating the monster who would leap from behind a door, or inside a wardrobe.

Kate hung her head. She was *so sick of it*.

Sick of being scared because of those men who had killed Hugo and left him in a pool of blood for her and Jack to find. The poacher who had carelessly shot an animal and left it to die in pain, in the path of her parents' car. The burglars who had smashed her window and broken into her home. Together they had done this. Created the shadows in her bedroom at night that made her start awake with a gasp and run to check Jack was OK. The creaking floorboards. The broken windows and muddy smears, the imagined footsteps on the stairs.

The people who made her and her child sleep inside a cage in their own home.

Kate watched the girls and saw her own fear transferred onto their faces as they tried to escape from the footsteps cracking twigs behind them in the woods.

Her footsteps.

The moon disappeared behind the clouds, shutting off the light.

Jack lay on his side on the trampoline, praying for it to return, listening for the footsteps of the Year Eight boys on the lawn.

He glanced at Mum's text message again, hoping she'd

sent another one. He lifted his head for the twentieth time, and scanned the fence at the bottom of the garden, as Gabe and Damon threw down cards and laughed more loudly than normal. He knew Gabe was as nervous as him but trying not to show it.

'Be quiet,' he wanted to say. 'If someone comes they'll hear us. They'll know we're here.'

'What's up, Jack-off,' Damon said, whacking his arm.

'Nothing,' he replied crossly, turning and looking at the trees.

'I'm going for a pee,' Damon announced, climbing out of his bag and jumping off the trampoline.

'Me too,' Gabe said, following him. 'Deal the cards, J.'

'Wait . . .' Jack said, trying to keep his voice calm, but they had already jumped off, making him bounce upwards.

'Your mum said we couldn't pee on the carrots. But she didn't say we couldn't do it on the flowers,' Damon was laughing.

Jack sat up nervously, and gathered together the cards.

Trying to focus on the numbers, he dealt them out, one by one, straining his ears for the other two to come back.

And then, he felt it.

The feeling from the river path. The heavy blurred shadow that emerged from the bushes and settled its weight on him.

He tried to ignore it. Tried to ignore the cramps in his stomach that made him want to run to the toilet again.

But this time there was something new.

There was a crack.

Jack spun round.

And there, looking through a gap in the fence, were two bright eyes.

Watching him. Not moving. Not blinking. Just staring at him through the crack.

The pain in Jack's stomach rose up for a second then stabbed down through it like a knife, making him bend over with an alarmed gasp.

Gabe and Damon were around the corner, giggling.

He grabbed his phone and looked at Mum's text message.

are you all right?

He wanted her here now.

But she was in London with that man.

So he kept his eyes away from the fence, and fixed them on Mum's words, shaking, as if she were here and keeping him safe.

Kate didn't mean to chase the girls, she just did.

As she came behind them, snapping more twigs in the trees, they moved as fast as they could along the path. Their panting was so loud she could hear it. The Spanish girl was whimpering.

She'd stop in a minute, she told herself. Just a minute longer to know what it was like to be on the other side.

'Who is it?' the Eastern European girl called out hopefully into the trees, but when Kate didn't reply, she carried on trying to run.

Kate kept a few feet behind them, in the pitch dark, on the other side of the trees.

Every time her foot crushed something with a crack, the girls' eyes flew back behind them. When they reached the top of the next path, they came to a fork. They backed into a tree at the side of the path, and looked left, then right.

Kate watched them as their faces turned towards her and caught a shaft of moonlight along the path.

They were terrified.

Finally the truth broke through to Kate from some place she had buried in her mind.

Is that what Hugo had looked like in his last moments: horrified. Eyes bulging, forehead sweating?

Is this what her parents had looked like as their car lay upturned in the river, the water rising?

Is this what the monster of fate had done to everyone she loved?

The truth would not leave her alone. As she watched the girls, she realized she had believed what she had wanted to believe, because it was all she could endure. That her parents had died instantly before the car sank in the ditch. That Hugo had fought those men to the end. Shouted at them. Charmed them. Been his big, brave, confident, ebullient self till the second when he had fallen fatally, at which point he had selflessly spent his last seconds thinking of her and Jack.

Now Kate looked at the fearful au pairs.

Was this the truth? The reality. Is this what these men did to people when they caught them? Left them frantic? Gasping? Desperate for help? Their dignity stripped away like animals, begging for life.

The girls were both whimpering now. The Spanish au pair opened her bag, and scrabbled inside it.

And pulled out a mobile.

She was going to ring someone.

Alarmed, Kate tiptoed forwards till she came silently to a stop behind the tree where the girls now stood, their backs against the trunk, watching the path.

If the girl rang someone, this would be over in minutes.

'Say him to ring the police,' she heard the Polish girl whisper.

Seconds, even. The police would ring the rangers straight away. The rangers might do a head count and spot Jago.

Can you do it, Kate? Jago's words came back to her. Have no morals? Even just for a few moments?

She smelt the girls' cheap perfume turning sour as it mixed with the sweat of fear.

The Spanish girl began shakily to tap numbers into her phone.

Predators have no morals.

Tap, tap, tap . . . One, two, three numbers . . .

Kate knew then what she was going to do.

Just once she was going to know what it felt like to be those men.

She began to lift her arms slowly, like a ballerina.

Tap, tap, tap . . . Four, five, six . . .

Kate continued her port de bras, until her fingers reached around the side of the tree.

No morals.

Just for a few seconds.

Kate shut her eyes, forced herself to see all the people who had hurt her family . . .

And then as the Spanish girl went to tap in the seventh number, Kate reached around the tree, sank her fingers into both the girls' hair and yanked their heads back tightly against the tree trunk.

'*Aaaa-ieeeeee!*'

Their screams sliced through the woods like lightning.

She held them there for three seconds, then let go, shocked.

As Kate stood gasping, the Spanish girl dropped the phone and, without looking back, the two girls raced off along the unlit path, frantically sobbing.

Kate fell back into the shadows.

What had she done?

She had to get out of here. She scrambled out onto the path, and hurried in the opposite direction to the girls, till, minutes later, the large patch of moonlit sky opened up ahead of her, telling her she was nearing the cricket field.

Tears started to form in her eyes at the sound of the girls' cries.

As she approached at a jog, she saw the distant movement of the bat-watchers and dropped again behind a tree. They were gathered in larger groups and heading back towards the hut. Checking there were no suspicious rangers walking around with torches to see where the scream had come from, she crept behind the cricket scoreboard and crouched down, waiting for Jago.

Nettles stung her ankle, but she didn't care.

She sat in the dark, heart thumping, incredulous.

Where the hell had that come from?

A hand suddenly appeared round the back of the scoreboard and grabbed her, making her gasp.

'Quick,' Jago whispered. 'They're going to do a head count.'

Jumping up, she followed him around the perimeter hedge of the cafe towards the rangers' hut.

'Did you hear the scream?' she whispered as they crept along.

Jago shrugged. 'It sounded as if it came from the road. Nobody took much notice.'

They reached the dark mass of the group, keeping their faces hidden inside their hoodies and looking at the ground as a ranger shone a torch over the tops of their heads, and counted.

'Twenty?' he said.

'Yup. Twenty,' the other ranger agreed.

Kate felt Jago grip her hand firmly as the rangers began to lead the group back to Onslow Gate, one in front, and one behind. She couldn't speak. Couldn't believe what she'd done.

Sickened by her own behaviour.

Surreptitiously, she kept looking for the girls, knowing, however, that they would be lost now, far over the side of the woods, about to be locked in for the night, with no torch, the Spanish girl's phone lying on the ground where she had dropped it.

The other girl might have a phone, she told herself. And if she

331

doesn't, they can listen out for the traffic and find their way to the fence. Climb over.

She gripped Jago's hand as they moved through the woods, a terrible sense of guilt descending on her, fighting the urge to go back for the girls and explain.

'What's up, J?' Gabe yelled, arriving back.

Jack was standing on the trampoline, desperately grabbing his sleeping bag and bed roll.

'What?' Gabe said, his nerves finally showing.

'I saw something. Over there. Someone watching us.'

'Where?' Damon shouted, coming up behind him.

Jack pointed, trying not to cry. 'Someone over there. Behind the fence.'

'Where?'

Gabe peered over. 'I can't see anything.'

Jack stood up. 'There is someone there!' he shouted at them. 'Stop telling me I'm LYING!'

The boys both looked at him, stunned.

They'd never heard him shout before.

'There,' Jack said dropping his voice.

He turned at pointed at the fence, his sleeping bag in his hand.

But the eyes had gone.

'You're just imagining it, Jack,' Gabe said, anxiety entering his own voice.

'Come on,' Damon said, sitting down and picking up his cards. 'Ignore him. Want us to call your mummy?' He sniggered. 'Oh no. That's right. You can't. She's in London with her boyfriend.'

'Shut up, Damon,' Gabe said, looking at Jack.

'Sorry,' Damon said in a stupid voice.

'Come on, J, it's all right,' Gabe said quietly. 'Look, there's nothing there.'

Jack shook his head. He put his sleeping bag back down and picked up his cards, knowing they were wrong and he was right.

'Jack – look!' Gabe said again.

He grabbed Jack's shoulder and made him turn round.

The eyes were gone. And now nobody would believe him.

CHAPTER THIRTY-ONE

Magnus arrived back from Gabe's garden at 10.30 p.m., took off his jacket, and sat on the bed, satisfied.

The woman was in London and wouldn't be back till late.

The boy was on the trampoline for the night.

Lifting Kate's laptop up from the floor, Magnus climbed into Jack's bed, put the laptop on his knee, turned on the small reading lamp beside Jack's bed that no one could see from outside, and stuffed into his mouth a flapjack that he'd taken from the kitchen.

This was his third. He'd also had a spoonful of half a lasagne he'd found in the fridge.

As he finished the flapjack he gave a loud burp, then settled back down.

Right, it was time.

Magnus pulled up a blank document and thought for a long time what to call it. It had to be something the woman wouldn't notice, that could sit among the documents on her computer, unseen by her.

He thought of the perfect phrase in his own language, then translated it to the best word he could think of in English.

'Brr brr, brr,' he sang.

Then he carried on typing, carefully looking at each word, checking back on the handwritten note he'd brought from next door to make sure he had the English words right.

When he'd finished he sat back with a sigh, contented. He saved the document, and hid it among her folder called 'accounts'. The last time she'd looked in there was when she did her tax return in January.

Magnus lay back, shut the laptop and closed his eyes for a moment on Jack's bed.

He preferred Kate's room. It smelt of that nice vanilla hand-cream.

But after the blonde woman had nearly caught him in the house last Saturday night, he was going to stay in the boy's room, with the main lights off this evening, just in case she turned up again, sticking her little pointy noise into his business. It was nice and cosy here. He might just stay here for a while and think through whether there was anything else to do before he wrapped this up for good.

With a tinge of sadness he suddenly realized that tonight would be his last night in the woman's house.

He'd nearly done what he came here to do.

Magnus shut his eyes, just for a moment, saving himself for the last.

CHAPTER THIRTY-TWO

Apart from a few cars heading back from a night out in London, the M40 was quiet by the time Kate and Jago reached it, most people having already travelled to where they needed to be by Saturday night. The motorway stretched ahead into the black night, with just the odd glow of rear lights flitting by like fireflies.

Kate and Jago drove in silence for thirty miles. It was when they reached the hill that dipped steeply down, overlooking Chinnor and the lights of farms and villages spread for miles across the valley, that Kate realized she was looking forward to going home.

And by that, for the first time in four years, she realized with surprise that she meant Oxford.

Jago drove slowly, his arm on the armrest, watching ahead thoughtfully.

A lorry with Spanish number plates overtook them, making good use of the empty night road to deliver its goods north of London.

'Madrid', it said on the side.

Kate looked away, ashamed.

'What?' Jago said.

She moved her eyes across the valley. There was no way she

could tell him what she'd done to the girls' hair. She couldn't believe it herself right now. 'Nothing.'

'Kate, are you sure? Did something happen . . .?'

'No.'

'Kate, listen. Don't worry. It was a harmless prank.'

She watched the lorry disappear into the dark, its brake lights flashing back at her like dragon's eyes. Kate rubbed at a raindrop on the outside of the window, even though she knew she couldn't wipe it away.

She looked at Jago, his finger in his mouth thoughtfully as he drove with one hand. What would he think if she told him what she'd done?

And then she knew, she could never tell anyone.

What had come over her?

Jago turned and saw her face.

'Kate! Cheer up! They'll be fine. As far as they're concerned, they just got lost from the ranger. Their English wasn't very good – when they try to explain to people what happened, that's probably what they'll think happened too: that they just got lost, panicked, then freaked themselves out.' He touched her leg. 'Listen. This was about you, not them. Don't worry. It's not as if you hurt them.'

Kate looked up at the black sky. In the daytime, she knew red kites hovered over it, searching for prey, wings held aloft, menacingly.

The light caress of his finger on her leg sent an intense shiver through her.

'But it was interesting, huh?' Jago asked. 'Being a predator.' He growled when he said the word. His hand now rested on her leg, squeezed it tighter.

She kept her gaze on the dark sky, trying to ignore the effect his touch had on her. 'I don't know.'

The thing was, she had hurt those girls. She hadn't stabbed them or punched them, but for the rest of their lives, they would find themselves wondering who had touched them that night. She shut her eyes, running through the implications.

They might never go out at night again alone.

They might even give up their dream of living in London.

She thought back to the intense hatred she'd felt in Highgate Woods towards those men who killed Hugo. What had she let those feelings do to her? The preyed-upon becomes predator. The bullied becomes the bully. In some ways, she was as bad as those men.

Jago turned the CD player on. American alternative folk music drifted into the car.

'Anyway,' Jago said, 'I think we're probably pushing our luck now. Let's call it a day next weekend. One more step to finish off. And I'll make it a fun one, I promise. No more scaring people or breaking the law.'

She drew her finger down a whole line of raindrops.

'I can't do something like that again, Jago. Involving other people. They looked like sweet, nice girls.'

'Kate,' he said, lifting away his hand from her leg, to indicate to overtake a minibus. 'We won't, I promise. And remember, bad things happen to nice girls, as you well know. Seriously, don't worry about it. They'll be fine and you've proved a point to yourself.'

She lifted her head. 'Hmm, well, I don't feel like a very nice girl tonight.'

She wanted him to put his hand back on her leg. It felt cold where he'd taken it away.

As he pulled back into the slow lane, he reached out instead and stroked the bare flesh of her arm lightly. She turned and met the long look he gave her. 'Good,' he murmured, smiling.

She turned away, embarrassed at the intense waves even the

338

lightest touch or suggestion from him sent throughout her body. He continued to stroke her arm, slowly. She didn't want him to stop, yet wondered how much longer she could bear it. Forgotten sensations drifted over her, unsettling her. Sensations she thought she would never want again with anyone but Hugo.

But *more intense than she remembered*.

What was happening to her?

Had she ever felt out of control like this with Hugo?

As Jago casually lengthened his caress, from her upper arm down to her elbow, Kate struggled to maintain her composure, knowing she was close to throwing away her dignity and asking a man she had only known a short time to pull off the M40 right now, and take her down a dark country lane to a layby where nobody could see them.

She shook her head, astonished. What was happening to her? What had being in the woods done to her?

For the first time Kate wondered if the person she was becoming was actually that much better than the person she was leaving behind.

CHAPTER THIRTY-THREE

It was the screeching call of an alarm that woke him.

At first Magnus thought he was back in the prison cell, lying above Jan, a fellow burglar, and that it was the brutal early morning wake-up call.

Beep beep beep.

Magnus tossed and turned in Jack's bed. It was warm. He didn't want to get up.

'Do you want a drink?' he heard a woman's voice say.

Magnus sat upright in the pitch black.

Where was he? He put out a hand and felt the edges of a small bed.

A light came on downstairs in the hall, illuminating a corner of the Arsenal poster beside his head through a crack in the door.

The boy's room!

He'd fallen asleep.

'Have you got a whisky, by any chance?' he heard a man say in a Scottish voice.

Magnus froze. The skinny woman Kate was downstairs and not alone.

*

It felt so strange to see Jago in her house.

Kate dropped her bag on the kitchen table, horribly self-conscious of everything she saw as she looked around. Jack's football boots by the door, the pile of ironing in the kitchen, the photo Hugo had taken of Jack watching her plane, on the wall. She saw Jago look at it.

'Great picture. Great house, Kate.' He turned around. 'It's beautiful.'

She took off her coat. 'Thanks.'

What would happen if Jago became part of her life? she thought, turning to find two glasses in the kitchen cupboard. Would she have to remove the photos of Hugo? Take away his Georgian furniture? His CDs? How would Jack even start to understand?

As if he sensed she was lost in thought, Jago came up behind her. She felt his hands on her shoulders.

He leaned his face on her shoulder and inhaled deeply.

'I've got something to tell you,' he said.

She paused with her hands in mid-air. 'Hmm?'

'I saw Marla in London on Wednesday night.'

Kate tensed. No, please, she thought.

'She came on the Eurostar from Paris, and I met her in a bar at Waterloo.'

Jago stroked Kate's shoulder. 'She was in a state, talking about getting back together again and . . .'

He turned Kate round in his arms. She kept her eyes on his chest, unable to look into his eyes in case what she dreaded was present there. 'And I told her that I was seeing someone. And that I wouldn't be coming to North Carolina in August now, and I'd get a mate at the university to pick up my stuff from hers and get it shipped back here.'

Kate waited to be sure.

'Then she got the late train back to Paris.'

Jago was *hers*.

'Was that OK?' he said, peering down at her. 'To say that? That I'm seeing someone?'

Kate couldn't help it. She fell into him against the wall, knowing now that she was ready.

It had gone silent downstairs now.

Magnus gave it another second, then turned around in the dark. How had this happened? He scrabbled out of the bed, noticing too late that the boy's nightlight was on a timer switch that had turned it off while he slept. In the dark, he tried to throw the cover over the bed as he'd found it.

Turning, Magnus peered at the other end of the bedroom. There was only one thin slice of light on the wall coming through the almost-shut bedroom door. Using that as a compass point, he tiptoed sleepily towards where the wardrobe door should be.

His toe touched something springy.

Too late, he realized he was heading thirty degrees in the wrong direction.

He withdrew his toe quickly, and for a moment, thought he'd got away with it.

Then, in front of his nose, a breeze blew by, then the most almighty crash rang through the house.

Shit.

'Jesus!' Kate yelled, pulling back from Jago. The crash upstairs was ten times louder than the thud the other day. She looked up, startled. 'Oh my God, Jago. There's someone in the house. Please – I am not imagining this.'

Jago looked up. He took her shoulders.

'Kate, listen. Don't panic. Where was it? Upstairs?'

He appeared unruffled, just as Hugo would have. 'At the front. In Jack's room, I think. The big bedroom at the front.'

'OK, stay here and I'll go up . . .' he said, starting to walk out of the kitchen.

'No!' Kate yelled. 'No, Jago.'

Tears came into her eyes and for the first time in a long time, she didn't fight them. She *couldn't* let Jago go up there. It was all too much after Highgate tonight, and those painful memories of Hugo. 'You can't.'

He took her hands. 'Kate, it's OK. I'm just going for a look. If there's someone up there, they'll be as frightened as we are, and make a run for it. I can handle myself, OK?'

The memory of Hugo lying on the floorboards, blood soaking into them, rushed into her mind.

'No, Jago. Just stay here and call the police.'

He hesitated. 'OK, I tell you what. Get the phone, ring 99 – then if there is someone up there, which I'm sure there isn't, I'll shout, then dial the third nine, OK?'

'Please . . .' she felt the tears running down her face.

'Kate! Don't worry. I'm here now.'

He put her hands down by her sides, kissed her, then walked off through the dining room, picking up Jack's tennis racket from the hall as he went.

'The front bedroom?' Magnus heard the Scottish man shout, followed by his step on the stairs.

Desperately, Magnus put out his hand in the dark, found the old chimney breast beside the wardrobe and stumbled across the floor. Luckily, the doors were still open. He lay down on his stomach and aimed his feet at the hole behind him in the wall. Pushing hard with his long arms, he propelled himself backwards. He managed to get his calves through into next door, then, with another big push, his thighs.

The Scottish man was coming, up the stairs fast: *thump, thump, thump*. And the woman?

Magnus was sweating now, trying to force the rest of his body through the gap.

He went for one last push but something stopped him. Panicking, he moved his stomach off the ground. A jutting piece of shelf bracket had caught on his shirt to the right. *Shit, shit, shit.* He was going to ruin everything. He wriggled desperately to free himself.

The Scottish man's footsteps reached Jack's bedroom door.

Magnus's body was three-quarters through now; just his head and shoulders still protruded.

The Scottish man flung open the door. In the silhouette from the hall light, Magnus saw a tennis racket dangling close to the ground, twisting around. With one last push, Magnus forced himself backwards in the darkness, feeling the nail rip through his T-shirt and along the skin of his back. He gritted his teeth against the pain, looking out to see if the woman was running up the stairs too. There was a click and light flooded the room. Magnus looked up carefully, his chin on the ground, and saw a pair of man's boots walking around the boy's bedroom, presumably taking in the rumpled bed and the fallen CDs from the rack that Magnus now realized he'd knocked over.

The feet went to the right, then the left. They turned towards the wardrobe.

Magnus gulped, trying to listen to hear if the woman was coming too.

Was he visible with the light on, even down here on the ground? Should he come out? Put his hands up?

The walking boots moved slowly, edging closer towards where his head was stuck.

They stopped.

Right above where he was lying, he heard the Scottish man breathing, slow and deep.

From here Magnus knew his head must be sticking out an inch at least.

Magnus waited, waiting for the woman's feet to appear in front of his eyes too. For the screaming to start as she looked into the open wardrobe and saw the tuft of his hair sticking out from under the bottom shelf.

'Kate!' A Scottish voice suddenly shouted right above him. There was a faint reply from what Magnus now realized was downstairs. What was he going to say?

'You're OK,' the Scottish man shouted. 'A CD rack just toppled over. It was probably just a draught when we slammed the front door.'

And with that Magnus saw the tennis racket right in front of him move swiftly backwards. Too late he saw the tennis ball lying in front of the wardrobe doors, where it must have rolled after being dislodged by the falling CD rack. With just a second's warning he shut his eyes tight, as the Scottish man swung the racket forwards, whacking the ball into the cupboard with such force that it smacked into Magnus's jaw and knocked his glasses sideways. His mouth fell open with the impact and he had to stop himself yelling.

'Nope, nothing here,' the Scottish man shouted, slamming the wardrobe doors behind the ball, so hard that Magnus felt the shelf vibrate above his head.

Darkness fell.

Magnus lay in the dark. 'Bastard,' he snivelled to himself, tasting blood in his mouth.

*

Kate stalked back and forwards around the kitchen, waiting for Jago to come down.

How the hell had a draught knocked over Jack's CD rack?

The feeling of unease had soaked back into her bones, as it so often did in this house. Maybe they should move. Buy a new-build flat in the centre of town without these creaky old doors and draughty windows. Unsettled, her mind flew to Jack, lying outside in the dark.

Kate pulled out her phone and started to text, not caring what Gill or Jack's friends thought about it. He'd probably be asleep anyway.

how are you? ok?

His answer flew back.

no. bit scared

She stared. Oh God. She looked at the clock. It was 11.30 p.m.

why?

don't know

want me to come and get you? i'm home

His response brought a lump to her throat.

yes but don't because they'll laugh at me

Kate heard Jago on the landing upstairs, and her body, newly awakened, responded with a shiver. It was betraying her, begging her to make Jago stay tonight.

She just hoped he'd understand.

jack, i'm coming now. i'm going to sit outside in the car

i thought you were with your friend

you are more important than my friends jack – than anybody

Jago started down the stairs.

Jack's next text brought more tears to Kate's eyes.

i'm tired of being scared mum

oh i'm sorry jack. we'll sort it out together i promise

Jago walked towards her along the hall, that easy smile on his face.

346

She smiled apologetically. 'I'm sorry, I just panicked.'

'Is this the kind of thing you were telling me about?'

She nodded. 'I just hear things all the time here.'

'Well, it's an old house. Old houses make noises. The floor's quite uneven in Jack's room, I noticed. Do you want me to fix that catch on the wardrobe, by the way? It looked loose.'

Kate sighed and took his hand, hoping he'd understand.

'Jago, you don't know how much I want you to be here tonight, but I'm so sorry.' She held out her phone. 'I have to go. It's Jack.'

If he was disappointed he didn't show it. 'Oh, God, of course. Don't worry. We're not in a hurry here, are we?'

'Hmm . . .' she groaned playfully, the tone betraying that she wanted nothing more right now than for him to stay.

He kissed her head. They stood there for a second, then she pulled back.

'Right,' she said, grabbing her stuff. Jago picked up his coat and they headed together down the hall as she locked up behind them.

'Next weekend, I promise,' Kate said on the doorstep, turning on the alarm. 'Jack will be with his grandparents. And we will get there.'

'I know, and it'll be worth the wait, eh?' Jago said, kissing her ear, as he put his arm round her and walked her to the car.

She drove round the corner to Gill's at 11.45 p.m., fighting the urge to race after Jago, and parked in a space outside. Too late, she realized she should have brought a sleeping bag.

Crossly, she stared up at the dark house. Gill was probably snoozing away in there, stoned out of her tree, while Jack lay terrified outside.

She lifted her phone and texted.

i'm outside in the car

thanks mum. sorry

don't say sorry. i should have realized you were scared. i'm sorry. try to sleep and i'll stay here till the morning right outside

night mum

night x

Kate pushed back in her seat, thinking about her crazy night with Jago.

An unpleasant image of the au pairs in the woods came back to her. Where were those girls now? At home, crying, unable to sleep? Talking to their own mums tearfully on the phone, being comforted.

Jesus – *what had she done?*

Kate felt the cold creep into her body and allowed it to.

She deserved every freezing minute she was going to experience tonight in this car.

The bullied became the bully – but only if they let themselves.

Tonight she'd learned that's not who she was, and she needed to tell Jago that.

The child watched Mother screaming, then turned as a new sound started.

A piece of the red tiled roof started to fall forwards.

Father looked as if he was going to be sick. He crouched to his knees and hung his head between them.

The child willed Mother to go to Father. To touch him on the shoulder gently, like she used to do before the snake house. To rub his hair and tell him it was only a house. Only money. Money they didn't even have till Grandma died and gave it to her. They were happy before, weren't they?

Dad had only tried to do something nice by buying it for them.

But Mother didn't move. She took her hands away from her eyes.

As the bricks continued to tumble off the side of the house, now in ones and twos, Father kept his head down, as if he were trying to work out how to use his car jack to put all the pieces of the wall back together again.

Mother fixed her eyes on him.

'Mother!' the child whispered, but her eyes didn't move. Her eyes were the eyes of someone else now.

Then she leaned down, without removing her glare from the back of Father's head, and scrabbled about.

When the child turned round, Mother was holding a chunk of bricks in her hand.

The child tried to shout, to warn Father.

But nothing came out.

CHAPTER THIRTY-FOUR

The following Tuesday evening, as arranged, Richard arrived to pick up Jack.

Kate opened the door to find Helen there, too. She was perusing the hanging basket of flowers that she had bought for Kate and Jack last year. Luckily, Kate had just watered the bright pink pansies she tolerated to keep the peace.

'Hi. Come in,' she said cheerily for Jack's sake.

Helen gave her a small smile, the coldness of their last encounter three weeks ago still present. In the hall, Kate saw Helen's eyes reach upwards.

'It's gone, Helen,' she said.

'Some of Jack's school things that he left,' Helen said, holding out a plastic bag, as if she hadn't heard her. The word 'dear' was noticeably absent. 'I've washed them.'

Richard hung up their coats, still smiling, but analysing the situation with his busy eyes, as always.

'There he is! Hello, darling!' Helen said, wrapping Jack in her pastel-clad arms. 'Enjoying half-term? Ready for your holiday?'

Kate watched Jack fall into his grandmother. She thought again of him in Highgate Woods, giggling, as she chased him. It would be her soon that he fell back into with the same ease. She was determined. They were on their way back to each other already. Since he had returned, shame-faced, from Gabe's sleepover to find her waiting with dark bags under her eyes from a sleepless night in the car, she had seen a small but marked change in him. A softening. She caught him more than once, watching her with gentle eyes, and realized, with a lump in her throat, that he was touched about what she had done for him, grateful that she had helped him save face with his friends. That had been the hardest thing to deal with: that he felt the *need* to be grateful to her. That somewhere along the way, her little boy had just given up on having a mother who loved him more than she loved herself, and she'd been too preoccupied about keeping them both safe to reassure him that she would do anything for him.

Die for him.

Kate checked Jack's bag. She just had to stay patient.

'Looking forward to the seaside?' Helen chirped.

He nodded, beaming.

'Come and tell me about your sleepover, darling,' Helen said, leading him into the kitchen to fetch his coat. 'Sounds like you boys had a real adventure.'

Kate glanced at Jack, and to her joy he gave her a tiny, conspiratorial look.

In that second, she felt a little ownership return to her.

'OK, darling,' Richard boomed. 'We're heading down to Dorset tonight. Got the place till Friday, so – what, bring him back Sunday? Give you a chance to do some work?'

The doorbell rang behind him, and Richard turned without compunction and opened it.

It's my house, it's my door, Kate wanted to say, but didn't.

Saskia stood there, with pink cheeks, looking as if she'd been running.

'Oh, great, I was worried I'd missed you. I came to wave you off,' she said, walking in behind Kate and waving at Jack in the kitchen.

The dreaded triumvirate. Jack was disappearing in front of her eyes into their fold.

'Here's his bag,' Kate said, handing it to Richard.

Right then, she made a pledge to herself. This would be over soon. Next time she would announce to Richard and Helen that she was coming to Dorset with them, invited or not. They would start to follow her rules and respect them, whatever they were.

Jack and Helen returned from the kitchen.

'Well, we might as well head off, folks, if you're ready?' Richard boomed.

Kate stood in front of Jack awkwardly, aware of their eyes on her. She gave him a casual hug, resisting the urge to squeeze him tight and tell him to be safe. 'Have a good time. I'll miss you.'

Saskia gave him one too.

'Well, if they're all heading off, do you fancy a drink, Kate? Or have you got to go to north Oxford to see that friend of yours?'

She gave Kate a meaningful look. Shit, Kate, realized. It was Tuesday evening.

'No,' she lied. 'It's, um, no – she's on holiday.'

Saskia nodded. 'So . . .?'

There was a lot of movement in the hall but Kate knew everyone was pausing to listen to her reply. They were lifting bags and opening doors, but their ears were pointing directly at her. Jack glanced up, hopeful.

He wanted her to go, Kate realized, wanted her to make things better with Aunt Sass.

'There's the new pub on Magdalen Road,' she said, picking up her coat.

'Great,' Saskia said, barely able to hide her surprise, and they all left together.

The pub was packed when they arrived. At Saskia's request, Kate went to find a table.

Saskia returned five minutes later with a bottle of wine.

'We're getting pissed,' Saskia announced, sitting down. 'How else are we going to get through this? How long's it been since we went for a drink – three years?'

Kate raised her eyebrows and held out her glass, already dreading Saskia asking her about Jago.

'So,' Saskia said, with a challenging look on her face. 'You've done it, haven't you?'

Kate regarded her confused. 'What?'

'*You* know what. You've got this kind of sexy walk thing going on.'

She suddenly realized what Sass meant. It was the kind of sweetly guileless comment Sass would have made in the old days, and took Kate by such surprise that she laughed, and spat out her wine.

'Actually, I haven't!'

'Really?'

Saskia was trying. She could see that. Kate smiled. 'Not quite yet. Sass, it's been five years since Hugo. And Jago's just come out of a long relationship. I suppose it'll happen when we're both ready.'

Saskia took a sip of wine. 'This weekend?'

Kate made a face at her. 'Stop it.'

Sass sighed. 'But is it definitely over? Him and his girlfriend.'

Kate nodded. Saskia ran her finger down her glass, thoughtfully. Kate took a sip of her drink, and watched her. 'What?'

354

Saskia groaned. 'Kate. If I tell you something, will you promise not to tell anyone? I have to tell someone or I'm going to die.'

Kate tensed. She couldn't take any more bad news about Helen regarding Jack.

Saskia opened her mouth. 'Jonathan. The business I told you about him being bored with me. It wasn't exactly true. I mean, it was. He did get fed up with me moaning about working for Dad and not going back to do my degree, but it wasn't the reason he left me.'

Kate sat back. 'What?'

'I had an affair.'

Kate slammed her drink down on the bar. 'You are fucking joking! You?'

Saskia shook her head ruefully. 'You remember when Dad made the whole agency go on that terrible team-building week in Gloucestershire? I met him there, at the hotel, on the first night. He said he liked the ladder I'd made out of a tree trunk.'

Kate smiled before she could help herself. She'd forgotten how funny and self-effacing Sass could be.

Saskia hit her arm. 'Don't, Kate. Honestly. He was called Tony, and he came from Essex, and he'd just got divorced. He was on business, and he was lonely, and he was very sweet to me.'

'Oh, your dad would love that,' Kate smiled, imaging the snob in Richard being faced with the prospect of announcing at the golf club that instead of 'Jonathan from Surrey' Saskia was now seeing 'Tony from Essex'.

Saskia rolled her eyes. 'Exactly. Anyway, I just needed to get away from everyone – you know what Dad's like when he holds forth to a captive audience at the bar. I said I had a headache, and Tony asked me to come for a drink in the village. I told him about all the arguments me and Jonathan had been having, and I really don't know how it happened. I was feeling low and he

355

just kept telling me he was sure I would make a fantastic architect one day. I drank too much and we ended back at the hotel. And then it just kept happening that week. Honestly, I've never done anything like that before and I still don't really know why I did.'

Kate sighed, knowing that Saskia would never be able to bear the guilt of something like that. 'Please tell me you didn't tell Jonathan.'

Saskia rolled her eyes. 'I didn't realize how serious Tony was taking it. He started texting me when I got home. I tried to stop him, but when I didn't return his calls, he rang me at the house when I was out. Jonathan answered.'

'Oh Sass!'

'He looked so sick. And the worst thing was, Tony wasn't even my type. He had this spiky dark hair with too much gel in it. And he wore business suits. I honestly don't know why I did it.'

Kate felt a tug of the old affection for Saskia. She had been cast into the role of big sister to Sass when they first met, and as an only child herself, had cherished it. 'Maybe it's not too late. If you finish your degree and give Jonathan some time, maybe he'll come round.'

Saskia shrugged. 'No. Do you know, I'm starting to wonder if this is the best thing. I'm not sure Jonathan really wanted the best for me. Not the way Hugo did for you. So, now it's my decision and no one else's. And I'm going to tell Dad tomorrow that I'm going to apply to do my Part Two, then do my Part Three the year after next, and qualify as an architect. And that I don't want his money. I'll pay for it myself.'

Kate sat back, imagining Richard's fury. It had taken Hugo a year to tell his father that he'd swapped from a degree in architecture to one in architectural history and design, and would not be following Richard's dream for him to be an architect like himself. It was a sweet irony that Saskia, whom Richard had no plans for whatsoever, would be taking on the dream for his golden boy. Becoming Richard's equal. Kate sat forwards. 'I'm pleased for you. Actually, I think Hugo should have stepped in and made you do it years ago. I'm not sure he ever realized that being Richard's daughter was very different to being his son.'

Saskia gave her a searching look that made her avert her eyes. 'What's he done to you, Kate?'

'Who?'

'This man? He's changed you. Your eyes are shining.'

Was it that obvious? 'I'm not sure what he's done. He just seems to get what's going on inside my head.'

'Him and the therapist.'

Kate looked away. She and Sass had shared enough truths for one night. 'Yup.'

Saskia took a long sip of wine. A frown appeared on her face.

'What?'

Saskia blinked hard.

'Sass, what now?'

'It's nothing. It's just . . . I don't know how to say this, Kate. This guy that you're seeing. Jago?'

'Hmm?'

'It's just . . . well, I know Dad's always been worried.'

'About what?' Kate felt the tension from earlier return.

Well, do you remember when Hugo was ki— . . . when he died . . . there was all that publicity in the papers about the case? The tabloids kept printing things like, "The gang targeted Hugo Parker's million-pound home in Highgate" and "Hugo Parker's parents travelled from their one-and-a-half-million-pound house in Oxford to the hearing today . . ." And stuff like "It has been a second tragedy for his widow Kate Parker, whose parents were killed in a car crash on her wedding night on the way home to their house in Shropshire". That kind of thing.'

Kate did remember. She remembered the relentless invasion of it, the pain of seeing photos of the people she loved laid out on newspaper pages next to car adverts. 'So?'

'I'm just saying. It wouldn't take anyone long to work out there's a lot of money sloshing around. All the life insurance. The property you inherited. The business. And then a load more coming to you and Jack one day from Mum and Dad.'

Oh my God. Kate put down her glass. Saskia was talking about money. She was accusing Jago of being a gold-digger.

Saskia wasn't happy for her at all. She was still trying to control her, keep her trapped.

Kate bristled. 'Well that kind of doesn't surprise me at all, Sass – as Richard's whole life revolves around money, he can't imagine anyone having any other motive in their life. For your information, Jago's a visiting professor at Oxford, with a best-selling book in the States. He drives around in a hatchback and listens to indie bands, and goes mountain-biking. I'm sorry, I really don't think he needs anyone else's cash, and even if he did, he's not the type.'

Kate knew as she said it, that a boundary had been crossed. Her feelings about Richard had always been implied to Saskia, never spoken.

Saskia sat back, looking hurt.

'Kate. Richard is my dad,' she said quietly. 'I know he has faults, lots of faults, but he's still my father, and I won't sit here and let you talk about him like that, any more than you would have let someone talk about yours like that.' Saskia hesitated as if she desperately wanted to say something but knew, if she did, it could never be taken back. She was fighting it, Kate could see, and then her sister-in-law's mouth opened, as if the words were being pushed out of her by years of resentment. 'And can I remind you that if Dad hadn't lent you and Hugo a quarter of a million quid, he and David would never have got the business off the ground.'

She broke off. They both sat with an almost full bottle of wine in front of them that was never going to be drunk.

'We paid it back, Sass,' Kate said quietly. 'Hugo, David and I worked seven-day weeks at that first year.'

'You paid it back out of a business you couldn't have started without him,' her sister-in-law replied, the resentment undisguised at last. They both knew Richard would never have done the same for Saskia. He would never have placed the same trust and confidence in his daughter that he did in his beloved son.

Kate pushed back her seat, knowing Saskia was right and hating the conflict it created inside her. She'd never wanted to take that bloody money off Richard. It had been Hugo who'd persuaded her it would be fine. It was time to go. This had been a mistake. She and Saskia were never going to be friends again. There was too much between them now. It was over.

'Hugs would find this so sad,' Saskia murmured.

'He would find it unbelievable,' Kate replied. She touched Saskia's shoulder, feeling sorrow for Jack and his hopes for her and his aunt's relationship, and walked out of the pub.

She marched up to Hubert Street, Saskia's accusation about Jago ringing in her ears. She gave it a moment of thought, then dismissed it completely.

Crazy.

Jack sat in the back of Richard's car on the M4, looking through Jago Martin's book, even though it was making him car sick.

He kept flicking back and forwards, and then he stopped.

He looked down at a page on road accidents, then up at the motorway.

Something wasn't right.

CHAPTER THIRTY-FIVE

It was Friday afternoon, and the roads were unusually quiet, perhaps because the colleges were shutting for summer. Kate cycled into town, not believing what she had just done.

The sun was out again. The trees were a rich, dark green. The air was filled with the fresh smell of summer.

There were no numbers today.

She cycled easily up the High Street, going over what she'd just done in her head.

She dismounted at Carfax and walked towards the end of Cornmarket Street, enjoying the new-found energy in her step. She no longer had to force one leg in front of the other to get through each day.

Vaguely, she noticed a couple of people glancing at her as they walked past. It had happened a few times this week, mostly men. She kept her eyes straight ahead, curious to realize she was visible again in the real world, now she had colour back in her face and light in her eyes.

There was a buzz on her phone. She checked it and her stomach lurched again.

It was too late now.

An email sat in her intray confirming the two flights she had just booked to Mallorca for August.

She and Jack were going on *a plane*.

A frisson of excitement ran through her at the thought of the warm sun on her skin, and swimming in the sea. She forced herself mentally to sidestep the stat about skin cancer when it threatened to come by, concentrating on what it would be like to have so much time with Jack on his own to talk.

Richard and Helen would be nowhere to be seen.

They could discuss their memories of Hugo. Perhaps take some of their old photos with them. They could talk about their future. She could even bring up the idea of Jago.

The thought of Jago sent a thrill through her.

She crossed the street, swinging her bag of ankle boots, recalling each word of their phonecall last night from London.

'Kate, I had to tell you,' Jago enthused down the phone. 'That psychologist guy in the States rang to see how you were. I told him what we'd been up to and he was fascinated. He mentioned us doing an interdisciplinary paper together on this anxiety disorder theory of his – I'm going to stop off and see him in New York when I go to Utah in the summer.'

'That's brilliant,' she'd said, pleased.

'But he thinks we should stop after this weekend, so we don't go too far. And he said that you're welcome to ring him to discuss the kind of cognitive behaviour therapy he would recommend if you want to try a different kind of counselling in Oxford.'

'Thanks, Jago,' she said, touched by his effort. 'Thanks for doing this for me.'

'You're very welcome.' He paused. 'Although, of course, I have dodgy ulterior motives, which would be seriously unethical if I was actually a psychologist. But we statisticians are allowed to be as dodgy as fuck as long as we can count . . . so I was thinking, that if you fancied it, maybe we could sneak you into my room at Balliol on Saturday after we get back to Oxford.'

She had hesitated, feeling a spark between them along the telephone line.

'I mean, if you can steal a boat and terrorize young girls in a wood, that'll be old hat for you by then, missus.'

She smiled. 'No, I'd like that.'

'Good,' he said.

They had arranged to meet at 8 a.m. tomorrow at an M25 service station.

And it was after that phonecall, which had made her feel so positive about the future, that she had, terrified, decided to book the tickets to Mallorca.

Kate arrived at the heel bar a minute later, squeezing past an umbrella stand. The old man was working behind the bar again, as irritable looking as last time.

'Hi,' Kate said, taking out the boots.

He lifted his head slowly again and peered at her.

'Sorry, but I picked these up from you last week and when I got home, I realized that the heel had been shortened by about this much.' She held up her fingers. 'I can wear them, but I really preferred them the height they were. Could I ask you to redo them, please?'

The old man turned with effort, took the boots from Kate, and peered through his glasses. He put them down on the counter.

'He asked me to do it. The bloke.'

'Who?' What was he talking about?

'The bloke that brought them in.'

'Who?' she said, confused. 'A Scottish bloke?'

The old man shrugged. 'Can't remember.'

She frowned. 'I'm sorry, but no, I mean, why would he?'

'Seen it before,' the old man said, tucking in his tortoise neck.

'Sorry?'

'Some blokes don't like it. When their wife is tall. Ask me to shorten their heels.'

Kate shook her head not believing what she was hearing. 'I'm sorry.' She smiled. 'First of all, I'm not his wife. And secondly he's about six foot, and I'm five foot seven. Even with heels on, I'm shorter than him.'

The old man scratched a veined cheek. 'Some do it to keep their women in their place.'

Kate had to stop herself laughing out loud. 'Excuse me, I'm sorry, but I find that quite offensive. How could you . . .'

He turned away from her, putting his hand up between her face and his. 'I'll redo them if you want. But he did ask me.'

'OK. If you say so,' she muttered, peering in the back of the heel bar, to see if there was anyone more rational here. The old guy was even madder than she'd first thought. She gave him her name again, put the boots on the counter and walked out, cross, as the uneasy feeling she had so often at Hubert Street crept over her again. How bizarre.

She walked back up the street to her bike, distracting herself by concentrating on what Jago might have planned for this weekend.

Kate arrived home an hour later, holding a bag with some new holiday clothes for Jack and her, to hear a commotion on the pavement.

She looked up to see the tall student with the glasses and spiky hair leaving the house next door, with two large holdalls. A small mousey woman in her twenties was standing in the doorway, talking to him with a harassed expression in her face.

'But we need it before you go, Magnus,' she was calling out. 'None of us can cover your share, and there's the electricity bill too. That's due soon.'

'I send it to you!' he yelled, placing the keys in her hand and waving in the air.

'But we don't have an address for you and . . .'

'I send it!'

He turned, then stopped when he saw Kate. She noticed he had a bruise on his face that ran from under his eye down the side of his face.

Some connection began to register in her mind, then slipped, like a foot off a pedal.

'Hey. I'm leaving!' he shouted.

Kate looked sympathetically at the girl, to show her support if she needed it, but the girl just turned away.

'Too many crazy fucking people round here,' the spiky-haired student called out.

He stomped off down the street, leaving Kate standing on the doorstep.

Oh, well, perhaps Saskia had been right. At least, that was one thing less to worry about, having him next door.

Inside the house, Kate walked up to Jack's bedroom, and put away his new summer clothes.

Then she sat on her son's bed quietly, and looked around.

Jack's world, where he had lived on his own for so long while she had been lost in her head, worrying about how to keep them both safe.

With one hand, she reached up and took down the little snowdome. Jack had loved this when he was a baby. Asked for it again and again. She shook it and a glittering snowstorm rained over the little plastic mountain inside, swirling glittering rain, feeling like her life for the past five years.

She lay back and thought of Jago.

With him, there could be a real possibility of something. She sensed he felt it too.

Just one more step in this experiment.

The glitter settled.

And then life would really restart.

But first she had to be honest with Jago about who she really was.

'No!' the child screamed.

Mother went flying at Father's head, brandishing the clump of bricks that had fallen off the side of the house.

Father turned round and looked up to see Mother coming at him, her face contorted with fury.

'You stupid, bloody bastard!' she shrieked, holding the bricks aloft. She waved a hand at the hole in the side of the house. 'Everything my father worked for just thrown away in this pile of shit. He said I should never have married you.'

The child ran at her, trying to claw the bricks away from her. 'No!

A creaking noise stopped the three of them in mid-movement.

They turned to see the end of the roof starting to sway. With a groan, the main beam began to slide to the left, bringing tiles down with it.

The roof collapsed into itself. More crumbled away.

The child's bedroom fell apart, taking with it the rocking horse and the cuckoo clock from Aunt Nelly.

The child jumped back, dropping the snowdome on the rubble.

Mother dropped the clump of bricks down beside Father's foot and stood, shaking.

The child watched in shock as she turned away feebly, starting to sob.

'You stupid little man.'

Father's face was going purple. The veins in his neck stood out.

The child gasped.

'Enough!' Father screamed, turning round, his big arms swinging. With one punch he knocked Mother across the jaw, sending her flying onto the grass. Before the child could open his mouth, Father picked up the block of wall with a huge roar, and threw it down on Mother's head.

The was a crack like an axe on wood.

Blood seeped into the hillside and ran down it like a stream.

CHAPTER THIRTY-SIX

It was 8 a.m. on the Saturday morning as Kate pulled in to the service station on the M25, nervous about the last step of Jago's experiment. In fact, she had been so preoccupied, she'd hardly noticed the lorries behind her on the M40. Instead, she'd found an old Johnny Cash CD in the front compartment and played that, his comforting mellow voice drifting out of the window she had opened to let in the already-warm June air. To her surprise, she had noticed a small sense of joy descending upon her.

She spotted Jago immediately as she circled, looking for a parking space.

He was standing at the main door of the cafe area, a coffee in hand, sipping it carefully as steam drifted up into a blue sky that, if all the bike carriers and boat trailers were anything to go by, was already summoning a weekend crowd to the outdoors.

Kate found a cramped space beside a 4x4 topped with mountain bikes, and turned off the engine. She sat back and observed Jago furtively in her side mirror.

He looked even more tanned, as if he'd been out cycling in the sun. He wore a slim-fit grey T-shirt that showed off the taut muscles of his arms and torso, and a black top tied around his waist. He was wearing tracksuit trousers and trainers, as she was.

He had been specific about that on the phone. 'Something comfortable,' he'd said. 'Something you'd go running in on a cold day.'

So. This was it. After today, when they saw each other again, it would be a normal date. How would that feel? Would she be able to do things with him that were planned ahead, without trying to control things again?

At least now Kate knew she had a chance.

She felt a tremor in her stomach, remembering something else.

Tonight she would sleep with him. She looked at him again, something niggling her mind.

But first it was only fair, before she took that step, to tell him what she had done.

She climbed out of her car, and crossed towards him. He spotted her and picked up a coffee he'd clearly bought for her, as she crossed the line of arriving cars to reach him.

'Hello!' He put out his arms, coffee in each hand, and kissed her. There was no awkwardness on his part or hers now. She fell into him, his body still familiar from last week in her kitchen.

'You smell nice,' he said. 'How are you?'

'Hmm . . .' she growled, prodding his chest gently. 'You'd better have a good reason for getting me up at 6.30 a.m., mate.'

'Ahah!' He kissed her again. 'Let's go and find out, shall we?' He pointed at her car. 'Can you drive?'

'Uh, yes, but how did you get here?' she asked, as they crossed back over the road.

Jago opened the passenger door. 'Someone gave me a lift on their way to London this morning.'

'But I thought you just *came* from London,' Kate said, climbing in her side and starting the engine.

Jago grinned.

369

'What?' she said, putting on her seatbelt and reversing out. She followed the exit sign back onto the M25, waiting for his reply.

'Kate. I haven't been in London.'

She did a double take. 'I thought that was where you've been – working?'

Jago sipped his coffee. 'No. My classes finished at Balliol the week we went to Highgate Woods – the Oxford summer school doesn't start till next Monday.'

Kate accelerated onto the motorway. 'Oh, sorry. So, where have you been?'

Jago lifted her coffee up for her to have a sip. She took it, realizing she was getting used again to these small intimate gestures of affection that people in relationships shared.

'Now, that's what we're about to find out.' She threw him a worried look.

'Come on. One more step, then you can relax. We can relax. Actually, I was just looking at those mountain bikes back there, wondering if you fancied coming cycling with me in the Cotswolds next week – someone at Balliol told me about a good trail.'

She tensed, waiting for the numbers to fly at her about bike accidents, but nothing came. 'Um, yeah.' It was easy to say yes. 'I suppose so. That sounds nice.'

And it did sound nice. Cycling outdoors in the sunshine in a beautiful part of the world. She took the cup from him and had another sip, their fingers touching for a second.

'Thanks.'

'Great. And we'll find a proper country pub this time.'

That sounded nice too. As Jago looked for a radio station, a thought occurred to her. How much of life had she missed in the last five years, tiptoeing between safe corners, frightened of shadows?

They turned off the motorway at the next signpost, then Jago directed her onto a two-lane country road surrounded by high hedges. He found an alternative music station and sat back, tapping his fingers on his leg. They carried on for ten miles, chatting about Kate's new plans for the foundation, then turned into a much narrower country road that soon disappeared behind high hedges.

'Why is this making me uneasy?' said Kate.

'Oi. Stop trying to predict.'

'Sorry.'

As she took her time, it dawned on her that Jack would be home next weekend. How would she explain the Cotswold trip? She glanced at Jago, wondering. Would it be too weird?

'Jago. Could I ask you something? Would you mind meeting Jack?'

He dropped his head to the side, as if listening to a strange noise.

'I'd just introduce you as a friend.'

'Yeah, absolutely. When?'

'Really?' He hadn't even hesitated. 'Maybe next week?'

'Absolutely,' Jago repeated, tapping his fingers to the music as the car re-emerged from behind the hedges. 'Take him to the Cotswolds, if you like. Does he like cycling? I take my niece, Clara, sometimes in Scotland. She's about the same age.'

'Do you?' She loved the way he talked about his family. Like Hugo. 'He'd love that, actually. I never take him cycling.'

'Great. He and I can talk science.'

The joy in her heart expanded a little. 'Thanks. That would be amazing. I'm sorry, it's just . . .'

He shook his head. 'Kate. My sister – Clara's mum – is divorced. I know a bit about what it's like.' He started singing along to the radio. He was so relaxed. So relaxing to be around and . . .

371

She glanced again.

. . . But actually, something was different. She had noticed it at the motorway station but now it was becoming more obvious. Jago's fingers were tapping incessantly. His legs and buttocks were tensing, too, in turns, moving half and inch up and down, like a boxer on his toes before a fight.

'So. Come on,' she said. 'What are we doing?'

Jago froze mid-tap.

Then, without warning, he threw himself forwards and put his head in his hands. 'Ah!' he groaned.

'What?' Kate said, alarmed.

Jago threw back his head. 'You're going to kill me.'

'What?' she exclaimed, swerving at the last moment to avoid a pheasant.

'OK. Right. Well, can I just say, when you start shouting at me, because you will, that it's your own fault.'

What was he talking about?

Jago turned sideways to face her. 'OK. Well, when you mentioned it last week, I realized it was something that I'd always wanted to do. I had this week off, so I thought, Why not? I've just got a royalty cheque through from my American publisher, so I went for it.'

Kate slowed down as they approached a bend, desperately searching her memory. What had she said?

'Jago?' she said nervously. 'Talking about what?'

'There,' Jago grinned pointing. Kate looked ahead and saw a field with a hangar appearing on their right.

The yellow wing of a small aircraft came into view.

It took her a second to register what was written in large letters on the sign in front of them.

'WELCOME TO BINDWOOD PARACHUTE SCHOOL'.

CHAPTER THIRTY-SEVEN

Jack woke up at 10 a.m. that Saturday morning, not knowing where he was.

At first he thought he was in the white bedroom with the sloping roof in the thatched holiday house in Dorset, but then he saw Dad's old Arsenal posters on the wall and remembered he was back at Nana and Granddad's. They'd arrived back at ten last night after getting stuck on the motorway for hours.

Then he remembered something else.

The computer!

Jack sat up with a gasp and looked at the clock. He hadn't meant to sleep in so late, but Aunt Sass had been here to meet them with some dinner she'd cooked for them last night, and said it was too late for him to use the computer before bed. After that, he'd lain restlessly, counting down the hours till he could run to the kitchen and check to see if he was right. And now he'd slept in.

Jack jumped out of bed and ran to his bag on the floor, yanking out clothes and brushing aside the shells he'd collected with Nana, to find Jago Martin's book, hidden at the bottom.

He ripped it open triumphantly.

At first, he'd just made one red mark when he'd noticed something odd about the book.

In Dorset, he'd noticed more.

Now the margins were covered in red marks.

Triumphantly, Jack hoped Dad was watching him.

Saskia sat at the computer in her parents' kitchen, a cup of coffee and a plate of toast by her hand, reading the email message she had just received, unable to believe it.

She had an interview next Tuesday to do her Part Two work placement at a small architect firm in Banbury.

She sat back, excitement and worry weaving together inside her. How the hell would she tell Richard? 'Dad, I'm leaving your agency. Oh, and by the way, I'm stealing your big dream for your beloved son Hugo, to be an architect like you . . .'

The kitchen door opened, and she jerked back, thinking it was Dad.

Jack stood there in his pyjamas, his hair sticking up, holding a book determinedly in his hand, glaring at her. He looked so cross, she laughed.

'Morning, Snores, what's up with you?'

'Can I get on the computer?'

Saskia looked at her email. 'Can you give me a moment? This is important.'

She started to type her reply, assuming Jack would fetch his breakfast, but when she looked up, he was still there. His normally tranquil green eyes raged like a rough sea.

'What's the matter?' she exclaimed. 'It's not your Facebook, is it, because I'm a bit worried about what I've been reading on . . .'

'It's NOT THAT,' Jack said loudly.

Saskia stopped mid-chew. She'd never seen him like this.

'Mum's got a boyfriend.'

Saskia hesitated. She tried to sound casual, as she picked at her toast.

'Oh. OK. Did she tell you that?'

'No,' he said, staring hungrily at the computer like he wanted to rip it from Saskia's hands. 'I worked it out.'

His eyes switched back to her, intently. 'Is it true?'

Saskia rolled her eyes. Great. Another Kate mess to sort out. 'Snores – I can't . . . your mum has to . . .'

'So it is true?'

She sighed. 'It's your mum's business, Jack. If she hasn't told you, it's because she's not ready to do that yet.'

To her shock, Jack yelled, 'Well, it's not! Because there's something wrong with him.'

'Who? The boyfriend?'

Jack pulled out a book from behind his back and lowered his voice. 'Look.'

Saskia read the front cover. '*Jago Martin* . . . oh, that's him. This is his best-selling book, is it?' she said, remembering what Kate had told her.

Jack nodded. He flicked over a couple of pages and pointed at the red pen in the margin.

Saskia peered. 'They're statistics. The chances of things happening to you.' She looked at him. 'So?'

'They're all the same.'

'What do you mean?' she replied, patting Rosie as she lay her head in Saskia's lap, hoping for some toast.

'They're all in a different order but it's the same list of numbers all the time.'

Saskia shrugged. 'Well, does that matter?'

Jack banged his hand on the table. '*Yes*. It doesn't make sense. They're just fake numbers to fill the space.'

Saskia put down her toast and took the book from Jack. He'd always been good at maths, just like Hugo. Following his pen marks, she flicked through. That was odd. He was right. The same twenty or so percentage figures kept appearing, as if they'd been copied and pasted in repeatedly. She sat back uneasily.

'Is this a proper book?' She looked at the cover again, and then at the publisher's imprint on the title page: New Maine Publishing. 'Perhaps it's just an early proof.'

Jack shrugged. 'It's a book.'

Saskia ran a finger down the front inside cover. Something wasn't right here. Something that she couldn't put her finger on. 'OK.' Not even knowing what she was looking for, she pointed at the laptop. 'Put "New Maine Publishing" in Google, Snores. See what it says.'

Jack sat up straight. She leaned over and watched the page as it loaded. A home page for an American publisher of popular science books came up. They clicked on the 'Authors' page and saw a long list of names, including Jago Martin.

Saskia frowned. She opened the front cover again, scanning the title page.

Then as she moved her eye to the page on the right, she saw it.

A tiny sliver of a page, just a millimetre thick, running between the title page and the first page. The remains of a page. . . sliced out.

'There's a page missing,' she said, turning the book over. She scanned the back cover, and there, right at the bottom, where she wouldn't have noticed, was a tiny logo in a box. 'Underline', it said.

'Jack – put "Underline" in,' she almost barked at her nephew, feeling unease creep steadily through her. 'Underline Books, or Publishing, maybe.'

Immediately a page flew up on the screen in front of them. 'Underline Publishing – the home of quality self-published books.'

Silence fell as Jack and Saskia read what was underneath.

'Always wanted to get that novel published? Turn that special holiday or event into a beautiful photo book? Underline Publishing is a self-publishing website with an array of pre-designed formats to choose from . . .'

Rosie whined and looked at Saskia with big soft eyes.

Saskia shook her head, confused. 'This is not a real book, Snores. It looks like one but it's not. He's made it himself.' She turned it over. 'How's he done it?'

'Give it here,' Jack said, pushing in in front of her at the screen. With an expert flick of the wrist, he returned to the New Maine Publishing site and clicked on 'Authors'. First he clicked on 'Jago Martin' and a profile came up. Randomly, Jack then clicked on another author's name. A new author profile came up that looked normal. Then he clicked on another. They both gasped. The two author profiles were the same, even the photo. They tried a third and found the same. 'He's made that site up,' Jack said, excited. 'It's not real. He's tried to make it look real.'

Saskia nodded, trying to hide her growing concern. She moved to let him take half of her seat, amazed, as the little boy then continued to work his way easily around the internet, bringing up Amazon, and typing in Jago Martin's book title. Popular books about statistics with similar titles popped up, but not Jago Martin's. Jack pointed at two.

'Look – he's copied the cover of that book, and the title of that one.' He then clicked on a third book that offered the option of 'Look inside'. Saskia read the first ten pages in silence onscreen, as Jack clicked through them for her.

'Wow, that is weird,' Saskia said. 'He's used some of these pages, too.'

'But he's changed the headline and some of the numbers,' Jack said.

Saskia sat back, trying to work it out. 'It's as if he's scanned different bits of all these books, then put them together in a self-published book and put his own name on it. Then he's cut out the real title page that would presumably say "Underline Publishing" and put the name of a pretend publisher, New Maine. Only he couldn't get the "Underline" symbol off the back cover. He must have hoped no one would see it. Why would he do that?'

'I want to tell Mum,' Jack said triumphantly.

Saskia blinked, starting to feel uneasy.

'Look, hang on. Let's Google him.'

They did, and Jago Martin's own website came top of a list of five websites that mentioned his name.

'Click on that one first,' Saskia said, pointing to it. They both stared as it came up, with a small photo of a smiling man wearing black sunglasses and a helmet on a bike. 'Bio, journals, press . . .' Saskia muttered. She pressed on a few links to other sites. They all looked impressive. She blinked heavily.

'Try the next one,' she said. It took them to Jago Martin's entry on the University of Edinburgh's website.

Saskia stared at it. Something wasn't right here. A word in the title was spelled wrongly: 'One of the worlds top universities'.

'Hang on . . .' She leaned over Jack and put 'Edinburgh University' in Google.

She pressed 'enter' and waited, feeling Jack's nervous breathing on her neck.

An almost identical page came up, but with 'world's' spelled correctly.

Saskia typed 'Jago Martin' into the real University of Edinburgh search engine.

'0 results', came the reply.

'Oh my God,' she muttered.

'What?'

Saskia searched two more newspaper and education links in Jago Martin's own website. They all went to the other four listed webpages in the Google search, all of which mimicked real ones.

'I can't believe it: he's . . .' she turned and saw Jack's confused face, and hesitated. She patted his shoulder. 'Listen, there's probably an explanation.'

She tried to sound calm. 'Really, don't worry. When I take you home tomorrow, I'll tell Mum and she can ask him. Have you met him, Jack? Has he been to the house?'

Jack shrugged. 'I think so, because sometimes I can smell this horrible aftershave smell in my room.'

'In your room?' She paused. 'But you haven't met him?'

'I've seen a photo.'

'That one?' Saskia pointed to the website.

Jack shook his head. He flicked to the back page of the book.

'Is that him?' Saskia gawped, grabbing the book.

She peered at Jago Martin. And then she looked again. Inside, she felt a line of barbed wire start to wrap around her. As it spiked into her, the blood drained from her face.

'What?' Jack said sounding scared.

'Jack? Is this a joke?'

He looked bewildered.

Saskia tried to stand up unsteadily. 'Right. Jack,' she said, trying to keep her voice normal. 'Leave this with me. You've done really well. Why don't you go and have a shower, and get dressed? Then later you could take Rosie out for a walk and get some bread for lunch at the shop. Nana's making soup, I think.'

'But . . .'

She put her hand on his shoulder, knowing there were only so many seconds she could keep her face composed.

'Jack. Please.'

CHAPTER THIRTY-EIGHT

'No, Jago,' Kate said, braking on the single-track country road, right outside the airfield. She knew her action would block traffic. She didn't care. 'Not a chance in hell.'

She put her hands on the top of the steering wheel, and tensed her jaw.

Jago snorted with laughter.

'What?' she snapped.

'I was just thinking I was glad you didn't have a brick in your hand.'

She realized he was trying to stop smiling. She shook her head, determined not to be coerced into joining him. He took both her hands in his.

'Listen. Hear me out,' he said.

She sat stiffly. 'I can't believe this. Why on earth would you think I would do this?'

He held her hands tighter. His tone softened. 'Kate, listen. You mentioned skydiving. I've always wanted to do it. After the canal boat, I looked it up on a whim, and found this course. I had nothing else to do last Sunday, so . . .'

She looked out of the window at a small plane taking off, praying for him to say this was a joke. That they were now driving on to some nearby village pub for lunch.

'. . . So I came here and did a one-day static-line course. Did my first jump on Monday.'

She looked at him, disbelieving. He lifted his hand and she realized he was trying to hide a beaming grin.

What had she done? *She should never have told him.*

'Please tell me this is a joke.' But then she saw his tapping fingers, the wired tension of his body, and realized she'd seen it before. Hundreds of times, at the parachute school in New Zealand.

He wasn't joking.

'Four times!' Jago exclaimed, making her jump. He laughed at her reaction. 'Sorry, I'm completely wired. The adrenalin just . . .' He blew out his cheeks. 'Whoo! Sorry, I've hardly slept. I'm completely high on it. Addicted. Do you know what I mean?'

Kate let her head fall helplessly. She knew exactly what he meant. It was how it had been for her the first week she'd jumped, too. Weakly, she shook it. 'Jago. Please tell me you don't think that I . . .'

There was a loud beep behind them. She looked in her mirror to see a lorry approaching from behind.

'You'd better, um . . .' Jago said, jerking his head towards the opening to the airfield.

With no choice, Kate took off her handbrake and turned into the long driveway. Before she could pull in again, a minibus appeared from behind the lorry, and followed her up the narrow drive, forcing her to continue towards the airfield.

Jago perched on his seat, like a schoolboy who'd done something naughty and got away with it.

'OK, listen. I know you're mad, but it's going to be amazing.'

Was he mad? 'I'm not jumping, Jago,' Kate said resolutely, as they bumped along the driveway into a half-full car park. She swung round in front of three brown hangars, and put her foot on the brake hard, without turning off the engine.

Jago kept tapping his fingers.

Ten small two-seater aircraft, their wings like flattened rabbit ears across their little mousey noses, sat in the grass airfield beyond the fence, signposted to keep spectators OUT. A group of grinning charity jumpers stood lined up on the other side in matching T-shirts, having a photo taken.

Hang on. Kate swivelled around. She knew this place. This was where she had done her refresher course five years ago, with Hugo and Jack in tow.

This was real. Not a joke.

Jago leaned over carefully, put the car in neutral, pulled on the handbrake for her and turned off the key.

'Kate. Come here,' he said gently. She was so shaken, she let him, yet keeping her body rigid in protest as he wrapped his arms around her. 'Right, listen. First of all, I'm doing it with you. And, second, it's incredibly safe. We did all that stuff on Sunday about how to deal with line twists and cell-end problems, and you know yourself that even if the main parachute did malfunction, you have a reserve. Kate, you know all this. I mean, how many times have you jumped – twenty?'

Kate kept her eyes on the floor of the car, shaking her head gently.

'Twenty-six.'

'Shit. Have you really? Well, there you go.'

Panic pulsed through her at the thought of what he was asking. 'No,' she exclaimed. She jerked out of Jago's arms, pushing them aside. 'I'm not doing it. There's no way.'

But he wouldn't let her go. He grabbed her hands again. 'Listen. You're not doing a free fall from 12,000 feet like you used to. This is just a little static-line jump from 3,500 feet. A piece of piss for someone who's done free fall. All you have to do is jump, let the static line pull out your chute for you, then enjoy it.'

She looked past Jago's shoulder to the canteen garden, where she saw a man and woman doing the 'pre-jump dance' she recognized from New Zealand, sucking too fast on their cigarettes, turning randomly one way, then the other, as they waited for their jump, grinning at each other manically.

She felt Jago's eyes on her. 'Come on, Kate. Step Five. *Face the Final Fear*.'

'Jago, it's just not that simple,' she said, her shocked brain desperately looking for a way out. 'I can't just jump. I don't have my licence.'

He sat back. 'OK, well, don't be mad but I gave them your details and they found it on the international register.' She stared. He was serious about this. 'As long as you match the online photo, and you show them a bankcard or something. And they want you to do a half-day refresher course one-to-one with an instructor, too.'

A droning noise approached. Kate saw the nine-seat Islander far above them. A little figure appeared mid-air. There was a burst of yellow in the bright blue sky as the static line from the plane pulled out a parachute. She watched the tiny figure wriggling for a moment then relax back into the jump.

Right at that moment, Kate had a flashback to New Zealand so powerful she almost gasped.

She was up there, thousands of feet up in the sky.

Hearing the loud drone of the propellers dropping away into silence.

Feeling the wind whistling on her face.

Her limbs losing all resistance.

Relaxing like never before.

Falling into the void.

384

Utter euphoria descending.

Flying like a bird.

And, all of a sudden, unbelievably, Kate wanted that feeling again.

Jago pulled her to him again, and this time she did not resist.

She had *loved* it.

'Oh my God,' she whispered.

Jago murmured in her ear. 'Listen, you were going to do it after your parents died. This time it's even more important. You need to restart your life, Kate. You said yourself, Jack needs you.'

She watched the jumper gracefully turn in a semicircle back towards the white arrow on the landing field.

Could she do that again?

Jago carried on. 'And for us, too. Let's make it the start of how we plan to go on. Having fun together.'

She let him move even closer and nuzzle into her ear. He kissed her cheek, once, twice, three times, playfully. For a second, she thought of Jack and the way they used to show their love to each other so unabashedly when he was a toddler, and how she wanted that again. She imagined telling Jack she had jumped out of a plane today. Seeing the pride in his eyes as he told his friends. His mum was not weird and anxious. She was fun and brave.

'What are you asking me? We jump once and it's over?'

Jago's eyes shone with delight as he realized she was considering it. 'Once and it's over. Then we head straight back to Balliol and lock ourselves in my room for the rest of the weekend.'

His words reached inside her and unlocked a door. She felt the anxiety rush out of her, and turned and met his lips full on. The waves that had started in her kitchen last Saturday when he kissed her pulsed back through her body.

As Jago kissed her, she thought of what he'd done for her.

He'd faced his own fears up in that plane, to help her return to life. He was giving her a chance to jump back into the real world, faster than she'd ever imagined, and he was going to do it with her.

'OK,' she whispered.

CHAPTER THIRTY-NINE

Jack ran around Nana's garden, kicking his ball, realizing that he was going to do something bad. He didn't normally do bad things, but today he didn't care.

Aunt Saskia said they would tell Mum about Jago Martin tomorrow. He wanted to tell her now.

'Jack, darling?' He heard Nana shout from the house. 'It's nearly twelve. Could you pop to the village for some bread, darling?'

He ran in and found Nana at the Aga, where she was making soup.

'Of course, Nana.'

'Good boy.' She turned to find him some money. Aunt Sass was still at the computer, looking a bit lost in her head, like Mum did sometimes. 'And can you get Granddad his newspaper, and another pint of milk?'

'Sure,' Jack said, grabbing the money and Rosie's lead. Rosie leaped up at him and pawed at his leg.

To his relief, Aunt Sass didn't even look up. Jack shouted, 'Bye,' and ran out, through the garden gate onto the river path and set off past the boats, with Rosie pulling ahead. He rubbed his stomach, realizing to his surprise that the cramp was gone.

'I'm going to look after her, Dad,' he said under his breath.

He waited till he was out of sight of Granddad's house, then took his mobile from his pocket and pressed his mum's number. Would she be pleased with him, or cross?

It went straight to voicemail.

He took a long breath.

'. . . Mum. It's Jack. Don't be angry with me, but there's something wrong with that man Jago Martin. I've got his book and all the numbers are wrong in it. He's stolen bits from other books on Amazon and made then into a book with his name on it and he's pretending it's his. Don't be angry at me, but he's weird. Sorry, Mum . . .'

Back at the house, Saskia got up, feeling nauseous. She picked up Jago Martin's book.

'You OK, darling?' Helen called from the Aga.

Saskia looked at her guiltily. Helen had been so upset about the divorce, so embarrassed about all the gifts that had been given by family and friends and hardly used. If she ever found out that Saskia had brought it upon herself, that she had caused this so foolishly . . .

'Uhuh,' Saskia lied, then walked into the sitting room and shut the door. She picked up the phone and rang Kate's number.

'. . . Kate, it's me. You have to ring me back straight away. Fuck, I don't know where you are or how to tell you this but that guy Jago Martin . . .'

She spoke for another whole minute before putting the phone down.

She sat staring at Jago Martin's photo in the book, hoping to God she was right, because, if not, this would really be the end of her and Kate for good.

She tried to imagine him for the twentieth time in a suit, with black gelled hair, and hoped that this wasn't a horrible mistake. That last time she had seen this man, he really *had* been called Tony, and really *had* come from Essex.

CHAPTER FORTY

Kate couldn't believe how quickly everything came back to her.

'I'll wait for you in the canteen,' Jago had said when they arrived, after introducing her to her instructor, Calum, an ex-army man, and giving her a reassuring kiss.

'Right, this should be a doddle for you, Kate,' Calum said, 'let's go.'

At his request, she demonstrated flaring the parachute before hitting the ground, then pointed to the altimeter, her reserve chute handle and the slider, telling Calum what each was for. She pushed her riser straps apart and kicked to demonstrate how to remove a line twist, and mocked up reinflating the cell-ends with the steering lines. Five times, he made her jump from the dummy plane to check she knew the positions and how to breathe. He made her jump five times in a harness from a twenty-foot-high scaffolding rig to show she could land with her feet together and roll.

All through the morning, as Kate heard the planes droning above, and saw the jumpers pulling on their suits, she waited for the figures to come and scream at her

390

- **1 in 80,000 jumps will end in a 'serious incident'.**

But she knew that that would most likely be because if she did something stupid, like not buckling up her chest strap.

- **The chances of both chutes malfunctioning are
  1 in a million.**

And probably better than that here with qualified packers who checked and rechecked.

The figures came . . . and then they went, half-hearted, on their way again.

They had absolutely no control over her.

They would not stop her doing this.

And, even better, to her astonishment, she was *looking forward to it*.

'Right, you obviously know what you're doing, Kate,' Calum declared at the end of the morning. 'We'll have to get you to come back and jump with the club jumpers one day.'

It was funny, she thought, this stranger's perspective of her being a brave person.

'That's great that you can access my international licence online. Is that new?' she said as they crossed the concrete area back to the canteen.

Calum frowned. 'Can you? Never heard of that before. I thought you had to bring your licence and show it – but then I don't work in the office . . .'

They shrugged at each other as he dropped her off beside Jago, who was sitting outside reading a newspaper at a table.

'Right, you guys, we'll jump at 1 p.m. – we'll take the Islander up. It'll be you and two others. I'll give you a shout,' Calum said, walking off to the canteen with a wave.

Jago gave him the thumbs-up and took Kate's hand, beaming, as she sat down.

'You did it! How was it?'

She saw him check his watch.

'Good, actually.' She sniffed, wiping her nose.

'Seriously?' He grinned.

She nodded. 'How are you?'

'Shitting myself,' Jago said. The irony hit them both and they laughed.

Kate took the sip of his coffee that he offered. 'I can't believe I'm doing this.'

'It's amazing, honestly. I'm proud of you,' Jago replied.

She reached out and took his hand, no longer self-conscious. 'You know, I'd probably never have done this again, if you hadn't made me. I just remembered today how much I loved it.'

He leaned over, kissed the side of her face, then stood up. To her surprise, she saw him check his watch again. He really was nervous. 'Can't tell you how pleased I am to hear you say that. Right. What do you want? Coffee?'

'Thanks.'

Jago walked off to the canteen queue.

As she waited, Kate looked around the garden. Most tables were busy, dominated by an air of tension and excitement. She'd missed this. This world of people with adventurous purpose. The horse riding. Travelling with her friends. Skiing. Working at the parachute school in New Zealand. There had always been an element of it in her life till her parents died, and then Hugo.

She'd forgotten.

This was part of *who she was*. However crazy Jago's methods, he'd really helped her. She was here. She was getting better.

Kate stretched back, feeling the sun on her face, watching an experienced-looking group of free-fallers walk towards a larger

Caravan plane with the heroic gait of firemen or helicopter doctors. The club members that Calum had mentioned, she suspected. She saw the beginners at the tables around her watch the group with admiring glances.

That had been her once.

She thought about Calum's offer.

Was Jago right? Could it be again?

There was a soft buzz in Kate's bag. She pulled out her mobile, and saw that two voice messages had arrived when she'd been training with Calum: one from Jack, one from Saskia.

What would they think if they knew where she was now?

She lifted the phone to her ear, looking through the window at Jago standing with his back to her in the canteen queue, holding his own phone to his ear.

Vaguely, she wondered who he was talking to.

'Mum. It's Jack. Don't be angry with me, but there's something wrong with that man Jago Martin .. . .'

As Jack's message continued, Kate sensed a cloud pass over the sun. The temperature dropped.

When Jack's message finished, she pressed Saskia's.

And when that message stopped, Kate looked up and realized there was no cloud. The sun was exactly as it had been before.

Jack walked slowly back from the village shop, clutching the bread, newspaper and milk in one hand, and Rosie's lead in the other. He didn't normally do bad things and now he was worried. Would Aunt Sass be cross with him that he'd told Mum about that dodgy book before she did?

He strolled under the canopy section of trees with Rosie, not even thinking about the strange feeling he normally had under here of being watched.

So when a very big man stepped out of the bushes, he nearly jumped in the air. The man was wearing a black beanie even though it was a nice day.

With a gasp, Jack stumbled over a twig. He tried to right his footing and race ahead, but Rosie saw the man, and strained her lead in his direction.

'No, girl,' Jack said, his chest pounding. He pulled her too hard, too scared to look behind him, and marched forwards.

'Jack!'

He stopped.

'Hi! It's me. Your neighbour, Magnus! From Hubert Street. You recognize me? What on earth are you doing out here?'

With relief, Jack recognized the man from outside his bedroom window. He looked around but the path was still empty. What should he do? He didn't want to be rude. 'My grandparents live here.' He pointed vaguely down the river path.

'Oh. That's funny. Hey, nice dog!' the man said cheerfully, coming over. 'Jack, listen, this is good I bumped into you – can you maybe help me, please?' He pointed at the road behind the trees. 'I've broken down in my car back in the lane. I was just walking to the village to find a bus back to Oxford. The phone in my house in Hubert Street is not working and I need to phone my housemates to come and pick me up. Could we ring your mum, and ask her to go next door and knock on my friends' door? Tell them where I am? Then I won't have to get the bus home and leave my car here.'

Jack hesitated. Rosie whined, pulling him.

'Can't you ring the AA?' he said.

The man laughed. 'Good idea, but it costs money. I'm a poor student, you know?'

'Um. OK,' Jack said awkwardly.

The man leaned down and patted Rosie. Rosie ignored him,

whining and pulling away in the direction of her walk. 'Your mum was telling me in the garden that you're an Arsenal fan, huh?' the man said.

Jack nodded shyly.

'Me, too! You think we're going to get the championship next year, huh?'

Jack shrugged. The man stood up.

'OK. Listen. Do you know your mum's number?'

Jack nodded.

'Well, could you tell me, and I'll ring her. Maybe you could speak to her for me? My phone is back at the car, actually – could you come with me?'

Jack shrugged again, wondering if he should offer his own phone for the man to use. But the man was already walking towards his car.

Jack decided to follow him. He was their neighbour, after all.

Kate sat frozen in the canteen garden, staring at her phone.

Her mind whirled trying to think what possible motives Saskia could have for making this up.

'Kate?'

She turned to see Calum walking out of the canteen with Jago, who was carrying coffee.

'Ten minutes in the packing shed,' Calum called, with upturned thumbs, before walking off.

Jago sat down. 'That's interesting.'

'What?' she whispered.

'He was saying that they're filming a stunt for a Hollywood film here next week.'

Kate kept her eyes fixed on the table, trying to calm the rush of confused thoughts in her head.

It had to be a mistake.

Why would Saskia say this? Because she was bitter? Could she have really made this up? Involved Jack? She wouldn't dare.

Why on earth would she say Jago was Tony from Essex?

She felt a hand on her arm and looked up to see Jago watching her. 'Oi, mate. You're not flaking out on me, are you?'

She kept her eyes down. Shook her head.

'No,' she said, trying to sound normal, starting to stand up. She'd ring Saskia right now, that's what she'd do. 'I'm, uh, just going to ring my sister-in-law and check Jack's all right. I want to speak to him, tell him I'm jumping. If anything happened and . . .'

Jago's hand came out of nowhere and settled on her arm. Firmly.

'Kate. You're joking, aren't you? You'll just worry him.'

'No, but I . . .'

Jago shook his head and grabbed the phone out of her hand. 'I think it's a really bad idea. Poor lad's been through enough. You don't want to make him more anxious, do you? Tell him when you get back down – then he'll be really proud without having to worry about you.'

Kate shrugged, uneasily looking at her phone in his hand. 'OK. Well . . .' She looked around. 'Actually, I'm just going to get some sugar for my coffee . . .'

Jago jumped up before she could move an inch. Her feeling of disquiet intensified. Why was he not letting her do what she wanted to do? 'I'll get it. Stay there. Least I can do after making you jump out of a plane!' he grinned.

She tried to smile back. As he walked off – still with her phone still in his hand, she noted – she sat rigid.

Saskia. Why would she lie? Why would she tell Jack the book was fake?

Jago's small leather rucksack lay in front of her.

His phone.

She couldn't wait. She *had* to ring Saskia.

She glanced into the cafe and saw him rummaging by the till among the salt and pepper. He was still looking at his watch. Kate prayed he wouldn't see her. Quickly she grabbed it and opened it, looking for his phone and . . .

Something red caught her eye. She blinked, taking a second to compute seeing one of her own possessions in Jago's bag.

Slowly, she pulled it out.

How the hell did Jago have this?

She heard the tinkle of the cafe door and turned to see him emerge.

Their eyes met.

His eyes fell to the object she held in her hands. The one she kept in her study drawer.

He ran so quickly she couldn't move. But this time he sat beside her, on her bench, throwing the sugar on the table.

'I don't understand,' she stuttered. 'Where did you get this?'

She placed her international skydiving licence on the table. Jago said nothing. Just sighed, and reached over for his coffee.

'Jago,' Kate whispered. 'Please tell me. What is this all about?'

'Hmm?' He sipped his coffee.

She looked about her, seeing the couples around her, feeling a crack appear in the dream of a future. Wanting to be wrong, but knowing she wasn't.

'This?' She looked at him finally, motioning about the airfield with her hands.

He shrugged. 'Er, jumping out of an aeroplane, back to life, etc.'

There was a new tone in his voice she hadn't heard before. Hardened, cynical.

'No,' she said quietly. 'You taking things from my house? And pretending to be a professor of mathematics from Edinburgh. What's it about, Jago – the money?'

She lifted her eyes and met his. At first she saw the familiar warmth and humour in his blue eyes, as he registered what she knew. Then a cloud of icy mist passed through them. They froze in front of her like an Arctic icefield. She tried to look away but couldn't. She saw dark crevices where the dark irises were, ice floes form in the intent of his pupils, so cruel and inhospitable that they made her shudder.

As a reflex, she leaned back. Yet Jago came with her, so close to her face that she could smell coffee on his breath. She tried to move away but realized he had placed his hand on her upper arm and gripped it tight.

'Jago. Let go of my arm.'

'No. So, what did you say – is it about the money?' Jago said. She blinked. What was wrong with his voice? He was speaking in a different accent. English. West Country. Stripped of the paternal Scottish warmth, this new voice was infused with the threat of a stranger. 'You mean, the one-point-eight million pounds?'

Kate froze.

She looked around the garden frantically, but the jumpers were talking in tight-knit groups, lost in their own world of facing their own fears.

'Get off me,' she repeated. Yet Jago's grip just tightened. Tears formed at the back of her eyes as it began to hurt. 'I said, let me *go*,' she said, but it came out so weakly it was hardly there at all. She summoned everything she had. 'Look. If you don't let go of my fucking arm, I'm going to scream.'

Jago pulled her so close she thought the bone would break in her arm.

'Uhuh, and if you do, I'll tell my friend the Viking – whom

you might know better as the bloke next door – to throw your son in the fucking river.'

Kate tried to call out 'No!' but the word stuck in her throat.

Jack walked beside the man back to his car on the lane. It was a black car.

He opened the door, and Jack glanced around nervously. The man saw him do it.

'Hey, please, don't worry, Jack. Your mum told you not to get in cars with strangers. That's good.'

He waited nervously as the man brought out a phone.

'What's your mum's number?'

Jack told him and watched the man put it in with his big fingers. That was strange. It looked different to Mum's number.

The man looked up. 'This is great, Jack. Really helpful.'

From the front, Kate knew that Jago's hold on her must look like an embrace. A boyfriend hugging his nervous girlfriend before her jump.

'Why are you talking about Jack?' she said.

Jago's phone rang. He checked his watch. 'And, finally, on cue . . .' he said. He took it out with his free hand and answered it away from her. He murmured something into it, then turned to her. 'Someone who wants to talk to you.'

She took it, with shaky fingers.

'Kate!' a man's voice said in a Scandinavian accent.

'Who is this?'

'Magnus next door. I have your son, Jack, here by the river. He's just giving me a hand.'

Kate's eyes opened wide. She shook her head at Jago.

'What are you talking . . .?'

'Mum?'

'Jack! Where are you?'

His voice was timid. 'By the river near Granddad's house. Magnus said, can you go next door and tell his friends to come and pick him up. His car's broken.'

Jago hissed in her ear. 'I would advise you strongly to say yes.'

Kate shook her head, and tried to pull away from him. 'Jack!' she started to shout.

'If you don't want him to end up going for a little swim right now in Granddad's river, say yes.'

Kate's heart began to thump so hard in her chest she thought she would vomit it out of her mouth.

Jago mouthed at her. One, two, three . . .

'Yes, Jack. That's fine. I'll do it,' she said. Jago began to pull the phone away from her face, she gasped, 'Jack, Jack . . .'

But he was gone.

She sat on the bench, as Jago put the phone back in his pocket, fighting the urge to scream for help and knowing she couldn't risk it. Desperately, she tried to think straight. They had kidnapped *Jack*. 'Jesus, is this really about the money? Have it!' she exclaimed. 'I never wanted it in the first place. Just let Jack go.'

'Oh, it's always the same with you lot,' Jago said, sounding disappointed. 'You don't care because you've always had it.' He turned his voice into a high-pitched whine. 'When I was a teen-ager I used to go skiing and jump five-bar gates on my pony.' She shuddered at hearing her own words. 'But the thing is, Kate, if it wasn't for me, you wouldn't have had half of it.'

'What?' she said, hating Richard and Helen with every part of her for letting Jack go to the shop alone. How long before they realized he was missing?

Jago shrugged. 'Where do you think the quarter of a million

pounds came from that Richard gave Hugo to start your business?'

Kate thought at first she'd misheard him. 'How could you know that?' she stammered.

'How do I know?' Jago continued. She looked at his mouth, unable to believe these vicious words were coming from those gentle lips. 'Because I know everything. I know Richard and his partner Charley Heaven, the builder, took every penny my dad had one night in the pub and sold him a piece of shit house on a hill with rotten foundations that fell down. And because of that, our lives fell apart. My father killed my mother, then killed himself in jail. When I was nine.' He pulled back, as if to enjoy Kate's horrified expression. 'And then Richard Parker took the profit and started his business. Fucked off out of Cornwall as soon as he could. That's how I know, Kate. Richard Parker ruined my fucking life.'

She felt a creeping sense of horror. 'This is about Richard?'

He loosened his grip, but just a little. 'Well, to be honest, Kate, it probably should have been Charley. But the fat fuck died of a heart attack on the beach in Portugal, so I'm afraid the finger of fate chose your Richard. So yes, it is about Richard.'

Kate stared, fighting back frightened tears. 'I'm sorry. But he's not my Richard. It's not my fault. Or Jack's.'

Jago sighed. 'I know that, Kate. But, the thing is, I don't care.'

She saw him look over her shoulder and wave. Calum was summoning them.

'Shall we go?'

'No,' Kate exclaimed, but he pulled her up, keeping his arm around her as they walked to the giant open-fronted packing shed. Calum pointed to the jumpsuits and their parachutes.

In shock, Kate did as she was asked, desperately trying to think as she pulled on her overalls and chute, with shaking fingers. Without being asked, Jago did up her chest strap, holding her tight when she pulled away, reviled as he touched her breast. He shuddered suddenly, as if he was experiencing a little thrill. 'You know, this is a big day for me. I've been planning this one for five years.'

'What do you mean, "this one"?' she asked, terrified.

'Well, it's not easy. The important thing is that Richard doesn't find out that it's about him. Because that way I can keep going right to the end. So I mean this step. First the dog . . .' he murmured. He put his hands up like two little paws desperately scrabbling in the air, and began to whine.

It took Kate a horrible moment to register. '*Hugo*'s dog?' She remembered Hugo talking about the dog, how he'd never wanted one since, he'd been so upset as a teenager. '*You drowned his dog?*'

Jago put on his own helmet. 'That's what gave me the idea. Honestly, seeing Hugo's face. Seeing the cracks in Richard's face, not being able to fix it for him. It just helped, you know?'

Kate put her hands to her face. 'Jago, I'm sorry; this is crazy. You're telling me you drowned Hugo's dog because of Richard. But that was twenty years ago!'

Jago held out a helmet for her. He was so calm.

'I know it's hard to understand, but what you're seeing today, Kate, is my life. What I do for my parents. Putting cracks in Richard Parker's world, and then watching it crumble, brick by brick. Just like he did to ours. Trust me, it's nothing personal against you.'

Kate stared. Then, with an explosion of understanding, she reeled backwards.

'*What else have you done?*'

Magnus waved goodbye to Jack and he set off home, relieved.

'Snores!' he heard Sass shout as he came up to the house.

402

'Here,' he said feeling guilty.

'Are you OK? Why did you take so long? Granddad's gone that way down the lane looking for you.'

'I was helping that man.'

'What man?'

They peered back out of the gate.

'Oh,' Jack said. That was weird. 'He's gone. His car must have started working again.'

Saskia followed his eyes. 'Well, never mind. Listen, I think I'm going to take you back to your mum's this afternoon. I need to speak to her not in front of Nana or Granddad.'

'What about?'

'Don't you worry.'

He hoped when she found out what he'd done she wouldn't be cross.

'I said, what else have you done?' Kate repeated, weakly.

'Guys, over by the manifest, please,' she heard Calum shout. He held out a small cloth bag. 'I'll need to take your mobiles, keys, anything loose that could fall out – in here, please.'

Jago put his hand on her back and firmly guided her forwards. Kate's brain felt under fire. Bullets of information that made no sense flew at her from all directions. Shaken, she found herself clutching at her car keys, to stop them dropping from her damp palms.

As they approached Calum, and the open valuables bag that he offered, she looked over and saw their plane waiting on the field. Jago was taking her on a plane. Telling her things that made no sense. Taking her up in the sky. Why?

Jack!

THINK, Kate yelled to herself in a panic.

Pull yourself together.

Jack's in trouble.

THINK.

She forced a long deep breath through her body in a desperate attempt to calm herself. And, then, from somewhere through the fug of shock, in the tiny space she created for herself, Jago's voice miraculously drifted into her head. Not the Jago standing in front of her, the frightening stranger with the unfamiliar West Country accent who had stolen her son, but kind, sweet Jago from last week. From the night in Chumsley Norton, from the canal boat, from Highgate Woods. 'Trust your instincts, Kate,' said the kindly Scottish accent in her head. 'Trust your *instincts*.'

She had to.

She had to stop trying to work out what he was saying to her, and work out how to survive this, for Jack's sake.

Jago stepped in front of her. As he moved forwards, she took her keys into her shaking right hand.

Jago dropped his phone into the bag, then turned to her. Calum, too, watched Kate expectantly.

'Anything, Kate?' he asked.

'Yeah,' she said, quickly, sticking her closed right hand quickly into the bag and dropping her car keys in heavily.

Jago placed his hand on her back. This afternoon, the touch of it there had sent a shiver of anticipation through her. Now it felt like a steel rod.

His eyes fixed on hers, cold and hard.

STAY CALM, she thought. She searched for a phone, any phone. Grasping the smallest in the bag, as subtly as she could, she formed a cage around it with sweaty fingers.

'Is it safe to jump? It seems more windy suddenly,' she asked Calum, to distract Jago.

''Course it is, darling,' Jago interrupted, the steel rod pushing further into her back. He winked at Calum.

Praying, hating him, Kate gently pulled out the phone.

KEEP YOUR NERVE.

Jago blinked.

'You'll be fine, Kate,' Calum said, tying the top together. Jago's face broke into what she could see was an attempt at a relaxed smile. 'Now, could you follow the others over to the manifest board?'

She felt Jago's fingers between her vertebrae, prodding her forwards, as they walked to the manifest area, where the other two passengers were writing on their names, checking they were doing it right. He took his arm from behind her back, put it around her shoulders and whispered intently into her ear. Kate glanced at the others. She knew what they saw: the kind boy-friend, soothing her nerves.

'Anyway, now back to my story – do you remember you used to meet Hugo in a pub in Archway when you were at college? Your local?'

Kate felt her legs start to shake uncontrollably. She gripped the phone.

'Well, I used to watch you there.'

What was he saying?

THINK, she screamed in her head. *Breathe*.

'Well, one day, you left, and Hugo watched you,' Jago sneered into her ear, 'and I could tell he was dreaming. Thinking about you. The future. And then I thought, what could I do to take the smile off his big fat face?'

'No,' Kate said. 'No,' she shook her head. 'No.'

He pulled her in more tightly. 'What could I do that would make Richard's son's marriage shit from Day One. What could I do to put a great big fuck-off crack through it?'

A cramp in her stomach now. Nausea. She bent her middle finger hard, and pointed it hard inside her palm, pushing the bottom of the phone inside her sleeve to keep it safe.

'. . . Something that no one would trace back to me.'

She shook her head. 'You can't have,' she whispered. 'Their car hit a stag . . .'

Jago rolled his eyes. 'If you're as pissed off as me, honestly, Kate, anything's possible. Remember, I lost my parents, too. No, it wasn't easy, but I shot it with one of my dad's old poaching rifles, dragged it onto my truck tailgate with a rig, and waited till dark.'

The words came out of her mouth, broken into pieces. 'You caused my parents' car crash?'

One of the two other jumpers, a middle-aged woman, came over with the pen. Jago pulled back and smiled.

'Nervous?' she asked.

Kate nodded.

'Me too,' she said sympathetically. 'We'll be fine.'

'Well said,' Jago said, taking the pen from the woman with a wink.

As she walked off with the other jumper onto the field towards the plane, he took the pen and wrote both their names on the manifest board.

'And then . . .'

Kate's mouth flew open as a new horrific vision came into her head. 'No,' she repeated. She tried to turn, but he pulled her close again and shouted in her ear above the passing noise of a small aircraft that was taxiing to another part of the field. Tears came into her eyes again.

She fought them back.

STOP CRYING. THINK.

'Every week. Sat on the bench outside your house in Highgate, bought with my family's blood money. Saw him bring that car home. Saw him looking to see what the neighbours thought.'

'But those men . . .'

He kept his nose pressed hard into her ear. 'The Viking gathers information when I need it, and he gives it to people too. He opened his big mouth beside them in their pub one night about this fifty-thousand-pound sports car his neighbour had bought. All I had to do was slip in after they'd left with his keys. The door was open. Hugo was just about to phone the police.'

Kate held out her hands, aimlessly, as if she were trying to fight off something she couldn't see.

'And, you know what the best bit was?' Jago said, putting down the pen, and guiding her onto the field behind the others. 'I told him all of this. Told him it would be you next. But I'd give it another five years. Because first I wanted to enjoy watching Richard trying to keep the cracks together with his big, smiley, desperate face. Waiting until you'd had enough of the cold nights. Were ready to be warmed up again.' He forced Kate to look at him. 'Hugo particularly liked that detail. Actually, it was a long wait, so I practised on your sister-in-law, and caused Richard and Helen a little embarrassment in the process . . . *crack* . . .'

Kate took his hand, beseeching him with her eyes as she started to realize what was coming. '*Please, Jago.* Please. Not Jack.'

He shook his head as if soothing a child. 'Kate, honestly, I'm not going to touch him. I've worked it out. I reckon his foundations will be so rotten after I've finished with you lot, I can sit back and watch him fuck up his own life.'

'What do you mean, finished with . . .?'

'Well, his grandparents, his father, and now . . .' He pushed her along as Calum marched ahead to the plane fifty yards away, her feet almost off the ground.

She looked at it up ahead. 'No,' she said desperately. 'There are people all around us. You can't.'

'I know, which is why, when you jump out, you're going

to . . .' Jago whispered something in her ear. It was something that in this morning's safety refresher Calum had reminded her never to do.

She pulled back, horrified. 'But my chute will get entangled.'

Jago shrugged. 'Kate, don't worry. There's a note on your computer called "Sorry", explaining why you did it. That you were a shit mother and you knew it.'

She shook her head, trying to suck in air, but he kept pulling her towards the plane. Forty yards, thirty . . .

He was telling her to jump out. Sabotage her own chute.

THINK, her brain screamed. Stop listening to him. Think what you're going to do.

Jack NEEDS YOU.

Jago's arm pulled her faster towards the plane. Twenty yards, ten . . .

'The thing is, if you don't do it, Kate, if the Viking doesn't hear you did it, in twenty minutes, Jack's going to dive into the river to save Rosie. I'll be out of here before you can check. And, thanks to the money the Viking took out of your internet account yesterday, I'll be gone for a long time. But when they stop looking for me – and they will – I'll come back for you, anyway. This way, you save your son at least. If you don't, he goes in the river and I come back for you. It might be a year, or five. In a wardrobe, behind a door, in a window, who knows?' He kissed her ear and said in a playful scary voice: 'The monster in the dark.'

'Get off me,' she gasped, as they finally reached the back of the plane.

He embraced her, making her want to retch at the forced intimacy, hiding her from Calum who strode ahead to talk to the pilot. 'It's a shame you had to run off last Saturday and that we couldn't finish what we started in the kitchen. But it doesn't matter. Because one day, when Richard is an old man, lying in the ruins of his family, just like my mother was, I'll tell him about today, and your sad, scared face. Watch his.'

'All right, Kate?' Calum said, coming over to check her equipment. She saw him note her expression. 'You sure?'

Could she tell him, shout for help? Tell him she'd lost her nerve, didn't want to jump?

But what if Jago was telling the truth? What if they hurt Jack?

She forced herself to shrug casually, her finger touching the phone in her hand.

THINK.

It had been Jago, the whole time, for the past eleven years.

He had killed Hugo and her parents, and had been frightening her ever since.

None of it had been imagined.

She had been right. Her instinct had been RIGHT.

And now he wanted to kill her.

THINK. Her instincts. She needed to use her instincts.

Kate forced herself to breathe deeply, to keep the oxygen coming. To remember the power she'd felt in Chumsley Norton, in Highgate Woods.

Her eyes danced about. She was nearly out of time.

She thought about everything that had happened. Meeting him in the cafe, the book, the waitress, the dog, the canal boat, the woods . . . And then, a thought came spinning furiously into her head.

An image of Jago's book. Locked in her shed.

She looked him in the eye. Slowly. She saw him register her revelation. Saw the ice melt, momentarily. 'I've got your book!' she said, as Calum looked over her straps. She saw Jago glance at him, checking if he'd heard.

'No, you don't,' Jago said casually.

'Yes, I do. You left it in the juice bar. The waitress gave it to me.'

Jago dropped her gaze. He turned round as Calum now checked his straps.

'No. I went back. Twice. She said I didn't leave it there.'

Kate remembered the waitress's earnest expression. 'Interesting guy.' Had she known something was wrong about Jago? 'Well, she lied,' Kate said.

Jago shook his head again. He waited till Calum walked away to check the others. 'No, Kate. The Viking checked your house, top to bottom.'

He had faltered. A moment of weakness. She felt new power surge into her.

'It was locked in the shed.'

Jago turned his face further from her. Trying to hide his disquiet, Kate realized.

'Yeah, nice try, Kate.'

'Jack has it,' she said triumphantly as Calum called out to them that they would board in three minutes. 'And this morning, he gave it to Saskia and she recognized you. Tony from Essex, she said. She's showing it to the police right now. She thought you were after my money.' The words tumbled out. Desperately, she hoped her face wouldn't give away her bluff. She saw the middle-aged female passenger, her shoulders shaking hysterically, laughing nervously with her friend.

Highgate Woods came back to her. There was no such thing as the hunter and the victim. Anyone could be both. It was their choice. He'd taught her that.

Be the monster.

She pointed to the gate where he'd been looking. 'So, I expect they'll be here by the time you hit the ground,' she yelled.

'Yeah, yeah.' He shrugged, but she knew he was rattled. It gave her strength.

'And another thing, Jago, even if I do what you ask of me, Jack will be fine. Because he has this sweet heart, just like his dad. He's had so much love from all of us. And I'm sorry. What happened to you was awful, Jago, but what you've done is so much worse. What you have done is evil. People who are bullied have a choice whether to do it themselves.'

He sneered. 'You did it, Kate. I watched you. Hurt people just like you'd been hurt, and enjoyed it. I know what you did to those girls.'

She nodded. 'I did, Jago, and the difference is that I felt bad. And that was what I was going to tell you tonight, before we went back to your pretend room at Balliol. About who I really am. And who I am is not someone who can hurt and scare people like that. I was going to tell you that I bought the old man a rowing boat this week and had it delivered when he was out. And yesterday, I sent a note via the Highgate rangers to tell the girls that they were safe. That it was a student prank gone wrong, and we apologize. I sent the same note to the health shop and asked them to tell the woman with the dog next time she came in. So you're right, I felt what it was like, and I didn't like it.'

She touched the black plastic inside her sleeve with one finger, more certain now. She had him on the back foot. Now was her chance, her only chance. But who would she ring?

Richard and Helen? Saskia? The police? But the weirdo might throw Jack in the river before they could get there. Same reason she couldn't call for help from Calum.

As she thought, instinct told her to keep distracting Jago. 'The thing is, I am not like you,' she said, trying to keep thinking. 'And my son would never be like you, and if your mother could see you now, she would thank God she didn't live. You have a choice how you let life affect you and we don't all make the same choice as you. Monsters are made, not born.'

Jago grabbed her arm again, and pulled her close against the back of the plane. With a growl, the engine on the wing burst into life in front of them.

'You know what, Kate,' Jago shouted above the noise. 'Let's see, shall we? See what happens if you don't do what I say?'

Calum waved the first two jumpers onto the plane, then turned to Kate.

'OK?' he yelled over the engine.

There were only seconds now.

USE YOUR INSTINCTS.

And then, suddenly, Kate knew who to ring. She pushed Jago's arm off and climbed in the door of the plane, knowing she only had seconds.

As Jago started to follow behind her, she spun round.

'Calum, could you just recheck Jago's altimeter? I don't think he's reset it right?' she shouted, pointing at Jago's arm.

Angrily, Jago tried to follow her onto the plane but Calum blocked him.

'Let me have a quick look, mate.'

Kate moved forwards into the tiny long tube, with her back to Jago, knowing Calum would not let Jago on till he was happy. Ignoring the smiles of the other passengers, she frantically pulled her phone from her sleeve.

JACK. She would ring Jack.

Without any of them seeing, she texted Jack's number with shaking fingers.

its mum – where r u?

She turned and saw Calum was carefully checking the little machine on Jago's left arm. Jago was glaring at him, his fury no longer disguised. His hands gripped firmly onto the side of the plane door, waiting to climb on.

A message pinged back.

at nana's – u get my message?

'Oh,' Kate gasped.

He was safe. Jago was lying.

She held the phone tight inside her hand as Jago climbed on behind her, followed by Calum. She felt him come up behind her but kept her back to him.

Calum checked their hooks were connected to their static lines, then gave the pilot the signal. With a roar, the little plane powered up the runway like an angry fly.

'Nice day for a swim,' Jago said.

Calum talked into his radio with ground control.

As the plane buzzed into the air, bumping on the currents, Kate gripped the floor.

Jack was safe.

Now what?

Jago shuffled up behind her, his legs touching hers.

'We should go out on the river later,' he said.

Just don't think about it, she thought. Not till you're on the ground. Concentrate.

The plane flew upwards, till it was at 3,500 feet. Kate looked ahead as Calum opened the hatch.

She was going to jump out of a plane.

'Right, guys. You're up!' Calum shouted over the rasping engine noise, signalling from the open hatch.

Kate began to shuffle forward. She felt Jago coming behind her.

'NUMBER ONE!' Calum shouted, signalling to Kate.

Kate turned behind her, to see Jago. Calmly, she took the phone from her sleeve with Jack's text message, and lifted it to Jago's face.

'Before you hit the ground, I'm going to get someone to ring the police,' she mouthed clearly over the engine so that he could understand every word.

Then she saw it. The ice cracked. Fear flooded into Jago's eyes. He put his hand out but Kate was ready for him. She moved swiftly forwards in front of Calum before Jago could touch her.

She looked back and saw a man alone, stranded alone in a terrible life, and she was no longer scared. Hugo's love and her parents' love and Jack's love wrapped tightly around her.

'Sorry, Calum, I did forget to put this in the bag,' she shouted, handing the phone to Calum. He frowned and waved her forwards, taking it from her hand.

Jago tried to lunge forwards again, but Calum was in the way now, helping Kate to the door.

She shuffled along to the edge, refusing to look back. As Calum did her pre-jump check, she pushed her legs into the powerful wall of air that rushed past the open door of the plane, feeling calm descend on her, remembering that this was who she was. She knew how to do this. She placed her left hand on the door, her right on the floor, ready to push off.

She looked down and saw fields 3,500 feet below her.

She saw death and knew she could face it, just as she'd faced it 26 times before.

'Go!' Calum shouted.

And with that she lifted her arms, flung back her head and jumped.

'ONE THOUSAND!' she yelled to make herself breathe. 'TWO THOUSAND! THREE THOUSAND! FOUR THOUSAND!'

Her parachute exploded into life above her, and she felt the welcome tug.

'CHECK CANOPY!' she yelled, looking up. A beautiful billowing parachute greeted her. Her lines were clean, her slider down, her cell-ends inflated.

She pulled her brake toggles down a couple of times to be sure, then leaned into her flight.

It all came back so suddenly, but as if it had been yesterday.

Hearing the loud drone of the propellers dropping away into silence.

Feeling the wind whistling on her face.

Her limbs losing all resistance.

Falling into the void.

Utter euphoria descending.

Flying like a bird.

She flew for a couple of minutes, gently pulling her steering line to take her towards the arrow on the ground.

She could see for miles in every direction.

Patchwork fields and road and trains, and places to go.

The world laid out before her, waiting for her.

Relief surged through her.

It had all been Jago, the whole time.

Her instincts had been right.

She had protected herself and Jack, while everyone said she was mad.

She was going to be all right, and so was her son. She knew it.

She had kept them safe. Her and no one else.

'I did it, Hugo,' she whispered.

Then a movement below her.

People gathering. Pointing. Running backwards as if trying to see better.

Looking up at the sky.

She turned.

Jago was plummeting head first, upside down, towards the ground, his main chute wrapped around his legs. As he hit 1,500 feet, his reserve opened automatically, and she thought for a moment that it might save him, but it too became tangled in his legs and main chute, and flapped uselessly.

She looked down again.

Someone had a camera. Someone was filming Jago's fall.

And even though the monster had finally come out of the shadows, and shown himself, she couldn't watch his end.

So she looked up at the sky.

Heard nothing when he landed.

Just knew it was over.

The boy climbed out of the back seat of his father's Jaguar and ran up the hill to the ruin, holding his toy soldier aloft.

This was exciting. It was like a proper ruin that you saw in war films, that soldiers had hit with a tank. Broken walls and a collapsed roof and belongings strewn all around the ground.

The little boy turned and saw his dad talking to the fat man who'd come up the hill with them in the car. Dad was shaking his head. He looked worried and angry at the same time.

'His own bloody fault, Charley,' he was saying. 'Bought the bloody thing without a survey, or insurance. Trying to keep it together with a car jack, apparently. God knows what damage that did. Now we've got a bloody court case to deal with.'

The little boy shrugged. He didn't know what Dad and the man were talking about; he just knew that they were not smiling.

As he ran around the ruin, something shiny caught his eye. He bent down and pulled a little plastic dome from the rubble. He stood up, wiped the dust off it and shook it. It was a snowdome. Glitter exploded over a little mountain.

The boy smiled, then put it in his pocket.

'Hugo!' his father's voice came from behind him. 'Right, boy. Time to go.'

And Hugo ran off down the hill, with the snowdome, wondering about the boy called Peter who lived here before the house fell down, and wondering where he was now.

CHAPTER FORTY-ONE

Kate stopped in front of the juice bar mid-afternoon. It was a Tuesday and the auburn-haired waitress was behind the counter. She locked her bike up and went in.

The girl came over, her eyes widening.

'Oh it's you. Oh my God, was that the Scottish guy, on the news?'

Kate nodded.

The girl flung a hand over her mouth. 'That's so awful. I wasn't sure. It looked like him in the photo, but I thought he was called Jago, and on the news they said "Peter something"?'

Kate shrugged. 'It's a long story. But, yes, it was him. I just wanted to ask you how you knew there was something weird.'

The waitress rolled her eyes. 'I'm so sorry. The first time you came in here, he followed you in and gave me £50 to pretend that I fancied him to you, to say that he had a sexy accent et cetera. I thought I was just helping him out because he was shy. Then when I saw him do that thing with the dog, I felt bad. I'm sorry, I don't mean to be rude, but you looked so fragile and vulnerable, and he just seemed weird. I thought, if I gave you his bag you might find something in it that told you what he was up to, some strange porn or something. He came back twice looking for it, and to be honest, he scared me. He was so angry that it had gone, and I knew there was something odd about him.'

Kate touched the girl's hand. 'Well, thanks. You were right.'

'They said it might have been suicide? On the news?'

Kate shook her head. 'They don't know yet. He jumped in a way they teach you never to do. He knew what might happen if he did, so either he did it on purpose, or he genuinely made a very bad mistake then froze and couldn't release his main chute when his reserve opened. The odds of it happening are tiny, so maybe he was just unlucky.'

'Got to be someone, I suppose, eh?' the girl said.

Kate nodded, 'Got to be someone.'

She arrived home fifteen minutes later, and Saskia answered the door.

'He's in his room,' she said.

'Thanks.' She put down her bag. 'How are your parents?'

Tears filled Saskia's eyes, which were already red from crying. She shook her head. 'Dad won't speak to anyone. He just looks so gaunt, Kate. He can't even look at us. He keeps going out on his boat. It's horrible. I think Mum's too scared to come over to see you. She keeps saying that Jago Martin – or Peter or whoever he was – his dad was an alcoholic, and it was his fault because he took his wife's money without asking and bought that house off Charley for cash without a survey or insurance. They knew each other from the pub, apparently. It wasn't Dad's fault. That regulations were different back then.'

Kate avoided Saskia's eyes. Richard's monsters were his own to deal with now.

'How did you get on at the police station?' Saskia sniffed.

'They're telling Stan the taxi driver's family in Shropshire today. And the lawyers for the guys that took Hugo's car have filed for an immediate dismissal of the murder charges.'

'What about the weirdo next door?'

Kate shrugged, shivering at the thought of that horrible man so close to her and Jack. How Saskia had tried to warn her, and how she'd ignored her. 'They questioned him this afternoon and they're going to search his house later to find out how he knew all that stuff about me. He's a serial burglar – he absconded from prison years ago, abroad, apparently,' she said, rubbing her eyes, exhausted. 'The police think he came to London, and met Jago through some dodgy bloke they both knew. Jago helped him get a new identity, then the weirdo said Jago kept blackmailing him into doing shady stuff for him.' She rubbed her upper arm. 'He was so clever – the weirdo thought he was Scottish too, never even knew his name. He had me believing this whole incredible lie, too, about him living in America, and having a girlfriend there – I think to make me jealous and to distract me from what he was really up to.'

Saskia turned one way, then another in the hall, shaking her head. 'Oh God, all those people. Your parents. Hugo. It's such a mess. I'm so sorry, Kate.'

'It's OK, Sass, it's not your fault,' Kate said, pulling her into a hug, knowing it was what Hugo would want her to do. They held each other tight.

When Saskia left, Kate went upstairs and found Jack sitting on his bed, playing on the laptop.

She sat down, and smoothed down his hair.

'I have something to tell you.'

He waited.

'Well, I think we've had a really horrible time, you and me, Jack, and I think it's time now for us to put it behind us, and think about what we're going to do next. Think about the future. So I've arranged for all Dad's furniture to be picked up tomorrow to be put in storage for you for when you're older, and then you can decide what to do with it. And then we're going to turn the dining room into a games room with a pool table so you can have your friends over.'

Jack grinned. 'Really?'

'Uhuh.'

Then his smile disappeared. 'But wouldn't Dad be sad?'

'No. Absolutely not. And if you wanted to sell that furniture when you're an adult to pay for something you'd love to do, I promise you, he'd be delighted. Your dad was such a happy person. It's what people loved about him. He loved life, and he'd want us to get on with ours, too and enjoy them. Starting now.'

Jack watched her with his big green eyes.

'So, the other thing is, at the end of term, you and me are going to Spain for a month to stay in David's house. On our own. And, guess what, there's a sailing school there, apparently, and I thought we could try it together.'

'Woo-hoo!' Jack shouted, like Homer.

She laughed and leaned forwards to kiss him. She stayed there for a second, resting her lips against his cheek, as if he was a toddler, and to her joy, he let her. Just for a second.

'Mum?' he said pulling back.

'Hmm?'

'Are you going to go parachuting again?' he said.

'Why?'

'I just wondered.'

'Well, I'm going to think about it.'

'What was it like?'

She laughed, 'Jack. You've asked me that a hundred times now.'

'But that man died doing it.'

'Well, we think he might have done that on purpose. And if

not, he was just very, very unlucky, Jack. And I think you and I have had our fair share of bad luck for now, don't you? But, you know what, it might be over now.'

Jack appraised her, then turned over to go to sleep.

She went over to the wardrobe and peered inside.

'Checking for monsters?' Jack asked.

She turned and smiled.

'There's no such thing, Jack.'

Acknowledgements

Thanks to my editor Trisha Jackson for her enthusiasm and support for *Accidents Happen*, and to Natasha Harding, Harriet Sanders, Liz Johnson, Jon Mitchell and the rest of the team at Pan Macmillan. Also to Lizzy Kremer at David Higham Associates for her expert guidance, and to Laura West and Harriet Moore.

A special debt of gratitude to Sarah B, who steered me through the world of statistics and probability, and to Phillip Lloyd of Lloyd Projects, for help with period property restoration. And to Skydive Headcorn parachute school for a fantastic morning learning the safe way to parachute (I will be back to jump, I hope!). I am responsible for the use of all information in this fictional context, and for any mistakes.

Further thanks to Linda Thomas, Jon Hird, Tracey Smith, Laura, Su Butcher, Kim Mansfield-Davies, Mandy Cohen, Francesca Hillier, Bridget and Sita Brahmachari. And to my family, especially my mum, Tim, and my own real-life lovely in-laws, Hazel and David.

I gathered my statistics as Kate would have done: randomly from internet sites, some British, some American. While I have stayed faithful to the layout of central Oxford, I have taken licence with the waterways, along with my fictional account of the fantastic bat-watch run by the real and very committed rangers of Highgate Woods!

I borrowed the story of the amazing Frano Selak from real life. He famously became known as 'the world's luckiest man', after cheating death seven times, then winning £600,000 on the lottery – which he then gave away . . .

If you enjoyed reading
Accidents Happen, here is a taster of
Louise Millar's incredible debut novel

The Playdate
LOUISE MILLAR

ISBN: 978-0-330-54500-6

You leave your child with a friend.
Everyone does it. Until the day it goes wrong.

Sound designer Callie Roberts is a single mother. And she's come to rely heavily on her best friend and neighbour, Suzy. Over the past few lonely years, Suzy has been good to Callie and her rather frail daughter, Rae, and she's welcomed them into her large, apparently happy family.

But Callie knows that Suzy's life is not quite as perfect as it seems. It's time she pulled away – and she needs to get back to work. So why does she keep putting off telling Suzy? And who will care for Rae? In the anonymous city street, the houses each hide a very different family, each with their own secrets. Callie's increased sense of alienation leads her to try and befriend a new resident, Debs. But she's odd – you certainly wouldn't trust her with your child – especially if you knew anything about her past . . .

A brilliant and chilling evocation of modern life, in which friendships might be longstanding but remain superficial.

'I started reading and couldn't stop . . . a must-read that will tap into every mother's primal fears'
                                                    Sophie Hannah

FRIDAY

Chapter One

Callie

The water is cold. I knew it would be, despite the disco ball of early summer sun that twirls through the willow trees onto the dark green, velvety pond. I pull my foot out quickly and rub its soft, icy edges. A small yellow leaf sticks to my ankle. I'm not sure I am up for this.

'There's something slimy in there,' I say.

Suzy adopts the pout she uses when she's trying to get Henry to eat broccoli. 'Come on – it's yummy.' We both laugh.

She stands up, towering above me at her full five foot ten. With one swift movement, she pulls her grey towelling dress over her head and kicks off her flip-flops. She stands at the water's edge in a black bikini and looks out. An elderly lady glides towards her with smooth, long strokes, a blue rubber hat perched on wire-wool hair. Suzy smiles and waits patiently for her to pass.

I sit back on my elbows. There are about twenty women on the grass, in various small groups or alone. Some are reading, some talking. Two are lying close together, laughing, their legs entwined. I look back at Suzy, who is still waiting for the old lady to move safely out of her path. It takes me a minute to realize I am staring at her body. It's not that I haven't seen it a hundred times before, marching naked round the swimming baths' changing room after the kids, or whipping off her top in her kitchen when she gets gravy on it. No, what is strange is to see her body unfettered by children. In the two and a half years I have known Suzy, there has almost always been a child attached to it: feeding at a breast, astride a hip, wriggling under an arm.

Suddenly I notice how young she is. It's amazing how well her body has recovered from three children. She has a thick waist, and a flat stomach with no hint of the soft pouch of flesh that Rae has left on mine. Her substantial bust sits high, politely accepting the support of the bikini, but not really needing it. Her skin is creamy and smooth, her frame strong and athletic. Taking a deep breath, she lifts her arms with the confidence of a girl who's spent her childhood lake-swimming in the Colorado mountains, and dives into Hampstead Ladies' Pond, ejecting a startled duck.

I lie back and try to concentrate on where we are. A fly buzzes at my nose. There is an air of calm around the pond. A hidden world behind the trees of Hampstead Heath, where women swim and stretch and smile; far from the company of men. Perhaps this is what the inner sanctum of a harem feels like.

Yes, I think. What could be better than this? Sitting in the early summer sun on a Friday afternoon with no kids and no work to worry about.

Yet that is not really how I feel at all.

The hot sun pricks my face a little unpleasantly. I try to focus on the sounds around me to relax. I used to collect interesting sounds, storing mentally the tiniest hum or echo, or whisper of wind that I heard and liked, in case one day I might need them. Today there is birdsong from a warbler, the soft swish of Suzy's strokes, the crack of a squirrel on a twig.

It is no use. However much I stretch my legs out, the tension that makes my buttocks and thighs clench won't release. My

430

mind is racing. I need to tell Suzy. I can't keep this secret from her. There is enough I hide from Suzy already. I sit up again and check where she is. She's travelled to one side of the pond and is working her way back.

Oh, what the hell. I am here now. I stand up and walk over to the ladder, and begin gingerly to climb into the murky water. The noticeboard says there are terrapins and crayfish in here.

'Good girl!' Suzy calls across, clapping to encourage me.

I roll my eyes to show her I am not convinced. The water is cold and earthy as I lower myself into it, shivering. Bit by bit, the icy ring moves up my body until I am almost immersed.

'Just swim,' calls Suzy. Her bright American tone echoes out across the pond and the female lifeguard looks over.

I launch myself off the edge. I am not a good swimmer. Suzy approaches me.

'This is so great,' she says, turning on her back and looking up at the clear sky and treetops. 'Next week, I'm going to book us a day at that spa you told me about in Covent Garden.'

My legs dip, and water goes in my mouth. I splutter, kicking hard. I can't touch the bottom.

'Hey, you OK?' she says, holding my arm. 'Let's swim to the middle then turn back.'

I take a breath, clear my nose and follow her.

'Suze,' I say, 'I can't spend money on stuff like that at the moment.'

'Don't be silly, hon, I'll get it,' she replies. I know she means it. Money is never an issue in the Howard house. Jez's business is thriving even in these uncertain times. For Suzy, money does not have the emotion attached to it that it does for me. It doesn't hang around her house like a critical mother, interfering in every decision she makes, squashing dreams, telling her 'maybe next year'.

Satisfied that I am OK, Suzy leaves me to swim alone. I wonder which direction to take across the pond. It is a strange sensation swimming in a natural pool, with no tiled edges to aim for, just gentle slopes of black earth veined with slippery tree roots. There is no rectangular structure to measure my lengths. It is lovely, Suzy is right. It's just that right now my mind aches for corners and edges, for beginnings and ends.

I hear a splash and turn round. The old lady is climbing the steps out of the pond. Stunned, I realize she is about ninety. Tanned, loose flesh hangs like draped curtains from strong old bones. I think of my own grandmother, sitting for twenty years after my granddad died, watching telly and waiting for the end. How does that happen? That one old lady watches telly and another walks to an open-air pond on a summer's day and floats around among water lilies and kingfishers?

The woman's lack of self-consciousness about her body gives her an air of confidence as she walks past two young women gossiping animatedly, eyes hidden behind overlarge designer sunglasses, thin limbs spray-tanned the same dulled bronze. Probably business wives from Hampstead. I decide the woman could be an old suffragette or a famous botanist who spent her younger years travelling round remote South America on a donkey, finding new plants. Whatever, I sense she has no time for young women like them. And me. She's probably earned the right to spend her days doing such wonderful things. She knows someone else is paying for ours.

This is not right. This has to end. Taking a deep breath through my nose, I swim as fast as I can back to the steps and reach up to the railings with dripping hands. Pulling myself from the water, my body feels oddly heavy. Heavy, I suspect, with the weight of my own guilt.

I have to find the words to tell Suzy. I can't do this any more.

It became apparent at Easter that Suzy had a lot of plans for her and me. She has never had a daylight hour without children, she claims, since she moved to London. Even when Jez is home, he says he can't manage all three of them together, so she always has one, whatever she does.

So since Peter and Otto both started private nursery in May, and Henry and Rae are now reaching the end of their first year at primary school, Suzy finally has the chance to do the things on the list she has been compiling from *Time Out* magazine and her London guidebook. All through June, we have been out most days. She knows I have no money, so we have done free things. We have rollerbladed in Regent's Park, ignoring the sign that says 'No skating'. 'They'll have to catch us first,' said Suzy furiously when she saw it. She has waited too long to take long, gliding strokes through the flat paths of the rose garden unhindered by our children's buggies and scooters. I don't like breaking rules, but I go along with it.

Another day, we ate sandwiches in Trafalgar Square after a visit to the National Gallery to see Botticellis and Rembrandts. We've peered through the railings at No. 10 Downing Street and seen Big Ben up close. Suzy even made me come with her to the Tower of London, insisting on paying the entrance fee. As I stood waiting among German tourists to see the Crown Jewels, I had to smile to myself. These are not the things I did with friends in London before I had Rae, but I remind myself that Suzy is from America and not Lincolnshire, like me, and that she wants to do the touristy stuff in the way that I wanted to climb the Empire State Building when Tom and I spent that one precious weekend in New York.

And today it has been Hampstead Ladies' Pond. 'We should come here every day,' Suzy says, as we get ourselves dressed. 'People do.'

Sometimes when she says these things I feel like I did in the pond today. I flail around, trying to find something solid and familiar to hold on to, but there is nothing.

It is 3.25 p.m. It has taken Suzy sixteen minutes to race from Hampstead Heath across North London in her yellow convertible to Alexandra Park. She skids to a stop outside the kids' school, completely ignoring the 'No drop off' sign.

'Go get 'em, pardner,' she shouts to me over the horrible American soft-rock music she likes to play loud in the car, oblivious to the looks we get from mothers walking through the school gate.

I laugh despite my embarrassment, and jump out. We both know the routine. I pick up Rae and Henry, she fetches Peter and Otto from nursery. We do it without speaking now, guiding each other through our shared daily routine like dressage horses, with a gentle nod or a kick towards school or soft play or swimming.

'I'm going to take them to the park,' I say, shutting the door.

'Coolio, baby,' shouts Suzy cheerfully, and drives off, waving a hand above her head.

I turn and look at the arched entrance with its century-old brick 'Girls' sign. Instantly, my shoulders hunch up. The massive wall of Alexandra Palace rises dramatically behind the school, like a tidal wave about to engulf the little Victorian building. I run through the gate, turn right into the infants' department and smile my closed-mouth smile at the other mums. Everyone told me that having kids is when you really get to know your neighbours in London. They must have neighbours different from mine. A few mums nod back, then continue arranging playdates with each other in the diaries they carry around. I've tried so many times to figure out what I've done wrong. My best guess is that it's because in Rae's slot on the class parent contact list 'Callie' and 'Tom' sit separately at two different London addresses; unlike 'Felicity and Jonathan' and 'Parminder and David' and 'Suzy and Jez'. Suzy says if the mothers are not going to be friendly to me because I'm a divorced, unemployed, single mother who lives in a rented flat, she and Jez won't accept their invites to stupid drinks parties in their double-fronted Edwardian houses in The Driveway, the only road apart from ours with a guaranteed catchment into this tiny, one-form-entry infant school. She says this is the price we pay for 'getting our kids into a posh, oversubscribed primary school' and that 'they're a bunch of stuck-up, middle-class cows for ignoring me', and that I am much better than they are.

I try to believe her, but sometimes it's difficult. Sometimes I think it would be nice to belong. Sometimes I think that if one of these mothers invited Rae to her house for a playdate, I would fall on the floor and kiss her feet.

The classroom door opens and Henry and Rae burst out looking grubby and stressed. 'What have you got to eat?' Rae murmurs. I give them the rice cakes I always carry around in my bag. She has red paint in her mousy hair and her hands are greasy as if she hasn't washed them all day. As usual I search her eyes for signs. Is she overtired? Too pale? I scoop her up and hold her too tight, kissing the side of her face till she squirms and laughs.

'Are you all right, Henry?' I say. He looks dazed and wired, checking behind me to see if Suzy is there. If she were, he would be whining by now, making his disapproval of her abandonment apparent. I put Rae down and hug him to show that I understand. He leans into me a little, and sighs. Then the pair of them head out of the outer door, gnawing their food like puppies.

At the school gate, Henry starts to run. He does it every day, yet I am so busy trying to shove their scribbled drawings into my bag that it still catches me unawares. 'Henry!' I shout. I chase him along the pavement, grabbing Rae who is following him blindly, dodging round a man, a woman and two girls. The man turns. It is Matt, a divorced dad from another class. Or The Hot Dude That Callie Must Get It On With, as Suzy calls him. And I have just shouted in his ear.

'Sorry,' I say, lifting a hand to emphasize it. He smiles coolly, rubbing his hand over a new crewcut. Embarrassingly, I blush. 'Stupid, stupid, stupid,' I mutter. As if.

I catch up with Henry at the play park behind the school. 'Henry,' I say, 'you mustn't run like that. Remember, Rae follows you and it's dangerous for her in case she falls.'

He shrugs a 'sorry', jumps on a swing standing up and throws himself in the air with violent jerks, as if trying to shake out his excess energy like ketchup from a bottle. Rae sits on the next swing, playing with the tiny doll that she manages to keep hidden about her person however much I search for it before we leave for school. I am going to look up her sleeve on Monday. They don't talk much, Henry and Rae. But, as their teacher says, they seem joined together by an invisible wire. Wherever one is, the other is never far away – just like me and Suzy. I wonder what Rae feels about that sometimes. I wonder if she feels like me.

I watch Rae, and I think about Suzy, and I can't even bring myself to imagine what it will be like for them both when I'm not here.

extracts reading groups
competitions books new
discounts extracts extracts discounts
competitions new events
books new books
events books extracts discounts
extracts new titles reading groups
interviews events
reading groups books events extracts events books
new books events interviews new books extracts
discounts
events new events
discounts extracts discounts books
www.panmacmillan.com
extracts events reading groups
competitions books extracts new